# LADY OF ICE AND FIRE

# LADY
# OF ICE
# AND FIRE

## COLIN ALEXANDER

**DONALD I. FINE, INC.**

New York

*This book is for my parents and for Cello, who believed in what I was doing.*
*My thanks to Don Gastwirth, friend and agent, for his unstinting support.*

*Library of Congress Catalogue Card Number: 94–061912*
*ISBN: 1–55611–449–4*

*Manufactured in the United States of America*

*10  9  8  7  6  5  4  3  2  1*

*Designed by Irving Perkins Associates*

# IN THE BEGINNING

AMSTERDAM (Reuters). *American scientist Dr. Henry Davenport was reported missing today after failing to appear at the Fifth International Congress on Biotechnology. Dr. Davenport, of the NaturGene Corporation subsidiary of Intergroup Resources and Technologies, had been scheduled to address the congress on the use of computer systems in developing so-called designer enzymes. Dr. Davenport's talk was expected to highlight significant advances in a much-heralded technology that has, so far, failed to live up to its promise to deliver easy and environmentally safe ways to obtain complex industrial and medicinal compounds. Company officials had no explanation for his failure to appear and emphatically denied that any questions had arisen concerning the validity of the technique. Neither they nor the police claimed to know his whereabouts. Amsterdam police were quick to point out that there had been "absolutely no suggestion of foul play."*

THAT WAS THE COMPLETE story, as it was perceived and published by the press. It received, as might be expected, little media exposure. After all, there had been no violence, no bodies bleeding in the street. No television station or newspaper had been called with a ransom demand or a political manifesto to be read. With "absolutely no suggestion of foul play," a private citizen missing a speaking engagement was not very big news, even when the topic was supposed to be scientifically important. Mrs. Paula Davenport, when she inquired, was told only that he would probably turn up in a few days, and was asked whether her husband was prone to occasional "flings."

European papers covering the congress printed the Reuters bulletin as a footnote to their main articles on the meeting, then dropped it entirely. Their interest was focused on the important discoveries that had been announced rather than something that was not reported. The major American papers reported the Congress only as a footnote, where they mentioned it at all. They showed no interest in such minor side-issues. In fact, only the Cleveland *Plain Dealer* ran the Reuters report at all, and that only because NaturGene was a Cleveland company and the paper happened to need a filler that day. All of which only proves that making sense out of what material is printed is only half the battle. There was, actually, a bit more to the story.

# PART I

---

## BOY MEETS GIRL

# CHAPTER 1

## CLEVELAND, OHIO

SLAM!

THE DOOR TO Herb Blalock's office crashed shut with the delicacy of a howitzer. The sound spoke eloquently of the thickness of the wood, and the force with which it had been closed. The lack of reaction elicited from the secretary sitting at the nearby desk gave an equally precise indication of the frequency of such events. The solid construction of the door was clearly a necessity.

George Jeffers, now standing on the secretarial side of that massive barrier, knew that Blalock would still be in the same state of apoplectic rage that Jeffers had found on entering the office not very long before. That, by itself, did not surprise Jeffers any more than the thunderbolt door closure surprised the secretary. He had learned over the course of three years that such attacks were Herb Blalock's typical reaction to the intrusion of unpleasant reality into whatever his current fantasy might be. Jeffers had made acquaintance with these attacks within three weeks after first joining the then-NaturGene Company. It had taken little longer for him to ascribe them to the whims of a spoiled and only child, from which point he ignored them. Blalock clearly had no intention of firing Jeffers, or of having a real stroke, so why pay attention? If anything about the outbursts surprised Jeffers at all, once he understood them, it was that Blalock continued at the head of NaturGene and, since its recent acquisition by Intergroup Resources and Technologies, continued to run it as a division. That was, no surprises until this time. Blalock's explosions usually developed over experiments that took longer than planned (longer than the time allocation in Blalock's daily planner, that is) or, Heaven forbid, gave results that were different from expectations. Blalock's tirades over expenses, those unconnected with the front office, were legendary. Jeffers planned for these as a necessary part of presenting any status report. Jeffers personally, however, had always been immune. Never before had Jeffers himself been the subject of Blalock's ire.

And why he should be angry with me, God only knows, Jeffers thought, as the reverberations from the door died away. It certainly seemed that if

3

anyone had a right to be screaming and turning purple it was Jeffers. He kept those thoughts to himself largely because of the second surprise he had encountered, the two men who had been with him in the office and who now stood outside with him. The usual Blalock tirade, as Jeffers knew, had as much lasting effect as a desert thunderstorm. Everyone kept right on doing whatever needed to be done, which was how NaturGene survived. The presence of these two men, however, argued that there was more than just Blalock involved this time.

One of the men was Jim Thompson, the head of security for IRT. Thompson had practically moved his office to NaturGene after the acquisition; certainly he seemed to be there almost every day. Aside from creating a *de novo* security system for a company that previously had not even had a "confidential" rubber stamp, Thompson had spent a large amount of time chatting with Jeffers. Jeffers had taken that as his due, he knew his importance to the company, but he had also felt that a real friendship had developed over that time. Thompson was what Jeffers pictured himself to be when he projected himself into the thriller fictions he enjoyed. Tall, athletic, even-tanned, Thompson seemed the very model of the dashing secret agents whose fictional exploits Jeffers admired. In fact, it was rumored that Thompson had worked for the government before "retiring" to the corporate world. Jeffers did not understand why Thompson had been present. Yes, security was Thompson's responsibility, but the problem was in Europe, for God's sake, not in Cleveland. Worse yet, Thompson had seemed to agree that it was all Jeffers's fault.

If Thompson's presence and opinion confused Jeffers, the other man in the room added unease to the confusion. Charles N. Oliver had been introduced, precisely by name, and then ambiguously by function, as a representative of the federal government. Jeffers could agree with Oliver that the disappearance of Dr. Henry Davenport was a concern of the government. Of course, it should be. But to term it, as all three of them had done, an issue of national security with Jeffers's enzyme project the primary focus, that was patently absurd. This bit of ridiculousness, Jeffers was certain, originated with the government employee. He found it easy to support this conclusion by simply looking at Oliver. The man was no taller than Jeffers, which would list him at five-ten. Where Thompson could have modeled the dark pinstripes he wore for a fashion show, the design of Oliver's body seemed to have been taken from a Bartlett pear. His face was full and fleshy, with a coarse gray moustache that shagged over his upper lip and would have looked better if it were denser. It reminded Jeffers of the old joke about a football moustache, one with eleven men on a side. Hair to match the moustache drooped limply across his forehead. The clothes matched the man, the shine of the suit leaving no doubt as to its composition.

"Why don't we get some coffee?" Thompson suggested. The idea received ready assent from the other two. Regardless of their reasons, standing in front of Blalock's closed door under the gaze of Brenda, the world's nosiest secretary, was undesirable.

Their walk to the cafeteria was in silence. An observer unaware of the men's backgrounds could easily have mistaken the procession, with Jeffers sandwiched between the two men in suits, for a miscreant being escorted off the grounds. One short corridor and two flights of stairs brought them to the side entrance of the cafeteria. Jeffers noted sourly, as he did almost every time he went there, that the doors had been installed with the push bars on the outside. A minor point, perhaps, but one that mattered when trying to exit to the lab with a full tray. Just another improvement to the building, courtesy of IRT, he thought, and then glanced around to be sure he had not said it aloud. His customary invulnerability to gaffes was seeming a bit shaky. It being well past lunch, they had the cafeteria almost to themselves and soon settled at a corner table, each with a styrofoam cup of coffee.

"God, George," Thompson said finally. "That was really dumb."

"Dumb!" Jeffers burst out. "What the hell do you mean, dumb? My enzyme is missing, my best friend is missing, nobody knows what's going on, and you're calling me *dumb*?" He ended on a rising note, as his gesticulation sent hot liquid slopping across his hand.

"That is precisely the point," Oliver put in softly. He regarded Jeffers critically, as if not quite believing what he saw. Thompson had briefed him quickly about Jeffers before the meeting. The man was a brilliant scientist, Oliver had heard, with an impressive record of achievements. In confidence, Thompson had told him that IRT had long been interested in Jeffers's project and that it had been Jeffers's expertise that IRT had primarily wanted when it bought NaturGene. Knowing that, Oliver had pictured in his mind a more distinguished-looking person than the one in front of him. Jeffers looked younger than the thirty-two years he claimed. His frame was rail thin, no fat in evidence anywhere. The face was thin, too, its planes being defined by high cheekbones, sharp jawline and cleft chin under short, curly, brown hair. It looked as though it could skip a day's shave without it being noticeable. It was not really the physique, though, that bothered Oliver, but what garbed it. Thompson had mentioned that Jeffers was informal, a man who rarely wore a tie. For the special meeting, though, Jeffers had added a purple knit tie to his green plaid shirt and khaki shorts. Over this he wore a knee-length lab coat adorned with a welter of smudges and stains. This was worth buying a company for, lock, stock, and crazy president? Oliver had to wonder.

"Maybe," Oliver started again, "it would be a good idea to go over it again, without all the histrionics." He nodded in the direction of the administration wing. There was no dissent. "All right. Dr. Henry Davenport left here, personally carrying your enzyme. He got on the flight to Amsterdam, and has not been seen since. Now, is it correct, as Blalock told me, that Dr. Davenport had with him your entire supply of this material? That sounds like a rather unusual thing to do." Oliver's tone clearly indicated that he expected a denial.

"Unfortunately, yes," Jeffers answered. "But at the time he left, I was not expecting a fire in 312-B."

"Ah, right. That happened the next day. How critical was the damage?"

"It really shouldn't have been," Jeffers frowned. "The actual damage was bad—don't get me wrong. It destroyed our stock, our precursors and our producer lines. Thing is, the experiments planned on the stuff Hank took are nondestructive, we can easily recover the material, and there was more than enough to do the work we wanted to do here. After that we were going to move on anyway. This was just a starting point. Now, though," he shrugged, "it could take nine months just to get back to where we were."

It was Oliver's turn to frown. "All of which makes the timing of this look even more suspicious. Don't you agree, Jim?"

"It looks more than suspicious, I admit," Thompson answered. "However, we've gone over that lab quite thoroughly and I know what happened. Apparently, a hot plate had been left on, and then forgotten. It started a fire in some scrap paper that had been left on and around it. There were several large jugs of flammable solvents left out, against regs, and the place went up. We're actually lucky we didn't lose the entire building. On the surface it sounds fishy, Charles, but that was the regular state of affairs up there. George knows that. I've discussed it with him before. Basically, that lab was an accident waiting to happen."

"Regardless, it came at a most inopportune time, leaving Davenport with the only material extant," Oliver pointed out. "I don't argue that it could have happened any time if the lab was chronically kept dangerously, so you can stop covering your butt, Jim, but you'll grant that the coincidence is still suspicious."

"The net result," Oliver directed at Jeffers, "is that you sent a valuable material, in fact a unique material that was a trade secret, by an amateur courier with no security provisions whatever. And you wonder why you are called dumb when it disappears."

That was too much for Jeffers. "Well, screw you, too," he retorted. "If the company thinks I screwed up that badly then I guess they can fire me, but they haven't done it yet. Anyway, why should whatever part of the government you work for care about what I did with the enzyme? I mean, why should you care about the company's problem? I thought you were here because Hank is missing."

"No, I'm here because the enzyme is missing," Oliver said. "Dr. Jeffers, this country has developed and then lost the lead in all sorts of fields, from steel to computer chips. Biotech is one area we still dominate, at least for now. This designer enzyme technology of yours could determine leadership in the field for the next ten years, just like genetic engineering did before. We do not intend to let it get away."

"Oh, my God! Tell me you really believe that! I mean, of course I think it's important—I wouldn't work on it otherwise—but this is a prototype! The reaction it catalyzes just makes a blue color so we can measure it. Don't start telling me that you believe the fate of American industry turns on it."

Do I believe it? Oliver wondered. Certainly Herb Blalock believes it. Blalock had convinced Senator Answard that it was true and Answard was an old friend of the director; they had gone to Yale together. Consequently, Oliver doubted that it mattered whether he believed it or not.

"It doesn't matter whether I believe it or not," Oliver told Jeffers. "Other people do and what I do believe is that to leave a valuable material floating around unguarded can create a great temptation."

Jeffers's eyes narrowed. "Just what are you suggesting?" he demanded.

"Only that it would be very easy for Davenport to simply abscond with it and sell it."

"Oh, come on!" Jeffers half jumped out of his chair. "Hank's a scientist, and he's worked on this project with me, and he's a damn good friend of mine. There's no way he would do something like that."

"That's your assumption, Dr. Jeffers. It may or may not be correct. Incidentally, why was Dr. Davenport going to the conference with this enzyme rather than you? It was your project. In fact, why was he taking it to the conference at all? That seems a bit unusual."

"Yeah." Jeffers looked unhappy. "IRT wouldn't allow us to discuss very much of the project, so said the patent lawyers. Hank was responsible for the computer modeling we used to work out the structure we wanted. They were willing to let him talk about the technique."

"So he wasn't just a courier?" Oliver demanded. "He actually knew many of the project details? That might give him more incentive, make him more valuable, as it were."

Jeffers could feel himself flushing. Normally, he avoided arguing or asserting himself, except on scientific topics where he felt on firm ground. Not this time. The words rose, without hesitation, to his mouth and out. "Money has nothing to do with it. You guys are always assuming that everything and everybody has a price tag—well, you're wrong! It would never occur to Hank to try to sell something we worked on. Anyway, he only handled the computer models. There's a long way between that and making it work in the lab. And as for why he had it with him, Hank was carrying our working sample because he was going to see Max Fruhling at the conference anyway, and it seemed safer for Hank to carry it instead of shipping it to him."

Oliver's reaction to the outburst was anything but pleasant. "Dr. Jeffers, am I to understand that this enzyme was to be *delivered* to Max Fruhling?"

"Yes," Jeffers responded with some irritation, "I think that's exactly what I said."

"Terrific. Well, if Davenport hasn't gone into business for himself, I'm sure Fruhling has seen to it." Oliver glared across the table. "You do realize, I hope, that there is sometimes a fine line between stupidity and complicity."

Jeffers sat with his mouth open, suddenly deprived of speech. Now they were going to accuse him of sabotaging his own project! It was not to be believed. He looked over at Thompson, seeking support but not finding any. Finally, with the realization that Thompson was not going to say anything in his defense, he found his voice. "What is wrong with collaborating with Fruhling? I've got a signed secrecy agreement with him. Hell, the IRT lawyers approved it. Or don't you trust people who don't wear the American flag on their underwear?"

"Max Fruhling," Oliver ground out, "is a totally unreconstructed Nazi who would go to almost any lengths to support a number of quasi-legal right-wing causes in Germany. He's the founder of the SRG Party which, if anything, is even more radical than the Republikans. The German Republikan Party, in case you didn't know, is a fascist party."

Jeffers said, "Just like here, huh?" but neither man laughed at his joke.

Oliver went on as though Jeffers had not spoken, "Are you going to tell me that you are totally unaware of Fruhling's politics?"

"*Professor* Max Fruhling," Jeffers shot back, "is an absolutely top-notch biophysicist. He has one of the best labs on either continent, and he is the perfect person to carry out the experiments we needed for this project. Yes, yes, I have heard rumors about his political views, but I don't really believe all of that and it certainly has nothing to do with his science."

"All right, Dr. Jeffers. Calm down." Oliver had both hands stretched forward as if to push Jeffers back into his seat, which might have become necessary as Jeffers was leaning almost completely across the table. "I believe your motivations. But I have heard more than rumors about Fruhling and I do not share your rosy view of science and scientists. I also doubt that any written agreement will do any good when enough money or politics is involved."

Thompson, silent since the beginning of the argument, stepped in as a peacemaker. "You're both reasoning okay," he said, "it's just that you're coming from opposite points of view. George does science, Charles. Period. I've been here long enough to realize that. But," he added, turning to Jeffers, "you need to realize that Charles deals with the rest of the world, and it plays by different rules. He knows what he's talking about. Particularly in this case, since I happen to know there's a likely buyer for that enzyme."

His last sentence got the complete attention of his two companions. Thompson leaned forward, into the silence that had formed at the table, and continued in a conspiratorial tone. "We haven't filed for patents on this yet, have we? Neither the process nor the substance itself?"

"No, we couldn't have," Jeffers replied. "We need these last studies even to get narrow coverage, and the lawyers wanted me to extend the work before we filed, to give us a broader patent estate. Some of the computer stuff is copyrighted, of course, but you could work your way around it. That's why they would only let us talk about the modeling work. Keeping that under wraps isn't so important."

"Yeah." Thompson frowned. "Look, George, say somebody else got hold of the enzyme and the information that went with it, especially if they also had Davenport's computer skills. They could do those final tests, maybe reverse-engineer the process, at least enough to file a patent on it, not necessarily in the U.S. Fraud is not likely to stop them. And then, there you are. Bye-bye technological superiority. Now just listen for a minute before you say this is crazy. You both recall that Helvetica-Chemie had also been interested in acquiring NaturGene but was outbid by IRT?" Both men nodded. It had not particularly mattered at the time to Jeffers whether it was IRT or the giant Swiss chemical concern that ultimately purchased Natur Gene, but he had been aware of the activity. Oliver had no direct memory of the events, not having been involved then, but he had noticed the fact in the database during his background review, prior to going to Cleveland.

Thompson went on. "Therefore, you know that Helvetica-Chemie had to be aware of many of the details of Dr. Jeffers's work. After all, it was his work and the spinoffs from it that gave NaturGene its real value. Anyway, I have, in my estimation, highly reliable reports that several H-C officers are heavily shorting IRT stock." He sat back, and looked from one to the other to gauge the impact of his statement.

On Jeffers, there was none. "Would you mind telling me what the hell that's supposed to mean?" he asked.

"Jesus, George, some day you're going to have to move out of your head and into the world." Thompson had used that phrase before, usually when he found Jeffers's academic detachment getting in the way of the necessities of life—identification cards and sign-in sheets, to name but two examples. "Shorting a stock," he explained, "means selling it short. You do it by borrowing stock from someone, and then selling it. Since eventually you have to return what you borrowed, you make money if the stock price goes down. That way, you can buy back the shares for less money, and keep the difference. Obviously, bad news, like having a major research project vanish, can make prices drop. If a competitor, not naming names, then moves ahead in that area, you can compound the drop. It can still work even if an actual marketed product is not involved, because so many traders buy and sell on hype and Wall Street has been sold on this technology for years. Obviously, they're sure the bottom will drop out of our stock, and how would they be so sure unless they knew they were getting the enzyme?"

Oliver was saying nothing, but inside his mind was racing. He would have given his eyeteeth right then to know how Thompson had that information. Sometimes, he thought there were more industry spooks than "real" ones. The director had been concerned about a foreign firm suddenly appearing with the patent, but Oliver had assumed that had come from Blalock's lobbying with the senator. Thompson's information gave credence to the story.

"I think," Oliver said carefully, "that we will want to take that into account when we look into this affair." He wanted to ask for the source, but restrained himself. There was no way Thompson would mention it in front of Jeffers. Probably would not even if Jeffers were elsewhere.

Jeffers was there, however, and he quickly latched onto a different implication of Oliver's comment. "When you look into this affair," he repeated. "Meaning you are going to be doing something to find Hank and my enzyme?"

"You can be sure we will do whatever is appropriate," Oliver replied, trying to sidestep the issue. In fact, he had made no definite plans, but habitual caution prevented him from giving out any information.

"Well, whatever you're doing, I want in," Jeffers stated emphatically. As soon as he said it, he was as surprised as Thompson and Oliver looked. He had not really meant to say it, the idea had just formed in his head. Then, next thing he knew, it was out his mouth. It was all very unlike George

Jeffers. Usually he had all his arguments perfectly lined up in his head, but could never manage to say any of them.

"Dr. Jeffers, be reasonable. You are a scientist, not an investigator, certainly not a field agent. You should leave this to people who know what they are doing."

Oliver's words were sensible, but they did carry a note of paternalism. Jeffers had endured sufficient condescension for one day.

"Listen, I'm getting tired of all this unworldly George crap. I'm a big boy and I'm perfectly capable of taking care of myself. You sit here and act like this is all my fault, well, if it is then you can damn well let me help fix it. And if you won't, then I'll bloody well go to Amsterdam and fix it myself!"

Oliver felt tempted to ask if Jeffers planned to hold his breath until he turned blue if his demand was not met. It was a difficult urge to stifle.

"George, why don't you let me talk to Charley alone for a bit, and we'll get things settled." That was Thompson, again intervening before the conversation lurched toward open warfare.

Matters were definitely not settled, Jeffers thought angrily as he left the cafeteria. If Thompson thought he was going to go up to his lab and forget all about it, then Thompson was wrong. Jeffers had no clear idea of what a search would entail, but he intended to be part of it. Oliver obviously thought of him as a fool—no, worse, a child—and Jeffers was also beginning to wonder what Thompson was thinking. To go back and say, "You're right, Mr. Oliver, this is no place for me," was impossible. George Jeffers was not going to give in, and he was not going to be placated by whatever smooth line Thompson would undoubtedly come up with. Hell, Jim had been almost as bad as Oliver with this "go to your room, son, while we adults talk" paternalism. Christ, and he had thought Thompson was his friend.

"So, why did you leave?" part of his mind asked.

"I had a choice?" he answered himself.

Jeffers took the stairs in twos and threes, arriving four flights later, his breath labored but his anger intact. The lab was exactly as he had left it. His two technicians were using equipment elsewhere in the building; they would be gone all day. Jim Phillips, the associate scientist he supervised directly had taken the day off. The other scientists on his project team were in their own labs. There was no one there to share his rage and hurt. Hank, the one other person he could have shared his feelings with was gone, into the center of this dilemma. He looked at the phone, then away. There was no one worth calling.

Usually, the clutter in the lab was comforting. Flasks and bottles on the benches spoke of work in progress. Scraps of paper here, there, and everywhere with jotted notes recalled observations that would not wait for him to exhume his notebook from his desk. It was no good. He was too wound up to work. A note, taped to the overflowing bucket of dirty glassware in the sink, caught his eye as he looked around.

It read, "George, this time you can wash them. I am not your mother. Kim."

It was a good thing Kim was elsewhere. Jeffers was in no mood for further swipes at his ability to cope with daily living, be it so humble a problem as dirty glassware. He had a sudden urge to toss the bucket in the trash, which he controlled only with some difficulty.

"Why in the hell did I leave academia?" he asked the glassware, his hands on the edge of the sink. The question was really rhetorical, so it did not matter that no answer came from the collection of round bottoms and Erlenmeyers in front of him. He had left because of guaranteed funding for his research, because of modern equipment he needed. He had left because he was tired of having his aspirator back up every time a toilet was flushed in the building and the water pressure dropped. He had left because he was tired of trying to have the maintenance people fix that, or anything else. Most of all, he had left because in spite of his publications and awards, he was not going to get tenure. He stood there thinking that NaturGene had solved those problems for him, but had given him others in the form of secrecy and market analysts and salesmen with no understanding of what science was or how it was conducted. He could easily believe Thompson's theory, that corporate machinations were at the bottom of this problem, too.

Staring at the sink, in the long run, proved uninspiring. He simply had no desire to do anything. Finally, he wrenched his lab coat off, and tossed it into a corner. It landed, with its radiation badge, on top of the scintillation counter. Jeffers gave a short barking laugh at the sight. IRT Health Physics could call him next month to tell him that he was dead, after they read the badge that was now being ruined by the radiation from the vials in the counter.

He walked halfway down the hall to the room that he and Hank always called the theater. There was indeed a movie screen in what, otherwise, looked like an ordinary conference room. Other than the screen, the only equipment in the room was a PC on the table. The screen was not used for viewing movies. Jeffers booted up the computer, then sat down next to it. He clicked through a number of selections until a model of a molecule, his target molecule, showed on the monitor. Another click and the image showed on the movie screen. Another click and a complex net of lines wove itself around his target. He put on a pair of glasses that had been lying by the computer. Suddenly, the target seemed to pop off the screen to hang in midair between Jeffers and the far wall. The network of lines also grew off the screen, extending out and enveloping the target. Those lines were an outline view of his enzyme. More clicks and the stick figures were clothed in colored sheaths representing the energy surfaces of the enzyme and its target. Jeffers rotated the enzyme, looking at it from all different angles. Then he moved his point of view, zooming in along the energy fields of the enzyme, molecular surfing he and Hank had called it. He watched it flex, make contact with the target; the colors changed as the energies around the target changed and then the target was cut in two. He and Hank had dreamed of this project; they had made it a reality together. They had done a lot together. Unexpectedly, he found tears welling up in his eyes. I have to get out of here for a while. The thought rang through his head.

Going home was not much of an improvement over the lab. Jeffers occupied a one-bedroom apartment in a highrise near a shopping mall in Cleveland Heights. The apartment was his alone. He had not tolerated a roommate since his sophomore year in college. Normally, that state of affairs suited him, and his work hours, perfectly. The apartment was for coming home to read, or watch the VCR for a while, and then going to sleep. Having a roommate would have imposed unwelcome restraints, although this day it would have been nice to talk with someone. Jeffers was never in his apartment at mealtimes, his concept of work hours running from before breakfast to after dinner, and he did not entertain. Consequently, when he opened the refrigerator there was nothing but a bottle of soda gone flat and a forgotten sandwich gone moldy. The emptiness disappointed him; he would have liked a snack. The half-filled cup of black coffee he had left by the sink that morning was still there. He swirled it once, looked at the liquid briefly, then downed it. It was not quite what he wanted. He halfheartedly poked through the stack of empty pizza boxes on the kitchen table, until he realized what he was doing. There was nothing there, and he would not have eaten anything he found anyway. He wandered, instead, into the living room. That area, equipped with the VCR and with his computer, received more use than any other part of the apartment. The stacks of books and journals on the floor around his armchair testified to the position in the room he usually occupied. A James Bond novel, that he had half-finished rereading lay on the footstool. He picked it up, but closed it again after reading only a page. Concentration was out of the question.

Damn that Oliver! Looked like a fool and talked like a fool, making assumptions about people he had never met, and about ideas he himself would never understand. This monkey in polyester was going to make the decisions about recovering Jeffers's project. Hah! Jeffers found himself regretting the manner in which he had shot his mouth off earlier. His original demand to be included had come on impulse, but now all the good solid reasons for his participation occurred to him. The more he thought about it, the more urgently he wanted to take part. It was his project, after all. Since he refused to believe Hank might have had a role in the loss of the enzyme, he had to consider that something might have happened to Hank. Foolish or not, it had been Jeffers who had sent Hank off with the enzyme, so Jeffers was responsible for what happened to him. Fat chance they would let him do anything, though, after that tantrum he had thrown.

"Damn it, I am responsible, and I am going to fix it. Somehow." Talking to himself was not going to do it though. He would have to call Thompson, plead with him if necessary. At that point the phone rang.

Oliver and Thompson sat quietly at the table, until they heard Jeffers's footsteps on the staircase. Only then did Oliver speak up.

"Jim, I seriously hope you aren't about to say what I think you're about to say."

Thompson put his hand up. "Charles, the man is crucial to the health of this company."

"No. Absolutely not. You can't expect me to use him for anything. Look, I don't doubt he's a real scientific hotshot, but he's also a goddamned spoiled child who hasn't the faintest idea what the world is really about, and I'll be damned if he's going to help us with an intelligence operation. I don't know whether this patent is going to break anything but your company, but the director is convinced and that's all there is to it. You know that. I won't be put in a situation where he can screw things up."

Thompson waited until Oliver had finished before saying another word.

"Look, Charles, there's more to it than just the operation, at least from my end of it. I have to find a way to keep George happy. That's my job and I'm damned serious about it. If George splits on top of this, NaturGene isn't worth near what we paid for it. So, keeping George happy, even if he is a spoiled brat, is important to IRT." Thompson let out a long sigh. "Of course, keeping George happy is really Herb's job, he's the f-ing president, but you can guess how good he is at it. QED, I wind up doing it. I've probably spent enough time in his lab to be on the payroll as a technician.

"I'm not going to tell you again that he's the only one who can identify the enzyme. I can't do it, and you sure as hell can't. What's more, I know Jeffers, and unless we do something to make him happy we could have a real problem on our hands. Both of us. Anyway," he went on, "I think there's a way we can do this without taking any risks. George will get the feeling that he's doing something and that we respect him, and we'll get on with our business while he comes back here with enough warm fuzzies to keep him quiet." He spoke for about ten minutes more, detailing the idea he had developed a little while earlier.

Oliver listened, without much enthusiasm. Of course, Oliver had difficulty working up enthusiasm for any part of his current assignment, Thompson or no Thompson. Head of the newly created Special Technology Section, oh please! Come on, Charley, he had been told, this is a promotion. This is a plum position, a new section and one that would be especially important in the next few years. Yeah, sure, he had thought, even as he had smiled to accept. He should have been put in charge of operations, which was what he had expected. Unfortunately, the official line now was that the collapse of the Soviet Union had eliminated the significant military threat to the United States. Charles Oliver, and others like him, who believed that the new world was more dangerous, not less, were simply cold warriors who did not want to admit their time had passed. Oliver supposed he was lucky. He still had a position. Still, there were nukes in the Ukraine, neo-Nazis in Germany, and a near civil war in Moscow while he ran around spying on nerds and chasing silicon chips. Or this, whatever it was. And, here he was in Cleveland, in person, because of a political friendship. Suddenly, he realized that his mind had wandered from the conversation. He had not heard part of what Thompson, had said and had to ask him to repeat it. The second time around did not make it any more appealing, but, ultimately, he found himself agreeing.

It was going to be a nuisance, but he had to recover that enzyme, no question about that, and Thompson had made it clear that he would need Jeffers's participation in order to identify the enzyme when he found it. Thompson obviously had his own reasons for wanting to keep Jeffers happy, but Oliver suspected that the identification problem was real. Oliver doubted that he would recognize an enzyme if one bit him. If that was what it took to get Jeffers's cooperation, they could play a little game for George. For a short while. Once he realized that he was going along with it, he began to mentally review his resources and options. They were more limited than he liked to acknowledge, God bless the Congress of the United States! Don Lorenzo was the one agent he had who was available, and, just as important, was already in a good location. He got up and excused himself. If he hurried, he could reach his office by telephone and have the necessary arrangements made, before all the good little bureaucrats went home.

\*    \*    \*

Jeffers moved quickly to answer the phone. Aside from the occasional wrong number, the only times he received calls at home were if there were major problems at the lab. Since the last such call had been to report the fire, the ringing hit him like an electric shock. To his surprise, the caller was Thompson.

"George? This is Jim. Christ, I've been looking all over for you. Since when do you go home in the middle of the afternoon?"

"I don't," Jeffers answered. "Today was different."

"Yeah, I know. Oliver's not exactly in the diplomatic corps." His tone indicated that the apology was a necessary ritual that he had to get through. "Bottom line, though, is that I got most of what you want." His voice seemed to brighten considerably on the last sentence.

"What do you mean?"

"I mean I got Oliver to agree to work with you, that's what. Now it's probably not everything you want, but getting any concessions out of Oliver is tough. In fact, you're gonna owe me for this one, pal."

Jeffers thought for a moment. Thompson was saying that they were going to include him. Having brought himself to the point where he was convinced they would not, it was difficult to mentally change direction.

"George, are you still there?"

"Yeah, I'm here. I appreciate your help. So, what's the deal?"

"For now meet us at Jersey's. We'll go over the details then. Be there at eight. Okay?" It was okay.

Jersey's was a moderately upscale grazing location in Cleveland Heights. Jeffers had met Thompson there before on a few occasions, for beers. The place was nearly full when Jeffers arrived, five minutes after the scheduled time. Thompson and Oliver had taken a booth in the rear, where there could be neighboring patrons on only one side. Oliver was pointedly looking at his watch as Jeffers came toward them. A coffee in front of each was the only concession to the real function of the establishment.

"All right, I'm here," Jeffers said, settling onto the bench opposite the other two.

Oliver was the one to reply. "Your friend Mr. Thompson has convinced me that you should have a role in what we are going to do. All I can say is that I sincerely hope none of us winds up regretting this. Enough of that; this is what we are going to do. The agent who will carry out our investigation will need a thorough briefing on your material: what it is, how to recognize it, how to handle it, anything you can think of that would be useful in recovering it. The agent will also need to know everything you know about Dr. Davenport and about Fruhling. He is not going to meet you here. If that fire was not an accident," he shot a glance at Thompson, "then there may be somebody here who is watching things. You and Davenport collaborated with a Dr. Antonia Chu at MIT. Under the circumstances, your going to see her will cause no suspicion. Jim has already arranged for you to spend the next two days in Boston. You'll meet our agent the first day. Your responsibility will be to make contact and deliver a satisfactory briefing. Make sure you see Dr. Chu the second day and talk about your discussions with her when you return here. Are we clear so far?"

"I thought," said Jeffers, "that I would go to Amsterdam as well. Whatever the reasons, Hank is missing. I have to find him." That sounded, he thought, like a perfectly cool, rational approach.

"George, I don't think you understand," Thompson replied. "The deal is as Charles put it. You do not go to Europe, not under any circumstances. I understand your feelings, but this is as far as we can go. Either accept and you're in, or refuse and you're out. There is no possible bargaining."

Jeffers swallowed hard. "Okay. I'll take it as is." Screw Europe anyway. That hadn't been one of his brighter ideas. The smart thing was to leave the heavy stuff to the pros.

"Good." That was Oliver again. "This is how it will work. Your code name for this operation will be the Cleaners. Your contact is the Tailor." Jeffers started at that, but held his tongue. It would be too easy for Oliver to withdraw even this limited offer if he made some wise-ass remark about the choice of code names. "You will make contact tomorrow at 6:00 P.M. in a bar called the Kettle Drum. It's located at Kenmore Square, you should have no trouble finding it. Be at the bar. The agent will come by and mention that he is the Tailor. When you hear that, you tell the agent that the Cleaners are looking for the Tailor. If there is no contact by 6:15, the agent will park outside in a purple Monte Carlo. Find the car, and tell the driver that the Cleaners are looking for a Tailor. If there is still no contact by 7:15, try again the next night at the same time. If there is still no contact, we'll consider it a failure, and make do without you. Which would not be good, since the briefing is necessary, and we have given it over to you. So, don't fuck it up. Clear?"

Jeffers nodded, and, at the nod, Oliver walked out. The concept of using a purple Monte Carlo for a secret contact was occupying Jeffers's mind. A car like that would stand out like a neon sign. Their confidence in his ability to carry out instructions was obviously not high. The realization hurt.

"Hey, George, wake up." Thompson's baritone intruded on Jeffers's thoughts.

"I am awake," he replied irritably.

Thompson chuckled. "I know that faraway look of yours. Your mind gets out around the orbit of Mars. Don't let Oliver bother you, because there's another part to the deal."

At that Jeffers looked sharply at Thompson.

"Thought that would get your attention. What I'm telling you now Oliver doesn't know. This is company business too, not just the government's. Any job like this needs money, not just personnel. Since it's covert, everything is a lot easier if there's no government money in it. So, Oliver's supplying the manpower, we're supplying the money, and he does not want to know about it." Thompson reached into his pocket, and pulled out a sealed envelope. "This contains the key to a lockbox in Zurich containing the funds that will be necessary for this operation. There is also a letter of authorization for its use. It's in the Crédit Suisse branch at this address." Thompson put a folded slip of paper on top of the envelope. "Memorize the address, then get rid of this paper. Whatever you do, don't carry the address along with the envelope. You are to get this to your contact, and nobody else. Absolutely no one else gets it. Before you leave him, make sure he knows the address. Don't write it down for him." He handed it to Jeffers.

Jeffers stared at the envelope for a moment before putting it away. "How much money?" he asked.

"That's something *you* don't need to know." Thompson chuckled again. "Let's just say that if you fuck up it will be rather unpleasant for me too, since I have signed for the key and guaranteed its transfer. Which is one reason you're not going to Europe. I want you back here when you're done, to tell me that the transfer went properly. I don't want a phone call. I want *you*, in forty-eight hours. Got it?" There was no humor in his voice when he finished and left Jeffers at the table.

I suppose, Jeffers thought, I should feel flattered that he's willing to trust me with this. I do, I guess. Of course, Hank trusted me, too. Look where it got him.

# Chapter 2

## BOSTON, MASSACHUSETTS

BOSTON'S JUNE WEATHER IS a variable thing, switching from sun to clouds to rain with scant notice to those who need to conduct their business in it. In any case, the temperature is warm, and the humidity is high. On this particular day, it had moved to an extreme. The sun burned in a pale blue sky, devoid of any cloud cover, bringing the temperature above ninety degrees Fahrenheit. This was a day when the metal seat-belt fasteners would sear the hand that, unwarned by the sauna within the car, proceeded to grasp them. The humidity had kept pace with the rising temperature, so that any movement, however trivial, would raise a stream of sweat.

The heat seemed to make no impression on the woman who stepped off the E train at the medical complex exit, regardless of how it wilted her fellow passengers. She ignored it the same way she ignored the traffic. The road crew tearing up the street in front of the corner drugstore hailed her with a series of whistles. If a woman was young, which she was, and tall, which she was, and had a figure worthy of modeling fashions, which she had, then wolf whistles were a fact of life. She ignored them, too.

She strode down the street, past the medical school, then turned left before Brookline Avenue. Halfway up the block, she felt in her pocket for a little, blue plastic card. She looked at it with distaste. Across the top, in big white numbers, was her identity. Below that, in much smaller letters, was her name, starting with the last. REDDING, it said, right over her thumbnail. She scratched at it for a moment and some of the white came off. Too bad I can't just run my finger over it and wipe it out, she thought. Smooth out all those raised numbers and letters. A stupid thought, really, she knew. She could destroy the card easily enough, a match would do it, but it would affect neither the charts nor the reality one whit. They would just give her another one. She shrugged and headed for the door.

When she reached the front desk of the proper clinic, there was an unfamiliar woman there. She took the card, stamped some forms, and said, "You can wait back in room 11, if you like, Miss Redding."

Thank God for an unfamiliar face! That meant no silly chitchat with old Jane, no bake sales, tag sales, group this or that, or whatever else Jane had dreamed up. An impersonal "Miss Redding" was fine for now. She worked on a smile, to have it ready for whichever doctor showed up to see her. Smile at the man, or woman as it might be, tell him just what he wanted to hear and nothing that he should not and hope to God that he does not want a recitation of my life story. It was supposed to be in the chart anyway. Those damned charts! The whole truth and nothing but the truth, so help me God. Not likely. A whole hour's conversation, she knew, could show up as a one-line entry, just enough to satisfy the insurance company, while what was not in the chart could be heard occasioning merriment in the conference room. No, don't think about that stuff now. If the visit went as planned, she would be out of there by the end of the afternoon. Of course, there was always the chance she would not be leaving. Don't think about that either, she told herself. Think nice thoughts for the good doctor.

By late afternoon the clinic was quiet, the front desk manned by a different woman. Jane Farley was slightly on the plus side, both of plump and of her "early" forties. She was beginning to show a few streaks of gray in her short, brown hair. Her principal occupation, as always at that time of day, was checking the roster of scheduled patients against those who had been seen, entering the data from their visit, their future appointments, and their charges into the computer. Occasionally the phone would ring, interrupting her work until she had taken care of the caller. If there was a single indispensable person in the clinic, it was Jane. Aside from her value to the logistics of the clinic, she also liked to believe that, in many respects, she knew the patients better than their physicians. This was doubtless true, for she was always there with a smile and time to chat, even if she was answering two calls and making several notations while she did. She could also glean a fair amount of information about the patients just from the outside of their charts. The shiny, new, very thin folders were either brand-new patients or those who had only been seen once or twice. A battered folder, edges frayed and gray from handling, with a thick sheaf of papers inside signified a patient who had been around for a while. The accretion of paper was as accurate a gauge of hospital activity as tree rings were of a tree's age. Sometimes the chart was a stack of folders, held together by a rubber band. The one remaining in front of Jane on the desk fell into that category. The name on it matched the sole remaining name on her appointment list. Taylor Redding. Now, there was a name from the past, Jane thought. She had not seen the girl come in so, presumably, it had been during her lunch.

Taylor had been coming only every six months in recent years, and it had been some time since Jane had thought much about her, although she had once known the girl quite well. Perhaps it was the quiet afternoon, or perhaps just the recent advent of her own gray hair, that put Jane in a mood to reminisce about the past. Whatever the reason, she found herself recalling the time Taylor had first come. Taylor had been fifteen then. Arriving with her parents, she had held onto her mother with one hand, the other being firmly clamped around a stuffed teddy bear. A bright, bubbly teenager, everyone had fallen in love with her from the first. She would chatter, with little urging, about her major goals in life, namely the pursuit of boys, rock groups, her learner's permit, and, God help her parents, flying lessons. Jane had found this friendly, outgoing girl a delight and they had become fast friends. After a while, Taylor would always stop by to visit when she came into town, even if she were not coming in for an appointment. In between times, she would write. On occasion, they would go to a show, or even to Fenway Park to groan as they watched the Red Sox lose.

The girl that Jane remembered, though few others did, had become history. As Jane recalled, the transition had been relatively abrupt, although exactly when it had occurred escaped her. Taylor had become much less communicative. At times she seemed to radiate cold, the way others did warmth. She had begun to come in alone, without either parent, a very unusual thing for a teenager to do. The letters, once as expectable as the sunrise, dwindled in frequency. When she finished high school, Jane had learned, she had not even applied to colleges, although her grades and the prep school she had attended should have guaranteed her admission almost anywhere. She had taken a trip alone that summer, to Europe. Jane knew that much because she had received a card, from Reykjavik of all places, recounting Taylor's plans. That had been the last time Taylor had written. No, not quite the last. Jane had gotten a letter from her a couple of years ago. That one had been brief and to the point. Taylor had been having difficulty making travel arrangements; could her appointment be postponed for one month? The letter had been postmarked in Nairobi, and the forwarding address was an American Express office in the same city. Jane had made a point of checking the papers, and had found news of a coup in one of the nearby countries, as well as considerable unrest throughout the region. What had Taylor, fastidious Taylor, been doing in an area like that? A call to her parents had revealed only that they had not the faintest idea of where their daughter was. In the absence of other information, Jane had simply done what Taylor had requested. The only reply had been Taylor's punctual arrival on the rescheduled date.

These days, the appearance of Taylor's name on the clinic list tended to bring a chuckle, and a groan, from the senior physicians. They chuckled because the chore of dealing with her could be left to one of the junior people; rank hath its privileges. They groaned because there was always the possibility that a junior colleague would ask for help. One result of this state of affairs was that Taylor saw a different physician almost every time she came in, just the opposite of the way the clinic was supposed to work. It occurred to Jane, as she thought about it, that Taylor might be actively abetting this process. The lack of consistency would make it that much harder for any one person to know her well.

As she pondered this insight, Jane saw a door open down the corridor and a figure step out. The lights over the midportion of the hallway had gone out at midday, leaving just one set of lights at the far end. This produced a silhouette of anyone standing in that area, obscuring their features. There was no mistaking Taylor, though. She was tall, five-ten at least, and rather slender. That impression was heightened by the width of her swimmer's shoulders which exaggerated the taper to her waist. She walked gracefully, although her gait was not quite smooth. A casual glance might miss that, but Jane knew to look for it and it identified Taylor as surely as fingerprints. As she came forward into the lighted section, the rest of her features became clearly visible. Jane thought she could still see that long-ago girl in the face, a little on the thin side perhaps, with high cheekbones and a slight upward turn at the tip of the nose. She wore her auburn hair below her shoulders and pulled back into a thick, elaborately braided pony tail. A fair complexion was well matched to pale gray eyes. There was nothing girlish, however, about the tautness of her face, and her eyes held a daunting coldness.

If there was no surprise about her appearance, there was also none about her outfit. Taylor always wore long baggy pants and a long-sleeved blouse. Only the colors and patterns varied from visit to visit. This day the pants were black, the top solid yellow. The shirt was open to the waist, revealing a tan T-shirt bearing a silk-screened black eagle and the word BUNDESWEHR beneath it. Jane could make nothing of the shirt, but then she had never pretended to follow all the new rock groups. With this, Taylor wore a yellow silk scarf knotted at her throat, and a floppy felt hat planted on her head. Privately, Jane deplored Taylor's choice of clothes. Had Jane such a figure, she would have reveled in fashions to show it off, not in loose outfits that half hid it. Unconsciously she tugged at her own sweater to smooth it over her chest.

"How did everything go, Taylor?" Jane asked as the girl reached the desk. A brief nod served as the reply. "So, when are you coming back? Six months again?"

"Yeah. If I show up." The voice was a low contralto. Taylor reached across the desk top, anticipating the small white appointment card Jane was filling out.

Jane did not react immediately to the remark. It had become almost a ritual for Taylor to add that qualifier whenever the subject of her next appointment came up. After so many years, Jane had learned to take it with several grains of salt. Instead, she searched for a way to keep a conversation flowing, as if time travel were possible.

"I heard you weren't planning to go back to school." She finished with the card as she spoke.

"Never said I was going to go to school. I can't think of anything more boring, or useless, to do with my time." She picked up the card without looking at it and tucked it away.

The hand that took the card caught Jane's eye. Engraved gold rings encircled the middle and little fingers. There was a large ring set with a turquoise rock on the index finger. Having noticed the rings, Jane then also saw the long, thin silver earring dangling from the left earlobe, and the small diamond set in the right. Taylor's fondness for jewelry had never diminished. Abruptly Jane realized that in the moment she had taken to look at the rings, Taylor was turning away from the desk.

"So, what are you up to now?" she asked, trying to tether her with the question. Taylor stopped.

"Meaning, 'What is crazy Taylor up to now?' "

"I never said you were crazy, Taylor," she said defensively. "You're just different. And I was just wondering what you were doing."

"I do a variety of things," she answered. "Something always turns up."

"Anything interesting?"

"Well, what I do isn't fattening, obviously, so you can figure it's either illegal or immoral." She smiled as she said it, but it was an odd half-smile that involved only the muscles around her mouth and left out the rest of the face.

The answer left Jane puzzled. Taylor had always been hard to figure out, even as a kid. Now she was downright cryptic. Jane tried to ignore it. "You planning to go to any of the Sox games?"

"No."

That "no" was so flat, so final, it put an abrupt end to the conversation. Before Jane could think of a way to restart it, Taylor had turned and walked out.

Jane felt put down and hurt. She had only been trying to be friendly, but it was so hard reaching out for someone who was not really there. So, why the hell do I bother? It was a question she had to ask herself. Certainly, nobody else did. Not any more.

Taylor Redding, for her part, was in a huge rush to get outside. She walked rapidly through the corridor, past the elevators and the security station to the front door. The wall plaques, commemorating generous donations, did not merit a glance, nor did any of the people who bustled through or sat in the front lobby. She had a very limited tolerance for the place, and she was rapidly reaching that limit. From the moment she came in, every time she came in, her body mounted a protest centered in her stomach. It began with a vague uneasiness just below her navel that gradually increased in sharpness and intensity. It could easily have been attributed to a tainted lunch, but she never ate beforehand and such an explanation could not account for its occurrence every visit. Eventually, it grew into a tumultuous pitch of nausea that threatened to burst through to the outside. She hated the idea of being sick, with the loss of control it represented, even more than the nausea itself. The slight delay old Jane had imposed shrank the thin margin of safety with which she operated almost to the vanishing point.

At last the automatic door swung open before her as she stepped on the rubber mat. The hot, sticky blast of summertime Boston that met her was as welcome as any cool mountain breeze. Almost immediately, she could feel her knotted guts begin to loosen. Taylor crossed the short driveway that ultimately led to the above-ground parking garage, and stood for a while on the sidewalk. Almost lost it this time! God, she hated the place, hated having to appear at regular intervals, as if to be checked in by a parole officer. She hated the furniture, the pictures, the little group notices posted on bulletin boards. Most of all, she hated the expressions she saw on the faces of people who saw her after reading through her chart. She could even tell who was properly doing their job, reviewing her chart beforehand, and who was just winging it. All by looking at their faces. She hated all of it.

After standing for a few minutes her discomfort completely subsided. Against the glare of the sun, she donned a pair of reflecting sunglasses. Their silver surfaces easily held as much warmth as the eyes they hid, and matched her unchanging expression. Her face might have been constant, and her stomach finally quiescent, but an undercurrent of unease persisted. She thought about it as she stood in the sun. After some analysis, she decided that it was the present absence of plans, the lack of irons in the fire, that was bothering her. Why should that be so? The rule was always that one waited patiently, and watched. Inevitably, opportunities arose. She had always been patient. The inevitable periods of idleness were merely the necessary price for finding good prospects. Predictable, readily available work—read dull—was only for when the cash flow demanded it. However, mentally reviewing the rules wasn't enough to make the mental itch go away.

She needed to do *something* right away; sitting around was suddenly anathema. Taylor took a brief look at her watch. If she wanted, in a couple of hours she could undoubtedly find Sean the Mouthpiece at the Plough and Stars. Sean always had an angle and would probably have something for her if she made the slightest noise about being available. The problem was, what Sean would have to offer would not be particularly attractive. The thought of another run to Bolivia or Peru, or wherever, to bring back some god-forsaken baby was enough to make her gag—not that the money was bad, an important point, but the undertakings lacked flair and importance.

Briefly, fantasy intruded. Wistfully, she thought of the escapade years ago when Perot had busted his people out of an Iranian jail. *There* had been a job with all the desirable features! Now, why could she not be called for a job like that? She shook her head, oblivious to passersby who were unaware of the line of thought she was discarding. Fool, she thought, you know perfectly well why you don't get calls for jobs like that. No one important enough to offer such jobs has the slightest idea who you are. Even if they did, of course, they would not give a job like that to a woman. And even if they would, they would not give it to you. Besides, you like operating alone anyway. Nothing like rationalizing it away, right, Taylor?

Ah, well, life was unfair. The acknowledgment of that formed one of the basic tenets of Taylor's philosophy. Sometimes though, like these times, the translation of those principles into reality was very frustrating. She was not going to call Sean, though. Not yet, anyway. That decision, at least, was clear in her thoughts. Better to poke around town and see what was cooking. Taylor had other contacts to tap, contacts that promised more interesting possibilities even if they lacked Sean's dependability.

# CHAPTER 3

## BOSTON, MASSACHUSETTS

"HEY, TAYLOR KID, I told you. I just don't have anything for you right now." The speaker was William O'Brian, Billy to the papers and the police, a large man with a shock of hair, once red, now resigned to gray. His face, large and heavy-jawed with a network of fine wrinkles at the corners of eyes and mouth, held none of the harshness that one might have associated with the delivery of such a comment. O'Brian might have been a handsome man, but at some time in the past a gash over his right eye had been poorly sutured. The resulting band of pink scar tissue, stretching from temple to mid-forehead, gave him a visage at odds with his conservative, well-tailored suit. It was more in line with his rather rough-edged syntax.

They sat facing each other in the booth of a diner, not far from the Government Center T stop. Most people seeking O'Brian's patronage would have expected to find him at one or another of the offices he maintained in downtown Boston. They would have been wrong. O'Brian saw people at his office by his choice only. To see him on an impromptu basis one had to know, as Taylor did, the coffee and lunch stops where he would hold court. Needless to say, such meetings derived only from prior association, or connections.

"Understand, please, I'm not trying to shut you out. Got no interest in doin' that." He leaned forward slightly to emphasize his sincerity. "Fact is, I know there's nothing going now that you'll touch. Or have the rules changed?" His voice underlined the last sentence, and let it dangle between them.

Taylor shook her head slowly no. O'Brian had a wide range of political and business interests, some legal, some not, and parts of both unsavory. There had always been an understanding that Taylor would not deal with certain aspects of his affairs.

"Still picky about how you get your hands dirty." O'Brian shook his head also. "If I didn't feel like such a father figure to you, I don't think I could put up with it."

Taylor grinned inwardly. Whatever else was true about the man, and she had no illusions about that truth, O'Brian had not been joking about his perception of their relationship. She never mentioned that she found little use for any father figure. Her daddy, she thought, would probably have lost the remainder of his graying hair had he heard either of those two opinions expressed. Father figure or not, there were actually two other good reasons she could think of for O'Brian to go along with the limits she set. One was her good reliable work. The other was his not having to worry about a stab in the back. She saw no need to point out either one. The issue had arisen before.

"Well, never mind that." O'Brian swept the crumbs off the table with his big-knuckled hands. "What does make me wonder is why you're asking. Long as I've known you, ever since whatshisname recommended you to me, you've never asked me for a thing. Even when you were so broke you weren't eating every day, yeah, I know just how flat you were, all I heard was, 'Taylor's available.' You never came around asking. So why the change in my girl who's otherwise 'constant as the Northern Star'?"

"No change really. I'm just looking for something to do."

" 'Looking for something to do'? Hmm. Kid, are you in trouble? If you're into somebody big, you let me know now. I may not be able to fix it, but I can probably help. Especially if it's money. And you don't have to pay me interest, you know that." A blunt index finger aimed at Taylor's chin accompanied the last sentence.

"No," she shook her head again. "It's not money. I'd just rather get moving sooner rather than later."

"Since when is time such an issue? You getting old on me, Taylor?"

The corners of her mouth gave a small twitch at that. "Not a chance."

"Hell." O'Brian arched his back to stretch a little. "Same old Taylor. Colder'n ice and harder'n rock. Look, kid, what can I say, but I'll let you know if I have something. If you're around, and you want it, you say so. Same as always."

"Fair enough," Taylor said, and stood to leave. She had no intention of pressing any harder. Nicky, a die-stamped bodyguard type who had been with O'Brian as long as Taylor could remember, watched her go from a stool at the counter. If she had any reason to suspect O'Brian's words about the nature of their relationship, the distance Nicky kept when she was around would dispel it.

As she crossed the expanse of brick paving between city hall and the T stop, she paused to reflect on the afternoon. It had been pretty dismal. No doubt, had she told O'Brian she would take any kind of work, something would have been forthcoming. With it, however, would have come the kind of invitation she should feel flattered to get, and O'Brian would be angry to have turned down. Which was exactly what would have happened, because she had neither any intention of doing what she did not want to do, nor was she interested in becoming a wholly owned subsidiary.

"Impatient, that's what you are," she muttered to no one in particular. "Where's your goddamn sense of timing? 'The strike of a hawk breaks the body of its prey because of *timing*.' Twenty-five hundred years ago they knew that. It's not as though timing were a new discovery." The collector at the token booth may have wondered what she was talking about, but Taylor could not have cared less.

Impatience was a mistake; it was clearly against her rules. She always waited for opportunities to develop, never tried to force them. Even Billy O'Brian, bless his black heart, had said as much. Maybe I just need to take some time, she thought, go back to Margret's farm and relax. Of course, it wasn't Margret's farm, it belonged to Margret's father, but that was the way Taylor thought of it. She tended to think of them as her family, more so than her real one. She had not spoken to anyone in her family for—how long?— three or four years, probably, and had not seen them for longer. Much as she wanted to see Margret and the others, though, she doubted that watching sheep crop grass would make her any less impatient. She wanted to do something *new*.

Making the rounds of old contacts suddenly lost its appeal. Doing so would just compound the error she had already made. Billy would say nothing, she knew, but others would bruit it around that Taylor Redding was asking for favors. A *very* cold day in Hell that would be. And, for sure, she would stay away from Sean. Working for Billy could frequently be problematic from a legal perspective, but it was unlikely to be dull. Working for Sean . . . for Chrissakes, she would rather go back to school. The best solution for the present was going to be to find a noisy bar, one she did not frequent, and watch the evening slide by. Maybe something interesting would happen.

Evening on a hot, sticky Boston day was a relief only in the absence of direct, glaring sunlight. The air still had the consistency of meringue topping, and the relative decrease in temperature simply made objects feel damp. Just as sundown had done nothing for the oppressive weather, it had also failed to cure Taylor's malaise.

She had found an unfamiliar bar, not hard to do in Boston, and had settled in for an evening of people watching, her favorite spectator sport. The bar was located in Allston near Commonwealth Avenue, an area she did not usually frequent. It was a curious neighborhood, boasting a high proportion of students and academic camp followers, all mixed in with recent immigrants from Asia. The sidewalks featured rows of tightly packed little shops offering wares from genuine antique furniture of dubious heritage, to greasy pizza. A large proportion of the signs were not in English, direct evidence of the size of the immigrant population. Given the shortness of the pockets of many of the inhabitants, many of the buildings—and the people—looked in need of a sandblast and a coat of fresh paint. All in all, it was a decent place to watch people.

The bar she had found was fairly typical for the region. It consisted of a single large room on the ground floor, with hardwood floors that at one time might have been polished. The bar itself, with its attendant row of stools, was set at one end of the room on a section elevated a few inches above the rest of the floor. Several small tables were grouped on the elevated portion. There were more, and larger, tables below, as well as a cleared space for dancing. The larger tables presumably compensated for the greater distance from the bar and the proximity to the gyrating bodies. There was no band, but a pair of speakers suitable for a Billy Graham revival in Yankee Stadium supplied an adequate volume of music. Like most bars situated in student areas, this one catered to the student population with the usual amenities of low-priced drinks, munchies, dancing and a liberal interpretation of the legal age. This basic arrangement had endured through several changes of management.

Taylor enjoyed a bar, almost any bar. Most people had no conception of how ridiculous they acted when drunk, especially when they were 'holding their liquor.' Consequently, they frequently provided splendid free entertainment. Add in the unpredictability of the man who has 'held' enough liquor, and an interesting evening was assured. She tended to avoid student bars, however, primarily because of the students. Taken as a group, they were of interest only to each other, sober or drunk. Why, then, she had landed in this one was a mystery. Most likely the reason was it had been there when she felt like sitting down and having a beer; having once sat down she then saw no compelling reason to get up. It had not been a banner day.

Unfortunately, her luck was not ready to change. She had been midway through her second beer, relaxing as she watched the floor show, when she acquired a companion. Michael was tall, moderately handsome and markedly extroverted. One minute the only other chair by the table had been empty, the next he was in it and talking. Being the good-natured sort, he was unlikely to let an attractive female rusticate alone at a table. He had just finished his first year of law school at Boston College, a fact with which he was greatly taken and impressed upon Taylor almost before his rear was fully settled on the seat. She heard the rest of his life story within, approximately, the next thirty seconds. From her point of view, this left only the problem of how to get rid of him quietly. This naturally ran counter to Michael's own designs.

Finding Taylor unmoved by the vicissitudes in the life of a first-year law student, unamused by the traps into which his classmates (never he!) fell, and unimpressed by his moment of glory in moot court, Michael fished around for some other means of keeping this potential relationship alive.

"How about somethin' to eat?" Original he was not.

"No, thanks. I'm quite comfortable here."

"Hey, no problem!" Michael grinned as though he had scored a debating point. "They serve food here. I'll have a large plate of fries," he shouted to flag down a waitress. "And the young lady here . . ." He ended the sentence with a flick of his hand at Taylor.

"Chopped meat," she said sardonically. Michael missed the intonation, and the point, entirely.

"So, what do you do, Becky?" he asked when the waitress left. "You haven't told me anything about yourself."

Even assuming I wanted to, Taylor thought, who could get a word in edgewise? Aloud she said only, "I'm a nurse." Taylor was no more a nurse than her name was Becky, but it was a convenient role she could assume easily.

"A *nurse*? Thank God!" He grabbed at his chest. "I think I need emergency resuscitation."

"You're out of luck. I don't do that kind of work." Events were starting to get out of control. Had the scenario been unfolding at a neighboring table Taylor would have been amused. As it was, she was annoyed.

"What kind of nurse are you, then? And where do you work?"

"Mass Mental," she replied. "I work with kooks."

While Michael paused to consider her statement, the fries arrived. After half-drowning them in ketchup, he offered the plate to Taylor, who refused.

"You know, Becky, I was thinking." As he thought he finished a few fries, and another glass of beer. "We really ought to go back to my place. I've got steaks and Heineken in the fridge, and a great sound system. I really would like to get to know you better."

No shit, Taylor thought. "Sorry, Michael. Not interested," she said. It was time to put an end to this.

Michael had never really disguised his purpose for the evening, which was to pick Taylor up, preferably get her drunk, and definitely take her back to his apartment. He had merely been, in his view, politely indirect up to that point. It was a program Taylor had little interest in. Bars, in her view, were for watching people, not meeting them, and she always went home alone. She did not regard herself as a tease, not in the least. She always paid for her own drinks, was careful to make her attitude clear early. Inevitably, however, her figure attracted attention, and there were always men who regarded a frosty demeanor as a challenge. Michael had not struck her as the hard-headed type initially, but he was proving persistent.

"Come on, Becky, why not? We'll have a good time." He finally abandoned any attempt at finesse.

Taylor looked at him with distaste. She had started out by wanting to brush him off gently, and now she was regretting it. "Michael," she sighed, "are you drunk?"

"Never that drunk!" He straightened in his chair, giving her a broad grin and a wink. "So how about it, Becky?"

Taylor pushed her chair back slightly from the table, causing the legs to squeak loudly on the floor. "Since you're not drunk, you'll understand what I say. I have no interest in fucking you. Absolutely none. There's plenty of available meat floating around here, and there's a lot of time before closing. I'm sure you'll manage to get laid."

"Hey, is that any way for a nurse to talk? If I said something wrong, I'm sorry. Can we start over?" He looked surprised, as though he had been really making progress and this was a totally unexpected reversal.

Taylor had been sitting in a semireclining position, with most of her weight on her right leg. Her left hand hooked the back of the chair, the right had been left on the table. Michael reached a decision of his own, drained his beer, and reached over to take her hand in his. "C'mon, we can take a walk and talk about it. Let's go, huh?"

Taylor suppressed a small shudder. She hated being touched under any circumstances. More importantly, there was a fine line between a bold attempt at seduction and impulsive rape. Michael was drifting toward that frontier. She smiled at him, then, and stroked his cheek with her free hand. Then she leaned forward, freeing the other hand, to run the fingers of both through his hair. He smiled back at her, with the gratification that the direct approach was paying off. At the smile, she grabbed a double handful of hair, and yanked downward. Caught off guard, he had no chance to resist the force of her move. His head snapped down, ending with his face in the plate of ketchup-covered fries.

He leaped up quickly, physically unhurt, to find that Taylor had used the interval to gain her feet and pick up an empty beer bottle by its neck. He faced her across the little table, his face flushed as red as the ketchup smeared across it. A single french fry stuck to his left cheek. His empty hands stayed down at his sides, intermittently clenching and opening. A stillness rippled out across the room, broken only by the bartender as she moved toward the telephone.

"What the hell was that for?" he demanded.

"Because you're too damn thick to understand that a polite 'no' still means no," she told him. She watched his hands and eyes, oblivious to the stares from other occupants of the bar. "Now, as far as I'm concerned, you can either leave in peace, or in pieces. The choice is yours." She tapped the bottle against the edge of the table for emphasis.

The confrontation ended abruptly. After emitting some gargling noises, Michael suddenly turned on his heels, and dashed out. The sensation of pressure in the room dissipated quickly. The barkeep let go of the phone, and within minutes the normal level of bustle and chatter resumed. Taylor was left standing alone, holding the bottle.

She set it down carefully on the table, and walked over to the bar. There, she found an empty stool at the end of the railing, where it intersected the wall. The positioning of the stool gave her a good view of the room and the entrance. It also had the added benefit of moving her away from most of the smokers. Putting up with cigarette smoke was the price she paid for hanging around barrooms, but it was a loathsome thing, in a class with physical contact. Seated with her back comfortably against the wall, she signaled the bartender for service with her index finger. The woman brought a fresh beer, and favored Taylor with an admiring smile.

"On the house," she said. "You're a cool one, aren't you? I loved the way you handled that situation."

Taylor took a draught from the mug without replying. The beer left a cold streak on the way down, with just a slight burn at the back of her throat from the carbonation. Beer had been an acquired taste, but she had come to love that sensation, which could not be reproduced by any other drink. She finished the swallow and shrugged at the barmaid. It had not been all that spectacular.

"Do you think he'll be back?" the woman asked.

"Nah." It was always possible, of course, but Taylor did not really believe it. Had she thought otherwise, she would have finished him with the bottle while his face was still in the fries. There had been enough times when the reverse had been true for her to be confident of her judgment.

The bartender, finding her uncommunicative, soon moved on and left her alone. The incident continued to nag at Taylor's mind, though. Not because of any serious implications—it had none—but because it should not have happened in the first place. Men! Always the same old problem. They were fine for business. In fact, Taylor infinitely preferred conducting business with men. Old Sister Angelica had been an exception to that rule, but was the only one Taylor could think of. The problem was that, business aside, the male mind seemed to move along a single sidetrack—at least, as best Taylor could tell. Any meeting, any *conversation*, was a potential spring-board to sex. Perhaps there was additional erectile tissue within the male brain to account for the phenomenon. She thought she had made her position clear enough. Looking back, though, she wondered what her real intentions had been. She could hardly claim either youth or naïveté as reasons for overlooking the fact that Michael's mind had been on his dick. Hell, he had not even had to open his mouth to broadcast his thoughts. So tell me, Miss so-streetsmart Taylor Redding, why did you let that circus act develop? She concluded that she was just too eager for some action to turn up. She had foolishly let him talk, hoping there was something else behind the transparent pickup. Wishful thinking. She knew she had to be patient, and here she was trying to force the issue. Why?

To be eager enough to listen to a law student, even briefly, told her how badly she wanted to be active, but not why. Money was not the cause. Not so many years ago too much idle time would have left her the choice of going to Daddy for money or not eating. The two options were about equally palatable. Now it was no longer an issue. There was enough stashed in various places to maintain her comfortably, if not quite in the style she preferred, while she waited for events to develop. Anyway, there was Sean if matters were that desperate. If not money, what? Maybe she was just getting itchy about sitting around as she got older. Had Billy not said something on that order? It had been a while since she last worked. She had wound up the venture a little early and, knowing she had a fixed date in Boston, had done nothing for a few additional weeks. Getting very possessive of my time, she thought. She squelched that idea as soon as it arose. For the present, she could do as she wished. If she kept up that line of thinking, she would wind up feeling sorry for herself, and that was not permitted. Ultimately, she decided to table the "why" of it. She wanted action, and eventually it would find her. It never failed.

As far back as she could remember, Taylor had a gift for being around when there was action. Her mummy used to sum it up succinctly for friends and relatives with the phrase, "Taylor has a knack for trouble." Possibly there had been a distinct point in her life at which this talent originated, although just as likely it was congenital. Questions of that nature were hard to answer. Memories of specific events in her early childhood were clouded, and the innate self-centeredness of the child made it impossible to recall whether she simply happened to be around when things occurred, or whether they occurred because she was around. What she could recall was the sing-song Mummy had made up for her.

"Taylor, that's a capital T which stands for trouble, Redding!" For some years she had delighted in reciting it whenever she was introduced to company.

She did remember when she first became aware of this "knack" as a real talent. She had been ten years old at the time. She had gone to the mall with Mummy, or more exactly had been dragged along, it being a perfect day for softball. A young man had caught her eye in one of the stores, for what reason she had never been able to say. Despite an unremarkable outward appearance, something about him had nibbled at her, tugged at her, refused to leave her alone. The feeling had been strong enough, and persistent enough, to act on. Unwatched by Mummy, who was absorbed by the makeup counter, she had sauntered over and kicked the young man in the shins with the edge of her new hiking boots. He had screamed at the unexpected strike and dropped the newspaper he had been carrying, and along with it the pistol it had concealed. There had been action aplenty then. Mummy had been hysterical, of course, but to set against that there had been the ride in the police car and her picture in the paper. Taylor, with a capital T, really did stand for trouble.

As she grew older, she came to view it as a special sixth sense. It was impossible to explain, and trying to do so led to predictable responses from friends and family, but it was there. It was not uniformly perfect, but eyes and ears were known to play tricks as well. Her Uncle Cyrus, great-uncle really, had been the one person who had been impressed with her intuition. He had seen plenty of action of his own in the past and had told Taylor about much of it, including things that he probably should not have said. Young Taylor had always listened carefully to Cyrus. She paid attention to her intuition. Too bad it had been asleep on this night.

The beer finished at about the same time the thought did, and the bottom of the mug offered no further inspiration. It occurred to her that if it was going to be a long wait for "something to turn up," she would be more comfortable in her usual haunts. Ah, a decision she could make! It was settled, the next evening she would start off at the Kettle Drum, a bar she considered to be much more her style. For the moment, she ordered another beer and settled back to watch the Red Sox bullpen let another game get away.

# CHAPTER 4

## BOSTON, MASSACHUSETTS

SHORTLY AFTER HIS ARRIVAL in Boston, Jeffers knew that he was a victim of Murphy's Law. He had planned carefully enough, or so it had seemed in his eagerness to be off after Oliver had capitulated. He was to meet his contact, this "Tailor" individual at 6:00 P.M., so what more natural thing than to take an early flight and spend an afternoon of leisure in the Hub?

For one thing, he had not reckoned on the stifling Boston weather. He desperately wanted to be taken seriously in this affair, after his experience with Charles Oliver and a few of Thompson's remarks, so he had dressed uncharacteristically in good slacks, a conservative shirt and tie, and a sport jacket. As a result, he was uncomfortable from the moment he stepped out of the terminal building. The shirt collar, wet with perspiration, chafed at each turn of his neck no matter how he tugged to loosen the tie. A river of sweat, collected from tributaries at his neck and shoulders, snaked down his spine to a reservoir in the band of his undershorts. Even with his jacket off there was no relief, and there seemed to be no casual or comfortable way to drape the unfamiliar garment.

As much as he had erred on the weather, he had done worse in gauging his own mental state. Planned from afar, the trip had no visceral impact, and the chance to see Boston at company expense, prior to taking care of business, was not to be missed. The plane flight and the simple reality of his arrival forced him to focus on the many uncertainties of his venture. Indeed, the only facts he knew—that both his enzyme and his friend were missing—did little to inspire calm. The previous day's anger at the accusation of his friend and at the implication of his own responsibility for the loss of his material had cooled. In its place, speculation as to their fates took over, with speculation about his own following shortly after. The fact that he was on the street with the key in his pocket to enough money to make Thompson nervous did nothing to calm him down. Consequently, instead of strolling casually around the historic downtown area, he went in search of relief for the dull constricting ache that had formed in a band

35

above his eyes and ears. The aspirin he gulped did little for his stomach, which appeared intent upon twirling itself around the inner aspect of his umbilicus, and created a sense of urgency unjustified by the trivial amount of food he had eaten.

Jeffers was not accustomed to anxiety. The last time he could remember feeling anything like it had been over a decade ago, before he had taken his qualifying exam as a doctoral student. He elected to skip lunch, procured some Mylanta from a druggist and took a cab uptown to the university. In so doing, he arrived in front of the Kettle Drum at three in the afternoon, a full three hours early. Even in his state of mind at the time he recognized the impossibility of sitting in the bar, doing nothing for three hours while remaining inconspicuous. He retreated, therefore, to the university bookstore, a large structure with sufficient diversity to permit him to spend the afternoon apparently browsing.

Under other circumstances he could easily have spent that amount of time looking over books without thinking about it, but this time he was unable to divorce his thoughts from the upcoming meeting. He was half afraid the Tailor would laugh at him and send him away, probably on Oliver's instructions. Then again, maybe there was no Tailor at all. Maybe the key in his pocket fit Thompson's bicycle lock and the authorization was phony. Then, when he went to the Kettle Drum, there would be no one there. He would return to the company to hear Thompson laugh and tell him the whole exercise had been designed to get the issue out of his system and that it was the best thing for him.

"They'd be just about right, too," he muttered to himself, and then knocked over a rack of books as he turned to make sure he had not been overheard.

After that, with the conviction that the bookstore manager would remember his face forever, he decided he could wait no longer. His watch showed it to be only a half-hour from the appointed time, and he figured he could nurse a single beer that long if he had to. The air conditioning in the store had dried him off, and if the evening was not cool, the heat was at least less intense, so he was able to muster a bouncy stride as he crossed the street to the bar.

A purple Monte Carlo was nowhere in sight, so he took a seat at the bar and signaled the bartender for a draft. The Kettle Drum was a small affair with perhaps a dozen tiny tables and a bar on the street level. A flight of stairs led down to a dance floor in the basement where a band would play later in the evening, the rising vibrations being a factor in the bar's name. There were rooms above as well, judging from the windows looking out onto the street, but there seemed to be no access from the main barroom. The place was not very crowded, but a steady stream of people drifted in as he sat there.

As he sat with his beer, working in small sips around long pauses to maintain appearances without the necessity of a refill, the inflow began to fill the bar up around him. The increasing density of the crowd was puzzling to him, as he was unaware of the Kettle Drum's proximity to Fenway Park and of the Red Sox's being at home. The crowd remained a distant phenomenon that did not directly impinge on him. The noise sounded muffled, as if filtered through earplugs, and the visible world constricted to the mug of beer in front of him and his watch. The bartender drifted in and out of this narrow field, his expression as he passed Jeffers plainly stating that the rate at which he was drinking did not justify the prime space he was occupying. The single, consuming thought in Jeffers's mind was the problem of actually making contact. It was very nearly six-thirty, but he had heard no one say anything resembling the code. Should he ask the bartender if he knew the Tailor? Oliver had mentioned no such variation. As for the barkeep, as much as Jeffers could tell from appearances, which he assured himself was not much, the man would greet any request, save for more alcohol, with an invitation to leave. His preoccupation with this predicament made him oblivious to the din around him.

"Can I getcha somethin' else?"

Jeffers started and looked up at the barkeep, who had evidently wearied of waiting for Jeffers to reorder voluntarily. At the question, Jeffers suddenly realized that he had finished his beer and had been staring at an empty glass. The barkeep was a heavy-set man, with thinning black hair and a mole by the right corner of his mouth. He looked like the wrong sort to argue with. Mutely, Jeffers signaled for a refill.

It was, therefore, entirely inadvertent that he became aware of the girl to his right. He had not noticed her working through the press to reach the bar, but he had not noticed anything for a while, and she had not been there the last time he had glanced in that direction. However she had gotten there, she stood at the bar in the rather narrow space between Jeffers and the occupied stool on the other side, holding two dollars out on top of the wooden planks. Her eyes were on the bartender as he prepared drinks at one end of the bar. Looking to catch the bartender's eye and flag him down, she was turned partly away from Jeffers. The first look was enough to shatter Jeffers's mental isolation. His gaze, having come to rest on her tall, well-proportioned figure, refused to move elsewhere. Overall, she had the look of an athlete. Her clothing had an expensive designer-label look to it. Rich kid, Jeffers catalogued subconsciously. Further examination reinforced that view—

those were not plastic mood rings she was wearing. Just the pretty Long Island princess who went to school in Boston, or so Jeffers had always heard. God, she was more than pretty, though! The outfit gave just enough hint of curves and tapers to start Jeffers imagining what was underneath. Unlike the rest of the clothes, a T-shirt under the mostly open blouse fit snugly, drawing Jeffers's attention that way. It took a moment before he was able to see it well, and when he did he saw that it advertised the German army. How did such a woman come to wear such a shirt in Boston?

It was crazy to go to the expense of those clothes, not to mention the jewelry, and wear them with a cheap T-shirt. Obviously, she had no thought for value. *Spoiled* rich kid, he noted mentally. She probably pumped premium gas into her economy compact and charged it to her parents.

His conclusions about the girl's lifestyle and upbringing did nothing to diminish his interest in looking at her. Extrapolating her behavior from her clothing led, naturally, to further speculation about her. What did she do? What did she do for fun? Was she dating someone? What might she think of George Jeffers? As he sat there, eyes engaged and most of his brain in neutral, a small mental guardian hammered out a different theme. "Fool," it said. "Idiot. Mind your damn business before you screw up good." It was too little, too late.

The way his mind saw it, the part of it that was off enjoying itself, he caught her attention and smoothly introduced himself. The line he used he could not quite remember after he said it, not surprising because Jeffers never had any such line. To brazenly speak, unbidden, to a strange woman was an art he could never manage, no matter how much he thought about it. In daydreams, however, such problems are not important and whatever Jeffers said worked. They spoke for a while and she moved closer to him. At first he felt just the wispy touch of her outer blouse, then his arm was around her waist, his hand over the crest of her hip, her skin warm through the shirt. She said something he could not quite hear and laid her head on his shoulder. Then reality set in.

"Something you wanted?" she asked. Given time, and the time interval had been long only in the subjective sense, the girl had reacted to the pressure of his stare. Turned now to face him, the gaze from her hard gray eyes burned into his brown ones the way dry ice burns by extreme cold. Her voice, now that he heard it, was contralto. Her tone implied that the question was rhetorical.

Caught off guard, Jeffers said nothing, his fanciful scenarios evaporating as he sat. Tongue having gone on strike, he shook his head no. She left it at that, turning back to the bar, though all the while keeping Jeffers in her field of view as though she was not entirely willing to discount the idea of his making a move at her.

"Jackie," she yelled at the bartender as he turned their way. "A Lite when you can." Her voice, when she raised it, penetrated the noise with ease.

"You got it, Taylor," Jackie answered, fishing a glass from under the bar as he headed for the tap.

The name shot into Jeffers's head where it set off alarms. *This* was his contact? Not possible! Yet, how much more a fool could he make of himself than if she were his contact, and he sat there as she came and left?

"W-wait a minute," he stammered, forcing the words out. "You're the Tailor?" His voice rose an octave as he finished the sentence, which triggered a flush across his cheeks. "You're the Tailor?" he repeated. He could not keep the incredulity out of his voice. On any other occasion he would have given almost anything to start a conversation with a girl like this one, never mind be handed an opening line, but not this night. The concept that she was his contact was impossible. "I think there's been a mistake."

At the question, and the negative answer he gave it himself, a quirky smile crossed her face. Her beer had arrived and she could leave, but Taylor Redding's sixth sense for trouble was twitching.

"You asked for the Taylor, you got her," she announced. "The one and only, in fact, Taylor Redding, world's greatest female adventurer." She tossed her head lightly, flicking the braid from one shoulder to the other. She stuck her hand out. "If you're looking for a problem solver, we should talk it over." It was pure guesswork on her part that any problem existed, but that was where her knack came in. The man looked totally out of place, not to mention nervous enough to bolt at a wrong word. People going about their legitimate business did not look like he did. It added up to something clandestine, which Taylor's mind translated as: action.

Jeffers took the proffered hand. What else was there to do? He could not think of anything to say.

"Well?" Taylor asked. "I'm more than happy to fix hassles, look for treasure or head for parts unknown. All on a fee-for-service basis, of course."

Jeffers did not answer right away. His face, however, told Taylor a great deal of what she wanted to know. There was no question he was involved in something, right to his chin. There remained two important issues for her. Where did it—whatever *it* was—rate on the Taylor Redding scale of interest, and was she going to get a piece of it?

Jeffers had questions on his mind, too. His, however, were rather amorphous. On the face of it, it seemed odd that the government—much less the company—had sent a girl to do this job. Still, Thompson and Oliver had been vague about the contact's gender. The question had never even been raised. Probably he should have asked. Thinking of it now did not do him a world of good. He had thought the entire routine, with contacts and codes, was pure Hollywood—but, of course, had he objected they would have dropped him from their plans. So what to do now? James Bond worked with beautiful female agents all the time. Surely that worthy would never have been caught tongue-tied in a situation like this. Damn your eyes, Taylor Redding!

"Look, Ms. Redding—"

Taylor chopped him off with a sweeping hand motion. "Taylor'll do. I can't see any use for formality."

"Okay," Jeffers tried again. "All I know, Taylor, is I was supposed to meet the Tailor here. How do I know that's you?" He fished for a means of deciding who she was without either revealing too much, or looking too stupid. Jeffers had a code sequence designed to precisely establish that point; however, under the pressure of the moment he had forgotten it.

Taylor considered the question briefly. It was possible that someone she knew had steered this mark her way. Unlikely, but possible. How many people knew she was in town? At least a few. For her it was an important question. If he had been sent, she would take on almost any job; if she did not, the next interesting problem might not come her way.

"All I can be sure of is that you've got a problem and you need help with it. As for who I am, you approached me, not the other way around. Remember?"

Jeffers did remember. He had also remembered the code he was supposed to use. Hearing it in his head it sounded abysmally corny. Hell, he thought, if she were not his contact, why would she pursue him like this? It would not make sense. What would Sir James do?

The thought sparked him to another tack. "Jim Thompson told you nothing, nothing at all about this?"

The name Jim Thompson was not a familiar one to Taylor. *Ergo,* this man was not a referral. She could have easily dropped the matter then; she had no real information to go on. Her intuition kept nibbling at her, though. There was something about the man, about his manner, his obvious reluctance to discuss what was bothering him that told her to stay interested. With luck she would be able to get enough information to decide whether to commit herself before he caught on.

"Hey," she said, "I can understand your not wanting to talk here. We can go elsewhere." A sudden grin lit up her whole face. "Hell, take me to dinner. If it's no sale, I go Dutch."

"Go elsewhere, huh? In a purple Monte Carlo?"

The question took Taylor completely by surprise. The moment she heard it, she knew she had tripped over a recognition code. Annoying as it was, the presence of such a verbal booby trap confirmed the importance of the party she was trying to crash. She was not about to let go.

"No car," she replied. "There's a place we can go just a few doors down. That way you won't feel trapped once we leave." It was not a terrific reply, but it was the best she could do on short notice for being direct and evasive at the same time.

The answer probably would have sufficed had Jeffers not caught the momentary look of uncertainty on her face before she spoke. Oliver had been specific about the car. If he could be vague about a person's gender, but specific about their car, then the car had to be important. He fastened on that thought and made up his mind.

"Listen, Taylor, I'm really sorry, but I've made a mistake here. I don't think you're the person I'm supposed to meet." Jeffers slipped off the stool with the intention of beating a hasty retreat. "Oh, shit!" He had backed up trying to find an escape route and stumbled over one leg of the stool. His elbow caught the recently refilled glass sending beer cascading across the bar. That brought Jackie hustling over with a towel and a frown.

Taylor showed no sign of backing away. "Wait a moment," she said, trying to retrieve her position. "What idiot told you to expect that kind of car? Could you honestly see *me* in it?" The more the conversation stumbled along, the more determined she became to keep her foot in the door. Having been caught unawares, she resolved to brazen it out. It was an inexcusable choice of car, anyway.

"Listen, friend," she continued, "I can't help if you're going to cut and run. If you don't trust me yet, fine. We can talk here. Crap, it's private enough." She gestured at the surrounding crowd, none of whom had even glanced at the two of them, save for the instant Jeffers had spilled the beer. "Now, first off, who the hell are *you*?" She smiled broadly again to take the sting out of the command.

"George, George Jeffers," he answered automatically. He did not think at all of why he should answer her question, only that it might be worth dying to see that smile one more time. With a mental wrench, he disposed of the thought. It seemed that he had done nothing right, and daydreaming was not going to help matters. He conceded in the same moment that she was his contact, although the lingering effect of the smile may have had more to do with the conclusion than logic.

"I think I would prefer to go into this over dinner." It had occurred to him that she was right about privacy; leaving was not essential. Unless someone were literally leaning over his shoulder, any conversation would be lost in the swirl of noise around the bar. Deciding to leave, though, was a way to assert himself, if only a little. After his string of embarrassments, his ego would take any bolstering it could get.

With Taylor following close behind him, he threaded his way to the door. He reached it and inhaled with relief. The night air was not very cool, but at least it did not have the stench of too many bodies in too little space. He was about to ask her for directions when he spotted a purple Monte Carlo parked at the curb a little way from the bar entrance. In spite of the darkly tinted windows he could see a figure seated behind the wheel.

Ye gods! Twice a fool, he thought. He aimed a derisive snort at Taylor, then sprinted around the front of the car to the driver's door. The man did not move, so he yanked the door open. When he did, the man flopped against him. Too late, Jeffers noticed a small hole by the left temple, a blackish burn next to it. A portion of the rear of the skull was gone, splattered across the interior of the car by the bullet that had killed him. A gelatinous mass of brains and clotted blood rolled down the neck and dropped into the man's lap. Screams from behind told Jeffers that others in the street had also seen what just happened.

Jeffers gagged and spun away, bent over at the waist. It was that reflex response to the horror in the car that saved his life, for just as he turned, the windshield shattered, followed immediately by the report of two shots.

"George! Get down, and get back here!" Taylor had been trailing him as he went for the car and had also seen the body fall out of the door. As the shots rang out she leaped forward to grab his wrist and pull him between two cars. Her move was just in time. Jeffers had escaped the first two shots by chance; his mind saw nothing but the head. Had she not reached him the third shot, closely following the others, would have had him. As it was it merely punctured a tire.

Crouched between the two cars, Jeffers struggled to keep his mind from going blank. Taylor was not the contact Oliver had sent. He knew that. That man was dead in the front seat of the Monte Carlo. When the shooting had started, though, she had not hesitated to move for him. Why hadn't she run off screaming, the way he would expect a stranger to do? It made no sense. And why was somebody shooting at him in the first place? That made no sense either.

Taylor had no questions about her own actions. To be involved in something big and dangerous was what she had been looking for. A killing and a sniping—in daylight yet—certainly fit the bill. Now, she wanted to know why it was happening.

The shots had initially cleared the street but after only a little while people began to come out of doorways to see the cause of the commotion. Seeing an opportunity, Taylor pulled Jeffers toward the door of the Kettle Drum. "Come on, come on," she urged him forward. She anticipated more shots as they dashed across the sidewalk, but none came.

"Jackie, I need the upstairs key," she shouted as they got inside.

She caught the tossed key without breaking stride and pushed through a swinging door into the kitchen area. Jeffers followed her. Outside the back door of the kitchen was a staircase leading to the second floor. By the time Jeffers reached its base she was already at the top, unlocking a door. Taking two steps at a time, he ran up the stairs. The door led to a short corridor on which several other doors fronted. One of them had been opened.

Taylor confronted him, slamming the door as he entered the small studio apartment. "Okay, secret agent man. What is going on?"

Jeffers hesitated. At that point, he was actually not certain he could answer accurately.

"Look, I'm not kidding around," she said. "Whatever you're into, it's deadly serious. I like action, and if there's money in it I like it even better, but I have got to know the story." Jeffers stayed mute. "Come on man, you have got not one but *two* gunmen after you. There's no other way to look at it since the shots at you came from a rifle fired from God knows where, while your friend in the car got it point-blank. Probably with a small-caliber weapon."

Mention of the murder got Jeffers talking again. "How can you be so sure of that?"

"All you had to do was look at him to know." Jeffers shuddered at the idea. "The black mark by the entry hole is a powder burn. You only get that if the gun is up close. Everything was normal on the street up to the time you pulled the door open, so the shot could not have made too much noise, just a small bang. Then, you know, firing a bullet, even a small-caliber one, gen- erates a lot of gas. It comes right behind the bullet and, in a situation like this one, follows it into the entry hole. Being gas, it expands rapidly and blows off the back of the head. Simple. It must have happened just before we came out. I know what I am doing, but I need to know what you are doing."

Jeffers looked at her to take his mind off the nausea and fear her textbook analysis had raised while he considered what to say. Time was moving too fast for his mind. He needed a mental break.

"How old are you, Taylor?" Odd question under the circumstances, but he asked it to gain time for his mind to start thinking again.

"Twenty-five, if it matters. I'm not joking about this. If I were, do you think I would still be here?"

"No," he shook his head slowly, "I guess not. What would happen if I told you that I was doing something illegal?"

That brought a short laugh. "Chance I take. If I don't like what you tell me, well, I'll deal with that when it happens. Besides, I don't believe it. Not from you, secret agent man."

"Dammit, I am not a secret agent." Well, maybe I just became one, he thought. But he did not like the way she said it. Jeffers took a deep breath and made his decision. "Have a seat, Taylor, this will take a minute."

"Try not to make it too many minutes," she said. "There are some people out there with guns that I'd rather avoid meeting." Wrong thing to say, she thought, as she looked at Jeffers's face.

"Goddamn it!" The words burst out of Jeffers. "I don't understand any of this. Maybe some of those guys are secret agents, I don't know any more. I was working on a project for my company, it's good science and maybe it'll be really useful some day, but it isn't right now. I mean, it's a designed protein that we made in the lab, but that's all it is. My friend Hank who worked on it with me was taking it to someone in Europe and then it disappeared—or, I mean, he disappeared with it and all of this shit started to happen. And then I get mixed up with you because your name is a goddamn homonym of the stupid code they gave me, but that guy is, well, out there."

"Jesus, George, get a grip. You come apart here and you're going to be in even deeper shit than you are now."

Taylor had no expectation that her words would have any effect. She fully expected him to dissolve into uncontrollable shakes or babbling. It did not happen that way, though. Unlikely as it seemed, Jeffers reacted to her words with a start, then the wildness left his eyes and he clamped his jaw shut.

"I'm sorry," he said. "I'm not going to come unglued." He almost did not believe his own words. He remembered the body in the car, the gunshots that followed. "Look, I can tell you the details later. Let's just say I've got to find my friend and my project. I was supposed to meet my contact here, and brief him. How it would be handled from there, I can't say."

"That you can leave to me, if you're hiring me—which, by the way, I recommend if you ever want to see your friend again. Speaking of which, what *is* the money situation?"

Jeffers colored. He had not mentioned Thompson's stash. He remembered Thompson's warning about the money but he had no enthusiasm for playing any kind of games with Taylor. "There's cash in a lockbox in a Zurich bank. I have the key. It ought to suffice."

"Then, I'm in!" she leaned forward on her chair. Of course, she was in. What fabulous luck!

Taylor did not stay in her seat for very much longer. Almost immediately after the conversation concluded she bounced to the window overlooking the street. She leaned against the back of the armchair, looking out through the gap between the shade and the pane. Once in the position she wanted, she froze. The still-life portrait had begun to develop an air of permanence, and Jeffers was almost ready to scream, before she finally straightened up.

"Looks like we have a good crowd sign, now. It should be a good time to go."

"Wait a minute." Again there was sudden fear in Jeffers's voice. "How do you know that guy with the rifle isn't still out there, just waiting for us?"

"I don't know," she answered, "but that's the point of the crowd. You've got the police, bless their blue-flannel brains, a mob of spectators and just now the Actioncam pulled up. All of that really increases a gunman's chance of getting caught, so he probably won't try. Of course, in some personal or religious vendettas people are pissed off enough not to care. I can't see how there could be anything like that involved here."

Jeffers had the momentary impression that she was fishing, to see if there was more to the situation than he said.

"Strictly company sponsored, then, with maybe a little help from the feds?" she asked. Jeffers nodded. "Okay." Her frown turned to a quick grin. "I don't suppose you work for H. Ross Perot?"

"No. What does he have to do with this?"

"Just an old fantasy of mine. Come on, time to go. We can't stay here forever." She headed for the door, Jeffers once again trailing behind.

A substantial crowd had gathered on the sidewalk, held away from the cars and the street by wooden barriers, yellow tape, and several police. An ambulance had arrived and the body from the Monte Carlo, features mercifully hidden by a blanket, was being loaded into the rear. The crew from the television station was using the scene as a backdrop for the reporter's story, providing a platform for various people to signal to their mothers. Most of the policemen were engaged in examining the cars and the bullet holes in them. The two policemen nearest the Kettle Drum were involved in a dispute with the owner of the car immediately in front of the Monte Carlo. The gentlemen clearly wished to leave, and was finding the police less than understanding. The attitude of the bystanders was split more or less evenly among these activities. No one paid any attention to the couple who left the Kettle Drum and headed toward Boston University.

At least, Taylor had initially *thought* no one had paid attention. They had gone less than a block before she thought they had acquired a tail. The man was not following too closely, but in the crowd of people present his business suit was an easy marker to spot. Once she had picked him up, she noted that he never took his eyes from them. That was a mistake Taylor had no intention of copying. Not once did she ever try to look directly at him. It took another block for her to be certain. No question about it, someone was interested enough in Jeffers to hang around, even in the face of the police. The knowledge raised her inner estimation of the stakes, but none of it showed on the outside. She swung along the street with a casual long-legged gait that could easily have been headed for an ice cream. Jeffers concerned her far more than the tail. He walked with a hunched look to his shoulders, as though anticipating a shot in the back, and was continually looking to the rear. Jeffers might have spotted the tail himself, though Taylor doubted it. He was so jittery there was no point in enlightening him if he had not.

"Taylor, where are we going?" The words came out with a slightly unusual enunciation; the muscles along his jaw were too taut to permit easy speech.

"Right now we're going to pick up my BDM."

"What the hell is that? A weapon?" It was an effort to keep his teeth from chattering. In spite of the heat, he felt chilled and shivery.

"Not exactly a weapon. BDM is short for Boston Driving Machine. This town requires a special kind of car."

Precisely what she meant by special Jeffers did not understand, and she did not offer further information. He had never driven in Boston himself, and on his one previous trip he had religiously avoided the taxicabs on the basis of friends' advice. Those old comments, plus the very real danger of the evening, began to fuel his imagination. In his mind's eye he saw the BDM as a miniature tank equipped with machine guns behind the headlights—he remembered the image from an old movie—with armor plate on all sides. He was vastly disappointed when Taylor turned into a sidestreet and stopped by an ordinary-looking car.

"This is it?"

'It' was an old Ford Falcon, quite possibly older than Taylor herself. At one time the car had been a uniform shade of sky blue. Now the paint was faded in patches, and rust showed through along the lower edges of the doors and wheel wells. The left-rear fender had been repainted; it did not quite match the rest of the car. A crease running across the front grille caught his eye. Whatever had created it had also tilted the front bumper slightly so that it thrust upward like a jutting chin. A bumper sticker proclaimed, IF YOU DON'T LIKE THE WAY I DRIVE, GET OFF THE SIDEWALK.

"What happened here?" he asked pointing at the grille.

"Don't know," she replied. "It was there when I got the car. I like it though. It gives the car an aggressive look, don't you think?"

Taylor had opened both doors and slipped into the driver's seat while Jeffers was still staring at the grille. "Are you planning to get in? Or are you waiting for the guy following us to catch up?"

"What!" Jeffers reacted as though he had been slapped and practically dove into the front seat. "Where is he and why didn't you tell me?"

"He's over there, and I didn't tell you because you're hyper enough as it is." She pointed out the man, still about a half block from them as she swung the car into the street. He was reaching into his coat, but what came out was a cellular phone, not a gun. He spoke into it as a late-model Ford turned onto the road behind them.

"Ah, no wonder he didn't try to close in at the end. I guess it's a good thing I didn't park any farther down."

She accelerated rapidly down the street and then made a sharp left, slamming Jeffers against the door, onto Monfort Street, parallel to the turnpike. The sedan copied her and was soon visible again in the rear-view mirror.

"Well," she said with annoyance, "at least he didn't get a chance to pick up his chum."

Taylor slowed and drove west for several blocks at a snail's pace. While she did so Jeffers twisted around to watch the sedan, now directly behind them. When they reached the intersection of the road with Commonwealth Avenue, Taylor brought the old Falcon to a stop at a red light. Behind her, the sedan stopped as well. Without warning, Taylor stomped on the accelerator just as she saw cross traffic beginning to move. Trailing smoke and twin streaks of rubber on the pavement, they shot straight across six lanes. The car fishtailed as it turned left, straightened out, and then fishtailed again as Taylor threw it into a hard right onto the Boston University bridge. The driver of the sedan must have been waiting for just such a move because he followed immediately. The sound of smashing glass told Taylor that he had failed to run the intersection cleanly—however, a look in the mirror showed the Ford still in pursuit onto the bridge. Its right-rear fender had been dented, the bumper torn partially away from the body, but it had not lost any ground.

"Damn, I really thought we'd leave him there. Oh, well."

After they crossed the bridge she turned west on Memorial Drive, then crossed back over the river on Western Avenue. The sedan managed to stay behind them the whole way, but the heavy traffic consistently frustrated their tail's attempts to draw alongside.

"So where are we going with this?" Jeffers asked.

"Zurich, eventually, but for right now I'll settle for getting to the airport."

"And where is the airport from here?"

"Back that way," she said, pointing over her shoulder in an easterly direction.

"You mean we're going the wrong way!"

"Relax, George. Just leave the details to me."

Jeffers subsided and went to fasten his seat belt. It was not there.

At length Taylor, now acting the model driver, arrived at Beacon Street, where she turned east. Traffic was moderate, and with only an occasional traffic light interruption they moved along at a steady thirty-five miles an hour. By weaving in and out of the flow of cars Taylor managed to prevent the trailing sedan from drawing even with them. She wondered, though, whether that was her skill showing, or whether the other driver was merely content to tail them. That he had made no attempt to fire at them did not really surprise her. Duels between speeding cars in traffic were a Hollywood fiction, not reality. Still, it was possible that he was only waiting for more help to arrive. Alternatively, he might only be interested in where they ultimately went, having reserves to bring in once they had left the car. The possibilities made for good questions, the answers to which she lacked.

As she drove down Beacon Street, with Jeffers apparently lost in his own thoughts, her mind pondered the adventure she had landed in. Jeffers had seemed to downplay the importance of his project, but he had been close to hysterical at the time, so it was hard to know whether to believe him. There had to be more to it. Maybe Jeffers's friend was important. Jeffers had mentioned money, and that could be the key. She had seen perfectly rational people go giddy and weird when enough money was involved. It could be as bad as pheromones for an insect. Could Jeffers be lying? He did not look to be the lying type, but such assumptions could also be wrong. In the end, though, it did not really matter. Whatever the cause, be it money or not, the promise of excitement, of real action, of achievement, was there. Her knack had not played her false.

Beyond the job itself, though, was the matter of her employer. Oh, my dear sweet Lord, a scientist! To Taylor, scientists had always ranked among nature's most harmless and inoffensive creatures. If kept in a properly insulated environment they needed little care or attention. For a mild-mannered scientist, however, Jeffers was now attracting a great deal of attention. Keeping him alive, not to mention functional, in the harsh, real world was going to be a major job in its own right. Too bad she could not park him with a baby sitter, but she could not think of any safe way to arrange it. Besides, Jeffers was the key to the problem, literally, so when it came to the lockbox.

Therefore, taking the job meant bringing Jeffers along and keeping him, if not safe, at least out of the clutches of the opposition, whoever they were. Not a bad-looking fellow anyway, not that it would matter to her.

With a shock she realized she had been driving on autopilot and had not paid attention to how far they had come. The sedan was now directly behind them, in the same lane. In the mirror she could see the driver speaking into a telephone. He would have help coming soon. What she needed was a good opportunity to lose him. It seemed to present itself as they crossed the bridge over the turnpike, nearly completing a large circle from their point of departure. The police and the crowd were gone now. She saw the right lane open ahead to the light at Kenmore Square, just then turning yellow, and the sedan was a little more than a car length behind.

"Hang on, George!" she shouted, and hit the gas. The Falcon shot forward toward the yellow light, with the Ford in pursuit. The light turned red.

Kenmore Square is a traffic nightmare under the best of circumstances. Three roads—Commonwealth Avenue, Beacon Street, and Brookline Avenue—converge on the intersection from within a sixty-degree arc. A single divided road, with a bus terminal in the island, exits to the east. The eastbound side just past the traffic light is three lanes wide, if the parking spaces by the curb are excluded. The righthand lane was, as usual, blocked by double-parked cars, and the middle lane by a taxi busy discharging a fare. The traffic funneling in from Brookline Avenue had only the open left lane to aim for. Taylor cut them off.

"Aaaah!" The scream tore, involuntarily, out of Jeffers.

The car hurtled toward the intersection at ever increasing velocity. In seconds, they were past the point where Taylor could have stopped, even if she wanted to. Jeffers clenched his eyes shut just before they reached the corner, beyond which he had seen the intersecting line of traffic beginning to move into the road. His fingers dug deeply into the padding of the dashboard, as though with his arms he could brace himself against the coming collision. Eyes closed, he missed the view as they veered sharply left to just miss the front of the lead car coming from Brookline Avenue. The driver of that car steered frantically away from them, directly into the rear of the taxi. The cab, idling in neutral with the driver's foot off the brake, lurched forward and began to roll into the extreme left lane, threatening to close off the opening. The Falcon, meanwhile, was aimed diagonally across the roadway, with the brick retaining wall of the bus stop in front of it. Taylor spun the wheel to the right. The right side wheels threatened to leave the pavement, but didn't quite. Like a small running back eluding a would-be tackler on a football field, the Falcon cut to the right, through the gap between the wall and the rolling taxicab. Several people in the act of crossing the street in the middle of the block dove for the relative safety of the curb. The Falcon straightened out and sped through the next light before turning left for Storrow Drive, along the south bank of the Charles.

The driver of the following car showed resolve at least equal to Taylor's. The surprise of the Falcon's rush had briefly frozen traffic in the intersection, giving him an opportunity to execute the same left to right maneuver. By the time he came through, though, the taxicab had come to a stop partially in the left-hand lane. The space between the curb and the wall was too narrow for the Ford. Undaunted, the driver jumped the curb and went for the opening, one set of wheels on the road, the other on the ten-inch-wide strip of sidewalk in front of the retaining wall. The side of the car kissed the brick wall, then scraped along it as the car bypassed the taxi. A trash can placed at the corner of a crosswalk, where the sidewalk ended, could not be avoided. It bounced off the bumper, scattering can, papers and shattered headlight across the road.

Jeffers had opened his eyes at the sound of shouts and squealing tires just in time to witness their passage between Scylla and Charybdis. "Goddamn it, Taylor. You're crazy!"

"That's been said before," she replied, never taking her eyes from the road.

Jeffers turned around at the sound of the noise behind them. The sight of the trailing car, shedding side mirror, paint and shreds of metal as it gave chase gripped him with a horrified fascination.

"I don't believe it. He's still with us!"

As they turned onto the riverside parkway, Taylor stole a quick look at the rear-view mirror to confirm it. "So he is."

Outwardly, she sounded nonchalant, but beneath the facade she was concerned. Had she harbored any remaining doubts about the value of the operation she had stepped into, the driver's determination would have resolved them. "Watch him," she said. "One of his front wheels is wobbling. Maybe it'll come off."

"Somebody could get killed like that," Jeffers protested.

"Somebody's already been killed, maybe by him. George, I guarantee you, he's not chasing us 'cause he's found your wallet and wants to return it."

Jeffers looked at the densely traveled road around them and decided he had been misunderstood. "It wasn't him I was worried about. There are a lot of other people out here."

"Boston traffic's always bad," she shrugged. "Believe me, this is nothing they're not used to."

As they approached the tunnel traffic began to thicken to the point where Taylor had no chance to maneuver further. Her options now fell into two categories. Either she could stay on the highway, looking to lose the tail as they moved out of town and traffic thinned, or she could simply run for the airport. It did not take long for the airport to win out. The possibility of being surprised by other pursuers had bothered her before, and it still did. Being stopped by the police was also possible. Such an outcome might prove as undesirable as being caught from behind. And unless she planned to drive to another major city, they needed the airport and it was getting late. As they drove through the tunnel, an idea began to form.

Logan Airport, the air gateway to Boston, is inconveniently located across a stretch of bay from the bulk of the city. The only direct road route from the city to the airport runs through the underwater tunnels. Faced with this natural bottleneck, the city planners had opted to place a toll plaza on the airport side of the tunnel. This arrangement had done for traffic what the Gorgon's head had done in the past for unwary travelers. As a result, the tolls had been removed in the direction from the city to the airport. This left a somewhat wider than normal section of road that was then rapidly constricted by a corset of concrete barriers just before the airport roadway.

Taylor brought the Falcon to the far left, accelerating as she came out of the tunnel as if she were planning to use the open highway to outdistance pursuit. Behind her, she saw the Ford speed up to match her. At the last possible moment, she swerved sharply, cutting off the cars to her right, to reach the airport exit. As before, the trailing driver copied her move. This time, however, her figuring proved correct. Subjected to the stress of the high-speed turn, the damaged front wheel collapsed. The car pitched forward and skidded, partly on its bumper. Another car piled in from the rear and helped to propel it into a concrete abutment by the exit.

Taylor viewed the result with satisfaction. Perhaps their position was known, but there would be no one on top of them when they left the car. She would settle for that.

Her satisfaction proved rather short-lived as she drove into the airport and saw what was waiting for them.

# Chapter 5

## BOSTON, MASSACHUSETTS

"NOW WHAT?" THERE WAS a perceptible edge of annoyance in Jeffers's voice. After all, in the last few hours he had found his contact murdered, been shot at himself and chased through Boston traffic. Now, to see a network news team at an airport was not in itself an event, but there were *multiple* trucks from a number of different stations clearly visible from the access road. There were also far too many visible police cars for an ordinary evening. With those sights as a tipoff, they had parked the car in the long-term lot, Jeffers staying behind while Taylor sauntered off to one of the terminals. The information she euchred out of a cameraman and a rookie cop was disturbing. The shooting at Kenmore Square was the prime topic of conversation. Neither the police nor the news teams knew what had really happened, but both had heard from unnamed sources that a man connected with the events might be trying to leave through the airport. Jeffers was unamused to learn that the description of the man matched him closely, and that he was being mentioned in the role of suspect rather than victim.

Taylor chewed on her lower lip while Jeffers finished fulminating about how unfair this was.

"It makes no sense," he cried. "If someone really wanted me dead, it would have been easy enough to do any time before now. I live alone, I work odd hours and there was no trouble at all before I met you."

"Listen, Jeffers," she said, "Don't start blaming *me* for this. If it was merely a matter of ruining your project, then yes, I would say that killing you anywhere along the line would probably have sufficed. But it's not just the project now, and *I* saved *you*, remember? Not only do you represent a possible lead to whoever stole it, you are also the key to a lot of money in a Swiss bank, either of which could be reason enough for them. From my point of view, and it ought to be yours too, the difference doesn't matter."

"I suppose not. But how can you be so sure it's a 'them' and not a 'he'?"

"Come on, that's obvious. Had to be a minimum of two people initially, one outside the Kettle Drum to tail us and the other in the car. Maybe the gunman drove the car, but if not, that's three. Then, look at the dog and pony show here. If I was betting, I would say somebody in the police has to be involved. Which means I would trust the cops even less than normal."

"Fine, I won't argue with any of that. But, it still doesn't get me out of here. If I try to board any plane, much less pass customs, I'm going to wind up going back downtown for questions. And I can easily imagine that a minor but highly fatal accident will have been planned for later." Jeffers had in the past felt an admiration for the way Thompson planned the operations they discussed over beers, but he was coming to the conclusion that Jim had blown this one.

Taylor, meanwhile, was happy enough to see Jeffers beginning to develop a realistic appraisal of the situation. She leaned across the hood of the car, elbows on the metal, chin in her palms, and broke into a broad grin. "That just makes it a little more interesting. If we want a plane to Europe, we'll just have to use another airport. We could try driving to New York—"

"No!"

"Now, just because I blew a light at Kenmore Square—"

"At fifty miles an hour!"

"—that's no reason to disparage my driving. But I agree anyway, it's a bottleneck getting out of here and that makes it too easy being spotted. My suggestion is that we go look at the private plane hangar. Maybe we can come up with something there." Her manner indicated this suggestion was not open for debate. She walked around to the trunk without waiting to see if Jeffers had any comment and pulled out a small daypack. Then she locked the car, carefully checking the doors and windows.

"Hey, Taylor." A disquieting thought popped into Jeffers's mind. It had been there all along, but he had been too busy to dwell on it. "What happens when they check this car? Unless the guy behind us is dead, they'll trace you easily. And then what?"

"Not to worry." She looked like a little girl, prepared to whisper a secret during class. "It's registered to an address in Roxbury, and the name on it is phony. Let 'em trace." With that she headed off to the walkway leading out to the road.

Jeffers followed, a role he was perforce becoming used to. As he did, he found himself noticing the slight but definite limp in Taylor's gait. It was nothing major, but he could not remember having seen it before. Probably he had become aware of it because he was watching her now as well as following her. By the time they reached the private hangar the limp had become a subject of concern. Had she hurt herself during the scramble outside the bar? When they stopped by the hangar, he pulled even with her and asked her about it.

"It's not a limp, that's just the way I walk." She turned away to look at the airfield, her hair catching the last rays of light. "Do me a favor," she said, "watch the pack until I get back. I'll meet you back here." Then she was gone, headed away from the hangar into the twilight.

Jeffers found a shadowed spot that he hoped would hide him from casual inspection and settled down to wait. Although the temperature had dropped enough to make his warm coat appropriate, he was far from comfortable, and waiting made the time drag slowly. Finally, when he noticed himself checking his watch every five minutes he stuffed it into his jacket.

The field was brightly lit, but the sky was fully dark when Taylor returned. "It's all set." She picked up her pack. "Time to get out of here."

She led the way through a gate in the chain link fence marked AUTHOR-IZED PERSONNEL ONLY, out onto the tarmac. Jeffers felt a twinge in his conscience as Taylor carefully swung the gate shut behind them. He, for sure, was not authorized to be where he was, and he had the idea she wasn't, either. However, she was urging him on.

Her destination, a short distance away, was a propeller-driven plane. To Jeffers it looked ridiculously small compared to the jetliners he was accustomed to flying in. Clearly visible in the glare of the field lights along the fuselage and tail was lettering for the NORTH SHORE 'CHUTE CLUB. Jeffers had never met a sky diver, but it seemed a safe assumption that one chosen at random would be crazy. After Taylor's exhibition of her driving skill, he could imagine her knowing a sky diver. Probably had no trouble talking the guy into this crazy adventure either, he thought.

The plane looked clean and well kept when Jeffers climbed in. There were two seats up front at the controls and room for four passengers behind. The dials and switches of the panel meant nothing to him, so he ignored them. They would be for the pilot when he arrived. Taylor was busy moving something in the aft space, so Jeffers continued a visual inspection of the cockpit. He really wanted to find some personal item that would give him a clue to the person who would fly the plane, but the cockpit was clean. Then his eye caught a sticker posted above the windshield.

SKY DIVERS, it read, GET BLOWN ALOFT. He smiled thinly. The humor fit what he expected of people who jumped out of airplanes.

"This is nice," Jeffers nodded approvingly when Taylor came forward. "Fly to New York in a light plane, then catch a transatlantic flight." For the first time in several hours he was not feeling pressured, and, whatever his opinion of sky diving, the plane's spic-and-span appearance was reassuring.

"A nice end run indeed," he was even willing to compliment Taylor. "Let's get our pilot and go."

"Pilot? Hell, I'm the pilot." Taylor laughed as she climbed into the other seat at the controls. While Jeffers watched with his mouth open, she made some quick adjustments on the panel. The engine roared then, and the plane began to taxi forward.

"*You* are the pilot?" From the look she gave him, he immediately regretted the inflection he had put into the sentence. After a few seconds of thought he was able to rationalize the concept. He could visualize Taylor running a parachute school. It also explained where the plane came from. It left him only the desire to restart the conversation to cover his gaffe.

"How did you learn to fly?" he asked.

"Got Daddy to pay for lessons. How else?"

"And this is your plane?"

"Lord, no. Don't be ridiculous. I can't afford a plane like this."

"Meaning you stole it."

"Of course."

Jeffers sagged back into his seat as the plane continued to pick up speed. As it cut onto one of the runways a loud stream of chatter from the radio made it clear that Taylor had not asked for permission to take off any more than she had asked permission to use the plane. The control tower's argument became academic, however, as Taylor smoothly took the plane into the air.

"I don't believe it," Jeffers said as they banked west. "I mean, this got us out of Logan, but how do we go about landing? They'll broadcast this all over."

"Relax, it's all taken care of." There was no hint of strain in Taylor's voice. "We won't have much to do for a while, and seeing as we've got a contract on this project, I'd like to know a bit more about it."

"Contract? What contract?" No matter how Taylor rattled him, she never gave him the opportunity to fully discuss any issue. She made her pronouncements and moved onto the next topic.

"Yep, contract. A promise for a promise as my asshole layer likes to say. You promise me money and a good adventure, and I promise to get your stuff back and find out what happened to your friend. That makes a contract. Actually, Sean's a pretty good lawyer. He just has a habit of getting his hand caught in the till."

"You mean getting caught with his hand in the till."

"That too. Actually, if he had ever been able to get his hand *out* of the till, he wouldn't have been caught. As it is, he's lucky not to be disbarred. Now he mostly does the ambulance-chase routine and brokers adoptions."

"I don't think I understand. The last part, that is."

"Oh, come on, George. There are plenty of couples here with money but no babies, and you better believe there are orphanages in South and Central America with babies they don't know what to do with. I've made those pickups for Sean a number of times. The pay's not bad, though I grant you running babies is not exactly high adventure." Sometimes, she added in her mind, it is necessary, just to pay the bills. She saw no need to bring that fact into the conversation.

"Do you ever, ah, run anything other than babies?"

"Meaning, do I run drugs?" She gave him a hard look. "The answer is no, never. There's plenty of money in it, of course, if you're sharp enough to get out before you get busted or killed, but that's something I don't touch. A girl has to be careful about her reputation, you know."

While Jeffers considered the seeming contradiction Taylor stretched her frame in the pilot's seat and continued. "Interesting as my life is, however, it is not the present topic of concern. I still need to know more about what we are going to do, which means I need to know more about what you do. You said you designed a protein. What kind of protein? Would I want it for breakfast?"

"No, it's an enzyme."

"Okay. I know that an enzyme is a protein that makes chemical reactions happen. So, what's the deal with this one? Will it make washday brighter, or what?"

That last sally finally brought a smile to Jeffers's face. It also started him thinking about his work, and that began to make him relax. Jeffers was never reticent about his work. "You have to understand what we were trying to do." He slumped into the seat with his eyes partially closed. Once he got going, he might have been talking shop over beers on a weekend. "Most of the products that are crucial to modern society, from drugs to plastics, are synthesized from raw materials by sequences of chemical reactions. The reactions necessary to get to many useful compounds, however, turn out to take place very slowly, or inefficiently, or they turn out some toxic crap you can't get rid of. These kinds of obstacles can make your product very expensive, if you can even mass produce it at all. This is where catalysts come in. A catalyst is just a material that speeds up a chemical reaction. Add just a tiny amount of a catalyst to a reaction that might take a week to complete, and, bang, it's through in fifteen minutes. Enzyme is just the fancy name for a type of protein that happens to be a catalyst. Without enzymes, very few of the reactions that keep you alive would work.

"The problem in a lot of industrial chemistry lies in trying to find the right catalyst for a particular job. A catalyst for one reaction may do nothing for even a closely related one, and it's very difficult to predict what a good catalyst might be. A lot of times it's trial and error. I remember one guy who had tried everything he could think of to get a reaction to run, with no luck, until one day he accidentally knocked over a bottle of glass beads and a few of them fell into the pot. Then it worked.

"It occurred to me, while I was still in college, that a good way around this would be if you could design an enzyme to catalyze the reaction you were working on. We know a lot about how natural enzymes work, and nowadays you can model protein structures on a computer. You can't have a chemist synthesize an enzyme—it's way too big—but it's not necessary to do that. Once you know the structure you want, you can synthesize an artificial gene for it. Splice it into a bacterium and let the bug make it for you. That's what we did. It's been a decade-long project. Right now there's just the one pure sample, which a European group was going to use for some studies. Never mind why it's the only sample. Hank was carrying it to the meeting because it seemed much safer than shipping it. He could just hand it to Max Fruhling—that's the head of the European group. I told you before what happened after he left." He sighed as he thought of how complicated it had become. "You know, ultimately it should be possible to use this technique to simplify many chemical problems, but this one is really just a prototype. I mean, it doesn't do anything very dramatic, it just breaks a target molecule to make a color I can measure. Granted, the target was set up so we could go ahead to make a cancer drug that people have had a lot of trouble synthesizing, but it's a little premature to be getting all wound up about it."

"Maybe somebody else doesn't agree with your assessment," Taylor put in. Jeffers had to nod in agreement. "Tell me more about what you did."

It was all the encouragement Jeffers needed. In Taylor he found a ready listener whose questions, although unsophisticated, showed a quick grasp of the ideas he spun out. The air time passed quickly.

It was nearing eleven o'clock when the radio came on. It had sputtered several times previously, and on each occasion Taylor had muted the volume to the barely audible level before turning it back up when the voice disappeared. This time she left it alone. Jeffers had worked himself deep into a discussion of how metal atom clusters could be linked to proteins, and he resented the intrusion. He reached out to turn it off entirely.

"No, don't do that. We need to hear what the situation is here."

That took little time. "Unauthorized private flight, this is White Plains control tower. You are cleared, and ordered, to land here. Please acknowledge." They made no reply.

# WHITE PLAINS, NEW YORK

IN THE TOWER AT the White Plains airport, flight controller Jon Gormann was both puzzled and displeased. As described to him, the whole situation was ridiculous. Stealing an airplane and making an illegal takeoff from one of the busiest airports in the country did not strike him as a particularly bright move. With that kind of intelligence, it seemed unlikely that the pilot was going to listen to reason—he had not, in fact, responded to any of the previous hails along his flight path, which gave Gormann no reason to believe it would be different at White Plains. Gormann's visitors, however, were insistent that Gormann establish contact with the airplane, an impossible instruction. Impossible instructions bothered Gormann.

Gormann's visitors bothered him as much as their instructions. It had been a peaceful evening until a young man in a dark blue suit had barged into Gormann's control room and identified himself as an FBI agent. The plane in question had not even appeared on Gormann's screen at that point, although he had heard enough of the news from Logan not to be too surprised at the appearance of the FBI. It was not bad enough that Agent Vanelli insisted Gormann make contact with the pilot. No, indeed. He clearly expected Gormann to talk the pilot into landing so he could be arrested. Fat chance of that. If this pilot had more than two brain cells to click together he would be heading for a prearranged open field and would not be interested in talking to Gormann or Vanelli. If, as Gormann believed, the pilot simply had a terminal case of squash rot and panic he wouldn't talk either and they'd be searching the wreckage in the morning. He tried to tell this to Vanelli, but the FBI man wasn't interested.

If Vanelli bothered Gormann, the man who joined him made Gormann nervous—not the man's appearance, short and pudgy, but his attitude. He had not introduced himself to Gormann, in fact, had barely acknowledged Gormann's existence. Gormann knew his name only from hearing Vanelli address him as Mr. Oliver. But what really got to Gormann was the deferential manner in which Vanelli addressed this Oliver. In Gormann's limited experience, FBI agents behaved that way only in the presence of rank.

After unsuccessfully hailing the plane several times, Gormann turned away from his microphone. He looked at Vanelli with wordless disgust, as if to make plain his feelings about the futility of what he was doing.

"Just keep trying, Gormann," Vanelli snapped. "Sooner or later he has to come down, so eventually he'll talk." Gormann withheld his opinion of Vanelli's comment.

"Unauthorized flight, please acknowledge."

"Gormann," Oliver said softly, and Gormann started at the sound of his voice. "Say that Agent Vanelli is here and would like to talk. Tell him that Vanelli can make a deal."

In fact, Oliver thought as he spoke, tell him anything that will get him down in one piece and where I can get at him. Anything that would help unravel the day's events. Some of it was clear. For one, Lorenzo was dead, no question about that. For another, no one had seen Jeffers since Lorenzo's death. Beyond that it was fuzzy. From what Oliver knew of Jeffers, it had seemed reasonable for the man to run straight to the airport. Oliver had contacts at the FBI in Boston, the sort that did not require him to go through official channels. They had pushed the city police to put men into Logan Airport to gather in Jeffers when he showed up. Surprise, no Jeffers. Probably Jeffers was dead as well and it would be just a matter of time before he bobbed up in the Charles. Thompson would be pissed, but what the hell—it had not been Oliver's idea. Then the plane. Occam's Razor told him the pilot had to be connected to the murders, and he wanted him. There had to have been a leak somewhere, and the pilot would know where. There was a score to settle for Lorenzo. So come on, come talk to Vanelli, he thought as Gormann broadcast the offer. If there was one bit of luck in this miserable day, it was that he had flown to New York from Cleveland on other business and could now deal with these events in person.

In the cockpit Jeffers stared across at Taylor as the transmission came through. "I thought you said everything was arranged." If that were so, why would a federal agent be offering to bargain? Maybe things had become unarranged. Being acutely aware that the plane was stolen, he began to sweat.

"Not to worry," Taylor reassured him, picking up the radio handset. "Just keep quiet while I'm sending. I know what I'm doing."

If Jeffers had doubts, it did not seem like a good time to voice them.

Taylor spoke into the microphone, pitching her voice higher than normal for her. "Who are you? Please help me."

The reply took Gormann by surprise. He pushed his chair back and swung around to face Vanelli. "Jesus," he said, "that sounds like a kid." Vanelli just stood there, useless.

"It does indeed, Mr. Gormann," Oliver said in place of Vanelli. "Why don't you answer her?"

The controller shrugged, and turned back to his desk. "My name is Jon Gormann. Who are you? Over."

"My name is Becky," Taylor's little girl voice came back through the radio. "Please help me. He made me get in here."

"Now what?" Gormann asked.

"Keep talking to her. Vanelli, get Boston on the line. Find out if anyone saw a girl, or if there was a Becky or Rebecca reported missing today."

A girl in the plane? The question was identical in Gormann's mind and in Oliver's. The similarity of thought ended there, however. To Gormann it suggested innocent people in the wrong place at the wrong time. Maybe more people dead in Boston. Oliver's thoughts were grimmer and more sharply focused. The ideas in his mind were "hostage" and "insurance." If that was what the killer had in mind, he was due for a surprise from Charles Oliver.

"Becky, talk to me, please. Come on kid, talk to me," Gormann pleaded. The intensity in Gormann's voice, and the sweat on his forehead, increased with time as each transmission was met with either whimpers for help, or silence.

While Gormann struggled with his one-sided conversation, Vanelli called to Oliver from the other side of the room. "I have one of our men in Boston. He does have some reports that claimed two persons were in the plane before it took off. It was dark, of course, and none of the descriptions are the same, but there probably were two in the plane. Logan also has a missing child reported tonight, but it was a four-year-old named Roger . . ."

Oliver had stopped listening. The girl on the other end was crying again. "Mr. Gormann," he said, "does anything strike you as peculiar?"

"Better ask me if there is anything I don't find peculiar. What are you driving at?"

"Just this. I can understand our man putting the kid on so that we know he's got her. For all I know, the schmuck enjoys listening to this. But enough is enough. I don't see why he's letting it run on. A pro would cut it off as soon as he'd made his point, and a psycho wouldn't be able to keep from gloating." Oliver tugged briefly at one side of his moustache. "See if you can get her to answer something specific."

"I can try." Gormann waited for silence, then hailed the plane. "Becky? This is important. I want to help you, but you have to tell me what's going on."

"I told you," was the petulant reply. "He made me get in here."

"Yes, but what's going on now," Gormann persisted. He was half expecting static for a reply if the man cut if off.

"Nothing." Gormann held his breath and waited. "A little while ago he was gaspin' an' sweatin', but now he's not doin' nothin'. I don't think he's breathing."

Gormann's head snapped around, his eyes meeting Oliver's. "Heart attack?" Oliver just shrugged. It would explain a lot. Unfortunately, it hardly made matters easier.

Aboard the aircraft, Jeffers watched Taylor with his eyes wide open. What in God's name was she up to?

"It's okay Becky, this is Jon. Tell me what your last name is, and how old you are."

"I told you my name is Becky. I'm nine and I'm scared."

Gormann was considerably older than nine years, but he figured he had to be at least as scared as the kid he was listening to. The way he was hearing the story made a terrible kind of sense. If the man they wanted was dead in the plane, the pieces fit. A bright nine-year-old could probably figure out how to use the radio. The problem was, could Gormann—or anyone—talk a nine-year-old through landing a light plane? He rather doubted it. In the background he could hear Vanelli on the phone trying to find a child psychiatrist. Waste of time that was, at least unless the psychiatrist was also a flying instructor. Gormann took a quick look at Oliver and saw skepticism on the man's face. That was all very well for Oliver—Gormann was sure the man would sleep perfectly well whether Becky crashed in the plane or not—but it would not do for Gormann. He had to believe what he heard, and he knew he would not sleep if he did not try to get the plane down.

"Becky, are you listening to me?"

"Yes," came a faint answer.

"Do you see the small steering wheel in front of the man?"

"Yes"

"Good. Is there one in front of you?"

"Yes."

"Good. Okay, Becky, what you need to do is take hold of that wheel, just like when you see your mom drive a car."

There was a pause. Then, "I don't want to! The plane moved when I did that!"

"Becky, you have to so we can land the plane." Come on, Jon, he thought, sound in control, sound soothing.

"No, I don't. I'm scared and you're not helping. I want you to come get me. I don't want to do it. I don't wanna talk to you any more. Just come get me!" The transmission ended with a click.

Gormann stared at his screen, incredulous. He had mishandled it somehow, and she was off the air. Now there was no chance at all. If the click paralyzed Gormann, it galvanized Oliver.

"Vanelli," he ordered, "get off the phone for a moment. That plane is going to come down eventually. If this little exchange we've heard is straight it's going to land real hard, but one way or another, it is going to land. When it does, you better have your people over it like flies on rice. I want those bodies, in whatever condition, and I want whatever's on them. Keep the local blue suits out of it. I want *you* to be able to tell me who that guy is, or was. Do you understand me?"

"Yes, sir," Vanelli answered. Then he hesitated. "Do you have the authority to issue those orders?"

"Of course I don't have the authority," Oliver snapped. Too true, he thought. "How could I possibly have any authority when I'm not here, and you haven't spoken to me? I am merely suggesting, in the strongest possible terms, the course of action you might wish to take on your own authority. I trust the meaning is quite clear. Even to Mr. Gormann. Isn't it Mr. Gormann?"

Gormann nodded silently. He would be more than happy to forget that he had ever seen Oliver. It would be harder to forget that little girl's voice.

"If you have just a few minutes, sir," Vanelli blurted as Oliver turned for the door. At the words, Oliver halted. "I think," Vanelli went on, "I've worked out a good explanation for this case."

Oliver's face developed a quizzical expression. "Mr. Vanelli, do you have information I don't?"

"No, sir. I'm sure you've gotten everything that's come through."

"In that case, son, let me mention to you an experience of mine you may find useful." Oliver paused while the younger man looked at him expectantly. "Several years ago I attended a church service and heard a sermon that I think is really appropriate here. It was titled 'Blessed is the man who has nothing to say, and does not say it.' " With that, Oliver inclined his head slightly and walked out.

After Taylor had cut Gormann off in the middle of an impassioned plea, she let out a whoop. Jeffers was silent, wondering if she was genuinely insane.

"What was that supposed to prove?" he finally asked.

"Well, mostly," Taylor said as she got control of her laughter, "it was fun to jerk his chain. But also you're right—it may help. Just think, at Logan someone is bound to have noticed two people in this plane. Maybe good buddy Jon Gormann will think *you* kidnapped some poor nine-year-old. Now instead of paying close attention to what we're doing, they may be busy trying to sort out the story I gave them. A little extra confusion on the other side never hurt. And, admit it. It was fun."

# CHAPTER 6

## WESTCHESTER COUNTY, NEW YORK

JEFFERS'S AMUSEMENT OVER THE disinformation handed the people at the airport, if he felt any at all, did not last long. For all the confusion they might have created, and the 'might' was mentally italicized, they were still in midair without any apparent prospects of landing. The night sky was nearly cloudless, but the moon was only a sliver, leaving the ground below a formless black mass, its uniformity broken only where there were artificial lights. Staring out the window at it, Jeffers could not guess where they might be, much less where they might safely put the plane down.

"I am waiting for you to tell me that you have a partner down there somewhere waiting to light up an open field so we can land." Jeffers said it confidently, hoping.

"Unfortunately, no. Hold on a sec, will you?" Taylor banked the plane to the south and visually checked the ground glow well to the south that was White Plains before she spoke again. "I never figured that we would be able to land, so we won't. We're headed south now, and this plane has enough fuel to get over the water before it goes down. The wreckage, they're welcome to. They can dredge around all they want looking for you and poor little Becky."

She unbuckled herself from the seat and moved into the aft compartment, grabbing two bulky packages and bringing them back to the front. "Know how to use a parachute?"

Jeffers stared at the sack with a horrified fascination. "Surely you don't mean to jump out of this plane. Do you?"

"Most surely I do. George, as you recently pointed out, there's no way we can land this plane at any airfield without inviting very undesirable consequences, and there's no way I'm crazy enough to try landing on an unlit field in the dark. The 'chutes are fine, I checked them before we left. I've got us over a relatively open part of Westchester. We're up north of the New Croton Reservoir, a ways north of White Plains. We should have good odds of landing okay, and I really doubt that if we go now there's any way those dirtballs can find us when we land."

"Dammit, Taylor, I've never parachuted before in my life. You should know this."

"Don't worry, it's easy. Just like falling off a log. Come on, I'll show you how this thing works." She frowned when Jeffers looked hesitant. "George, I'm jumping. If you don't want to, you're free to land anywhere you want, after I leave."

"*I* can't land the *plane!*"

"All the more reason to jump." She held up one of the packs. "Shall we get on with it?"

The girl was serious, no doubt about it. But the idea of bailing out of an airplane in the middle of the night paralyzed the thinking parts of his brain so he stopped arguing. His muscles moved automatically in silent acquiescence as Taylor showed him how to handle the parachute. It felt like a small backpack when it was strapped on. Jeffers stared at the buckles and the rip cord, scarcely hearing what Taylor was saying. Something hard banged against his leg as she stepped around him, but he paid it little attention.

"Just stay cool, George," she said as she made the final adjustments. "It's a piece of cake. Sky diving is really a lot of fun."

Finally, he found his voice. "Daddy pay for those lessons, too?"

"Hardly," she tightened her own straps. "I paid for those."

"You ever jump at night before?"

She shrugged. "Nope. Should be interesting though." She took time at the panel to check the autopilot—was not the world's most elaborate system, but it would hold course and altitude, and do a fair job with the trim. Now, she gave Jeffers a last dry run. "The area I have us over is not so heavily settled," she said. "There's lots of woods and open country so we're not too likely to land on a road or somebody's house. If we don't land together, which is a fair bet, I'll meet you at the Prague Inn off the Saw Mill River Parkway. The main roads near us should be Routes 100 and 35. Head south or east and you'll hit one of them. From there you should be able to get a ride to the Prague Inn without any trouble. It closes at three. If you're not there tonight, I'll check back the next two nights. After that . . ." She looked into his eyes, searching for a response.

Jeffers could feel beads of cold sweat standing out all over his body. His knees were starting to feel very unsteady. "Taylor. I told you I've never done anything like this before. It's too damn risky."

"Well, what do you want, George?" There was an edge in her voice. "In this business you have to take some chances. Anyway, you don't have too many choices right now." To punctuate the sentence, she popped open the door, and wind noise rushed into the cabin. "One last thing, George. If you shit your pants on this, I don't know you when we get to the Prague Inn." With those words, she turned away from him and tumbled out of the cabin.

Jeffers braced himself against the rush of air from the opened door. Intellectually, he knew she had left him no choice at all, but it was a long way from that realization to forcing his body out the door into free fall. In the end, it was the sting of her parting comment that overcame the fear. He felt cold all over, but he had control of his body again. His resolve crystallized, and with a terrible scream he leaped through the door, arms and legs windmilling against the sky. The roar of the engine and the wind was suddenly replaced by quiet. There was the sensation of hanging motionless in a vast emptiness between earth and sky, disrupted only by his stomach which told him that he was falling.

It was the falling sensation that brought him out of his reverie. He realized then that he had forgotten to count and, therefore, had completely lost track of the time since his jump. In the dark he had no sense whether the ground was, even as he looked down, rushing up to squash him. In an immediate, convulsive reaction he pulled the rip cord.

His first thought on pulling the cord was that the parachute was defective. He would continue to fall, until the ground interrupted his trajectory and sent him to wherever dead men go. This train of thought was halted when the parachute fully deployed, with a jerk that seemed intended to separate the shoulder girdle from the rest of his torso. He had failed to account for, of course, the necessary interval between releasing the parachute from the pack and its opening to brake his fall. While this is not, in absolute terms, a long period of time, it can be perceived differently by a man waiting in midair in the dark. Swaying then, in tie and jacket and feeling like a male Mary Poppins, he had a chance to reflect on his day. The pace and danger of his activities, viewed scientifically, resembled an exponential curve, with the slope of the line increasing most dramatically at the time he met Taylor Redding. How in God's name had he been talked into that mad dash across Boston, not to mention this harebrained airplane heist? It was altogether more appropriate to the cover of a pulp magazine than the life of a corporate scientist. It was an easy progression from such considerations to thoughts of how to deal with Miss Redding after reaching the Prague Inn. What the Prague Inn was he had no idea, he imagined it as a seedy, squalid shack identified only by a neon sign and a derelict or two in the parking lot. The vision seemed appropriate for the sort of place that would welcome the trade of a quick-talking, unscrupulous, airplane-hijacking, self-styled World's Greatest Female Adventurer. His mental image of the ensuing conversation was equally vivid, including a very creative use of language on his part. He was beginning to look forward to the encounter when he realized that not only was the ground approaching rapidly, he was on a direct line for the roof of a house.

The house was a two-story affair, with a slate-shingled roof and a tall brick chimney at one end. As was typical for that part of Westchester County, it was set on a large plot of land well removed from the road, with an extensive wooded area stretching out behind the backyard. Except for a light at the garage, the house was dark.

Jeffers vaguely remembered a comment by Taylor on how to alter the rate or direction of descent by selectively spilling air from the parachute. Either his attempts were too tentative or he remembered the procedure incorrectly, because nothing he did changed his course. Instinctively, he tried to pull himself up in the parachute, a useless maneuver in midair. Finally, just when it seemed he would have to audition for the part of Saint Nick, a gust of wind lifted him slightly and he cleared the roof.

Having spared him that obstacle, however, the wind proceeded to carry him into the trees behind the house. Leaves and thin branches slapped at him as he fell through the uppermost layers. These were soon replaced by more substantial buffets as he hit the lower limbs. Jeffers shut his eyes tight, less from fear than to avoid a blinding poke. Proceeding in this fashion, he never saw the tree trunk into which he was carried. The first warning of this barrier was the impact, from head to toe, that knocked the wind from his lungs. Grappling frantically for purchase on the trunk, he then slid six feet straight down the tree, suffering total body abrasion along the way. It was a few minutes before he realized that he was actually on land again, and a few minutes more before he had assured himself that nothing critical was broken. The lights in the house remained out. No one knew he was there—for the moment.

From the war and spy stories he had read in the past, Jeffers knew he should bury the parachute. However, although he was able to pull it free of the tree, he had nothing with him that would permit a decent burial. In the end, he settled for hiding it under a pile of moldering leaves that had accumulated around a fallen log. While not perfect, the site would do. Then, carefully picking his way around the house to avoid any possibility of being spotted from a window, he made his way to the road.

Taylor had assured him that obtaining a ride to the Prague Inn would be a simple undertaking. Jeffers rapidly discovered otherwise. Aside from the initial problem of getting someone to pick up a hitchhiker who looked like a gang-war victim, no one had heard of the place. Jeffers concluded that his delay, either in jumping or pulling the ripcord, had taken him away from the roads Taylor had mentioned. Alternatively, of course, Taylor might have completely misfigured their location. Even if she had not, he had no idea which direction east, or south, might be. Finally, Jeffers reached a twenty-four-hour gas station on foot. There, after persuading a trucker he had been involved in a motorcycle accident, he was able to obtain a lift to an intersection of the Saw Mill River Parkway. A completely drunk pair of college students picked him up next, the first people he had met who had heard of the Prague Inn. They delivered him directly there, intact if shaken. By then, it was well past two in the morning.

The Prague Inn was a far cry from what Jeffers had imagined during his jump. The building most resembled a converted barn, the beam above the door at the level of the second floor adorned with gargoyles in imitation medieval style. Despite the hour, a half-dozen cars were parked outside. The door itself was massive, solid hardwood two inches thick. Inside, the inn was richly appointed. A large three-sided bar occupied the center of the first floor, with tables and booths arranged around the perimeter. Two side staircases led up to a mezzanine which had more tables. At this hour, the mezzanine was closed and dark, the remaining customers grouped either at the bar or at tables along one side of it.

The figure that advanced through that door in the wee hours of the morning bore no resemblance, other than that of physiognomy, to the one who had so uncertainly entered the Kettle Drum half a day before. Jeffers's face was grim, his hands partially clenched in front of his body, as he strode forward. His jacket hung in tatters across his chest. Several buttons had been torn from the sport shirt underneath, leaving it to flap open in the middle. His left pant leg was missing below a ragged margin at the knee. Multiple small patches of skin showed bright red where they had been scraped by the tree.

He had taken only a few steps into the room when he saw Taylor Redding sitting at the bar. She looked, with the exception of some mud on her Reeboks, exactly the same as she had in the Kettle Drum. Even the floppy hat was mounted at the same angle. She gave no sign that she had seen Jeffers enter, being engaged in conversation with a young man sitting on the adjoining stool. The man's back was to Jeffers, but he seemed to be about the same age as Taylor. He wore a T-shirt with the sleeves cut completely off, the better to exhibit his broad shoulders and densely muscled arms. Each had a half-finished drink on the bar in front of them.

Jeffers advanced on the pair, saying nothing. His carefully crafted conversation was gone from his mind. He had come to the inn with the idea of telling her off, yet it somehow angered him that she was sitting with someone else and not paying attention to him. Only the bartender, a carbon copy of Jackie from the Kettle Drum, watched him walk up. He straightened, putting down the glass he had been drying, looking like he was expecting trouble. It was the bartender's movement that alerted the young man to Jeffers's intrusion. By the time he turned around, Jeffers was standing scarcely an arm's distance away.

"Whaddaya want, Jack?" the man asked. His face matched his shoulders, with straight brown hair falling across his forehead and ears. A slightly crooked nose was accompanied by a faint scar that ran from the bridge down onto his cheek.

"I'm here, Taylor," said Jeffers slowly. "Let's get going."

"Hey, the lady is with me. 'Less you wanna get hurt worse'n what looks like already happened, why don't ya go buy somethin' to play with? 'Course, maybe you're better off playin' with what you already got—sucker." Taylor sat there quietly, not moving. Her gaze took in both men at the same time.

For a moment, Jeffers had a sense of déjà vu. He was back in college at a fraternity party where Dave Reihner, a major component of the conference championship backfield, had moved in just this easily on Sue Donovan. Reihner had slopped beer on Jeffers's pants, then stepped on his foot. When Jeffers had failed to protest, he had started talking to Sue. Jeffers had been dating Sue most of the semester, but she had slept with Reihner that night. He had said nothing then, even as he saw the situation developing.

He said nothing this time either. What was done was done, he thought, and really, he mostly wanted to be rid of Taylor anyway. He dropped his eyes and turned away from the pair. As he did so, his motion brought him past a small table on which someone had left a half-finished bottle of Guinness stout. Jeffers could not then or ever after remember what happened next, but as he turned he grabbed the bottle by its neck. He pivoted quickly, completing a full circle, and clubbed the other man across the side of the head.

The bottle remained intact but the force of the blow knocked the man unconscious. His head snapped sideways and landed with a thud on the bar. It rested there momentarily until, muscles slack, the body slipped from the stool onto the floor. Jeffers stood there with the inverted bottle, the spilled beer puddling on the floor.

"An old friend of yours, I hope," he said to Taylor. She was actually smiling.

The bartender looked from the mess to Taylor. "Not a problem," she said and tossed a bill on the counter. Then she got up, pulling her pack from under the bar.

"If you say so, Taylor," he said, picking up the bill. "I'll see that he's taken care of after you leave. Damn drunks are always tripping over their own feet." He chuckled softly at that.

Jeffers did not wait to see if she was going to come along. As he walked out of the bar the other patrons turned away, not one showing any desire to interfere with a lunatic who was demonstrably violent. He was out the door and across three-quarters of the parking lot before he realized he was alone. When he turned back to face the inn, he was half expecting an empty expanse of gravel. Instead, he saw Taylor moving to catch up with him. Her walk was slower than he remembered from the afternoon, the limp more evident. The gravel surface of the lot might have accentuated the limp, or perhaps she had not landed as smoothly as he thought. Watching her come toward him, Jeffers recalled that when she had helped him into the parachute, he had bumped against something hard at her left knee. A brace? He wondered about that. If she made a habit out of foolish stunts, he could well believe she had absorbed some damage along the way. The hell with that. Once again, he just wanted to be rid of her.

"George, where do you think you're going?"

"Kennedy Airport, if you remember." The question brought all the anger and frustration of the evening to a head. "The more I think about it, the more I think I'll go alone." Even in the dim light of the parking lot, he could see surprise on her face. Well, what the hell did she expect? "I've had just about as much of being hustled from one insane situation to another as I can take. I may not be James Bond, but I know what I have to do, and I am going to do it. And I am going to do it without any suicidal heroics from the world's greatest female adventurer. If you're looking to get killed, why don't you do something useful and try blowing up Iraq? I have business to take care of, and it's not providing one last joyride for you."

Taylor was shocked by the outburst. It had never occurred to her that he could resent the way she had taken control of the situation, but he had and now he was threatening to take off by himself. That was foolish from the perspective of getting his job done. It was worse from her perspective—it meant being left out.

"Wait, now, just wait a minute and slow down. I am not trying to get killed, and I am not trying to get you killed either. The risks we took were necessary. Just think a moment about what happened earlier if you don't want to believe me. If you go ahead by yourself, you're almost sure to wind up dead. I'm not going to guarantee that I can pull it off either, but at least with me you have a chance. Just think for a minute, how were you going to get out of Boston by yourself?" The urgency in her voice was genuine. She could not allow herself to be left out.

Jeffers hesitated. His anger was cooling almost as fast as it had exploded. "Tell me something, Taylor. What's in it for you? I partly created this mess, so I have to try and straighten it out. But what about you? I know you brought up money before, but I've known some real mercenary people and they would always want to see some money up front. You can't really know what's in the lockbox, because I don't know either. So it can't be just money. Why are you so hot to be in on this?"

Taylor took a step back and cocked her head slightly to one side. She could sense that the conversation had reached a decisive moment. Jeffers was ready to make a final decision, and if she said the wrong thing he would leave. There would be no retrieving it then. She was sure of that.

"I think," she said softly, "this is going to be an adventure worth having."

"It can't be worth the risk of getting killed."

"I don't happen to see it that way. And don't discount the money completely. I have expensive tastes." Taylor drew a slow breath. Jeffers had not left, but he had not decided to take her yet either. They stood, waiting on his decision, for a minute or two. Carefully, she said, "Well, are we going to Kennedy?"

Jeffers scuffed at the gravel, and let out a sigh. The more he thought about the situation, the less sense any of it made so there was no logical decision to make. He had never been very good at saying no to people. Taylor wanted to go along. Her reasons made no sense to him, but she definitely wanted to go along. And when it came to actually saying something, he could not turn her down. After a few more minutes he nodded his head with a brief, "Sure," and hoped he would not soon regret it.

"Great!" said Taylor, very much her confident self again. "I think we can do better for transportation than walking."

"Taylor, we are not going to steal a car." One half-day's association was enough for Jeffers to see where her mind was heading.

"But . . ."

"No!"

## KENNEDY AIRPORT, NEW YORK

THE DESK CLERK AT the airport hotel was probably less surprised by the appearance of a man and woman at four-thirty in the morning than he was by the woman arranging for separate rooms. ("Daddy's American Express card?" "No, *my* American Express card.") The arrangement elicited no other comment from Jeffers. By that time he was dead tired.

For all his fatigue, once he laid down on the bed George Jeffers had trouble falling asleep. His insomnia was not the fault of the hotel; air conditioning held the temperature at a pleasant seventy-four degrees Fahrenheit, and the two queen-sized beds were equipped with luxurious mattresses. While Jeffers had never been one to fall asleep immediately after going to bed, neither had he been accustomed to staring at the ceiling counting the ticks of his clock. What kept him awake was Taylor Redding and his continuing inability to decide, once and for all, what he wanted to do about her.

By his own choice, Jeffers fell into a category of dedicated scientist, frequently referred to by others as a "lab rat." Such people wedded their laboratories much the way a monk weds his church. These were people who would skip a meal, two meals, maybe a night's sleep as well, rather than interrupt an experiment. Having taken his vows, as it were, at his doctoral defense, he had subordinated everything else to his research interests. He did not consider himself antisocial, though. He bet the football pool regularly, followed the news if irregularly and was pleasant enough at work. He also participated in outside activities, at least if he had nothing going on in the lab. The problem was that he usually had something going on in the lab.

This mental attitude ideally suited him to rise rapidly in academia and to be a sought-after scientist in industry. It had made him the real "asset" IRT had obtained in buying NaturGene. It also left him woefully ill-equipped to deal with the likes of Taylor Redding. Again, it would be wrong to assume that he had nothing to do with women. Indeed, in conversation over a beer or at a cookout, a common theme of his was women, or more precisely, the lack thereof. A causal relationship, however, between the jealous demands of the laboratory and this state of affairs consistently escaped him. Moreover, the women he met were much like himself, absorbed in their work and career ambitions. Dinner conversation, frequently in the cafeteria, tended to run along the lines of "homonuclear J-coupled spectra" or the like. The women were not gorgeous, did not dress to emphasize their looks, and most certainly did not cause internal surges when they smiled.

Now, on the other hand, there was Taylor. Lying in the bed, his feelings about her oscillated wildly. As much as he had been furious at her, he would have regretted it had she accepted the exit he offered her. He would have regretted it even more had he stomped away and left her. His anger was kindled alternately at her and at his own desire to stay with her. He told himself that any attraction was purely physical, and there was no denying the physical part of it. God, she was beautiful! He could easily picture the long frame, sculptured face and tawny hair in the darkened room beside him. What other reason could he have for wanting her around? A foolish reason it was, too. There was beauty in a king cobra, but it was best appreciated at a distance. She had a beautiful body *and* a dangerously warped mind; he was going to be rational and not let his gonads lead him by the nose. He could hold to that reasoning as long as he stayed angry. His anger lacked staying power, though, and as it ebbed he found other reasons for wanting her around. She had respectfully listened to him prattle on about his work without looking bored. She had also probably saved his life, a point that had become muddled by subsequent events. Ultimately he decided that he should not have yelled at her and he was not going to do anything about her. It was at that point that he drifted off to sleep.

Taylor Redding went through no such soul searching after reaching her room. She unzipped the pack and pulled out a small stuff sack that held her favorite nightgown. It was always nice to be able to have favorite things along. But along on what? She was still not certain what she had stumbled into. Industrial espionage? Maybe, but maybe not. It did not quite smell right. There was no point worrying about it, though. Whatever it was, it would still be there in the morning; for the remainder of the night it was not under her control. The Rules said she worried only about things under her control. Yet she was not entirely satisfied in that respect either. She had handled Jeffers's escape from Boston well enough, no reproach there. But the confrontation in the parking lot. That was bad. She really thought he was going to leave, exclude her from this new adventure. The thought was horrible, to have it pulled away from her just when she needed to be involved. Much worse, she knew that, for a brief moment, this need to be part of the action had overridden discipline, Rules, everything. She had nearly begged—pleaded—to be included. True, she hadn't actually done so, but she had come close. She had thought of doing so. That would never do, was not permissible. Such feelings could not be shown. Fire on the inside, ice on the outside, that was always the Rule. Ice and Fire.

She shook her hair loose and looked at herself in the mirror. "Okay, okay. You almost blew it. But only almost. And you made things happen in Boston." She smiled, then. Damn, it felt good to be back.

The image in the mirror rippled, then, and faded. At least, it did in her mind. When it reformed, the face she saw was fourteen-year-old Taylor's. The general design was the same as that of the adult looking into the mirror, but a few details were different. The cheeks were softer, with a gentle roundness. The hair was cropped above the shoulders and adorned with a baseball cap. The eyes held the same eager intensity, but no hardness. She was fifteen and ready to bat in her first high school baseball game.

They were losing two to nothing in the bottom of the third. She was ninth in the order, but leading off their half of the inning.

"C'mon, Taylor, make something happen." Coach Magliossi gave her a pat on the back as she left the bench. He added another line under his breath when he thought she was far enough away not to hear.

She had not been able to make out all the words, but she had not needed to. For all the local liberal posturing, neither the coach nor anyone else at the school had been happy with a girl going out for varsity baseball. Her parents had not been happy either; it was Taylor who ultimately called the newspaper to apply pressure, both at school and at home. Magliossi, at least, she gave some credit to. In spite of his displeasure, she had won the starting third base position during the tryouts, fair and square. No doubt it would have been easier to keep her on the team and on the bench. However, that did not mean Magliossi enjoyed having to ask a girl to "make something happen" with his team trailing.

The first pitch to Taylor had been right where she expected it, high, hard and straight at her head. She had figured it correctly and was able to coolly step back, seemingly at the last minute, to dodge the ball. The umpire jumped in, naturally, to threaten the pitcher and the other coach with ejection.

"Never mind," she told the umpire, loud enough so that everyone could hear. "Three more like that and I walk." The bravado covered the tightness in her chest. She had *felt* the ball go by her face; it had been that close.

The next pitch made it worthwhile. It came straight down the middle with nothing on it, as the pitcher lost the psychological game within the game. Taylor would never forget the sweet, solid feel of that hit. The ball had taken off on a straight line about eight feet high, toward left field. Then, somewhere in Taylor's mind, the fielder's approach to the ball told her it was time to "make something happen." She rounded first and kept going. It caught everyone off guard, gaining her a few more seconds. It was going to be close, very close, she saw, as the throw headed for the base. Running all-out, she threw herself headfirst into a dive, hitting the ground on her belly and tearing skin and uniform. She felt the base under her hand before the tag, though, and that was what mattered. She stood up on the base, the front of her uniform solid dirt, dirt on her face too and caked on her chin where blood from a split lip dribbled. It had been grand. Magliossi by the bench looked ready for a heart attack. Coach, she thought, meet Taylor with a capital T as in Trouble. I am where the action is. Taylor Redding makes things happen when it's important.

Baseball had been critically important. Once.

Suddenly the image was gone, and Taylor saw herself still looking into the mirror, wearing a pink Windy Rose nightgown that had seen better days. Had she been standing there long? No. Memories were funny, sometimes. They could come when they wished. That one, at least, had been pleasant. There were plenty that were not. She shrugged at herself, turned away from the mirror, then looked at the bed with distaste. The lines, "To sleep: perchance to dream: ay, there's the rub," ran through her head, and she wondered if she had remembered to stash a book in her pack. That way, she could read until the fatigue knocked her out.

# CHAPTER 7

## KENNEDY AIRPORT, NEW YORK

GEORGE JEFFERS AWOKE IN the midmorning after a brief and troubled sleep. His dreams had a recurrent theme, no matter how often his mind rose to the level of nearly awake and banished it. Over and over he approached a car with a man inside, his head shattered and shards of flesh strewn across the seat. Somehow, against his will Jeffers was drawn closer and closer to the car. As soon as he reached it the face on the head would transform into that of Taylor Redding. "You have to take chances in this business, George," she said from a head that was only half there. There were other details he forgot after he woke, but that much stayed with him.

If waking brought relief from his dreams, it also brought pain. He hurt all over—not the simple sore muscles of overexertion, but a multitude of different pains, all clamoring for attention. His first response, after a groan, was to lie back in the hope of escaping into sleep again, dreams be damned. However, a large abrasion by his left knee had oozed while he slept. The blood and tissue juice had formed a bond between his wound and the bedsheet which the movement tore apart. Pain rocketed in both directions through his leg, and Jeffers was suddenly very much wide awake.

It took a determined effort, and the conviction that sitting up would be less painful than lying down, to bring him up. He sat head in hands on the edge of the bed, trying to orient himself. The clock on the nightstand read a quarter to ten, a late hour for him to be in bed. Even on nights when he worked to near dawn, he was usually awake no later than nine. Last night, however, had not been a usual night, had it? Had it even been real? He had never been intoxicated enough to lose an entire evening, but the idea was attractive compared to what he thought he was remembering. He picked up the television remote control and turned on CNN. Sure enough, after waiting through several stories the announcer began: *"Authorities are investigating a bizarre case that began in Boston last night. A man apparently stole a light plane at Boston's Logan Airport, cut off a passenger jet on the runway and took off into the night. The pilot ignored all calls from air traffic controllers while flying in a southwesterly direction and ultimately crashing into Long Island Sound. Some sources have speculated these events were connected to the murder of an out-of-work building contractor named Don Lorenzo, who was shot in the head as he sat in his car near Fenway Park in Boston. Neither the Boston police nor the FBI would comment on these rumors, nor did they have any information regarding the identity or fate of the pilot."*

Dear God, Jeffers thought, it did happen. Which means that I *did* jump out of a plane in the middle of the night and I *was* in a bar in Westchester County. Dear God in heaven.

He was still in the same position ten minutes later when a rap on the door brought him to his feet. Until the previous day he would have simply bounded to the door and opened it. This day he kept the chain on and the bolt thrown until he had had a good look through the peephole. It was Taylor Redding.

"I guess you weren't just a bad dream," he said as he opened the door.

Taylor stepped into the room, looking for all the world to be dressed for a party, not a vestige of mud in sight.

"Good morning," she said. "I'm sorry for not making what I was doing clearer, but I'm not sorry for doing what I did to get us here. I did bring a peace offering for yesterday." She held out a small bag with the logo of the hotel's souvenir shop and I LOVE NY printed on it.

To Jeffers, the three sentences had the sound of a rehearsed speech. He took the bag, realizing as he did that he was also accepting it as the limit of any accounting he would get from her about the previous day. When he opened it, the bag proved to contain a purple and green rugby shirt also bearing the message I LOVE NY, shorts and clean underwear. The contents made Jeffers acutely aware that he was standing at the door wearing only his torn shirt and underpants. He turned bright red, closed the door and retreated to the bathroom.

"Good idea," Taylor said. "Right now, you look like we lost."

Shortly thereafter, the sound of running water was audible, admixed with occasional epithets. Twenty minutes later Jeffers emerged from the bathroom and found Taylor stretched out in the room's armchair, seated almost sideways with her right leg over the arm of the chair. She appeared totally absorbed in the texture of the ceiling.

She rotated slowly in the chair to face him. One hand held an airline ticket folder. "We have seats on the evening flight to Zurich, which gives us several hours to kill. As a start on that, how about brunch?" Her tone made it a rhetorical question.

Their sole option proved to be the hotel's utilitarian coffee shop. There

was little to distinguish it from any other similar establishment anywhere in
the country. There was the inevitable counter, with its row of stools and
stale doughnuts under plastic. Past that, beyond the PLEASE WAIT FOR HOST-
ESS sign, were several echelons of tables and a scattering of customers.
Taylor waited for no one. Instead she marched to a convenient table and
occupied it, rather like an army taking enemy ground. The hostess acknowledged the *fait accompli* with menus and restrained herself to a barely audible comment about reading signs which Taylor ignored.

After a few moments Taylor spoke up. "George, you look like you have
something on your mind other than breakfast. Why don't you let me in on
it?"

As she spoke Jeffers realized he had not taken his eyes off her from the
time they had sat down. "It was what you said just before we left the room.
I was thinking about it on the way down. Why the evening flight to Zurich?"

"That's the next flight out. It'll get us in early morning their time. We're
lucky to get the seats. Summer *is* a heavy travel time you know."

"It wasn't the time I was wondering about. It's the flight. Why Zurich?
The conference Hank was supposed to go to is in Amsterdam, and there are
only a few days left."

"The conference may be in Amsterdam," she answered, "but from what
you tell me, the money is in a bank in Zurich."

"Well, yes." Suddenly, Jeffers felt defensive. He was a terrible negotiator.
"But what's the rush? Or are you expecting payment in advance, or
something?"

"My payment has got nothing to do with it. This is going to be an expensive operation, even leaving me out of the calculation, and if you think I'm
going to schlepp you across Europe on my American Express card, you're
crazy. Rule number one, George, of any operation is to make sure of your
supplies at the start. I'm not saying you have to have everything with you,
but you have to know where you can get it. One of our most critical supply
items is going to be money." She thought of Montrose as she spoke—hell,
even he, who had sneaked into Scotland with three men and a mule and
made himself master, had reasonable expectations of where to find men and
supplies.

She continued: "The money is there *now* I assume, but that is no assur-
ance that it will stay there. Consider: once it is established the key to the
money has disappeared, it will occur to someone to be concerned for its
safety." As it was in the room above the Kettle Drum, her tone became
professorial. "The only real way to protect that money is to move it. You'll
see what I mean if you reverse roles for a second. If you're responsible for

the money, just telling the bank to prevent access to it is no good. The baddies know exactly where it is, have the key, and you can't know when they would try to take it. Also, that money is there for a purpose, and blocking it would make it that much harder for your people to get to it. So you have to move it. The question for us is, how fast? If your security people are really good, they could pull it today and beat us. But there are a lot of ifs. They didn't control your contact, Oliver did, and Oliver, so you tell me, doesn't know about the money. How fast will they pick up on the hit and your disappearance? They won't know you're gone for sure just from the news, but once they know, how fast will they get their asses in gear? The man in charge may know just what to do, but if he can't get his people to execute fast enough or doesn't have someone he can trust, he might as well be a dud."

The more Taylor talked, the more intense she became, and the more her voice dropped. Jeffers found himself leaning over the table to catch her words.

"There are a couple of items that let me make a guess, but that is all it is. First of all, the money is in Switzerland. That's fine, except the action is in Amsterdam. Why Switzerland then? Either it's an old stash, money for a rainy day, or somebody's brain is ossified. If it's always kept there for contingencies, they probably won't want to move it unless they have to. Second, even if they have heard about Oliver's man, they can't know about you. They'll probably wait a day for you to show up. All of that should give us the day it will take to get there, but I would not count on more."

She paused to chew on her lip for a moment. "All of that is an awful lot of reasoning based on not too many facts, but I want to let you know how I'm thinking. It would help sharpen it up if you can give me some details about your security."

"I don't know a lot about the security force as a whole, but I do know the guy who runs it." Taylor nodded for him to continue. "His name is Jim Thompson. He worked for IRT long before they acquired us. In fact, we really had no security before the acquisition, which is how I got to know Thompson. The lack of what he called 'proper security' really drove him nuts, so he spent a lot of time in Cleveland reorganizing us. I guess he's done a good job—Lord knows getting in and out is a real pain now— although I would never have figured we had anything that needed to be secured like that." Which is why I'm here now, he added silently. "Anyhow, Sir James is an absolute fanatic about details. Before IRT he worked for the FBI, or CIA, something like that."

" 'Sir James?' He's British?"

"No, no," Jeffers grinned. "That's a tag I hung on him because of the show he always puts on. You know, for Sir James Bond the superspy. Thompson hates it, I think, but now other people have picked up on it, so he's stuck."

"James Bond, huh." Taylor's voice had developed a wary tone. "You like that stuff?"

"Sure." Jeffers's grin was still in place. "When I'm not working on something, I read. I've got every Bond book Fleming wrote, also the ones written under his name. It's a little weird, thinking I've sort of fallen into one of them."

Fallen into a spy story! Just what I need, Taylor thought, an amateur spy and a James Bond freak to boot. Dear Lord, what did I do to deserve this? Aloud she said only, "James Bond aside, do you think Thompson has done anything about the money?"

Jeffers began to worry as he thought over the question until the answer struck him. He had to fight to keep from giggling—here Taylor was trying to work her way to an answer, and he knew it all along. "No, he won't have done anything with it. Not yet. The way he set it up, I'm not due to report back until tomorrow. Even if he's heard the news, I'm not overdue."

"Well, it's not a guarantee but I'll take it. Why don't you have a look at your menu, because that's what I'm going to do."

Once he had opened it the menu riveted his attention. Glossy photos of eggs and pancakes in various positions brought his hunger to the front of his mind. His stomach had not forgotten the twenty-four-hour gap since his last meal, even if he had.

His perusal of the offerings was interrupted by an "Excuse me" from Taylor's side of the table. Jeffers looked up to find Taylor glaring across at the next table. There was a man sitting there with a somewhat surprised look on his face. Jeffers was sure he had not been there before; they would not have spoken so freely with someone at their shoulders. A single glance at the man brought "Texan" to Jeffers's mind. He was middle-aged with a slight paunch and wore a string tie with a turquoise brooch. A white cowboy hat covered the place setting opposite him. Could he have heard something? Jeffers was doubting his recollection of the table having been empty when he noticed the man's stogie—the reason for Taylor's stare—which had gotten about halfway to his mouth.

"The little lady doesn't mind if I smoke, does she?" The drawling condescension confirmed Jeffers's first impression of the man's origin.

Taylor seemed to mind. "Light it, motherfucker, and I'll put it out in your left nostril." Her voice stayed low and even. She had not moved from the position Jeffers saw when he had first looked up.

The man's face, ruddy to begin with, turned beet red. "And supposin' I call that bluff?"

"Your choice; it's a free country. But I don't bluff, I don't like smoke and the no smoking sign is practically in front of your nose."

"I see." He picked his hat off the table and replaced it on his head. "Mister," he said to Jeffers, ignoring Taylor, "if you haven't married her yet, I'd think twice." Then he left.

Jeffers relaxed, one muscle at a time, acutely aware of how rigid he had been before. "Christ, Taylor, that's all we need. A little melée and a trip to the police station. What would we do then? Get your daddy to bail you out?"

"Ease up, George," she laughed. "You didn't think he was really going to do anything, did you? There are times you can push and times you can't. Trust me, I've never had to have daddy bail me out."

"Wonder if he would?"

"Bail me out, you mean? Yeah, 'trial and tribulation' though I may be, I think he would if I asked. But I wouldn't ask."

# PART II

---

## TRAMPS ABROAD

# CHAPTER 8

COMPARED TO THE JOURNEY from Boston to New York, going from New York to Zurich was surprisingly easy. At Kennedy Airport in New York Jeffers had no concerns about being recognized or shot. The stolen plane from Logan was on the front page of all the newspapers, but there was little more substance in their stories than there had been on CNN. And, after all, the plane had gone down over the water. There were no bodies in the wreckage, but where else would one expect them to be but at the bottom? That was the official view of the police, who could sense a no-win case when they saw one. Some papers, lacking any hard news on the story, constructed an interesting speculation that a large drug deal had been involved. Reading some of them made Jeffers wonder if they weren't writing about an entirely different airplane. One paper did send shivers down his spine with its theory of a late-night parachute drop to a hidden airfield, which the authorities spent a great deal of time debunking. The radio exchange that had taken place over Westchester did not exist in the public reports.

Once they had boarded, the flight itself, like almost any transatlantic crossing, was boring. At first Jeffers thought he would welcome any amount of boredom. That idea lasted only two hours. He had not thought to buy anything to read before passing customs, an unusual lapse for him. Taylor had picked a best-selling piece of trash fiction from the newsstand while he had been preoccupied with the papers. She stuck her nose in it from the moment they sat down and did not change position, it seemed, until she finished it—a remarkably short time, he thought. Once she was through, she tilted her chair back and went right to sleep.

Jeffers, unfortunately, had never been able to sleep on a plane. This constitutional problem was compounded by the two very nice Middle Eastern ladies in the row behind him who maintained an absolutely uninterrupted flow of chatter, one of them effortlessly and seamlessly entering the stream whenever the other needed to breathe. And when he reclined the seat, the young child with the women battered away at the lowered seat-back with his feet. Taylor was of no help during this ordeal. She snoozed, oblivious to her surroundings. Maybe not totally oblivious—she did wake up when the food trays came around, but she went back to her slumbers once the meal was finished.

With nothing else to do, Jeffers found himself watching Taylor sleep and envying her ability to do so. Eventually he decided he was just watching *her*. Asleep in her chair, she looked more sixteen than twenty-five, and a far cry from the Valkyrie of the previous day. The intensity in her face was gone, that was what made the difference. He had heard her merry laugh and seen her smile, but there was also an underlying hardness in her voice and in her eyes. With her face relaxed it was difficult to imagine any harshness about her. A sword in a velvet sheath, he thought. Still, the more he looked at her, the more he wondered if, perhaps, the adamantine side was the pose, rather than the reality. He almost reached over to stroke her arm but thought better of it, and it was probably good that he did.

After they landed Taylor steered them through the corridors of the Zurich airport with an ease that bespoke previous experience, which was fortunate for Jeffers. Although he had partially recovered his energy lounging around Kennedy, the night flight had left him exhausted again. The fatigue did not prevent a relapse of the jitters when the taxi dropped them off near the bank.

"Let me have a look at that letter you have before we go in," Taylor said. "Just in case one of us should have a different name, I'd like to know in advance."

Jeffers passed it over without comment. To him it seemed that the noise from her ripping open the envelope was loud enough to alert everyone in the city to what they were doing.

"Well, isn't that interesting. Take a look at this." Taylor stuck the sheet under Jeffers's nose.

"There's no name for the person," he said once his eyes had adjusted to the short focal length.

"Correct." She beamed. "It's a bearer document. It authorizes the bank to give the box to whoever has this and the key. What else?"

Jeffers shook his head. The note was short, and precise.

"Your friend Thompson isn't one of the people who signed it, that's what. He can't authorize anyone to go to the box, he had to get it from higher up. It's not dated, so this is probably his to keep for emergencies. I'll bet he is hoping you show up, otherwise he has to go back to his boss for another authorization. Now I'm sure the money is still there."

"So, we go for it now?" Jeffers asked.

"In a moment." Taylor held up her hand. "It would be best, I think, if I take the letter and go alone. I'll meet you back here at the café." She pointed past Jeffers's shoulder.

"No!" Did everyone in the world think he was naïve? "We go together."

"George, be reasonable. This letter gives whoever carries it the right to go to the box. I can use it as easily as you and there's an advantage to that. We're betting that no one—not Thompson, not even Oliver—can really know what's happening right now. However, if your Jim Thompson is covering all possibilities, which he ought to do, then *somebody* in that bank has instructions to call him if you show up. Nobody will be watching for me. True, the bank will have a record that the box was accessed, and may even have instructions to report it to IRT, but everything you've told me makes me believe that the bank doesn't know what's in there or that it's anything important. IRT won't set up anything that would call attention to it and that's why I don't think alarms are going to go off the instant we go to it. Now, you'll pardon my saying so, but the moment we walk out of there with the money, we and Thompson are not exactly on the same side anymore. So think about it. If you go in there, they know today that you're here. If I go in, we get a little extra margin and that could be important."

"I don't care," Jeffers said. "I've got people after me right now and if you take the letter and the key, they'll still be after me while you're on your way to Tahiti."

Taylor looked murderous, but all she said was, "Okay, we go together." Then she set off for the bank as though nothing had happened.

The moment of truth with the bank officer was more like a century for Jeffers. Under any circumstances, he imagined, trying to do business in a Swiss bank while wearing a rugby shirt would have made him uncomfortable. But George Jeffers was a marked man, wanted in the United States for the possible murder of a government agent, the theft of an airplane and the abduction of a little girl named Becky. Even if the bank official had not been alerted, he would surely notice the half moons of sweat appearing on the shirt under Jeffers's arms and pick up the phone. Nothing he had heard Taylor say, not even his own knowledge of what was true, could stem the rising tide of panic.

Taylor watched him with mounting concern. Her biggest worry, as she had told him, was that the money might be removed before their arrival. It was a concern that had been largely dispelled by the contents of the letter, yet the strain Jeffers was showing was another matter. If he was having so much trouble handling himself when he had legitimate documents, what would happen later if they had to do something questionable?

In reality, the banker spent only a few minutes examining Jeffers's documentation. Then, with a murmured direction, he escorted them to a small room, bare save for two chairs and a desk. He went out and returned with a large, traditional metal vault box. This he placed on the desk and withdrew.

"Well?" Taylor asked.

Jeffers shrugged in reply, and made no move to touch the box. Seeing him hesitate, Taylor took a deep breath, held it and flipped open the lid. The box was full of cash, packed tight with small stacks of bills, deutsche marks and U.S. dollars. The bills were not in small denominations. Counting the total amount would have been a chore.

"Bingo," said Taylor Redding.

"How much is in there, do you think?"

"Enough to kill a federal agent for, I think," she answered.

"Holy shit," said George Jeffers.

"Well, come on Mister secret agent. Staring at it won't get anything done." She began to pull stacks from the box and stuff them into available space in her pack.

"We're going to take all of it?"

"Why not?" Taylor answered. "I told you, this could get to be an expensive operation.

"You know," she continued, "your company must run a fair number of covert operations, which argues that they are used to some pretty nasty competition."

"What makes you say that?"

"This does." She pointed at the box, no longer as full of bills as when she had started. "Why would you stash this much cash in a Swiss bank and leave that kind of authorization with your chief of security? So you can pay for things in an untraceable fashion. This isn't money in an account, which can be traced in some situations, even here. This is nothing but cash in a box. It can't be traced at all. So what don't you want traced in this set up? Graft and espionage!" She paused briefly. "I must admit, I am losing a great deal of respect for your Sir James. Sure, we moved fast, but if *I* were running your company's security operation, I wouldn't have worried about inconveniencing my operations or even having to go back to my bosses. This cash would be long gone. Not that I'm complaining."

Before long, the available space in Taylor's pack was stuffed with bills. The box was by no means empty.

"What now?" asked Jeffers.

"Here," Taylor held out the same plastic I LOVE NY bag. "Dump the rest into this."

When the transfer had been accomplished they returned the closed, now empty box to the bank. Taylor strapped the pack to her back and, with Jeffers holding the bag in tow, strolled out.

"All right, now that we've got it, where do we put it?" Jeffers asked as soon as they were back on the street.

"Back into another bank, of course—this time into an account only we know about."

"Oh, like maybe that one?" Jeffers pointed at the Union Bank building in the next block.

"No, not there. Or any of these for that matter. It's not that I have anything against Swiss banks. They're perfectly safe. It's just that dear Uncle Sam has been pushing very hard lately to find out who has accounts, and what is in them. Eventually, he may succeed. In contrast, I expect the Bank In Liechtenstein to remain completely discreet."

"Liechtenstein! You mean we're just going to go ambling around like this?" He waved the bag in front of them for emphasis.

Taylor could see that he was beginning to lose control of his fears again, but she was not certain of how to calm him down. "Relax, George. This is Zurich, remember? Not New York. Absolutely nothing is going to happen." Inwardly, she knew that that was not quite true. Sooner or later the company would try to do something about their money and they weren't going to be very friendly about it.

"Relax, you say? How am I supposed to relax? I really wasn't supposed to *be* here in the first place. That authorization certainly wasn't for my use. But, heigh ho! Here I am making off with the secret agent's pension fund, or whatever the hell it was supposed to be for. Jim Thompson is really going to love this."

Jeffers's side of the conversation, conducted loudly in English on a street corner, began to attract attention. Initially, the looks from passersby had been only curious, but Taylor had to wonder how many of the minds behind the glances were following the conversation. Many Swiss spoke fluent English. Not for the first time, Taylor wished she had access to a good baby sitter.

"George," she spoke softly and rapidly, "that money was to bankroll this operation, right? You were never told that it was for anything else. So, we're going to use it as intended. I just want it where it's under our control. Now please try and calm down. This is a very public place, and we are attracting attention we don't need."

"Safely under our control? Oh, very good. And then I wake up one morning, and you're gone and so is it. That'll be a good one."

As out of control as Jeffers was, what he saw on Taylor's face stopped him cold. Pure anger stared at him from steel-hard eyes in a visage clamped tight as a vise grip.

"Dr. Jeffers, I earn my pay. It's a ridiculous little scruple that I have." It flashed through Taylor's mind as she said it that Billy O'Brian would have said the same, but with a different meaning. "If all I wanted was your money I could have it right now." Jeffers stepped back at the words, still low pitched but no longer soft. Her tone and stance left little doubt that it was within her power to do as she said.

"Excuse me . . . What is the problem here?"

Both of them looked up in surprise at the accented voice behind Taylor's left shoulder. What they saw was a large man in the uniform of the local police. Caught up in her own outburst, Taylor had failed to pay attention to her surroundings. Jeffers, although nearly facing in the direction of the policeman, had been solely focused on Taylor.

A perfect picture, Jeffers thought, as his mind cleared. They were going to be picked up by the police for disturbing the peace. All this, and bags of cash. The idea froze him into immobility.

Taylor could see the same picture but it did not inhibit her actions. Deftly she plucked the bag from Jeffers's hand, and turned to face the officer.

"Problem? Sure I can tell you what the problem is. My skinflint boyfriend is what it is." She stuck her arm out to point at Jeffers, the bag of money dangling from her fist.

"Skinflint?" the policeman asked, struggling with the word.

"Skinflint," she repeated. "You know, cheap. I mean, he makes like he walks around with all this money, and I'm from Brooklyn y'know and how often does a girl from Brooklyn get to Europe y'know, so I'd like to get a few things. But can we go shopping? Be real! All I've got is a couple of sweaters and a pair of those funny pants that end at the knee. Here, would ya like to see?" She thrust the bag in the direction of the policeman's face. "I bet you treat your girl better than this."

Whether he did or not was unclear, but that last sentence was the only part of Taylor's rapid-fire speech he was able to fully understand. Enough came through to convince him he had happened on a domestic spat between American tourists. His interest in intervening in such an argument was about equal to his interest in examining the no doubt sweaty bag the young woman was swinging around to emphasize her remarks, which was nil. He extricated himself from the situation by admonishing them to take their argument indoors. Then he walked off with the happy thought that the loud-mouthed American woman was still rare in Switzerland.

As soon as she could see the policeman turning away, Taylor turned and headed in the opposite direction. Jeffers, his motor function restored, hastened to catch up.

As he drew even with her, she laced into him, without breaking stride. "George Jeffers, if you ever pull a dumb stunt like that again, I will fold, spindle and mutilate you. You damned near blew everything acting like a fool, and I don't need that. I know what I'm doing and you don't, but you better start learning. Clear?"

"Yes. I'm sorry," he said.

"Dammit, I don't want you to be sorry, I want you to be smart."

Once they embarked, the trip to Vaduz, capital of Liechtenstein, was without incident, as Taylor had promised. The Bank In Liechtenstein was also accommodating, so the day was still relatively young when they stepped back outside, the cash safely divided between a lockbox and a numbered account.

"Now that we have spending money," Taylor said, "we need to get you a suit."

"A suit? What for?"

"So you at least look respectable. I realize you probably thought that a clashing sport jacket with slacks was formal wear, but that's because your education has been neglected."

Jeffers decided to let the slur pass. "When you say spending money, how much are you talking?"

"Oh, about three hundred fifty thousand in U.S. equivalents."

"What!" Jeffers wound up trying to inhale and swallow saliva at the same time, producing a coughing fit.

"George, you may be comfortable walking around with fifty or a hundred dollars, but I like to have some money in my pocket. Anyway, it's OPM, so what the hell?"

"What do you mean by OPM?"

"Other People's Money," she replied. "Don't you watch television? It's the best kind to spend, don't you know."

In spite of Taylor's insistence on the suit, they did not buy it in Vaduz. Instead she brought Jeffers back to Zurich, where she picked out a severe (to his mind) dark gray pinstripe from the first store they tried. Had he been less tired, Jeffers would have mounted a stronger protest over the style. As it was he had done more arguing than he wanted to already, and in any case he felt ready to go to sleep in the change room. She took pity on him then and booked him into a hotel room using one of her credit cards.

"Thank God—a bed!" Jeffers said on entering the room. "I'm so damn pooped I feel like I'm wearing lead socks."

"No problem. Now would be a good time to catch up on your sleep. Before you do though, do you have a phone card and a credit card through the company?"

Jeffers was ready to shut out the world, but the request was odd enough to raise a question from him.

"Fact is," Taylor continued, "there's no way of hiding that you came to Zurich. We had no time in New York to even think about getting fake passports and ID. We have to assume that Thompson's people learned you were in Zurich the moment we went to the bank." She hoped those were the *only* people who would learn that Jeffers was in Zurich, but she didn't mention that. "Even if you weren't traveling as George Jeffers, they're going to know that someone went to the box, and that will draw them here. However, there's no need for them to know about Liechtenstein. There's no record we went there except at the bank, and they won't talk even if they're asked. What I'm going to do is build a nice paper trail for you in Zurich that leads somewhere else. Nobody will even wonder if you might have been in Liechtenstein today, and they won't be looking in the direction we're going to go."

"Unh."

Taylor looked at him, leaning back limply on the bed, his eyes half-closed.

"Nitey-nite, George."


Taylor wasted no time after she left Jeffers. Outside the hotel she stopped at a store and bought a man's shirt and a pair of slacks. From there she walked down the street to another hotel where she found a public phone in the lobby and made a series of calls using Jeffers's card. One of them was to an old acquaintance who owed her several favors. She was grinning by the time she got into a taxi that took her to the Hilton Hotel near the Zurich airport. There she took a room for Jeffers for three days using his credit card and passport. In the room, she put the tags and wrapping from the new clothes she'd bought on the dresser, and heaped the clothes in her bag. Then she pulled out the telephone card. A travel agent booked a flight for George Jeffers from Munich to Berlin and a hotel reservation in Berlin for the following day. With a pen she made a check by the Zurich-to-Munich train on a much folded schedule that she pulled out of a pocket and left it by the phone. Several more brief calls followed. When she was done she hung the DO NOT DISTURB sign on the door and went downstairs.

From a lobby phone she made a few lengthy calls with her own card. On the last, though, she let the phone ring twice and hung up. She found a chair with a good view of the whole area and sat down to wait. About a half-hour later, a short man with dark hair entered the lobby. Their eyes met for just the briefest glance. He turned and walked back outside, now quite dark, with Taylor following a few minutes later. She caught up to him just past the hotel entrance and handed him Jeffers's cards and told him which train to take to Munich and where to get the tickets for Berlin.

"Why not just fly from Zurich to Berlin?" he asked. There was just a trace of German accent in his voice. "I don't see why I need to wait around in Munich."

Taylor shrugged. "I'll grant that the EC has gotten pretty loose about tickets and passports but this is still Switzerland, not EC, and somebody at the airport may look. You won't have time to pick up any documents here that will pass, but on the train it won't matter. You can get what you need in Munich."

The man shrugged in return. "You're overcautious," he said.

"That's how I was taught and why I'm still around. There's a time to take risks and a time to be careful."

"Fine." He did not seem disposed to argue further. "What do I do when I reach Berlin?"

"Have fun. Stay active and give those cards some exercise but not so much that the companies would flag them as stolen. Don't get caught."

*"Alles klar."*

It was far from a perfect deception, Taylor thought when he left, but it should be enough to send Thompson's men off on a wild-goose chase. It was going to be enough work finding Jeffers's enzyme without having the company cops chasing them to get their money back. Even more important, someone had already taken shots at Jeffers and she had no idea who that someone was or what his sources of information were. If they picked up Jeffers's track in Zurich, maybe they would also follow the trail to Berlin— maybe. She looked at her watch. There was still enough time to get a few hours' sleep before they had to start again in the morning. She would have almost preferred no such time at all.

# LANGLEY, VIRGINIA

IT WAS DARK WHEN Oliver pushed the last of the reports to the side of his desk and drummed his fingers on the wood veneer top. The Virginia countryside outside his window looked peaceful, for a moment a deer was visible, but the pastoral scene did nothing for his disquiet that had built up during the day. Don Lorenzo was dead. He would be remembered as others were, with a star but no name by the year in the Book of Honor at the entrance. For Oliver, though, this was the beginning, not the end. The fact that Lorenzo was dead argued in persuasive terms that there was more to this case than a political favor to a senator, more than a little game to keep an important scientist happy, more than either Thompson or Jeffers had told him. What had they hidden from him and why? How important could that damned enzyme be? Why had his agent been killed? Oliver wanted those answers, but as much as he wanted answers he also wanted revenge. He pulled a yellow pad off the top of a pile of reports and leafed through the pages of notes he had jotted down. He grudgingly admitted that the Boston police had been pretty thorough at the scene of Lorenzo's death. They had interviewed anyone on the street who might have seen anything and had also interviewed each one of the mob that had been packed into the Kettle Drum. Most of it was useless, of course. Some items, though, stuck out in a way that bothered Oliver. Jeffers had been in the Kettle Drum, no question about that. The bartender remembered him sitting there, staring at an empty beer glass. Just about what I'd expect him to do, Oliver thought. Jeffers had been there all right, but not with Lorenzo. A couple of people remembered Jeffers being with a tall young woman—arguing with her, it seemed, because he had knocked over his beer. The bartender curiously made no mention of a woman anywhere near Jeffers. Oversight or intentional? An older woman who had been on the sidewalk claimed that Jeffers had been alongside Lorenzo's car with the door open when the shooting started. The first shot, she said, hit the driver of the car. Or so she had told the police. She had also said that a tall young woman had been right next to Jeffers at the same time. Lorenzo had not been killed by the sniper, though. He had been shot point-blank with a handgun. The woman was wrong about the shot that killed Lorenzo. Was she also wrong about who was standing by the open car door? Jeffers and, apparently, the young woman were no longer present when the police interviewed the people at the scene. So who was this tall young woman? Had she been in position to shoot Lorenzo as she and Jeffers stood by the car? Possibly. Could the "girl" in the plane over Westchester have been a tall young woman? Part of Oliver's training had been to construct patterns from seemingly unconnected scraps of information. These scraps, however, refused to coalesce in his mind. His teeth clenched in anger at the thought—and at the thought that this case might be bigger than he had imagined.

# CHAPTER 9

## LANGLEY, VIRGINIA

THE NEXT MORNING OLIVER felt as though he had barely had time to get into his office, barely time to notice the stacks of work (much of it thoughtfully placed on his chair by his secretary so he could not fail to see it) and certainly no time to finish his coffee before the phone was ringing. It was Thompson, upset, wanting to know what was going on, a discussion Oliver would have preferred to put off, at least until he had finished his coffee.

"Jim, I am not trying to put you off," he said. "I literally just this minute got into my office and I haven't even had time to get my butt in the chair. I lost a man in Boston, remember, and I'm not real pleased with that. It also makes me think I haven't quite heard everything about the damn enzyme. Right? I know Blalock has the director convinced that the future of American biotechnology rests on this thing, but are you going to tell me that it really is important enough for someone to waste one of my men? What's the truth, Jim? What's your read on it? Not what Blalock or IRT want to tell us. What *you* think."

There was a long silence on the line and Oliver found himself hoping that Thompson would refuse to talk about it. That would give him a good excuse to hang up.

"Listen, Charles," Thompson said. "It may be an exaggeration, but maybe not much of one. What we expect to get out of Jeffers's work is a patent on the basic technology for making artificial enzymes. If you don't know what that means, I've talked to our patent people. They say it would be like owning the rights to all computer chips. Anybody who did anything in the future would have to come to us. If H-C has it, they'll blow us out of the water. I'm sure that's why some of their people are shorting our stock, but I would guess they're acting on their own just to cash in on the side, because that activity has tipped their hand."

"Jeffers didn't seem to think it was that important and he's the scientist."

"George doesn't understand the legal side of it," Thompson said. "And, frankly, he doesn't care. Never mind what George told you. This whole presentation in Amsterdam had been set up without any of our legal people knowing about it and, let me tell you, they went apeshit when they found out. We only let Davenport go because the abstract was already public and canceling would have caused us a lot of bad press."

"And now you're missing both the invention and the inventor. You're doing well, Jim."

This time the silence lasted longer than before. "I need Jeffers back," Thompson said at last. "At the very least I need to know what happened to him. This is urgent and I'm not exaggerating in the slightest bit."

"Okay," Oliver said. "Let's move ahead together, then. I assume you had him followed. What else do you know that I should know?"

"I had Jeffers tailed," Thompson agreed. "After the shooting, he left that bar with a woman, dodged the police and got into a car. No obvious coercion, but that doesn't mean anything. I can fax you her description and the plate number. Unfortunately, we lost them when they pulled out."

"You haven't had the plate run?"

"No. I'd prefer if the police didn't know I had anyone there. You always had good connections with the FBI, Charles. If the information came through that channel, I could keep a low profile."

"Are you thinking this woman is an assassin?"

"I don't know. Will you keep me informed of what you find out?"

"Up to a point." Oliver measured each word carefully. "You know, you're not exactly with the Company anymore. There are some things you may not need to know."

"I can accept that," Thompson said. "Just remember this is *my* case too."

"Okay." Oliver paused. "Jim, you mind if I ask you a personal question?"

"Charles, does this mean we're getting serious? What is it?"

"Well, you were one of our better case officers," Oliver said. "In fact, I would have figured you for Chief of Station by now, one of the major European posts. I'm curious why you left."

Thompson's reply started with a chuckle. "I guess I figured there were some things you guys didn't need to know. Hell, it's no big secret, though. I left after the Wall came down and Eastern Europe fell apart. I just figured the next war will be an economic one and I wanted a good position early. I was right, too. Shit, they've even got you chasing computer chips now, don't they?"

Much as it galled Oliver to admit it, Thompson was right. And Thompson seemed to be right about more than just that. By midmorning his call to the FBI had produced some results on the license plate. The car Thompson's man had seen was registered to one Abdul Rahman El-Kader. The registry had sent a car to check the address and found a boarded-up apartment building. So, there was a young woman who met Jeffers in the bar. She was at Lorenzo's car when he was shot. Jeffers had apparently left with her afterwards and neither of them had spoken with the police. She was driving a car registered to a phony name and address, which argued that this was no good Samaritan who just happened to pick up Jeffers. It certainly did not seem as though Thompson had expected her. So who the fuck was she and what was she after? The information was starting to make a nasty pattern, but there was still not enough to tell him what was happening. He needed more information.

# BERNE, SWITZERLAND

"THE MAN YOU ARE going to see is Werner Hochmann," Taylor said as they sat in the intercity train the next morning. "His position is essentially equivalent to an executive vice-president. I would think that he has some knowledge of any major operations that Helvetica-Chemie is engaged in and he's the logical person to know about anything covert. Getting him to tell you about it is the trick. Supposedly he's a real Young Turk; not much given to 'leisure time' pursuits. I'm afraid I don't know too much more about him."

"Yeah," Jeffers said slowly. "How many children?"

"Two. Why do you want to know?"

"No particular reason. I'd just hate to see what you consider a complete dossier." He shook his head as they left the railroad platform at Berne. At least now he knew some of what Taylor had been doing with the calling card the previous day.

The headquarters of Helvetica-Chemie proved to be a fifteen-minute taxi ride from the railway station. Situated on a flat, grassy meadow, it was all steel, glass and right angles—six stories worth. A row of glass doors at the main entrance opened onto a small waiting area which was blocked by a security checkpoint and a pair of guards. Beyond them, a lobby so modern as to be nearly bare stretched the width of the building under skylights.

Jeffers pointed to the guards with a tilt of his head. "I hate to throw a monkey wrench into the plan, Taylor, but what are we going to do about them? They're hardly going to show us in to see the executive VP." Unlike their American rent-a-cop counterparts, these men appeared young and trim. Their posture at the desk lent a military air to the establishment.

"Not to worry, George. Just hang loose." She headed straight for the guard desk.

The guards' discipline was not quite perfect; Taylor had their full attention from the moment she walked in. Jeffers could tell that, for the moment, they were completely ignoring him, but what was he supposed to do with the situation? He doubted the guards were so mesmerized as to let him slip by. He waited for a sign from Taylor, wondering even as he did if he was letting his chance slip away.

"Dr. George Jeffers, Intergroup Resources and Technologies, U.S.A." he heard Taylor announce to the seated guard. The response was almost immediate.

"*Ja, Fraulein.*" The man inclined his head slightly and, from a shelf below the desktop, produced a small card which he handed over to Taylor. Then he waved both of them through, toward the bank of elevators behind the security station.

Jeffers caught up to her at the elevator. Anxious as he was to see the card, he figured it would be unseemly to run after her. When he saw it, he found it to be a visitor's pass. Printed on it was Hochmann's name, and what had to be a room number. Prearranged! What else had Taylor been setting up? He started to ask her as they entered the elevator, but she cut him off by holding up her hand.

"No time now. Just listen, please. When we get to Hochmann's office, you're going to be on your own. Push him a bit, see what happens. Okay, boss?"

Jeffers nodded silently. What else could he do? He had had a similar feeling once before—on an airplane, wearing a parachute. Behind him the elevator doors slid open silently.

In the blink of an eye, Taylor changed. One hand came out of a pocket and popped a double wad of gum into her mouth. The other hand released the top button of her blouse, leaving a long bare expanse of skin between the silk scarf and where the blouse was still buttoned, then she set off down the corridor with an exaggerated wiggle. Her limp, normally close to undetectable on a flat surface, was pronounced as well, but somehow it seemed less like a limp and more like a provocative fling of the hips.

Jeffers went along, more ill at ease with each step. The paneling on the walls looked like real wood, the pictures on them were probably prints but the frames alone must have cost a small fortune, even the carpet felt rich. Power resided here, no doubt of that. The place reeked of it, far more than Herb's suite of offices did in Cleveland. Of course, Helvetica-Chemie was an international industrial power. Werner Hochmann, whoever he might be, had risen to near the pinnacle of the organization and was unlikely to be another Herb, safely ignored or even baited, on occasion, for amusement. Marching in to beard this lion in his den was one Dr. George Jeffers, who would have infinitely preferred to be back in his lab, and his companion, who looked as if she would have been at home on New York's Eighth Avenue. Push him a bit and see what happens, Jeffers thought. I bet that's not what King Saul told David before the big match.

The door they wanted was at the end of the corridor. It opened onto a huge front office. The room was large enough to hold the three secretaries who occupied it, several potted plants and a bank of files, and still give an impression of wide-open spaces. Each secretary's desk was set up as a computer workstation.

One of the secretaries, a robust dark-haired woman, came over to greet them. "Ah, Dr. Jeffers, Miss Aldridge." Jeffers managed to avoid looking surprised as she addressed Taylor. "I am Helga. I spoke with your office yesterday. I am sorry your visit was not foreseen, but Herr Hochmann has made time to see you." Helga's English was accented, but functional.

"Spoke with your office yesterday" ran a second time through Jeffers's mind. Spoke with our Zurich branch office would be more accurate, he thought. That calling card must have seen a lot of use. He could also imagine what kind of paper trail it had left. Perhaps Taylor did know what she was doing. With his confidence somewhat restored, he allowed himself to be ushered into Hochmann's office.

That small bit of confidence dissipated as soon as he saw Hochmann. It was not a matter of imposing stature—Hochmann was a smallish man—it was the face that did it, high forehead and skin stretched tightly over every bony prominence. All softness had been pressed from that face; it seemed all lines and corners rather than curves. The pale blue eyes set deep in their sockets would have done justice to a religious fanatic.

For coldness, Jeffers thought, those eyes easily matched Taylor's when he had first seen them. Taylor's eyes held nothing of that icy gaze now, he noted. If anything, they were vacuous. Almost before Hochmann had indicated the chair, she had settled into it. She sat tilted forward at the hips, a position from which Hochmann must have been provided a view down the front of her shirt.

"Dr. Jeffers," Hochmann began as soon as Jeffers had seated himself. "If you don't mind, we should dispense with pleasantries. I assume that when one has traveled from the United States on short notice the matter is of some importance. Nevertheless, my time is precious and arranging this meeting was difficult, so please state your business."

Jeffers was taken aback by Hochmann's nearly pugnacious tone. It had the sound of a man convinced he could more profitably be elsewhere. He looked at Taylor for a clue on how to start, and was rewarded with a loud snap of her chewing gum. At the sound, two spots of red appeared on Hochmann's face, one over each cheek.

"Georgie," Taylor turned to Jeffers, ignoring Hochmann, "you know how I hate sitting through business meetings. Is there some place I can get a drink and meet you later?"

Hochmann's visage virtually dripped contempt. "If you ask Helga, no doubt she can show you the lunch room." That the words got out at all was remarkable, given the minimal opening he permitted his mouth. He turned back to Jeffers. "You can pick her up at the security desk in the lobby, after."

He waited until Taylor had left, enduring the wiggle she aimed at him and the wink she gave Jeffers. "I would think, Dr. Jeffers, that on a transcontinental trip it would pay to bring someone more astute as a secretary. Unless, of course, she serves a different function. I gather from your office's message that she does not speak German, either. If that is true, she may get bored waiting for you. Now, why are you here?"

Had there been an available exit Jeffers would have taken it. Hochmann was in high dudgeon, and Jeffers could think of nothing to say other than his real business. Damn! Again Taylor had maneuvered him into doing exactly what she wanted.

"Herr Hochmann, first of all, it was hardly my idea to bring her." Ha, true enough. That for you, Taylor Redding. "I am here in regard to the disappearance of Dr. Henry Davenport of my firm, who was expected at the Amsterdam Conference several days ago."

Much to Jeffers's surprise, Hochmann actually appeared to relax. "Yes, I had heard of his disappearance. It even made the news for a day or two."

"I'm sure. I am interested in any information you might have in this regard."

"None, I'm afraid. If this question was the purpose of your visit, you have wasted your time and mine, I'm afraid. I do not see how this concerns Helvetica-Chemie at all."

"One moment." Jeffers put up a hand to halt Hochmann, realized he was copying a habit of Taylor's, and put it down. He took a deep breath. Now or never. "What may not have been in the news was the fact that Dr. Davenport was transporting an artificial enzyme—our total working supply, in fact. What definitely was not in the news was the fact that several of your officers are selling IRT stock short."

Hochmann turned a shade somewhere between purple and puce. "By implication, then, you are accusing Helvetica-Chemie of both industrial espionage and stock manipulation. Have a care, Dr. Jeffers."

"Herr Hochmann! Accusations are public affairs, this is strictly private. Both statements I made are true and verifiable. Why am I wrong to connect the two?" Jeffers was surprised at how smoothly it came out. It really sounded good.

"Very well," Hochmann said. Apparently he thought it sounded good, too. "If you know that Helvetica-Chemie officers are selling IRT stock, you know more than I. I do not oversee the financial affairs of any officer of this company other than my own. I suggest to you, however, that if they are selling the stock, it is for excellent financial reasons. Your company's management performance has been dismal, a fact amply reflected on the balance sheet. In my opinion your earnings are artificially inflated and the stock is ridiculously overpriced. Selling it would be a superb move. I would recommend that course to anyone interested in making money.

"As for the enzyme, it has been our view that the project will not generate sufficient returns to justify the time and money spent. I know this because we evaluated your company before it was acquired by IRT. Had we been interested we would have bought it outright at the time. I trust that explains the situation?"

For once, Jeffers mentally kicked himself for never looking at any of the company documents he regularly disposed of in the trash. He should *know* whether Hochmann was telling the truth about IRT. Then it struck him that Hochmann had no way of knowing that he did *not* know. In fact, since Hochmann probably knew Helvetica-Chemie inside out, he might make similar assumptions about Jeffers and IRT. Maybe IRT *was* a corporate basket case. He had always thought Herb was a schmuck for selling out, anyway. It would serve him right to sell out to a bunch of losers. Which left the other issue.

"You can't expect me to share your view of the artificial enzyme project. What evidence is there that you are still uninterested?"

"You have my word."

"Like I said . . ." Jeffers let the phrase hang in the air. Christ, he thought, if Hochmann gets wound up any tighter, I swear he's going to have a stroke.

Hochmann shrugged and stood up abruptly. "I would tell you to take it or leave it, except that I am sure further inquiries will come. As you know, even groundless accusations are damaging, which is why you sit here so smugly. What I will do is arrange for you to speak with Dr. Teuschlein, chief of our research and development unit. You may ask him what you like about our areas of interest. Since all scientists seem to enjoy chattering about their work as much as doing it, you should be able to satisfy yourself. Be warned, though—I will not restrict the areas of discussion, but should there be any, ah, leaks, I will know where they come from."

From his standing position Hochmann punched one of the buttons on his phone. When a voice spoke from the speaker unit, he replied in rapid-fire German. Then he looked back at Jeffers, every bit as icy as when Jeffers had first come in.

"One of the guards will conduct you to Dr. Teuschlein's office. I hope that you find speaking with him worthwhile. I say that because, privately between you and me, there is no free lunch, as they say in your country. I do not appreciate being insulted or compelled to act against my judgment. And I have a good memory. *Wiedersehen*, Dr. Jeffers."

Under other circumstances Jeffers would have enjoyed his conversation with Teuschlein. In his years at the laboratory bench Teuschlein had been an organic chemist, but he had always read extensively even in fields minimally related to his own. This had served him well in ascending Helvetica-Chemie's corporate hierarchy. Now, as the head of the company's research arm, the lines of inquiry on multiple disparate projects converged at his brain. He showed a keen interest in Jeffers's work, indeed he proved to have more than a passing familiarity with Jeffers's papers.

"Of course, I know your work," Teuschlein said. "It's really quite elegant. I haven't seen much over the past couple of years, though. You haven't given up on your artificial enzyme, have you?"

"No, by no means," Jeffers answered. "It's just that since I joined NaturGene the lawyers have been saying I can't publish until the patents are filed and, well, you know how that goes." Jeffers ended abruptly because he could not bear the thought of telling the entire sequence of events yet another time.

Teuschlein agreed with a grunt. The exchange, however, raised a question in Jeffers's mind. "I take it you are also interested in the concept," he said.

"Interested, yes," Teuschlein said. "Working on it, unfortunately, no. That has not been for lack of trying on my part. I proposed putting a project team on it when your papers in the area first appeared. Management thought it was too speculative then. Maybe they were right at the time, but technology has changed since. When it was clear that NaturGene was for sale, I recommended we buy it." He sighed. "They said the price was too high. Of course, when I again proposed starting our own group they told me we were too far behind. I didn't help my cause, I'm afraid, when I put through a grant to another scientist—you'd recognize his name if I told you—who had a proposal in this area. Nothing came of it, though. Since several of our projects have recently failed, however, I think Hochmann would go for it if he could buy it cheaply, or if I could convince him that there was no risk of failure. That isn't too likely, unfortunately."

If Teuschlein was discouraged about Helvetica-Chemie's prospects for competing in the field, it did not dampen his interest in discussing it. By the time Jeffers left they had spoken more about Jeffers's project than those of Helvetica-Chemie. Overall, Teuschlein tended to corroborate Hochmann's story and left Jeffers with the feeling he had made an enemy for no good reason at all.

It was midafternoon by the time a security guard escorted him back to the front lobby, where he found Taylor waiting.

"Well," he said, "I hope you had a good time."

"Hardly. I'm bored to tears. Why don't we go out and buy me something to compensate me for this dismal day?"

He gave her a sharp look, and was about to launch an equally sharp reply, when he saw that her lips were continuing to move, silently. She was saying that one of the guards spoke English. Behind her was a different pair than in the morning. The shift must have changed, and, likely as not, Hochmann had seen to it that one of the pair was fluent in English. Instead of his planned retort, he merely shrugged and headed for the doors. He had nothing to say that could not wait for a little while.

After the taxi left them in downtown Berne, Taylor broke the silence. "What did you get out of Hochmann?"

"Not a whole hell of a lot," Jeffers replied. "He said he had nothing to do with it, but, honestly, I can't see him saying anything different even if he was in it to his armpits. He did let me talk to Hans Teuschlein, he's the guy in charge of R and D, and what he said supports Hochmann's claims. But it doesn't *prove* anything. If Hochmann were running an espionage operation, Teuschlein might not know anything about it. Hell, somebody other than Hochmann could be running it, and Hochmann could be telling the truth. I mean, I'm sure I raised his blood pressure several points, and I sure got him angry enough at me, but did I really get anything out of it? I don't think so. It would have been child's play to hide almost anything from me."

He paused momentarily, and then added, "Did you enjoy your lunch with the girls?"

"As a matter of fact, I did." Taylor wore a sly grin. "After Hochmann threw me out, I had a very nice lunch with Helga and some of the other secretaries. It's an interesting thing. The way offices are organized, the secretary either sees or hears about almost everything that goes on. We had a good talk, and I got no sign at all of any funny business. Of course, that's not proof either. So after lunch, when Hochmann was away from his office, I slipped in to look through his files."

"You mean you burglarized his office."

"Yes, if you have to be crude about it."

"Jesus Christ, Taylor, don't you have any nerve endings at all?"

"I had them amputated when I was a kid. Actually, it was a good enough risk. Hochmann's schedule is so tight it creaks, so no question of his whereabouts, and he's not, shall we say, popular with his staff. I had a decent look."

"So did it pay off? After all of that, did you come up with anything?"

"Maybe something, maybe nothing." Taylor wore the mischievous grin of a child who has hidden her father's mail.

"Well, then, out with it already! The suspense is killing me." The irritation was surfacing again, too, in Jeffers's mind. He did not see himself as caught up in an exciting game, as Taylor no doubt did.

The outburst did not faze Taylor in the least. "As I told you, there was nothing to tie H-C directly to Davenport or to your enzyme. No surprise there. You'd hardly expect a memo on that sort of thing in a file. I did find a couple of items, though. There were some notes on a company called Sachsen Fabrik in Neu Mecklenberg that is working on a project like yours. H-C is trying to decide if they want to buy the company. Do you know anything about them?"

"Never heard of them. Teuschlein did say that he thought Hochmann would make a deal if it was a sure thing. I gather some of their other projects haven't panned out, so he needs something. I can't imagine this Sachsen Fabrik has much, though. I know most of the top people in the field. Where is Neu Mecklenberg?"

"No idea. Okay, we'll table it for now. The next bit is more interesting. What I found was a list of six scientists in your field who have received large sums of H-C cash in grants. Your friend Fruhling is on the list."

She stepped back as if to survey his face for reaction. Not finding any, she made a brief statement. "You're not impressed. Don't you think that's an interesting connection?"

Jeffers did not, and said so. For the first time in recent days, he felt on firm ground. "I'm impressed with how you got it, but you don't understand academic research, Taylor. Money is hard to come by. Scientists, even top ones, will take it anywhere they can get it, and H-C is known as a big supporter of outside research. There's nothing strange at all about Fruhling working with me on one project and his having money from H-C for something else. It just doesn't prove a thing."

"I didn't say it was *proof.* I said it was *interesting.*" Inwardly, Taylor felt deflated. She had not considered that such arrangements might be normal business. In that respect, Jeffers was quite right. The funding of academic research was not a specialty of hers. "Oh, well. Let me give you the other names, and see if one strikes a more responsive chord." Jeffers motioned for her to continue. "Martin Bieber, François Chireault, Helmut Jurgens, Franz Kleindorf, and Peter Zehner," she recited.

Jeffers shook his head after she finished. "I don't think that helps. While they all work in the same general field I do, only Bieber has been interested in this sort of project, and he hasn't done anything recently."

"Okay, you win," Taylor said. "But let's not forget the names entirely."

For himself, Jeffers had already dismissed the list. Most companies gave grants, and half an academician's job was figuring out how to get them. But if the list did not occupy his mind, the way Taylor had obtained it did. It had not been a serendipitous burglary.

"You planned that whole scene in his office, didn't you?"

"Sure." Taylor's grin returned. "I made a number of calls yesterday, and not just to set up the meeting. There's no point in meeting someone unless you know enough about him to have something to take advantage of."

Jeffers found himself shaking his head again. "You know, I have to admit your maneuver worked, but doesn't it bother you the way people must look at you when you carry on like that?"

"Like what, George?"

"Well, hell, you had to know Hochmann was sitting there thinking you were a—"

"Bubblebrained idiot or possibly a call girl." Taylor finished the sentence for him. "Why should I care what he thinks? I know myself pretty well, George, and of the various parts of me, good, bad and indifferent, idiot and call girl are not among them. So what did I do, really? I made a big show of chewing gum, gave him a fair view of my cleavage, such as it is, and acted like a bored child. That act should have raised his suspicions in this context, but it didn't. Hochmann, like most Swiss men and many men period, does not take women seriously in any but subservient roles. He was all set up to believe I was a fool, and when I made it easy for him, he swallowed it. I just let him fall in the direction he was already leaning. The result was that he tossed me out and forgot all about me; just what I wanted. Not that there's anything new about the basic idea. If you are strong, you want to look weak, and vice versa. The biggest part of manipulating someone is knowing what buttons to push, not how you look when you do it. End of lecture."

"That's okay, you make sense. And speaking of manipulating people, I noticed that you did a fair job on me."

Taylor shrugged, but kept her little half grin. "It's not hard to see that you hate being told what to do outright. You do much better when circumstances force your hand and you have to respond. Actually, that was the biggest gamble I took. If you hadn't reacted well and handled it—if you had fucked up—we would have been in more than a little hot water."

There was a compliment in there, mild and partially hidden, but present. Jeffers seized on it and felt warmed by the praise. It was the first time since he left Cleveland that he had felt that. Then he saw the hook.

"Damn it, Taylor! You're doing it again!" Her answering smile was genuine, and all Jeffers found he could do was to laugh. "What I want to know is where your buttons are."

"It doesn't matter. They're taped in the 'off' position."

They walked on for a while, at a slow pace, toward the railroad station. From what Jeffers could see, Taylor seemed to have given up Hochmann and Helvetica-Chemie for window shopping. Periodically she would pull the disinterested Jeffers over to look at an item, or a price tag. Finally, their progress came to a complete stop outside a jeweler's shop.

"Taylor, no," he protested. "We have to be at the station soon. For all our clever moves, we've gotten nothing solid at all today, and I would hate to top it off by missing the train."

"That's not true, George. We have actually picked up a most important item."

"And what might that be?"

"Since our visit to H-C, we've got another tail."

"What!" Taylor might have shown more emotion mentioning a change in the weather, but the word seemed to explode inside of Jeffers. "Not again."

"Easy does it, George. People are watching, one in particular. Relax and admire the merchandise, and don't look around. He is a stocky guy in a dark blue suit. I don't think he knows he's been spotted. That gives us a margin, even if we can't be sure what he's been told. Hochmann may still think I'm here just to give your manlihood some exercise."

Jeffers colored at that and wished he had not. "Then Hochmann really is the SOB we want," he forced out. It was an immense effort not to spin around and find the man for himself.

"That is not necessarily true, George. Say Hochmann's innocent, but put yourself in his place. Two characters like us show up; I would have them followed. So would you." Jeffers shrugged. "The difference will be in the instructions Musclebrain has. That's what tells us whether H-C is involved or not."

"Makes sense, but I doubt he'll tell you. Even if you ask real nice."

"Oh, he'll tell us all right. Just by what he does. If H-C is innocent, Hochmann will want to know what we are doing, but that will be about it. If H-C is guilty, he will have orders to interfere with us."

"Is that a delicate way of saying he'll try to kill us?"

"Reasonable assumption." Chin in hand, Taylor looked far more absorbed in the watch display than the conversation.

"Christ on a stick!" he said. "It sure will be great to know who's responsible after he shoots me. That's just terrific."

"Hopefully we'll nail him before it gets that far. But it's like I told you, in this business—"

"You have to take some risks," Jeffers finished sourly.

"I wouldn't get depressed about it, George. Hey, I know what will pick you up. You could buy me something nice. Like, maybe that." Taylor indicated one of the watches with a long forefinger.

"You mean the one with the telephone number on the price tag? Don't push your luck too far, Taylor. Come on, we've got a train to catch."

Jeffers had plenty of time to think on the train between Berne and Amsterdam. There was not much else to do. Taylor seemed to prefer sleeping while she traveled and had nodded off within minutes of leaving the station. That left Jeffers with the options of staring at her, at the farmer in the next seat or at the countryside of eastern France.

Trains, to his way of thinking, were a slow and outmoded form of travel. Aside from metropolitan commuter lines, he could not remember the last time he had traveled in one. At least this one moved along at a good clip, keeping to its timetable. The interior was clean, the seat covers intact and there was a total absence of graffiti. In first class, where they sat, the seats were of comfortable width, although they were covered with a green and red tartan pattern that would have been more at home in Scotland. The existence of first- and second-class sections on a train amused Jeffers. The difference in ticket price had not been that great, and the sole difference he could see in accommodation was a greater seat width and a different cover pattern. Of course, now that Taylor was spending 'other people's money,' Jeffers expected it would be first class all the way.

Then why take the train? If money was no object and time was important, air travel would have been Jeffers's choice. He had not thought to ask her before she went to sleep and he was unwilling to wake her. The hypothesis his mind liked best was that she had picked up a weapon, or weapons, and was unwilling to try taking them on a plane. He had slept long enough the day before for her to have done so. Taylor's battered daypack was stashed at the base of the seat, under her legs, even though there was room in the luggage racks. Moving it at all was sure to jostle her. Of course, she had probably placed the pack that way to safeguard the cash she kept in it. Being unable to check the pack served to keep his mind on the idea. Another possibility, as inaccessible as the pack, was on her person. The billowy clothes she wore would hide almost anything.

Thoughts of weapons also focused Jeffers's attention on the man in the dark blue suit. He had boarded the train with them and now sat just three rows away. His presence made the idea of Taylor having a weapon both comforting, because he was there, and terrifying, because it implied a weapon might be needed. As Jeffers sat, somewhere in Alsace, trying to watch the man without being seen to do so, he found another reason for taking the train. It made it easy to follow them. Taylor had claimed their tail would tip Helvetica-Chemie's position by his actions. If true, it would never do to lose him, so she had turned the tailing game around. Games within games. How many games did Taylor play?

He had no response to his own question. There was no way to know. Even trying to answer it ran him into the contradictory feelings he had about her. She could be arrogant, exasperating, highhanded and manipulative, but always she fascinated him. Naturally, it did not hurt that she was gorgeous. Would he feel the same way, put up with the same antics, were she homely? He had to be honest with himself. Probably not. His mind ran along, repeating the same ideas, until it wore a mental track through his head.

Taylor was awake when they reached Amsterdam, Jeffers asleep beside her.

# CHAPTER 10

## AMSTERDAM, THE NETHERLANDS

THE TRAIN LEFT THEM at the Centraal Station in Amsterdam. The plaza outside was crowded with people of all sorts, from business men in suits to unshaven teenagers in tattered jeans. They had to work their way around clumps of squatters who had seated themselves, apparently at random, across the pavement. Some of these sat beside backpacks and were presumably just taking a short break. Others seemed to have nothing but the clothes they wore; their bare feet and arms did not appear to have been washed for some time. At least some of the smoke in the air did not come from cigarettes. From the plaza, a dense river of walkers poured across the bridge over the canal, paying no attention whatever to the color of the traffic signal on the other side. Jeffers was nearly run down before he reached the other curb, not by a car but by a bicyclist who, with his girlfriend seated side-saddle on the book clasp behind him, plowed straight into the crowd. There was a hotel on that corner and Taylor went straight to it.

The choice of hotel was not to Jeffers's liking. He would have preferred to go out to the airport where, he was confident, there would be a modern hotel with none of the crazies who seemed to populate the city center. Taylor would not hear of it. For her it was essential to be near the center of town, close to the conference and to more than one potential means of transportation. The airport hotel was too tied to the airport, too much of an operational cul-de-sac. Jeffers thought that another equally important criterion for choosing the hotel was luxury, although he avoided saying so. In any case, he would have preferred air conditioning to classic architecture. If he felt manipulated by Taylor's taste for posh lodging, Jeffers was at least able to amuse himself with an image of what Herb's face would look like if the bill were to come through on a company charge.

To arrive at such a hotel without reservations at the height of the tourist season and obtain a room, to say nothing of two, is usually impossible. What passed between Taylor and the manager in French, Jeffers could not say. His French, good enough to fulfill a college requirement fifteen years before, was not up to the task. He did note the bills that passed between Taylor and the manager during the course of the conversation. They were undoubtedly more significant in securing the rooms than anything she might have said. For an instant, as the bills changed hands, he wondered if the bribe could appear as "miscellaneous expenses" when he filled out his report. Then he caught himself. The odds of an accounting were minimal. In the end, they had two rooms.

"Let's try to examine this logically," Taylor Redding said. "Especially since a lot of things about this business don't make much sense." She was draped across an overstuffed armchair in Jeffers's room when she said it. She paused briefly to chew on her lower lip before continuing. Then, one fist held in the air, she went on to enumerate the facts of the case, extending a finger to account for each one. "One, Dr. Davenport was on his way to the conference here, and your enzyme was with him. Nobody admits to seeing him, or it, since. Two, somebody in Washington acted like you had pissed on the flag when they heard about it. Three, you get set to look for Davenport, so somebody kills your contact and tries to kill you. That's basically what we know. The question is still, who is behind this? And that means we need to know who wants this stuff." She interlaced her fingers into a bridge to rest her chin on.

Jeffers had seated himself crosslegged on one of the two queen-sized beds. The position showed disdain for the integrity of the crotch seam in his new trousers. The suit jacket and tie hung from a nearby lampshade.

He had lost most of his enthusiasm for rehashing his problem. "I've already said a number of times that I can't think of anyone who would take it. Science is supposed to be 'publish or perish,' but not like this. Besides, I've told you this project is a long way from any commercial stage." He paused for a moment. "In the long run, of course, I expect it to be valuable. That's why the company is concerned about the patent. But right now? Who would go to so much trouble, take such risks, when there's no guarantee it will pay off? I just don't understand."

"Neither do I. But then there has to be *something* about that enzyme that *you* don't know. A disappearance and a murder, on two separate continents, tends to support that view. That kind of reach implies that a government or an international company is involved. We've had two leads. One was Helvetica-Chemie, and we checked them first. They were a likely possibility considering that they were once interested in buying you, and they have been fiddling with IRT stock. So far, no yield, although Mr. Blue Suit has also bribed his way into this hotel. Which brings us to lead number two, your erstwhile collaborator, Fruhling. From what Oliver told you, he has the right kind of, shall we say, wrong connections, and he knew about your project. You say it can't be. Before we see him tomorrow, I want to know how sure you are and why." As usual, when Taylor deemed a topic important, her voice hardened under the impact of the thought driving it.

Jeffers started to reply, but something caught in the back of his throat. After the coughing and sputtering subsided he tried again. "That is just the way I told it to Thompson and Oliver. It can't be. Max Fruhling has been involved in this project from the beginning. I was sending him the enzyme. Why steal it? There could be no possible gain for him. As for the politics business, they're just dredging up old stories from decades ago. Fruhling is a *scientist,* he is not going to get involved in some cloak and dagger shit."

Jeffers turned red at the look Taylor gave him. It had not occurred to him when he said it that his last sentence applied to him.

Taylor ignored Jeffers's embarrassment. She was still trying to clarify the picture in her own mind. Two reasonable possibilities remained in play. She had answer A, Helvetica-Chemie; or B, Max Fruhling. There was also possibility C, Helvetica-Chemie and Fruhling together. None of them was really satisfactory, which was why she had wanted to talk through it. Nibbling at the problem by herself, she found only paradoxes. There was a tremendous contrast between the extravagantly botched assassination attempt in Boston and the slick, quiet way in which Davenport had vanished. High-powered rifle attacks in the middle of busy streets attract attention. Davenport was just . . . gone. It was almost as if the operations were run by different people. The money in Switzerland also bothered her. That money was a more logical target for a mere thief than an exotic scientific project, but then how to explain Davenport except by adding more participants? She sighed. Maybe the correct answer was D, none of the above.

While Taylor drifted off with her thoughts, Jeffers got off the bed and began pacing back and forth across the room. "Can we leave all your possible scenarios for a moment and just talk about tomorrow? I would like to know if I understand how this is supposed to go." Taylor motioned for him to continue. "All right, tomorrow we head over to the conference. We have to talk to Leblanc, he's in charge of the organizing committee, although that will be useless. The man has the intellectual curiosity of a camel. Then we talk to Fruhling. Meanwhile, we have H-C's man tagging along. Presumably Fruhling will react to us somehow." How sure was he of Fruhling? He had not had doubts until Taylor reopened the argument. Could he bet his life on Max Fruhling? The sensation of being a target returned in full force. Once, long ago, he had been to a dog track to watch greyhounds chase a mechanical rabbit. During one race the rabbit broke down. He was unable to shake the image.

"We don't really have much choice, George. If it were just a matter of hiding from our esteemed adversary, it would be easy. I doubt anyone would know we were here if we didn't want them to. But hiding isn't what we are here to do. We have to find Davenport and your sample in a relatively short period of time. That means making waves. As Heisenberg once said, any interaction you have with a system perturbs it."

At another time, Jeffers might have enjoyed the pun. His concern, however, prevented it. "Yes, and we already have one perturbed individual following us, and are going to perturb another one tomorrow. How many balls can we keep in the air?"

"Quite a few, as long as we can create misdirection and keep the initiative." Taylor's eyes developed a dreamy look Jeffers had not seen before. "People's reactions to us give us information. Remember Hochmann at H-C. 'Agitate him and determine the pattern of his movements. War is based on deception.'"

Jeffers looked at her sharply. The phrase sounded like rote recitation. "Is that what they taught you in college?" he asked, breaking into her reverie.

"I never went to college. No, a Chinese general wrote that twenty-four hundred years ago. An uncle of mine got me interested in him back when I was—well, a lot younger." The dreaminess disappeared, to be replaced by the old, intense Taylor. "It still works," she added, as she pulled herself erect in the chair.

Just what I need, Jeffers thought. A nutty sky-diving partner who likes to quote ancient Chinese generals. No matter how she phrased it, they were setting themselves up as moving targets. He could see he had no options, short of trying to go home, but the realization was not comforting. It made him feel very lonely.

"You know," he said to Taylor, "I'm starting to wish that you hadn't set up that false trail in Zurich. Without that we would probably have met some of Jim Thompson's people by now. I mean, don't you think we could use a little help?"

"Help." Taylor's mind echoed the word. Sure, she could use some help. From Jeffers. Aloud, she said, "Yeah, it would be nice to have help. Don't expect to see any of it from your friends, though. Forget for a moment that we just walked off with a pile of IRT's money. We might convince them that we were entitled to use it, or at least that we were using it as intended. But look at things from Thompson's position. Your enzyme is already missing and he didn't want you over here in the first place. He's not going to take a chance on losing you too. If we hook up with his people, they're going to ship you back home packaged in bubble-wrap. Think about it. You know I'm right."

Jeffers had to agree.

"So, what's it going to be, George?" Taylor asked, trying to make her voice as gentle as possible. "Do you want to do this or not?"

"I'm doing it," he replied.

He was going to do it, he told himself. The idea might not make him very happy, but he was going to finish what he had started. He just did not want to think about it anymore, at least not for a little while. He did not want to speak of enzymes or companies or anything connected to them.

"Can we change the subject, please? You have me ready to draw a bull's-eye on the back of my jacket. Just for a while, I'd like to talk about something, anything, else."

"Sure. Name your topic."

"Christ, I don't know. You and me, maybe."

"George, I'm here to do a job, one you hired me to do. The better we analyze it, the more chances we have, and speed is important."

"All right, I grant you that. It's the middle of the night, though. Tell me how much we lose by taking a little break."

"Nothing vital, I would expect. One evening's delay ought to be harmless." The concession came reluctantly. "Trying to chase Fruhling down at night would be foolish. We'll do better at the conference. H-C are probably the only people who know we're here, so we should be safe for the moment. If their man turns hostile, we have our answer anyway."

"Like I said. So why don't you tell me what interests you?"

Taylor sighed, the reluctance showing on her face. "George, when I'm on a job, I should attend to details. I'd rather not talk about myself."

"You could try."

With that impetus, the conversation drifted away from their immediate problems. To Taylor's surprise, Jeffers turned out to be a good listener. Talking to him was easy, and Taylor proved rather talkative once she got started.

Jeffers had always considered his reading tastes to be eclectic, but once they began to talk, the obvious scope of Taylor's took him by surprise. The two of them meandered through various items of history, then jumped to philosophy and literature. The extent of their common ground surprised him as well. Jeffers frequently spent hours discussing a scientific problem with a colleague, but he had rarely, in his constricted world, met someone who could talk at such length about anything else. After a while the conversation began to remind him of late-night bull sessions in college.

The conversation ultimately led, as such conversations between relative strangers usually do, to personal histories. The life of a scientist was easily compressed into a few phrases, so that Jeffers found himself talking less, and spending more time listening to Taylor's tales. In spite of having spent nearly every waking hour of the past three days together, Jeffers realized that he knew very little about Taylor Redding. How many people did he know who would glibly mix Heisenberg with an author of Chinese strategy? Not many. Of those, how many would concoct and execute a plan that required stealing an airplane and parachuting from it in the middle of the night? Nobody. Nutty and perhaps suicidal Taylor might be; dull she was not.

Her story as she told it was conventional enough until she finished high school. High school had been a prestigious prep school in central Connecticut, a datum that revived a piece of Jeffers's first impression of her. She repeated that she had never gone to college, had not even applied. College, she said, would have been boring, all talk and no action. Taylor had headed out on her own instead, much to the horror of her professional daddy and mommy and their equally professional friends. The break seemed a little too sharp and clean to Jeffers. When he asked about it, she mentioned her uncle, the same one as before, whose stories of his adventures had shown her the path she wanted to take. Taylor gave no specifics about him, though. Cyrus was seven years dead, but she still honored his injunction not to repeat what he had told her.

Once out in the world, she had covered much of it in a few short years. Her reminiscences were focused as much on what she had seen as on what she had done, and there was a great deal of both in her talk. Images she was able to call up—the midnight sun, dropping to touch the rim of the volcano across Reykjavik's bay, Mount Cook reflected in a lake—this was the stuff of dreams to Jeffers. By comparison his laboratory, the physical boundaries of his world, shrank in his mind as she spoke of what it was like to be a jack-of-all-trades in the world. There had been adventures, not just against nature but against men as well. There had been money in some of them, fair-sized sums. Not all of it, perhaps, was legal. This blurred a bit in the telling, more from caution, Jeffers was sure, than from any bashfulness.

As the time passed a new question began to form in Jeffers's mind. Where, if anywhere, was the evening going to lead? The concept of romance intermingled with adventure was known to him from books, if not from personal experience. The idea was, however, curiously absent from Taylor's stories. She mentioned friends and enemies, occasionally by name, but never an intimation of anyone close. It was a problem for Jeffers because he really wanted to know what was on Taylor's mind. He knew what was on *his* mind, but without knowledge of hers, he couldn't make an advance. As they talked, he mentally chastised himself for his usual inability to make an active move where a woman was concerned, but his mind refused to go beyond the thinking stage. Same old story, he could hear himself say. Even in college with Sue Donovan, it had been her idea to go barhopping the first night. He had been blind drunk by the time they finally went to bed. If Taylor Redding had an interest in him that approached his in her, was it possible that she would not say something? Even if she did not, might it make a difference if he spoke up? Every time he had almost worked up his nerve, he came back to the realization that she had worked to get two rooms, and they were not even on the same floor. That put a damper on him, or perhaps it was only a convenient excuse. In the end it was easier to enjoy the conversation rather than say something that would spoil the whole evening.

Eventually, and again as usual, events took matters out of his hands. Taylor caught a glimpse of her watch, and stopped in midsentence. It was closing on three in the morning. She rose quickly and apologized for losing track of the time. Their bodies would no doubt take revenge later in the day. With that she smiled, said good night and was gone.

Jeffers sat on the edge of the bed filled with all the thoughts he now wished he had voiced. History, as always, had repeated itself. "You know," he said to the empty chair, "if it hadn't been for women's lib, I'd die a virgin." He tried again to convince himself that it was for the best. She was at best a little nutty, and at worst dangerous to his health. Previously, he had believed it. Sitting there without her he discovered that even if it were true, he did not care.

The time, forgotten for a while, began to make itself felt. Naturally they had agreed on an early start the next day—more accurately, later that morning. He cursed quietly to himself as he turned out the light.

# CHAPTER 11

## AMSTERDAM, THE NETHERLANDS

THE ALARM CLOCK RANG at precisely 7:00 A.M., followed almost immediately by the telephone. The concierge was calling with his wakeup call. Jeffers could not remember leaving a message with the desk, but it was just as likely Taylor had arranged it. He sat up with a groan, wondering if it was going to become his morning habit. At least the bruises and scrapes were receding. Most of them were only a little sore, and the only hindrance to his motion came from his left knee. The scab there still cracked apart whenever he flexed the joint. After a quick shower, he pulled on the parts of his suit and headed out to find Taylor.

As he expected, she was in the restaurant. The hotel served a buffet-style breakfast and she was halfway through an enormous one. There were several empty plates in front of her, coffee, a half melon and two pastries. Jeffers made a quick circuit of the buffet table and joined her.

"You keep this up," he said, pulling out a chair, "and you'll get fat. Or at any rate I will."

A low chuckle accompanied the disappearance of the melon. "I imagine we'll work it off. I always do." She pushed herself back as Jeffers attacked his eggs. "Soon as you're done we ought to get started."

The number four trolley took them from the Centraal Station out to the Rai Centrum where the conference was being held. The Rai was a sprawling set of several buildings connected to the main exhibit hall, which looked a bit like an airplane hangar. Two-foot-high letters across the front of the hall spelled out WELCOME INTERNATIONAL BIOTECHNOLOGY. On a large paved plaza in front of the buildings a well-built young man wearing nothing but a silver jockstrap was roller-blading back and forth. The only thing that struck Jeffers as odder than the man's appearance was that none of the passersby paid him any attention.

Inside, four thousand people milled around among the exhibits and conference rooms throughout the huge building. Finding Fruhling seemed to be a needle-in-a-haystack problem, but they had a bit of luck just then. The conference schedule showed that Fruhling was due to speak in less than half an hour. One of the staff in the room set aside for speakers remembered him and directed Jeffers to where Fruhling was sitting in the cafeteria.

Seated alone at a table in apparent communion with his cup of coffee, Fruhling truly looked the part of the mad scientist. Now approaching his seventy-third year, his short wiry hair had little black left among the gray. It no longer covered his scalp evenly, having receded to a wide fringe between his ears and jutting irregularly into the air. The face it framed was lined and cleanshaven. With its sharp, protruding nose and high cheekbones, it gave him a cachectic look. The way his gray suit and vest hung suggested that the underlying body was thin, too. Overall, it was a clear picture of a man who had led a sheltered life within the confines of a university laboratory. One would have been very wrong to come to such a conclusion about Max Fruhling, however.

Jeffers knew a bit of the reality that made up the man, and had passed this on to Taylor while he picked at his breakfast. Jeffers had not acquired his information from any careful research on his collaborator but because Fruhling's notoriety was sufficient that anyone in the field knew it. He had begun life as the scion of a wealthy South German family, a family with numerous ties to industry and banking, but none to science. The young Max had not even been favorably disposed to science, or to academia in general. Even in his current position as a prominent scientist, he refused to repudiate his earlier feelings, instead referring to them in arguments against the early specialization encouraged by modern education. What had roused the feelings of the then-teenager was the rising tide of jingoism in the early Third Reich. It swept Fruhling first into the Hitler Youth and then, as war approached, into the Wehrmacht where his family connections secured a lieutenant's commission. When war did come in the West he had led his unit against the French and British competently and bravely, always at the head of his men, always in the action. That campaign had ended, for him, on the road to Dunkirk when his company was enfiladed by machine-gun fire. Fruhling had taken out the machine gun single-handed, an action that brought him multiple wounds, months of painful recuperation and the Iron Cross. In the end his wounds probably saved his life; he was posted to the occupation units in France and was not sent east the following year with his old unit. When the relative quiet in the West came to an end with the Normandy landings, Fruhling had fought again—and again heroically— during the German retreat. It was to that retreat, or more exactly to the actions of the American general Patton, that he would ascribe in later years his ultimate decision to become a scientist. Patton's summer offensive shattered Major Fruhling's patchwork battalion. The broken remnants fled, leaving Fruhling, again grievously wounded, for dead on the battlefield. That he lived to reach a prisoner-of-war camp in England was mostly luck. It was his recognition of his luck, plus the obvious fact that the war was lost, that drove him to look outside the military for a career. He resolved to learn English, the language of his captors (and the biggest winners of the war), as the first step, and he accomplished this rapidly, becoming fluent by the time the war ended the following spring. Repatriation had been of little immediate interest to him then. Germany was a wreck. Family connections again proved useful, making travel to the United States, and a college education there, possible. The subsequent spirit of the Cold War made Germans acceptable allies to Americans, and Fruhling stayed on for graduate education. At last Fruhling returned, degrees in hand, to West Germany in time to join the major redevelopment of its science and industry.

That much, of course, was no secret. In another setting, with another man, it would have slowly receded from view the way most people's histories do. In Fruhling's case, however, he was dogged by persistent rumors that he remained an unrepentant Nazi who expended considerable money and effort in the service of West Germany's far-right political groups. These rumors had led to his ostracism in the 1960s by the American scientific community. In spite of this, Fruhling never commented, neither on the rumors nor on their effects—with one exception. One day an American visiting the institution where Fruhling worked had voiced his disapproval of the medals he kept mounted on the wall behind the desk.

Fruhling's fist came down on the desk. "That is not a Nazi decoration," Fruhling growled. "It is a *German* decoration."

The chief consequence of the incident was his being referred to as "Iron-Cross Fruhling" whenever his name came up at American meetings.

Jeffers had paid no attention to any of this when he first arranged his collaboration. Max Fruhling was a superb biophysicist who had the ability and the equipment to complete the studies in which Jeffers was interested. That was all that counted. Fruhling had also been eager when they discussed the project by letter and phone—maybe too eager, Jeffers thought as he walked toward Fruhling's table. Was there perhaps an obvious industrial application he had not realized?

Fruhling looked up from his cup as they reached his table. He gave Jeffers a brief glance, Taylor a longer one.

"*Ja, was wollen Sie denn?*" he asked.

"Excuse me, Herr Doktor Fruhling," Jeffers replied in English. He did not need any knowledge of German to understand the question. "I am Dr. George Jeffers. We have corresponded about the enzyme project."

"Ah, Dr. Jeffers," Fruhling broke into a smile. "It is good to meet you at last. Please sit down. I do not believe I know the beautiful young lady."

Taylor smiled in response to the compliment, but Jeffers had seen her enough to recognize it as ersatz. Her eyes stayed cold and she remained silent. Jeffers cursed himself for not having a suitable introduction ready for her.

"Why, ah, this is my secretary, Becky. Ah, Becky Aldridge, that is." Sorry to steal your character, kid, he thought, but I needed a name fast.

"Pleased to meet you," Fruhling nodded his head.

"Dr. Fruhling," Jeffers began, "I really had hoped to meet under more auspicious circumstances, but the reason I'm here is because Henry Davenport isn't. That is, because he didn't show up." God, I'm botching it, Jeffers thought. It hadn't been this difficult with Hochmann, except this time *she* was sitting here. "What I mean is, we know that Hank got on the plane and no one has seen him since." Jeffers went on to describe his meeting with Hochmann, omitting any mention of the money box in Zurich and of Taylor's exploits at Helvetica-Chemie. Then he moved on to their present position in Amsterdam. "We spoke to Leblanc at the conference headquarters. He was, as you might expect, no help at all. So I thought we would come to you. It was not general knowledge that Hank was bringing the enzyme to you personally. I wonder if he had called you or tried to contact you after he landed."

Fruhling pursed his lips, exhaled tensely and leaned back from the table. "I too was surprised when Dr. Davenport did not appear for his lecture. Initially, I thought there had been a sudden change in his plans, perhaps illness, and that I would hear from you shortly about the enzyme. Obviously that was not the case. What little was in the papers, and now you, clearly imply the presence of foul play. So what you are really asking is whether the *altekämpfer* is also an *Alte kakker*?"

Taylor was caught off-guard by the question. She had not been anticipating a play on words and had to fight to avoid grinning. Jeffers missed the connection and felt lost. He could see no sign from Taylor to tell him what to say. Her face might as well have been granite. He could guess at what Fruhling meant, at the risk of offending him if he was wrong.

"Dr. Fruhling, I do not think that you had anything, anything at all, to do with his disappearance. I was just hoping Hank might have been in touch with you or maybe you know where he might have gone after he got off the plane." When he finished Jeffers held his breath. He could only hope he had projected a sufficient amount of earnestness and sincerity into his words. Offending Max Fruhling was widely reputed to be a bad move under any circumstances.

Much to Jeffers's surprise, Fruhling showed no sign of taking offense at all. "Had you no suspicion at all of me, Dr. Jeffers, I would think you a fool. You are not, so let us not waste time on polite noises." Fruhling hesitated, looking as though he wanted to have the "secretary" leave. Seeing that Jeffers did not notice the nonverbal cue, he simply continued. "I did not hear from or meet with Dr. Davenport after his arrival. In fact, the last word I had was your letter saying that he would bring the sample and your notes with him. I have no way of proving this. You have only my word." Jeffers was thinking that he had heard the same thing from Hochmann when Fruhling spoke again.

"There is something else, though, which you should find interesting." Fruhling paused for effect. "You know Dr. Martin Bieber, I believe."

"I know him by reputation, if you could call it that." Jeffers knew that Bieber had been working along similar lines in the past. In spite of Bieber's standing as one of the young luminaries in European science and the wealth of funding he was able to attract, Jeffers had never been impressed by Bieber's published work—he had in fact turned down an offer of collaboration with Bieber several years before.

"He was here at the beginning of the conference," Fruhling went on. "I found it rather strange that he offered me almost the same collaboration as you and I had agreed on."

"That's ridiculous! Bieber hasn't come anywhere close to getting a functional active site. In fact he hasn't published anything on the topic for almost two years. Most of what he has published is purely imitative." Jeffers was not sure which idea he found more difficult to believe, that this man could be on the verge of duplicating his achievement or that Fruhling was implying Martin Bieber could have been involved in Davenport's disappearance. For a moment his conviction wavered. Could he have been blinded by a bit of professional jealousy? Then reason reasserted itself. Not a chance. As for any involvement with Hank's disappearance, Jeffers was willing to call Bieber a poor scientist, but not a thief. Then he remembered that Bieber's name was on the list in Hochmann's office.

Caught up in that thought, he had to ask Fruhling to repeat himself. "I told you I found it strange. He did say he had an excellent new postdoctoral fellow now and his work was progressing rapidly. He was quite high on this chap, said he had worked on a similar project for an industrial company in the old DDR. Bieber implied that he is now collaborating with them. I also note that the day after Dr. Davenport failed to show up, Bieber had to return to Frankfurt." Fruhling appeared to be lost in contemplation of his hands after he finished speaking. He folded them on the table in front of him, carefully probing a liver spot with a forefinger.

There was no mistaking the unspoken accusation Fruhling had made. His very silence seemed to emphasize the point. The George Jeffers of a week before would have laughed the idea off as preposterous—as far as Jeffers was concerned, Bieber could barely repeat an experiment someone else had published; to believe that he had managed a heist in Europe and arranged a killing in Boston was a bit much. However, the George Jeffers of the present had absorbed enough unlikely experiences to give it some consideration. Of course, if he was going to consider Bieber capable of these deeds, what should he think of Fruhling?

Next to Jeffers, Taylor had sat quietly through the entire conversation. She spent most of her time watching Fruhling while attempting to mask that activity from him. What she saw was satisfactory. The man did not fidget, did not appear nervous at all. She felt he believed what he said; whether what he said was correct or not was a separate issue. Either way she could see an opportunity to take the initiative. She too remembered Bieber's name.

"That is most interesting, Dr. Fruhling, as our schedule calls for us to visit Dr. Bieber in Frankfurt tomorrow," Taylor said. She had originally planned to say nothing—again the dumb secretary—but the chance was too good to pass up. It was worth stepping out of her role to take it. "Does Dr. Bieber know whether you and Dr. Jeffers have met before today?"

The question, and its source, puzzled Fruhling. His reply was somewhat delayed. "As I remember, we were both at a Society meeting in London a few years ago but I can't recall whether we actually met. I am sure you noticed that I did not recognize Dr. Jeffers until he introduced himself at the table. We have communicated only by letter or phone. Bieber would not know, one way or the other."

"Good." The idea would work. "We will see Dr. Bieber around midday. I wonder if you would be willing to call him tomorrow afternoon and tell him that we had this meeting today. When you do it, please also tell him you think someone is using Dr. Jeffers's name as a cover, that you don't think the real Dr. Jeffers was here today."

Jeffers had the sensation that he had been subtly but firmly relegated to the sideline. The action had shifted to the other side of the table. His annoyance dissipated quickly as he thought about Taylor's request. Whatever Fruhling did would give them information; he had no choice in the matter, since ignoring it was a response in itself. Whatever he said to Bieber would cause a reaction. More games.

There was a long silence at the table. Fruhling looked hard at the young woman, a gaze that was returned in both its steadiness and intensity. Two pairs of gray eyes, each probing the other, neither blinking. There was a tension that lasted until Fruhling spoke.

"It is nice, is it not, Dr. Jeffers, to have a secretary with an independent mind." Fruhling continued to keep his eyes on Taylor as he spoke. "It seems a most reasonable request. I will be glad to do so. Now, if you will excuse me, I have a slide talk to deliver."

He pushed back his chair and got up, a faint smile on his face as he turned to leave. His gait as he left the room was brisk, more a march than a walk, his back ramrod straight.

"I didn't know 'our schedule' called for a trip to Frankfurt," Jeffers said after they were alone. There was more humor in his voice than anything else.

"Well, just now it begins to seem like a real good idea. Don't you think?"

"I think, I think."

# CHAPTER 12

## AMSTERDAM, THE NETHERLANDS

AFTER THEY LEFT FRUHLING the remainder of the day disappeared almost without Jeffers being aware of it. There was the necessary, perfunctory visit to the police, who merely pointed out that IRT had already been notified of whatever information they had, that further information would be relayed as it became available and that Jeffers was wasting their time. The nonverbal implication was that Jeffers was being a nuisance.

"If there was any waste of time, it was visiting them," Jeffers complained after they were politely shown the door.

"Of course," Taylor answered. "It's about what I expected. It's probably just as well they're not interested. I hate spending any more time with cops than I have to."

"If that's the case, why did we bother?"

"Because if you were really just being Dr. Jeffers making inquiries for your company you would go to the police. It's a good idea to stay in character whenever possible."

It also seemed that no time had really been wasted because, having disposed of that chore, Taylor now put business on hold. She took Jeffers on a walking tour of Amsterdam, a welcome respite, for the good doctor, whose conversation with Fruhling had left him more unsettled than at any time since Thompson had called him dumb. If Taylor wanted to play tour guide, he was going to relax and enjoy it. She pointed out cathedrals, monuments, bridges and formal gardens as they walked, attaching bits of stories to each. She did it without a guidebook, indeed without a map, relying instead on her own apparently encyclopedic store of information.

Jeffers found it fascinating, his enjoyment tempered only by the occasional glimpse of the H-C man tagging along behind. It was those glimpses, multiplied as the afternoon drew to a close, that began to make Jeffers edgy. For all her talk of rapid, unexpected moves, Taylor had chosen to throw away a good part of the day. With such problems on his mind, sightseeing ceased to be therapeutic. Was Taylor intentionally giving the H-C man a

122

chance to strike, and would he do so in public? Jeffers would not have been Jeffers if he did not also wonder whether Taylor was doing more than just enjoying a quiet afternoon together, but he managed to push the idea aside. Taylor always had hidden plans behind the ones she actually discussed. In spite of Jeffers's concern and possibly in spite of Taylor's intent, the man did nothing but follow. They finally turned back to the hotel after Jeffers saw Taylor's limp becoming more noticeable. Getting Taylor to give in was impossible, he thought, deciding that if she were left to herself she would walk until the leg fell off rather than admit it bothered her. Instead Jeffers pleaded his own fatigue.

The next morning they boarded the train to Frankfurt. The H-C man turned up in the same car, prompting Jeffers to wonder how the man could track them so consistently. He had to sleep, too, did he not? How did he know when to wake up?

"That's simple enough," Taylor said. "He's bribed several of the hotel staff to warn him when we're going out. I know because I'm outbidding him. Besides, I'm being very careful not to lose him."

The hint of a smile on Taylor's face as she stressed the last sentence irritated Jeffers. She had said much the same in Switzerland. Spies were supposed to *lose* the people following them.

"Well, why not lose him? He's tipped nothing so far, we have other leads to follow and I'm tired of waiting to find out if I'm his bull's-eye."

"Easy, George. You know better." The gray eyes seemed to light up from the inside. "We're not quite ready to disappear from Amsterdam. If we ditch him H-C will just send somebody else, and maybe we won't spot him. I would rather deal with this one, at least until we know a little more than we do now. Meanwhile why don't you fill me in on this Bieber character?"

As with Fruhling, Jeffers knew Bieber by reputation and through third-party reports. As he laid it out for Taylor he became painfully aware of how skimpy his knowledge really was. Why had Taylor not done the same kind of homework she had done on Hochmann?

"Different situation, George. I don't usually deal with scientists, and neither do my contacts. Your information and opinion will be much more reliable. You're doing a good job, so keep talking."

The Martin Bieber that Jeffers sketched for Taylor was indeed the fair-haired boy of European science. A more complete antithesis of Max Fruhling would have been hard to find. Fruhling could claim credit for an impressive body of work produced over many years, yet he labored in relative obscurity, his name well known only to those who read his papers. Bieber in contrast occupied a prestigious post at the Frankfurt Institute in spite of being only a few years older than Jeffers and in spite of authoring a very limited amount of independent work. Jeffers attributed this strange disparity to politics, both present and past. While Fruhling's past made him anathema to American scientists, and rumors about his current connections were viewed unfavorably in Germany, Martin Bieber was in good odor in political circles. He was an editor for several European journals, the recipient of grants from the American government for his laboratory and an occasional science advisor to the German government. When Bieber came to the United States he was invited to lunch with congressmen and sought by the media for interviews, on topics not always related to science. Jeffers concluded sourly that this state of affairs existed because Martin Bieber was a more natural politician than he was a scientist; his career had long since lost any linkage to his laboratory. Rather, Bieber had developed a knack for coordinating the work of several other researchers, a position that allowed him to appear as a coauthor when the work was published without ever, as best Jeffers knew, having done any of the work. There was also a good supply of graduate students and scientists who had recently received their degrees who were unable to obtain funding or laboratory space on their own. Such people depended on established investigators for this and for guidance in their work. In return for the money, lab space and supervision, the established scientist appeared as the senior author on papers that resulted. The system was open to abuse where guidance and supervision were concerned. Conceivably a scientist could have his name appear on many papers to which he had contributed nothing but money. Privately Jeffers was convinced that Bieber operated in this fashion.

Jeffers had known for years that Bieber was interested in the artificial enzyme project, but from what he knew of how Bieber worked he doubted that Bieber could succeed in such a highly complex project, in which consistent oversight and long-range planning were essential. The prospect of it having happened was aggravating. No doubt it had also aggravated Fruhling. Jeffers pointed out the possibility that Fruhling would enjoy seeing Bieber smeared by Jeffers making an accusation against him. The idea made an unpleasant sort of sense.

# FRANKFURT, GERMANY

IF BIEBER WAS SURPRISED or taken aback by their arrival he disguised it well. He responded personally to the call from the guard at the front entrance announcing their presence by coming to meet them, and then escorting them to his office. He proved to be a big man—Jeffers estimated his height at six feet three—with a frame to match. His face was broad and very fair-skinned under a shock of blond hair. Pale blue eyes looked out at them from behind horn-rimmed glasses. Over his shirt and tie Bieber wore the long white lab coat that was almost a uniform for a scientist. The coat, Jeffers saw, was spotless; in fact, it looked as though it had been dry cleaned and pressed. Nothing, other than greetings, was exchanged until they reached the office and sat down.

Bieber's office picked up where the lab coat left off, an impression that bothered Jeffers. The office was *clean,* not merely in the absence of junk, but in the neat arrangement of its components. Bieber's large, glass-topped desk was almost bare, no loose papers in sight. The desk was dominated by a framed picture of a young woman. For lack of anything else on the desk to look at, Jeffers's attention fixed on the photograph. She was apparently in her twenties, her short dark hair cut in the punk style. Jeffers wondered, though not out loud, at the heavily made-up face and the purple top she wore, with its oversized, padded shoulders. Not the sort of girlfriend— wife?—he envisioned Bieber having. The very dominance of the picture reinforced the emptiness of the rest of the desk. An active scientist's desk, Jeffers felt, should not be so clear. Of course, the problem might have been entirely in his own mind. His own desk more closely resembled an archeological dig, with varying strata being exposed from time to time. Sir James, one afternoon, had bluntly called it an Indian midden. Maybe Bieber just had a thing about being neat. Damn! thought Jeffers, even the books were alphabetically shelved.

"Well, Dr. Jeffers," Bieber began, "it is a pleasure, though unexpected, to meet you. I have read all of your papers. What can I do for you?"

Bieber seemed perfectly relaxed, partially reclining in the chair behind his desk. Could the bastard really have made an enzyme?

"It's simple, actually. I met Max Fruhling in Amsterdam recently. He told me you had made a great deal of progress on the enzyme project and that I would find it interesting to speak with you. So, here I am." Jeffers was pleased with his opening. It shaded the truth a little, but not too much.

"Old Max Fruhling, eh? Yes, I saw him at the conference, too. I did discuss what we were doing here with him. He was very keen to collaborate with us."

"He asked to collaborate with you?" Jeffers asked. Not what Fruhling had said. He could not tell by looking at her, but he knew the contradiction would not have escaped Taylor either.

"Yes he did. I turned him down, of course. Not that there is anything wrong with his work, it is excellent you know, but it would be a difficult association to explain to too many people."

"I quite understand what you mean," Jeffers said, while wondering again if it had been Fruhling's sour grapes that had sent them to Frankfurt. "Now, he did not give me any details, but from what he said your work must be going very well."

"It is, it is," Bieber beamed. "We have now a functional enzyme, designed from the ground up. It was that news that brought me back from the conference." He leaned back to look at Jeffers with a smile of pure triumph.

Jeffers knew he could not completely keep his emotions from his face and would have been unable to keep them out of his voice had he replied immediately. Not bad enough that he should have been at the same stage, or would have been had his material not disappeared, but to be scooped by the scientific equivalent of George Villiers was too much to take. At last, he said simply, "That is quite an achievement."

"Thank you," said Bieber. He paused. "To be honest, a great deal of the credit should go to Gerhardt Müller. He's not your usual postdoctoral fellow. He's actually an experienced scientist with Sachsen Fabrik. That's a company in what used to be the DDR. They have been interested in this field as long as you and I but, until the reunification, they never had access to the technology to pull it off. Since then, they acquired the computer facilities to handle the modeling, an area where I have never had quite the right person, while I have the facilities and the expertise to handle the rest of the project. It has been a useful collaboration for both of us. Until Gerhardt's arrival my laboratory had been in the doldrums for a while. He has really gotten the project moving."

"You know, I was wondering," Jeffers said, with what he hoped was a casual manner, "what it's like getting funding in Germany for this sort of research."

"Similar, I should think to the United States," Bieber replied, "and getting harder every year. The reconstruction of the East is absorbing so much money that research funding is at some risk. It has been enough of a problem that the government has appointed a commission, of which I am a member, to study it. It has become particularly hard for our younger colleagues, a point I made to the minister of finance when we had lunch a few weeks ago."

"It sounds like, with your contacts, you shouldn't have any trouble. In fact, I heard you had a nice deal going with Helvetica-Chemie a while back."

Jeffers had no idea where the comment would lead when he said it. The startled look Bieber gave him was gratifying.

"I am sorry, Herr Doktor Bieber, I thought it was common knowledge. After all, I had heard about it, so . . ." He let the sentence trail off, and waited for Bieber. This, he thought, could get to be fun.

"Please, there is no problem. It was hardly a secret, we just never publicized it—at least I was not concerned about that. No, wait, I see I should explain." Bieber had recovered his composure, but now he had dug himself a hole. "You see, I made this deal with Hans Teuschlein of Helvetica-Chemie about three years ago. You wouldn't know him, but he is the head of their research and development group. Hans had been interested in the artificial enzyme idea for some time but he never had any success convincing the top management to make a commitment. We arranged that he would provide me with what was officially general purpose funding for the laboratory, and I would use the money to pursue the project. We never publicized the grant because it could look to his people as though he were circumventing their decisions, which of course he was. So, you see, the concern is his, not mine."

"I imagine Dr. Teuschlein must be quite happy also." Jeffers had to struggle to keep his voice dry.

"Well, perhaps not." Bieber's face flushed red. "We terminated our agreement when it did not appear to be leading anywhere. As I mentioned, Dr. Müller is with Sachsen Fabrik. By my agreement with them, they have the patent rights, or they will. We are working on the applications now. It's actually a bit of a struggle to get everything done just right and all at once and I think Gerhardt is feeling rather pressured. You know how hard it can get when a project gets hot this way."

"Yes I do. It really is a most impressive accomplishment for one man," Jeffers said, while thinking that "impossible" was closer to the mark. "I would like to meet him."

"I'm afraid Gerhardt did not come in today. There was a rather late celebration last night." Taylor laughed.

"I see," Jeffers said, staring at Taylor. "Well, I would be interested in seeing what results you have with it so far."

"You will have to forgive me, Dr. Jeffers, but we have not filed the applications yet, and you and we are rivals in a sense, and you work for a company, not for yourself." Bieber was staring at Taylor himself. "In any case, we are just beginning to analyze the tertiary structure and the reaction kinetics. Gerhardt has some preliminary NMR data . . . I will tell you about the reaction we have catalyzed. It is the same as the one you were aiming at!"

"What?" Jeffers had trouble getting it out. His throat could not have felt tighter if there had been a noose around it.

"It might as well have been public, what your target was, between your earlier papers and some of your colleagues who like to chatter. I decided that I was not only going to beat you to a designed enzyme, I was going to beat you to your own target."

"Why in God's name would you do that?" The only reason Jeffers's voice stayed as calm as it did was that he was having trouble breathing.

"I am well aware," Bieber said slowly, "of the conceit with which you view your own achievements and the disdain with which you view mine. I decided to beat you, what is your American phrase, in your face."

Jeffers sat in his chair without a word, incapable of bringing any of the thoughts that bubbled in his mind out to his mouth. When Jeffers remained silent, Bieber continued: "Perhaps I should not have said that. Chalk it up to frustrations that have accumulated for a few years and accept my apology." Bieber smiled. "Tell me, though, how did you come to be in Amsterdam? I was not aware you were planning to attend the meeting."

Jeffers doubted that Bieber really meant to apologize, in the same way he was certain that Bieber's desire to rattle him had been sincere. He also needed no special training to see that Bieber would not further discuss the enzyme. Calm down, George, he told himself. You came here to get information, not to throw a tantrum. Still, he was surprised at how level his voice came out. "I came to Amsterdam because Henry Davenport did not," he responded.

"I see," Bieber's smile did not reappear. "I heard that he missed his talk."

"He missed more than his talk. He is just plain missing."

"Ah. That is unfortunate, Dr. Jeffers. It no longer seems very safe for Americans to travel abroad. Have you been contacted by any group?"

"Not as yet."

"You know, maybe you should have asked Max about this when you saw him. He does, ah, have some unusual connections."

The air in the office crackled with tension, when Taylor broke the silence. "Dr. Bieber, could I ask you something?" She had put on her sweet, little girl voice.

"Yes, *Fraulein.*"

"This enzyme I heard you and Dr. Jeffers talking about, is it very complicated?"

"Well, in a sense it is." That brought the smile back to Bieber's face. He went ahead to give Taylor a broad, simplistic outline of the problem.

"I see," Taylor said when he finished. Her eyes were so wide they seemed to take up half her face. "It must be a very intricate thing to make. Could you show it to me, please? I promise I won't touch."

The look on Bieber's face changed to stupefaction. He turned to look questioningly at Jeffers, but got no help there. Jeffers was having trouble stifling a full-blown laugh.

"*Fraulein,* I am afraid that at the level at which one sees, it does not look very interesting. Just a white powder, really."

"I would like to see it though, really. I promise I won't be disappointed."

With a grin, Bieber capitulated. As Jeffers followed the other two through the connecting door between the office and Bieber's personal laboratory, he decided that Taylor had the dumb blonde role down to a science. Not only that, but she enjoyed it.

With Taylor in tow, Bieber crossed to a conventional refrigerator. From the freezer compartment he pulled a small vial. At the bottom of the vial, as he had said there would be, was a small amount of white powder. Coming closer, Jeffers could see that the lettering on the label was in German. Otherwise, it could just as easily have been his material. Taylor stuck her face right next to it, peering intently at the dust inside.

"Ooh! It's so exciting to think of how much work went into making that small amount of stuff. You must be very proud. And your associate, too."

Taylor continued to ladle out compliments as Bieber replaced the vial. Soon she had him purring like a cat having its belly stroked. When they parted, a few minutes later, it was most cordial.

"Taylor," Jeffers said when they were back on the street, "has anyone ever told you how nauseating you can be?"

"Many times. You should hear my daddy on that topic. But we can save that for later. More importantly, what do you think?"

"Of Bieber? Damned if I know. All I'm sure of is he has maybe thirty milligrams of what he says is an artificial enzyme, similar to what Hank was carrying. Do I believe that one person, experienced scientist or not, has magically transformed his lab? No way. Christ, the place looks like a model home. I can't see anyone working there. But if you ask me, do I think he has *my* enzyme . . . I can't believe it's my enzyme."

"But you don't think he's done it on his own?"

"No."

"Hmm. George, don't take this the wrong way, but are you being a bit conceited about your ability?"

Jeffers nearly went red again. "You mean like what he said?" Jeffers started to make a nasty retort but swallowed it instead. "Yeah, maybe I am and probably I've said some things I shouldn't have. But that's not the issue and that is not affecting what I think about this."

"Then what's he doing all the talking about and what's in the fridge?"

"I don't know." He paused for a second. "I think he's just blowing smoke. You notice he wouldn't show me anything, not one thing, to prove what it is. He wouldn't do it in spite of the fact that he wants to rub my nose in it and in spite of the fact that he has to know I don't believe him."

"Yeah, but wouldn't he do the same if it was yours?"

"Listen, Taylor, one man missing, another one dead. I can't see Bieber running an operation like that. It would risk his precious political career, even if he was up to it."

"Of course," Taylor added, "he may not be responsible at all. I noticed that nice hook he made into H-C, and, as I recall, Teuschlein was the man you spoke to."

"Wait a minute." Jeffers snapped his fingers. "That company you said Hochmann is thinking of buying—Sachsen Fabrik, wasn't it?"

"Yes, now that you mention it. I wonder if this is just an elaborate setup and H-C is just planning to launder your enzyme through Bieber and this other company the same way you launder money through a foreign bank. Which brings up obvious questions about Fruhling, too. I think we ought to chat with him again. Ah, our man from H-C seems to have finally noticed we are leaving. Good thing, too, we have to catch that train. I wonder if old Max is going to make that call."

## AMSTERDAM, THE NETHERLANDS

THE RETURN TRAIN FROM Frankfurt deposited them at the railroad station late at night. Except for the change in lighting, the station looked much the same as it had in the morning. The weather had changed, however. Heavy gray clouds began to gather in the afternoon and by the time they returned the clouds had formed an impenetrable layer of darkness. A moist wind greeted them at the exit from the station. The first raindrops, large scattered ones, began to fall as they crossed the street, prompting a sprint to the hotel. Jeffers covered the distance swiftly and arrived dry. Taylor, lagging behind, sported several damp splotches by the time she gained the doorway. Shortly afterward, the main event began. The booming thunderclap brought with it a falling wall of water that obscured the station across the street.

They reconvened in Jeffers's room, neither having said much since leaving the train. It was always his room, Jeffers noticed, never hers in which they would talk. He had in fact never seen her room, or even where it was in any of the hotels in which they had stayed. Taylor always left from his room at night and was always up before him in the morning. Idly he wondered if Taylor slept at all, or whether she spent the late night hours looking for more trouble to get into. He was ready to dismiss the idea as frivolous, when it developed into a more disturbing thought. Was there more to Taylor Redding—not that she was simple in the first place—than he was aware of? Could she be playing him false and be this cool about it? He busied himself attacking an imaginary spot on his jacket with a damp cloth while keeping an eye on her. The object of this scrutiny sprawled as usual in the armchair, intent on buffing an apple to a mirror shine. The more he tried to fight the suspicion down, the stronger it came back. Attempts to dismiss it for lack of evidence foundered on her secretiveness. Previous comments of hers came back in a different light. "War is deception," she had said. But who was being deceived? Would it suit her sense of humor to tell him about it while she did it? The more it circled through his mind, the more he tried to deny it. He would not believe it. And the basic reason was as simple as it was alarming: he had come to like Taylor Redding.

Suddenly there was a rap on the door. The exchange of glances indicated that neither had expected a visitor. Signaling Jeffers to wait, Taylor glided soundlessly to the hinged side of the door. When he opened it, she would be hidden behind the panel. With Taylor in position, Jeffers moved to the door. The ten feet of carpeted floor stretched out forever. There was a pounding in his chest that echoed in his ears. The image of the dead agent's half-head floated in the air before him. Cleverly, so cleverly they had worked to provoke a reaction. So carefully, they had given the H-C man a chance to strike, a chance to reveal his intentions. Too bad it was going to be a bullet through the doorway. In his anxiety he forgot about the peephole. On reaching the door, he yanked it full open. Professor Fruhling was on the other side.

He did not look wet; he looked saturated. Droplets ran in a stream from the tip of his folded umbrella to the hall carpet, where a sizable puddle had already formed. The umbrella must have been useless against the storm because his raincoat was uniformly soaked. The old-fashioned felt hat he wore had fared no better.

"*Guten abend,* Dr. Jeffers. For a moment I wondered if you would wait until I had dripped dry."

Jeffers gaped. He had imagined a wide variety of possible bogeymen during his trip to the door, but Max Fruhling had not been one of them. "I'm sorry. I wasn't expecting . . . any friends tonight."

"No doubt," said Fruhling with a wry smile. "Now, may I come in just a bit farther?"

Jeffers realized he was standing with one hand on the door and one on the frame, totally blocking the entrance. "Sorry again. Please." He backed away and invited Fruhling in.

Fruhling took note but showed no surprise as Taylor materialized behind him. What she might have planned for other circumstances, Jeffers did not know. For Fruhling, she took his coat and hat to the bathroom. Fruhling said nothing until she had returned.

"I imagine you are interested in the reason for my being here." Jeffers thought that was a mild understatement, and nodded for him to continue. Taylor, once again ensconced in her armchair, made no comment. "I made the phone call as you requested. Bieber was polite and brief, no more. But then I received a phone call this evening from a party claiming an interest in what they called industrial espionage. They were most anxious to meet with the American investigator and wondered if I would help arrange it."

Fruhling might have been discussing the weather for all the emotion his voice showed. Actually, he probably would have shown more emotion over the weather. His suit jacket was wet in several places, too.

Jeffers spent a moment on the implications of this. Wheels were finally in motion. "It was not Bieber who called you?" Fruhling had implied as much, but Jeffers wanted to be sure.

"It was not Bieber."

The only sound was Taylor crunching into her apple.

"So, what do you suggest we do?"

"My dear Dr. Jeffers, I brought information that I thought would be of interest, not advice."

"All right, what's the rest of the proposal?"

"If you are interested, leave the hotel at nine o'clock tomorrow morning, turning right from the main entrance. A man smoking a cigarette will be leaning against the first 'no parking' sign. There will be a blue BMW parked next to it." Christ, Jeffers thought, here go the idiot code words again. At least, there will not be a purple Monte Carlo. "Ask him if he has American cigarettes. He will take it from there, I am sure."

"It sounds," said Taylor, slightly muffled by the apple, "like it could be a trap."

"Most assuredly," agreed Fruhling.

"That's just great." Jeffers threw his hands up. "So what do we do? Call the cops, right? That would be a laugh. At most he'll get a parking ticket." Then he reined himself in. Both Taylor and Fruhling were looking at him as though they were expecting him to say one thing in particular. What were they waiting for? It occurred to him that Taylor had been talking all along about creating a reaction that would make their adversary surface. Now they had it, and it certainly did look like a trap. But whose? Taylor's eyes were still on him.

"Wait a minute." He said it loud enough to startle himself. "I think we ought to do it. Maybe it is a trap, but maybe also there's a deal here. Maybe our friends from H-C are finally ready to do something." Or, possibly, the friend in the room.

He saw Fruhling look up when he mentioned Helvetica-Chemie. "Yes, Dr. Fruhling. When I mentioned we had been to H-C, I omitted the fact they've been following us ever since."

"How interesting," Fruhling said. He was silent a moment, watching Taylor work on the apple. "You probably don't know it, but Bieber has always had considerable support from H-C for his lab."

"Also interesting." Taylor finished the apple and sent the core arching across the room, to land with a boom in the wastebasket. Then she got up to pace.

"Who would be interested in meeting the alleged Dr. Jeffers," she said. "H-C perhaps, someone working with Bieber perhaps. Anybody else you can think of?" She looked directly at Fruhling as she said it.

"Why, anybody connected with Dr. Davenport or the enzyme," he replied. "If you know who it is, there is hardly any point to this."

"Which we do not," Jeffers put in. He could easily add a couple more possibilities to the list. There were the always hinted at, unnamed cronies of Max Fruhling. Then the name Taylor Redding again arose. There was enough money at stake to tempt anyone, a point she had been fond of making. Had it tempted her? He refused to rule it out. Suddenly it occurred to him that Fruhling was talking to him.

"I should point out," he said, "that there are a number of groups operating who will trade information on anyone to anyone. Some are terrorists, some are purely mercenary. Your activities may have stimulated their interest as well. If it is these people who have information to offer, what do you plan to give them in exchange?"

"I'll buy it," Jeffers snapped, getting off the bed. Fruhling sounded as though he knew exactly what he was talking about.

"Buy it." Fruhling hummed a little. "People who sell such information generally have high asking prices, and they do not like IOUs. That will be true whether they are merely selling information, or willing to betray a present employer."

"I said I'll buy it. I have . . . Aghh!" The sentence ended in a yelp. Taylor had been standing next to him, and as he started to speak her right foot came slanting down across his shin to stomp onto the top of his arch. Jeffers sat down on the bed, holding his injured foot.

"Dr. Jeffers sometimes becomes excitable," she explained. "When that happens he is prone to develop foot in mouth disease if I don't prevent it. He was about to say that we have an adequate down payment and can easily secure whatever additional funds are required."

Fruhling grinned broadly at her. *"Touché, Fraulein.* I should not have inquired. I do wish to assure you that whoever will be there, they will not be associates of mine. In fact, if Dr. Jeffers is willing to go through with this, I am willing to help."

For a brief span of time there was no noise at all. Jeffers, on the bed, again found himself the object of not only Fruhling's gaze, but Taylor's as well. Dammit, why had he shot his mouth off? That was how he had been catapulted into this adventure in the first place. But if he backed out now he was going to have to do it in front of Taylor Redding. Instead, he mutely nodded his assent.

Taylor, however, was not going to make it easy for him. "I agree this is an excellent opportunity. I just hope you realize, George, that this could be very dangerous. If it goes sour or turns out to be a trap, you could wind up dead."

"Yeah," Jeffers shot back, "but if it was you who was going to be the target, you'd jump at it." Once the words were out of his mouth he wondered how he had come to say them. Of course, it had been the first time she had ever raised his safety as an issue. Too bad she had said it in front of Fruhling.

"Now that that has been settled," Fruhling interrupted, "may I ask if you will accept my word that I am not involved, and if so, are you interested in my assistance, limited though it must be?"

Without hesitation Taylor said, "Yes to both."

It now remained only to sort out their roles for the upcoming day. Jeffers's was already set. He was the person who would actually go to the rendezvous carrying a down payment. If a deal was possible, he would try to arrange one. Fruhling announced that he would remain, personally, apart from the proceeding. It was far from certain he would be unknown to those they would-meet, and he refused to risk an association. He said he had a young graduate student named Wolfgang who would go in his place. He was Taylor's age and, though imbued with more romanticism than experience, was eager to help. Wolfgang would be the driver and spare hands, at Taylor's discretion. He would pick up Taylor outside the hotel, and together they would tail the BMW. This was the major risk—they might lose their quarry, or their presence might be detected. In either case Jeffers would be left without any outside source of intervention if there were problems. If they were able to follow successfully, it would be up to Taylor to assess the situation and decide what action to take. Should there be trouble they would try to get Jeffers out. Failing that, they would contact Fruhling, who would turn to other sources of "help."

At the end of the discussion Fruhling pulled a small flask from his jacket pocket. "I thought we would be having a talk of this type tonight. I wanted it to have a suitable ending." He split the amber contents among three hotel tumblers. "To Dr. Jeffers and his success." They all took a drink. Fruhling held his glass up again, and turned to face Taylor. "Also to a very pretty young lady, who is more than just a pretty young lady."

"Both more and less," said Taylor under her breath. The others, in the midst of drinking, did not hear her.

Fruhling retrieved his sodden garments and headed back into the stormy night. Jeffers watched him go with mixed feelings.

"Do you really think we can trust him, Taylor?" he asked.

"Of course not." Her face had the set-in-stone appearance he had seen before. "You don't have to trust someone to work with them, or to use them. You just have to be aware of what you're doing."

"I don't know, Taylor." Jeffers upended the tumbler to get the last drop in it. "Do you trust anyone?"

"Sure. Me." She strode to the door but stopped before opening it. "George, there are some arrangements I'd better take care of before tomorrow. I suggest you get some sleep." Then she planted the felt hat on her head and closed the door behind her.

Arrangements, Jeffers thought. Arrangements. What in God's name needed arranging in the middle of a monsoon, and for whom was she arranging it? Once again he questioned his trust of her. The worst of it was that it would hurt very badly if it turned out he had misplaced his trust. Going to sleep turned out to be a fruitless endeavor. He was just as awake by morning as he had been when he retired. The only difference was that he was awfully tired.

# CHAPTER 13

## AMSTERDAM, THE NETHERLANDS

GEORGE JEFFERS HEADED TO the hotel restaurant the next morning trying hard to disguise his nervousness. He doubted that he was being successful. The active role he had taken in formulating a plan, and the key role he played in it, gave some lift to his spirits, but those spirits were overwhelmed by his assessment of his prospects for emerging in one piece. He also was not entirely sure how active he had been, as opposed to being once again neatly maneuvered by Taylor.

By the time he reached Taylor in the dining room, his stomach was in turmoil. As before, he found that tension robbed him of his appetite. A few bites of egg, part of a piece of toast, and a cup of coffee were all that he could manage. Taylor did not object. She simply finished off the rest of his breakfast, in addition to her own. Jeffers watched the food disappear, while one leg jitterbugged up and down next to the table leg.

"George, you're nervous," Taylor said, looking up from her plate.

"No shit." I am not made of ice, he thought, like the person having breakfast with me. Or, more exactly, the person I am watching eat my breakfast. Probably my last one, too.

"You worry too much. Now listen, we need to talk about the H-C man."

"Oh, Christ!" Jeffers sat up ramrod straight. "We forgot all about him."

"By no means. We merely did not discuss him in front of Fruhling. I told you I had some arrangements to make last night. Basically, you need to be in the lobby by at least five minutes to nine. The bell captain this guy thinks he has paid off has tipped him that you will be leaving through the lobby for a meeting at nine, so you can be sure he will be there. Just wait a bit. When it happens, you leave."

"When what happens?"

"You'll know it when you see it." She signaled to the waiter for the check. "You didn't eat much so I'll pay for breakfast, but you owe me dinner. Now scat, I'll see you later."

Jeffers wished he felt as confident as Taylor. At least she looked confident, and whatever might be underneath was hidden from the world. Jeffers was certain his worry was evident to all who happened to look his way. Definitely not the image he wanted to project.

He bought a paper in the lobby—not to read, but to have an object to manipulate in his hands. The H-C man was there, standing with one hand on an armchair, pretending to be waiting for someone else. It was seven minutes to nine. Jeffers did not notice the two boys entering the lobby. They were, perhaps, twenty years old, and by the dilapidated look of their clothes they did not fit in with the other people in the lobby of the hotel. They would have looked more in place with the people sitting in front of the Centraal Station. They were also, quite obviously, a couple, and in that sense they stood out as well. It was clear from the way the other occupants of the lobby worked to avoid looking at them that they were the center of attention.

"Hey, Hans," one of them shouted in German, clapping the other on the shoulder. "Look, it's Johann." He pointed to the H-C man. "Hey, Johann! It's us!" At the shout, Jeffers's attention joined the rest. He did not understand the German, but he did not really need to.

The H-C man at first looked behind him, not believing they were shouting at him. Finding only empty space and a wall, he turned back with a grim look on his face as he tried to watch them and Jeffers at the same time.

"God, Johann. Looks like you got a good job, doesn't it?" The one addressed as Hans led the way to the H-C man. Reaching him, he fingered the suit jacket admiringly.

As he did so, his companion came up on the other side and draped an arm across the H-C man's shoulder. "Have you forgotten old friends, Johann?" he said. "We ought to go somewhere for breakfast and get reacquainted." He leaned over, and kissed the man on the cheek.

"Bastard!" the H-C man exploded, swinging his arms wildly to try to get free of them. They clung to him, however, in spite of the buffets, and a wrestling match developed in the center of the lobby. As the trio staggered around, with all manner of epithets coming from the one in the middle, the one called Hans swept his hand under the H-C man's jacket. There was a thump as a semiautomatic pistol flew out, and slid across the floor. It came to a stop at the feet of a fat American matron. Seeing the gun, her eyes grew very wide.

"Terrorists!" she shrieked, at which point her eyes rolled up and she fainted. As she hit the floor, another shout was heard, "Help, someone's been shot!"

It was nine o'clock. The lobby was a bedlam.

The time, and the scene, were a marvelous release for Jeffers. He was no longer tense, he was exhilarated. He strode through the door, back straight and chin up. The paper he tossed into the trash. Sean Connery could not have looked cooler.

Once through the door, he turned to the right as instructed. There would be no slip-ups this time. A blue BMW was standing just a little farther down the block and, as promised, a man was leaning against the NO PARKING sign. Jeffers studied the man as he walked toward him. His contact was nearly six feet in height, and stocky. A white silk shirt was open nearly to the navel, revealing a rug of black hair. A loud plaid sport jacket was worn over it. Black hair topped a tan face, and as he drew closer Jeffers could see uneven teeth in the man's smile. There was a second man behind the wheel of the car. Of his features, Jeffers could see nothing. Again following instructions, he walked over to the man at the sign.

"Excuse me, do you have any American cigarettes?" For a second, he wondered what he would do if the man burst out laughing.

"No," said the man, his smile growing broader. "But I can take you to someone who does."

"Suits me," replied Jeffers.

"Good, get in." The man pulled open the rear door of the car.

Now or never, George, thought Jeffers, hesitating halfway through the door. Sean Connery had evaporated in the shadow of his contact's bulk. Jeffers could cut and run if he wanted to. On such a public thoroughfare they would be unlikely to chase him. However, the thought of explaining such behavior to Taylor was intolerable. He went ahead and entered the car.

Hairy Chest got in next to him, and handed him a pair of glasses, with instructions to wear them. They looked ordinary enough, but when Jeffers put them on they transmitted no light at all—he was effectively blindfolded, without that being evident to anyone outside the car. Once in the car, Jeffers found his nose assaulted by a noisome odor. It was cheap cologne, and it emanated from the man next to him. Beneath it was another odor, not entirely disguised. Jeffers thought the problem could have been solved more simply with soap and water. He hoped it was not going to be a long ride.

Hairy Chest checked the glasses by thrusting his fingers at Jeffers's eyes. There was no response. "All right, Klaus. Let's go."

The two men spoke sparingly between themselves, never to Jeffers. They spoke in German, at least that was the language Jeffers thought they were speaking, which effectively excluded him from their conversation. Whether they were largely silent from habit, or whether they were uncertain of Jeffers's fluency was not clear. Jeffers found it hard to endure the silence, plus the blindness, or what might happen when they arrived. His position brought home to him the fact that he had entrusted Taylor Redding with his life. It was a bad time to have second thoughts, but they bubbled up in his mind regardless. To counter what he was able to recognize as early signs of panic, he tried to time the intervals between turns, and their sequence.

At length, they came to a stop. The man in back gripped Jeffers's arm tightly. "I will help you get out," he said in English. "Do not take the glasses off until you are told."

Wearing the glasses, Jeffers needed the same assistance as a newly blind man. He moved only when there was pressure on his arm, and he had a tendency to shuffle his feet. The abrupt removal of the sun's warmth from his head told him that they were near a building. The procession stopped to allow the driver to open the door. As he started forward again, Jeffers caught his toe on a bit of uneven pavement. In trying to recover his balance, the glasses were jostled, giving him a quick view of the street. The big man next to him saw the glasses dislodged, and with an oath roughly shoved him through the door.

Once inside, Jeffers saw that he was in the front room of a small apartment. It had been overfurnished with gaudy, and inexpensive, items. There were windows on two sides, it had to be a corner apartment, but the shades were completely drawn. Diagonally opposite from where the trio stood, a door to another room was ajar. Aside from the door through which they had entered, and a steep staircase immediately beyond the entrance, there were no other exits from the room. Neither man seemed to match the room. Hairy Chest was gaudily dressed, but there was nothing cheap about his clothes. The driver of the car, the one called Klaus, wore a gray business suit. He looked to be in his early fifties, and reminded Jeffers of a nasty high school mathematics teacher he had once had.

It was Klaus who opened the discussion. "Let us be clear about what we are doing." He had a pedantic way of speech that reinforced the teacher image. "You are going to provide us with the information we want. Otherwise, things will be . . . unfortunate."

"Now wait." Jeffers found himself surprised that he was not surprised by Klaus's statement. "It was my understanding that you had information for me."

"Well, Dr. Jeffers . . ." Klaus gently rested his left hand on Jeffers's shoulder, the sort of intimate gesture friends use. With the suddenness of a snake, his right hand drove a sucker punch into Jeffers's solar plexus.

The air whooshed out of Jeffers's chest. He folded, partially, at his mid-section and sat down on the sofa in front of which he had been standing. Breathing had abruptly become a major struggle.

"I think that you misunderstood what I said before," Klaus continued evenly, "so I will clarify it for you. You have very little bargaining leverage. In fact, you have none. If you wish to end this day alive and free, you will answer our questions. All of them. If we are satisfied, we will let you go, and I will advise you to invent some story that will put an end to your hopeless probing. If not, well, I can leave that to your imagination." Klaus laughed. "The only information *I* have for *you* is that you would have done better to have stayed home."

Jeffers was still having trouble breathing when Klaus finished. Mouth open, he sat on the sofa trying to coax air back into his lungs. Slowly, each breath a little deeper than the previous one, he succeeded.

"I can pay for your information," he gasped out.

"With what?" Klaus asked. The simple mention of money drew the attention of both men.

"I have a sample here." Jeffers tossed the bills onto the floor. There was a pause while Klaus counted the money. "There's more where that came from," Jeffers said when Klaus finished.

"Very good." Klaus looked from the money to Jeffers. "I will make a deal with you. You will answer our questions. After that you will take us to the rest of the money. In return, we will let you go."

Jeffers could not help noticing that only moments before, Klaus had promised his freedom in exchange for information alone. The thought was chilling. These two were planning to kill him. It was only a question of whether he handed them the money first or not. Oh, Taylor, he thought, where are you?

"Now that we have a satisfactory agreement," Klaus continued, "I would like to know who you really are."

"I'm Dr. George Jeffers, as you know."

There was a loud crack as the back of Klaus's hand connected with the side of Jeffers's head. Jeffers reeled back on the couch, blood running from a gash where Klaus's seal ring had cut his cheek.

"Now, I will ask you again. Who are you? Please do not try my patience. We know that you are not Dr. Jeffers."

Taylor's gambit was coming home to roost. Even though he was Dr. Jeffers, with all his associated identification, they would never believe it. That, in itself, provided some information. Only someone who had spoken with Fruhling would "know" that he was not Dr. Jeffers. There was, however, no time to sort through the possibilities. He needed a name, fast.

"Wait a second," he managed to rasp out, holding up a hand. He needed a name, but not just any name. He needed one with a ready-made character he could appropriate. "Harry Flashman," he blurted out.

Klaus relaxed a little and began to address him as Mr. Flashman. Jeffers felt some of his tension seep away as well. The name of Fraser's famous poltroon evidently meant nothing to either of the men in the room. Of course, how many German thugs would be expected to have a knowledge of English literature?

If having secured a suitable identity afforded Jeffers a brief respite from violence, it did not permit him to relax very much. Klaus continued to ask questions. Some of them concerned operations or agents that meant nothing to Jeffers. Others regarded the enzyme: who was paying him to look for it, what kind of support he had, and to whom Jeffers had spoken. Anything he had the faintest idea about, he talked about in great, if fanciful, detail. Since Klaus responded to answers he did not believe with an immediate blow, Jeffers soon concluded that the man was swallowing most of what Jeffers was shoveling out. Where the subject was completely unknown to Jeffers, he said so, fearing that it would be too easy to trip himself up. This tactic caused him to absorb a few punches and slaps. The punishment ceased after Klaus evidently became satisfied with the flow of information and the apparent limits on Jeffers's knowledge. The willingness of the two to listen attentively to a stream of what was mostly nonsense, and the name Jeffers had hung on himself, gave birth to an idea.

Jeffers had come to the conclusion that unless he could keep Klaus interested in what he was saying until Taylor arrived he was going to be dead. A slight extension of that reasoning said that if for any reason Taylor did not show up, or could not rescue him, the only way he was going to stay alive was to make Klaus want him alive rather than dead. The name Jeffers had used had not been planned in any sense of the word. Harry Flashman had just popped into his mind. The character Fraser had invented had not been long on stoicism. Whatever it took to talk his way out of a jam, he would do. Putting the name together with his predicament, Jeffers began to speak in increasing detail about items he knew, embroidering wherever possible. The name Charles Oliver proved to be known to Klaus, and Jeffers rambled on at some length about the man's connections and habits. Then, Jeffers began to whine a little, mostly about how little money he was receiving from Oliver, and about how much he owed various unnamed people.

Klaus took a deep and, superficially, sympathetic interest in his financial plight. As the talk began to revolve less around the enzyme, and more about Jeffers's fantasy life he became bolder in his invention. When Klaus pushed harder for the names of people to whom Jeffers owed money, Jeffers let slip, or pretended to, mention of blackmail by a jilted homosexual lover. That, he explained, was how he had become so trapped. His former lover worked for Oliver, and Jeffers feared the repercussions if Oliver learned what happened. Klaus and his partner grinned at that. Then they wanted to know the ex-lover's position. Perhaps, they implied, something could be done for Jeffers, if they could be assured of his cooperation. Inside his head—and not, Jeffers fervently hoped, on his face—was exultation. Money and kinky sex were, according to all the novels he read, the means by which agents could be manipulated and turned. These two seemed to take to the bait as readily as the spies in the books. The spiel was definitely buying him time. If Taylor failed to arrive with the cavalry, it might even buy him a way out into the open.

Taylor Redding had left the hotel by a side door. She had not gone to watch the scene in the lobby. If she had done her work well, the H-C man would no longer be behind Jeffers when they were outside. It would only take one look to know whether it had worked, not that she had many doubts. The boys would show up, money and connections told her that. No matter how the scene then played itself out, the H-C man would be unable to tail Jeffers. She was more concerned about how Jeffers would actually function. She had been able to see the way he kept his jitters under control, more or less, in the dining room. Whether that control was going to hold up under real pressure was a good question. It had been a pleasant surprise to find Jeffers willing to jump into the role he had to play, without any urging this time, but it was going to be all for naught if he could not hold up his end of the plan.

She walked briskly to the location where Fruhling had said Wolfgang would be waiting with the car. A car was there as planned, with a youngish man at the wheel. She breathed a sigh of relief over the car. It was a tan Golf, commonplace enough in model and color to be almost invisible on the street. She had dreaded finding Fruhling's "enthusiastic" graduate student behind the wheel of a fire engine red sport car, ready to chase the enemy from there to Berlin at top speed. All it would take would be a glimpse of such a car twice in the rearview mirror to alert their quarry.

Wolfgang leaned over to open the passenger door for her. He was a picture-postcard North German, blond of hair, blue of eye and square of jaw.

He met Taylor's eyes only briefly, then his gaze seemed to fasten between her shoulders and waist.

"Good morning, *Fraulein*. Please have a seat. I am sorry about the car, it is mine. Herr Professor would not let us take his Porsche." His English was serviceable, no more.

Taylor slid in, thanking her stars as she did that Herr Professor had some sense in these matters. The boy—she thought of him that way even though their ages were similar—was pleasant enough but something about him made her uneasy.

Must be the language, she decided. *"Wir werden auf deutsch sprechen. Nur deutsch,"* she announced. She would not gamble that Wolfgang's English was fluent enough to avoid mistranslation. Even if it had been, the brief time needed to mentally translate from a language in which one did not think could lead to disaster, especially in times of excitement. She was comfortable enough in German anyway.

They pulled around to the front of the hotel to see Jeffers headed toward the blue BMW. Taking care to leave some distance between the two cars, they followed it as it pulled out. Almost immediately after leaving the curb the BMW made a right-hand turn, followed by two more right turns. Taylor tensed, recognizing the same maneuver she had employed, and instructed Wolfgang to permit more space between them after the second turn. Making three successive turns, in the same direction, was a simple way of establishing whether a car behind was following. The odds of an individual on unrelated business following that sequence was quite low. She held her breath after the third turn, but the other car made no evasive move. At each successive light, she expected the other to wait just for the stop signal, then dash across, leaving them behind. It did not happen. Either the other driver had not recognized them when he checked, blessed anonymity, or he was being inattentive. For whatever reason, he made no further move to shake them. Although the Golf's engine sputtered and wheezed ominously from time to time, they had no difficulty keeping the other car in view.

At length the BMW turned onto Prinzengracht and shortly came to a stop in front of a block of old canal row houses. They watched the two men bring Jeffers to the entrance to the corner building. As far as Taylor could see, Jeffers was intact so far. Then she saw Jeffers stumble, and the large man trailing him reacted by roughly pushing him ahead. Just that brief glance was enough to set off an alarm in her head.

"Drive past the building," she ordered Wolfgang, "then take that bridge left across the canal. Now left again, come back opposite the building."

There was just enough space there to park the Golf. From that spot they could see the BMW and the entrance, but with the canal between them and the house and the shade trees that lined both sides of the canal, it was unlikely that any watcher would spot them. The memory of that push itched at her brain, stimulating her trouble sense.

"Wolfgang, did Fruhling leave anything for me with you?"

"No, *Fraulein.* Were you expecting him to?"

Taylor sighed. When Fruhling had said limited assistance, she had not expected it to be this limited. "Fruhling did not leave a pistol with you?"

"No, *Fraulein!* Herr Professor said you had everything you would need. Are you going to need a gun?" A distinct tinge of fear had crept into his voice.

Taylor was not pleased, mostly with herself. She had not asked Fruhling for a weapon. Not knowing whether to trust him, it had seemed better to give the impression of not needing one.

Unfortunately, she had to make a decision quickly. Her instinct had started to sound loud and clear in her head—that Jeffers had walked into a trap and was in trouble. She was going to have to move fast, and needed to also decide how to use Wolfgang. The time spent following Jeffers's captors had revealed a great deal about Wolfgang. He talked too much, and too much of it was not related to the problem at hand. He was already converting this adventure into a story. That in itself was fine, but the story telling should wait until the adventure was over. In addition to that, he had thrown in various ideas for what they could do together later in the evening. After listening to his patter and seeing his reaction to the mention of firearms, it dawned on her that the kid was, in fact, a graduate student. Nothing more, and nothing less. That puzzled Taylor. She had assumed that Fruhling would have sent someone with skills in her field, rather than in biophysics. Yet he had not. Were the connections mere rumors, without foundation? She doubted it. Fruhling had not acted the part of an artless, ivory-tower type. Had she misread Wolfgang? Not a chance. Therefore, Fruhling had intentionally sent her out with an innocent, good for driving but not much more. She bit down on her lip and tried to sort it out in the scant time available. She could see only two possibilities. Either Fruhling was going to doublecross them, and he was clever enough to figure out she would be watching for any move by Wolfgang, or he was concerned enough that he was being set up, and willing to jeopardize their chances rather than expose his connections. She had expected Wolfgang to be armed and unless there was going to be a doublecross the gun would be available for her. As it was, she was not even sure if she had been doublecrossed, and had no gun to boot.

"You wait here," she instructed him. "If neither I nor Jeffers are back in forty-five minutes, you report to Fruhling. If they leave, with or without Jeffers, you follow and report their location to Fruhling. You do nothing else. Understood?" Most of her words were for effect only. If she was not back in forty-five minutes it probably wouldn't matter what Wolfgang did.

"*Jawohl! Alles klar!*" In the absence of any further mention of weapons, his enthusiasm had returned, and he threw her an exaggerated salute.

God, do we have to play soldier? *Alles* had damn well better be *klar*, she thought, as she stepped out of the car. She would have much preferred to use Wolfgang in a more active fashion. There was no guarantee that more people were not in the apartment house, and it was a near certainty that some of them would have guns. However, to make a plan that would rely on him was too much of a risk. It was better to go it alone. At least she was well aware of her own abilities and limitations.

It was a sunny morning. The street, if not thronged, was well populated with pedestrians and motor traffic. That would provide some cover in case there was a watcher in a window. Taylor walked down the sidewalk toward the BMW. As she reached it she pulled a handkerchief from her hip pocket. A number of coins, folded into the handkerchief, flew out and bounced on the sidewalk.

"*Verdammt,*" she muttered, for anyone who might hear, and knelt down by the front fender where she began to retrieve the money. The handkerchief remained in her right hand. Concealed within it was a small, sharp awl. A quick glance revealed no pedestrians too close. She jabbed swiftly with the awl at the sidewall of the front curbside tire. There was an answering slow hiss of air. She allowed herself a small smile, and picked up the remainder of the coins. There would be no fast exits from this place.

She assumed that the apartment was a safe house used by the two men they had followed, or their employers. For that reason, there had to be a convenient escape hatch for the occupants. Back ways out could become back ways in, for Taylor Redding. She saw the approach she wanted when she reached the street corner. The street was little more than an alley, barely wide enough for a car. Its other end, she could see, connected to the next street. The alley was deserted when Taylor stepped into it. From the refuse that littered it, she could tell that it saw little traffic. A dumpster blocked half the alley about twenty feet from the entrance. Just beyond the dumpster she came to a window set at approximately waist height. Anyone going in or out of that window would be screened by the dumpster. Jeffers could be on either the first or second floor. Since the odds were equal either way, she decided to start with the route presented by the easily accessible window.

Peering into the window, the shade of which was only half drawn, she could see a kitchen. It was unoccupied, and the interior light was out. The window gave easily at a quick test and slid smoothly in its frame with minimal noise.

She paused for a moment to ready her equipment. From a pocket by her right knee she took a thin, black Bakelite handle. A little pressure on its switch and a six-inch blade clicked into place. By feel she checked the small throwing knife, taped inside her left sock and positioned for a rapid grab. The knives were comforting, but she still would have preferred a gun in this particular situation. It was not a matter of accuracy—she could hit a rat with her throwing knife. A gun, however, could be fired more than once.

"Okay, kid, it's time. No use crying over spilt milk." She spoke only to herself. The old familiar tightening of muscles along her jaw and abdomen was there. The feeling came whenever she tried something dangerous for the first time. There was another component to the tensing as well. She had a partner inside who was her responsibility. Taylor had rarely considered those she worked with as partners, and certainly had not begun this adventure that way either. Jeffers had just been her ticket to adventure, expendable if a maneuver went sour, and that was all. She had felt that way earlier, but no longer. She was more tense about Jeffers than she was about herself.

She slid the window all the way open and waited. There was no movement below. Underneath the window was a sink and counter. The counter was a clutter of dishes, towels, and utensils. It offered treacherous footing at best, so, knife gripped between her teeth to free her hands, she eased herself across the sink. The door leading to the streetside of the apartment was partially open. Voices could be heard easily from the adjoining room, and one of them belonged to Jeffers. He was being addressed as "Flashman." When she heard enough to catch the drift of the story Jeffers was creating, she had to grin. Old George was doing damn well by himself.

She peeked through the open door, crouched low to avoid being spotted by a chance look in her direction. Jeffers was seated on a couch at the opposite end of the room. There was blood on his nose and upper lip and a swelling over his right eye. No major damage that she could see, but it confirmed her hunch not to rely on the good intentions of his hosts. Which left only the question of getting him out.

Neither his hands nor his feet were bound. That was an incredible stroke of luck. Their opponents had to be either stupid or overconfident, which amounted to the same thing. They were turned so that most of their backs faced her. At that distance, she knew she could put a knife in either one without much trouble. The problem was, the switchblade was not well balanced for throwing. They would be left with a single opponent, but he would probably have a gun. The odds of somebody getting shot in that scenario were fairly high. There had to be a better approach.

The kitchen door, she noted, opened inward. When it did so, it would create a small alcove bounded by it and the outside wall. That helped. Next, a stack of dirty dishes next to the sink caught her eye. The height of the pile suggested a week's inattention. They had been stacked without the remnants of food or silverware being cleared off. Consequently the tower listed badly toward the counter's edge, the pitch induced by the random presence of forks, knives, meat and potato skins between the plates. Yes, it would work nicely.

In the front room Jeffers's dissertation was interrupted by a crash from the room in back. A secondary, less loud, crash followed the initial one. It sounded like a waiter dropping a tray of dishes. Both of his captors started at the noise. Klaus drew a small automatic pistol from beneath his coat. He turned part way to the rear door, but kept Jeffers within his field of view. That was unfortunate, Jeffers thought, because the other man had turned completely around. There was no further sound from beyond the door.

"It's probably just some of the dishes, Klaus. You don't need to get so excited."

"Just dishes! Karl, you idiot, I'm sure it's just dishes the way you left them stacked, but you go make sure that's all it is." Klaus was not one to take a sudden noise at face value. There were beads of sweat visible on his forehead and upper lip. Jeffers could feel his own sweat starting as well. Unless the crash was strictly the result of Karl's poor housekeeping, it would likely be Taylor who was in the back room. Had Klaus turned a little bit further, he might have been able to jump him. The way it was, though, he had no chance.

"Karl! Your gun!" Karl looked sheepish. To investigate broken dishes with a drawn gun was silly. He did not argue, however, and drew his weapon as he moved to the back of the room.

So both of them were armed, Jeffers saw. Maybe it was just as well he had not had the opportunity to tackle Klaus earlier. But if Taylor was in the back of the apartment, she would shortly be facing a gunman. If she were similarly armed, Jeffers did not know it, having never mentioned his speculation on the train. He needed to alert her somehow.

Klaus appeared to divine his thought before he even tried to act on it. "One word out of you and you're dead now. I won't miss at this range." Reluctantly, Jeffers sat in silence.

Karl pushed the door open completely as he moved into the kitchen. Broken dishes covered the floor from the sink to the far wall. "Hell, it was that pile of dishes," he said. He stepped forward, eyes on the crockery, and the door swung closed behind him.

Klaus relaxed at Karl's comment, but when no further sound, or movement, came from the kitchen, he tensed up again. "Karl! What is going on?" he cried. There was no answer. Klaus was torn between two necessities. He could not leave his prisoner unguarded, yet he had to know what was happening in the kitchen. Both he and Jeffers, for different reasons, were positive that more than broken dishes waited beyond the door.

The question was resolved a moment later when the door opened, and Taylor Redding peered around the frame. Klaus's mouth dropped wide open. Surprised he was, but not frozen. His gun swung back to the door.

"Duck!" screamed Jeffers, oblivious to the weapon next to him. Klaus fired twice. The surprise was, perhaps, enough to ruin his aim. Both shots struck the wood frame. His target had vanished almost the instant he had fired, in any event. But not for long. Taylor was back in the door opening rapidly, but much lower down. She was in a catcher's crouch, right leg doubled under her, left leg extended, holding the frame with her left hand for balance. Her right hand held Karl's automatic, and it was blazing.

The stream of bullets sprayed across the other end of the room. The clock face on the wall above the couch exploded. So did a vase on an end table. Jeffers threw himself to the floor as slugs hit the cushions. Klaus had no stomach to stand there and fire back in the face of the incoming bullets. He dove for the front door, which was partially shielded by the staircase, losing his own gun in the process. Bullets followed him, tearing chunks out of the wall and door. With the jerky motions of a man in panic, he yanked the door open and fled. Not a single bullet had touched him.

Across the room walked Taylor Redding. The cuff of her right shirt sleeve was stained with blood. There was blood as well over the back of her right hand. Her face wore an expression of absolute disgust.

"Jesus Christ, Taylor!" Jeffers pulled himself to a sitting position on the floor with his back to the couch. "Am I glad to see you."

She nodded curtly. "Are you all right?"

"Yeah, how about you?" He indicated her hand. "What happened?"

"Don't worry, it's not my blood. As to what happened, I missed. That ought to be obvious."

"I guess you can't put shooting lessons on Amex." Jeffers had not planned to comment on her shooting. He was simply glad she had come for him. It did occur to him later that probably the safest spot in the room had been where Klaus was standing. But even had he thought of it then, he would not have said it. What he wanted to do was say something light, more in Taylor's own style, but it came out wrong. The look he received should have frozen the air between them.

"I'm a perfectly good shot. I just assumed I could do it one-handed. I was wrong, and I know it, and I don't need shit about it."

Jeffers had gotten to his feet by the time she finished. His face felt as though it was burning, and not just in the areas he had been hit. "Whoa, Taylor, please. I didn't mean it the way you took it. Believe me, I'm not mocking you. You just saved my life."

"Never mind about that." She dismissed it with a wave of her free hand. "I think we had better get out of here."

# Chapter 14

## AMSTERDAM, THE NETHERLANDS

It was indeed time to leave. The gunshots had to have been heard by passersby as well as other inhabitants of the row house. Even in American cities, where the tendency to avoid becoming involved in the affairs of others was most marked, the police would be called with at most a moderate delay. Amsterdam was not New York. Gunfire was most uncommon. It was therefore unlikely that there would be any significant delay in calling the police.

It was amazing to Jeffers how his views of this prospect had changed in so short a time. In the past he had looked on the police as a source of help and was almost compulsively law-abiding, a trait that extended to taxes and speed limits. Within the brief present framed by his acquaintance with Taylor, he suspected he had been involved in breaking more laws than he could count. Even as an unwitting accomplice, he had developed a preference to keep his actions to himself. Also, and decisively, there was the blood on Taylor's hand. It argued that major trouble would ensue if they were connected to the apartment by the police. He agreed immediately with her suggestion.

The front door was a poor choice of exit for the same reasons that required their departure. The risk of being identified was too high. The back alley route Taylor had used to gain entrance was a better bet. It was not perfect—they might still be spied by a nosy neighbor—but the odds were reasonable. Jeffers paused only to scoop up the pistol Klaus had dropped before heading through the kitchen door behind Taylor.

One step through the door confirmed his worst thoughts about the source of the blood on Taylor. Karl's body lay on the floor, tipped over on its left side, the throat slashed so deeply as to be almost decapitation. The body was positioned so that the head tipped backward, which accentuated the effect of the gaping chasm in the neck. Blood had geysered from this site under the force of the heart's pumping, liberally spattering the counter, cabinets and walls with red. It had also flowed widely over the floor, forcing them to step carefully to avoid tracking it with their shoes. Given the amount on the floor and elsewhere, it was surprising Taylor had as little on her as she did. She was seated on the counter above the body, beside her a bloody towel on which she had wiped her hand, an odd expression on her face, when Jeffers came through the door. Once he had caught up she wasted no time leading the way out through the window over the sink.

Fortunately, the alley was deserted. No shouts or commands to stop greeted them. As they walked, Taylor rolled the cuff of her sleeve over itself to hide the bloodstain. They reached the outlet of the alley and turned onto the cross street without incident.

Taylor was unsure whether they would need to walk back to the hotel or not. It was conceivable that Wolfgang would have pursued Klaus when he fled. Her instructions had been worded in a way that would permit that interpretation if stretched a bit, and Wolfgang was the sort of impetuous novice who might act on it. It spite of the considerable inconvenience it would pose, she half hoped it had happened. The fewer people she had to be around right then, the better.

Wolfgang was exactly where she had left him, however. As he explained to Taylor, one man running down the road, without either her or Jeffers, did not fit the criteria she had established. In truth, and it was quite plain even to Jeffers who was meeting Wolfgang for the first time, the sound of gunfire had eliminated his enthusiasm for any role more active than sitting as unobtrusively as possible in the car.

Taylor curtly ordered Wolfgang to return them to the hotel. Then she got into the back of the car and lapsed into silence. Jeffers planted himself in the front passenger's seat, where he soon felt totally ignored. Wolfgang was saying nothing, obviously aware that his fear had been detected by both of them, and was embarrassed by it. Jeffers had no problem with that, he had not really expected any important information from the driver. What he could not deal with was the total silence from the back seat.

His feelings about Taylor Redding had never been entirely consistent, but he now had to add a new element to them. Fear. It was a large emotional step to go from the intellectual realization that death might result, his or others, from what they were doing to the gut understanding that Taylor had done, well, what she had obviously done to Karl. He desperately needed Taylor to say something to him to take the feeling away. He had never known anyone he considered capable of an act like that, and the idea that he had thought fondly of her just an evening ago was now repulsive.

Feelings aside, he also recognized that there was still work to do. He knew they had been both lucky and successful thus far. The trap had been foiled, one enemy was dead and the other had been put to flight. However, the success was incomplete. Klaus might attack them again or he might communicate with his superior, and the identity of that worthy remained unknown. Jeffers did not believe for a minute that Karl and Klaus were the total of their opposition. Some action on their part was necessary, but although he saw the need, the answer escaped him. For that he needed help from Taylor, and he was not getting it. For all the response she made to his attempts at opening a discussion, she might as well have been back in Boston. She sat rigidly in the back, her face as taut as the rest of her body.

"One stupid remark," he muttered, though not loudly enough for her to hear if she was listening. "Just one, for God's sake." That she had taken such umbrage at a single foolish comment of his was unbelievable.

The Golf was still some distance from the hotel when Taylor broke her silence by indicating that Wolfgang should pull over to the curb.

"Let me off here. You should let Dr. Fruhling know what has happened." As an afterthought, she added: "On your way you can leave Dr. Jeffers at the hotel." To Jeffers, she said in English, "Wolfgang will take you the rest of the way. I'll meet you at your room this evening."

That was emphatically not what Jeffers had been waiting to hear. "Like hell we're splitting up like this now. If you have some burning desire to walk the rest of the way, I can walk with you. There are things to be planned and things to be explained, and they won't wait until evening, and you ought to know it. I'm sorry I said what I did, I told you I didn't mean it that way, but I really think it should not get in the way like this."

"What are you talking about? What did you say?"

"You know," Jeffers looked puzzled, "about your shooting."

"What? Oh. George, that has nothing to do with anything. Nothing at all."

"Well, if that's not the problem, then I want to know what is."

"Nothing." Taylor could see that Wolfgang was having difficulty trying to follow the conversation, and was glad of it.

"Like hell, 'nothing.' "

"I said, nothing." She could see that Jeffers had his hand on the door latch as soon as she did, and suddenly relented. "Forget the hotel, Wolfgang. Just report to Fruhling." Her voice had become very weary. When the car was gone she spoke again to Jeffers. "I wish you had gone with Wolfgang. I really do."

She gave him no opportunity to reply but turned and walked off down the street. Jeffers hurried to follow after her. Taylor was not acting like Taylor, a concern that overshadowed all else for Jeffers.

A little way beyond where Wolfgang had let them off was a small park.

It was partly screened from the street by shrubs and contained a small plot of well-groomed grass and several flower beds. A fountain with a large stone bowl played in the center of it. The garden was empty of other people. Taylor turned into the garden and walked directly to the back rim of the fountain. She put her hands on the wall of the pool, leaned over and was sick. Great, aching heaves broke from her, spilling onto the water below. When the spasms subsided she washed off her face with some clean water from another spot. She straightened herself slowly, a bit unsteady. When she looked up she saw Jeffers standing not ten yards away, staring at her.

"Well?" she said.

Jeffers at first thought it was better that he had stayed, if only so she would have some company on the walk back to the hotel. In spite of his efforts, however, she remained just as uncommunicative for the entire trip. He found her continued silence annoying. Also on his mind was something he had seen at the fountain. When she had raised her hand to wash her face, the same arm on which she had rolled up the shirt sleeve, he noticed a mark, what looked like a thin white scar running longitudinally along the inside of her wrist.

"Taylor, we need to talk. I can't take much more of this silence," Jeffers said, deciding to take a stand when they reached the lobby of the hotel.

"Can it keep for a while? I really need some time to myself." That, Taylor thought, was a mild understatement. The reality was that she urgently wanted to be alone. It was bad enough to have been sick. Had no one at all been there she still would have been very unhappy. To have been *seen* that way was horrible. The only consolation, and a small one at that, was that Wolfgang had not been there.

Jeffers was in no mood for any further delay. "No," he said. " 'The time has come, the Walrus said, to speak of many things: Of shoes and ships and sealing wax, of cabbages and kings.' Of our situation in general, and Taylor Redding in particular. We can either agree to go upstairs and talk, or I can follow you upstairs and bug you."

Seeing no way out, Taylor capitulated. After they reached Jeffers's room, however, she remained silent. She did not flop in the armchair either. Instead, she paced.

After a few more minutes of silence, Jeffers tried again. "Taylor, will you please tell me what is wrong."

"Nothing is wrong."

"Bullshit, nothing is wrong. Ever since our little showdown this afternoon you have been about as talkative as an embalmed corpse. You said it's not my stupid comment, so what is it? Then you blow lunch all over the fountain, and you tell me nothing is going on. Give me a break! Was it Karl, what you did, that did it?" Riled as he was, Jeffers still could not bring himself to be more explicit about the killing.

Taylor came to a stop at the window and stared out of it, her back to Jeffers. A small sigh escaped back into the room. "Did I get sick over cutting his throat, do you mean? Yeah, you could say that. It's funny, you know, I'm fairly sure it's not the first time I've killed someone, but it's different in a firefight. You pull the trigger and it happens a hundred yards away. This is more personal. It bothered me for some reason."

If anything, her statement reassured Jeffers. He tried to project that to her. "Look, you did what had to be done, and I'm damn glad you did. The bastard got what he deserved, and it turned my stomach too, but I wouldn't let it bother you."

"That's not what's bothering me."

The response took Jeffers aback. "What is bothering you then?"

"Nothing."

"But you just said." Jeffers came to a stop. "Taylor, don't bullshit me. What is going on?"

"You wouldn't understand it, so don't worry about it."

"How can you tell me I wouldn't understand it when you haven't told me anything. Now, what is it?"

"Ice and fire."

"What?"

"I said you wouldn't understand."

"Damn it, you haven't said anything."

Suddenly, Taylor whirled away from the window, and Jeffers could see anger in her face. "All right! I am not pleased that I got sick over butchering that turkey, but the problem is I let it out and let it get in the way. I'm not trying to blame missing Klaus on it, although I'm sure it didn't help, but I haven't been good for much since, and that is not permitted. Now will you please just shut up and let it go?"

"No, I can't." Jeffers knew that he could not—there was too much at stake—but he was a little afraid of what he would find when he pushed. "You're telling me that what's bothering you isn't what you did to Karl, but that you couldn't bottle it all up. Well, it sounds like a pretty normal reaction to me, and here you are telling me it is not 'permitted.' Whose permission do you need? And what do you mean by ice and fire?"

"Christ." She stood facing him, her face no longer angry, just unhappy. "You won't understand." She did talk to him about it, though. She found it hard to describe, strange she thought, for that was the way she lived. Then she realized that she had never really tried to put into words the rules she lived by, and what was crystal clear in her head was not so obvious when spoken in sentences.

"You have to understand about emotions, George. You have them, I have them, everybody does. You can't stop yourself from having them, and people who think they can are only fooling themselves, but you don't have to let them get in your way. Ice and fire are part of the rules I live by. Emotions are like flames. They flicker; they change shape. They can burn you if you let them, so the fire has to stay inside. Think what you like, feel what you like, but never, ever, let it through to the outside. That's ice."

Jeffers was silent when she finished. It was hard to know what to make of what she said. The whole idea sounded impossibly rigid. He wondered where it had come from in the first place, and then remembered the scar he had seen. Did that fit in as well? Taylor had mentioned nothing about it, and as much as Jeffers wanted to know he dared not ask. He wanted to be careful, very careful, at this juncture. If he said the wrong thing, as he usually did, he could believe that Taylor might snap. Aside from the immediate consequences to their job, he figured she deserved better from him than that.

While he was thinking, Taylor spoke again. "You know, I promised you the world's greatest female adventurer, but I'm afraid it looks like you got the world's biggest female mouth."

The pain in her voice decided him. The distance between them was no more than six feet. He closed it with a few steps, and put his hands on her shoulders. The flesh under the blouse was soft and warm, not quite the steel-plate image she projected.

Having moved that far before he could think, Jeffers ran into a problem. Where women were concerned, spontaneity was not his strong suit. He found himself at just arm's length from Taylor's gray gaze. Their eyes were nearly on a level, as tall as she was, and his angle of vision constricted to within a few degrees of the line that joined those eyes. Her face was smooth, expressionless. Jeffers could feel his mind start to blank. Mentally, he shook himself. Not this time.

"Listen. It's one thing to have rules to go by, but sometimes they are not what is most important. I owe you my life. More than once. You've delivered on all of your promises. I think that's a hell of a lot more important than a small chink in your armor. You're still my lady of ice and fire."

She looked at him, at first without speaking, and he could feel her relax under his hands. "Thank you," she whispered.

According to the novels he had read, not a small number, this was the point where the hero swept the heroine into an embrace both passionate and comforting. James Bond would not have hesitated. George Jeffers did not move. He was again divided against himself.

"Cretin," a part of his mind railed against the inactivity of his body. "What are you waiting for? You know what she'll think if you stand here like a goddamn coat tree. Oh, God. You couldn't do a thing at sixteen, and you still can't at twice that."

The main portion of his mind held out against it. Inaction was the best action just then. Taylor, it said, neither wanted nor would appreciate any further advance. Whether this was a correct assessment or merely a rationalization for cowardice, Jeffers was incapable of determining. The reality was that he did nothing. The tableau lasted for several hour-long minutes, until the telephone broke in.

Jeffers turned away with what might best be described as reluctant relief. He was able to feel his heartbeat from his stomach to his ears, and any diversion from the conditions that brought it about was welcome. Until he heard the voice on the other end.

"Dr. Jeffers?" Max Fruhling asked. "Good evening."

"Dr. Fruhling? I think so. I mean I think it's a good evening."

From the moment he recognized the voice, he waved frantically for Taylor to join him next to the phone. She came over quickly, all signs of her previous disquiet erased. Her personal portcullis had slammed back into place.

Fruhling chuckled a little at Jeffers's verbal stumble, but then went immediately to his intent. "It seems that I again have news you will find interesting. I have heard some information about your friend."

"My friend? You mean Klaus?"

"If that is the name he gave you, yes. He is the same one who contacted me the day before, and apparently one of the people you met today." Fruhling chuckled again. "I understand that you have put him into a rather agitated state."

If Jeffers could have strangled the old man through the telephone wire he probably would have done so. The amusement Fruhling found in the situation totally escaped him. But, Fruhling did not bother to wait for a coherent reply.

"What I have learned is that his real name is Reinhard Schwerin and, more importantly, he is, or was, an agent for the Stasi."

"What?"

Fruhling seemed to misinterpret Jeffers's exclamation. "Yes, that is a strange development, although I would assume that he has merely hired out to some other interest these days. Nevertheless, you should assume that he is dangerous in the extreme. I would very much like to know who he is working for and what their interest is in your enzyme."

"And what can we expect from you in the way of help?" Jeffers asked. "We certainly could have used some weaponry earlier today."

"Dr. Jeffers, I am, after all, a rather aging professor. I am not in the business of supplying weapons. This is not a conversation that should be continued further over an unsecured line. If you wish to meet privately, maybe some things I know would prove useful. *Guten abend*, Herr Doktor Jeffers." The click followed immediately.

Jeffers hung the phone up with fingers that were acutely numb. "Did you hear that?" he asked.

"Most of it."

"What's a Stasi?"

Taylor's face was grim. "Stasi is short for Staatsicherheitsdienst. That was the old East German secret police, certainly the spiritual if not the lineal descendant of the Gestapo. After East Germany collapsed and the Stasi headquarters were opened up, it turned out they had files on something like one-fifth of the population. Actually, they were drowning in files; it's a good thing they weren't really computerized. All sorts of people, East and West German, were informers for them. You can bet a lot of careers were ruined when all that came to light." Taylor gave a laugh that had no humor in it. "They also armed and trained many of the terrorist organizations and let them use East Germany as a base. I would agree with Fruhling. This Schwerin may be freelancing now, but that doesn't make him any less dangerous. We need to find out who he is working for and we better do it fast."

"How are we going to do that? Fruhling didn't seem to know."

Taylor shrugged. "I'm not sure, but this may be a start." She held up a leather billfold.

"What's that?"

"Karl's wallet. I thought it might turn out to be useful."

She dumped the contents onto the room's desk and began to sort through them. Most of it was prosaic: Dutch guilder and German marks; a Eurocard; a driver's license that gave his home as Leipzig. Tucked among the marks and guilder, however, was a folded slip of paper. Taylor spread it out on the desktop. It read, "Klaus and Dr. H. Schroeder. Neu Mecklenberg. 6 June."

"Hmm," she said. "Where have I seen that name before? Neu Mecklenberg." She snapped her fingers. "I've got it. Remember when I looked through Hochmann's files? Neu Mecklenberg is the town that company, Sachsen Fabrik, is in. Do you have a good road map here?"

"Yes." Jeffers pulled open a drawer. "I bought these downstairs just to be on the safe side."

"Good move." Taylor picked out one that showed all of Germany. After a few minutes she put her finger on a small dot. "Here's Neu Mecklenberg. About due north of Leipzig, which is where Karl was from, apparently. And supposedly Sachsen Fabrik was working on this designer enzyme project also."

"Yeah, and that's where Bieber's hotshot came from. June sixth, that was just three days before Hank left. I don't like this at all, Taylor."

"I don't either."

"All of this really makes me wonder if what is sitting in Bieber's refrigerator is my enzyme."

"I'd wonder about it, too, George, but right now we don't have time. We better figure out how to deal with Schwerin. Don't you think Bieber is Schwerin's boss?"

"Bieber hiring somebody like that?" Jeffers sighed. "I suppose anything is possible, but it doesn't sound too likely. You said the Stasi used to be the East German secret police."

"Correct."

"And if it came out that Bieber had someone from the Stasi working for him?"

"Could be a scandal. The presumption tends to be that if you have those connections, you used to be an informer. Or worse."

"Which would blow Bieber's precious career." Jeffers shook his head. "I can't see him taking that kind of chance. Of course, that assumes Fruhling is telling the truth."

"Always an assumption." For herself, Taylor thought Bieber ought to be the prime suspect, but Jeffers knew the man and she was hesitant to try to overrule him. She was suspicious, not certain. Fortunately, there was another lead. "Making that assumption, though," she said, "I'd bet our answer is in Neu Mecklenberg, maybe with this Dr. H. Schroeder."

"And what do we do now?"

"We take Fruhling up on his offer." Even as she said it, a suspicion that had been building within Taylor since her ride with Wolfgang became a decision in her mind. She could be wrong, she knew, but she was no longer uncertain. The prospect of more action washed away all the doubt and failure of the afternoon. It was like a powerful tonic.

Jeffers was not so sure. In fact, he looked aghast at her answer. "How can you trust him now? You just told me the other day you did not trust him, and look at what happened this afternoon when I went to a meeting he arranged."

"I could point out," Taylor replied, "that you were the one who told me to trust him in the first place."

"Yes, but that was when I thought he was just a crusty old German Herr Professor. You were right, not me."

Taylor threw her head back and laughed, a clear musical laugh. She was feeling much, much better. "You're learning, George. You can't ever trust someone completely, but there are indicators. Fruhling's information and actions have checked out pretty well so far. Anyway, even if they didn't, we need to get to Schwerin or his boss fast before he can get reorganized. And Fruhling may be able to help us do that."

Jeffers might have been willing to argue about trusting Fruhling; he would not argue about going after Schwerin. The thought of the man still being loose in the city made him shiver. On one point, though, he did argue. Taylor had emptied the clip on Karl's gun during the fight at the apartment and had not found a spare on the body. Jeffers had the gun Schwerin had dropped, and he intended to keep it. Whatever the reason for Taylor's inaccuracy, Jeffers decided that he would be happier with their only weapon. He was not totally unfamiliar with guns; he had fired a pistol at a range several years before, but did not bring his experience into the discussion. Taylor, to avoid a rehash of the afternoon, did not object too strenuously, although she did voice the hope she would not regret it. Leaving Jeffers with the pistol, she went up to her room to get her pack. Whatever the result, she did not intend to return to the hotel.

Waiting for her at the elevator, daydreaming, Jeffers was surprised by a light touch on his arm. It was Taylor. "George, I just want you to know I appreciate what you did this afternoon. I really do. I can promise you there will not be any repetitions. Please remember, though, what eventually happened to Achilles."

"I haven't forgotten. I just think we'll have to dodge the 'arrows of outrageous fortune' when they come."

Any reply she might have made was lost when the elevator arrived with a load of tourists, but he could see her smile.

# Chapter 15

## AMSTERDAM, THE NETHERLANDS

TAYLOR CAME TO A sudden stop just outside the hotel. It was abrupt enough that Jeffers almost walked into her. She just stood there in the middle of the sidewalk staring at a patch of sky somewhere over the Centraal Station, quite oblivious to the stream of people forced to walk around her.

"What's the matter, Taylor?"

"Something just struck me. You know, I was planning we would meet Fruhling and then probably switch hotels, just for safety. The more I think about it, though, we should leave for Neu Mecklenberg tonight."

"Tonight?"

"Yes. Think. You said Bieber is unlikely to be Schwerin's boss. If that's true, the logical place to find that person is Neu Mecklenberg. Right now, though, neither Schwerin nor anybody clsc has any reason to believe we know Neu Mecklenberg even exists. If we move now, we can get there before anyone can expect us."

"How? Is there a flight we can catch?"

"I rather doubt it. Besides, I'd rather not take a chance on security."

"You're not going to have Wolfgang drive us are you?"

"No." Taylor turned down the suggestion as though he had made it seriously. "For this, I would rather not have Boy Wonder with us. And there is no way we are going in that car of his. It needs at least a valve job and a new clutch. I can do without a midnight breakdown on the autobahn. No, we need a real car."

The implication slowly filtered into Jeffers's abused head. He recalled how Taylor had obtained an airplane not too long ago. "Taylor, we are not going to steal somebody's car to go to Neu Mecklenberg."

"Of course we are. George, this game is not played by the Marquess of Queensberry's rules. Anyway, aside from buying that suit you're wearing, we haven't done much that *is* legal."

"Sure. If you're going to slit somebody's throat, why should I quibble about a car? Well, Karl deserved what he got; I have no regrets. But we can't rip off some poor guy who has nothing to do with this." His voice rose as he went along.

Taylor threw her hands in the air and did a half pirouette. "For Chrissakes, George," she said with an air of exasperation. "One of these days your scruples are going to hang us."

"Scruples? Yeah, I have 'em, even if you don't. Honestly, Taylor, sometimes I think you have the moral sense of a squid." He leaned back against the brick front of the hotel. The face in front of his was stone. "I was not brought up to be a thief."

"As it happens, neither was I. I had nice upper-middle-class suburban parents, a ten-speed bike and my own stereo. So what? We're here and now and if we don't do what we have to do, we'll fail." Part of Taylor wondered why she was bothering. Justifying herself to people was not something she did often.

"Listen," she said, turning back to Jeffers. "I'm not going to make the mistake of having you do something you can't or won't do. I'm also not foolish enough to compromise our job. There's a little cafe halfway down this block," she pointed until Jeffers nodded. "Get yourself some coffee and food. Just keep a low profile and don't go back to the hotel. Remember, Schwerin is around somewhere. I'll meet Fruhling and I will arrange for a car. Please, just leave it to me."

"So the ends justify the means?" he asked.

Taylor shrugged. "That depends on what the means and ends are."

The cafe looked undistinguished. There were a half-dozen metal tables placed outside on the sidewalk, another dozen or so in the dimly lit interior. Jeffers had planned to sit inside, Taylor's parting warning about Schwerin clear in his mind, but it was just too hot and sticky there. That, he reflected, probably accounted for the fact that none of the inside tables was occupied. There were people at three of the sidewalk tables: a pair a giggly British girls at one, and two parties of locals at the others. Jeffers figured that his clothes, even with their recent, rough wear, looked no worse than those of the other patrons. The proprietor, however, was initially wary when he approached Jeffers, more likely because of the recent violence done to Jeffers's face than the appearance of his suit. A quick flash of bills won the man over. Jeffers's credibility thus established, he was given rolls and a steady supply of coffee. The caffeine made him feel more awake but it did nothing for his mood. His feelings were bruised, as much as his body was tired. It seemed that every time he was beginning to warm to Taylor Redding she did or said something to put him off. He was not even sure why he should care about it. She was, he tried to tell himself, nothing more than a replacement for the man killed in Boston. He knew nothing about her other than the few days they had been together and the stories she had told. How much could one rely on that in judging character?

"Just my luck to run into a female mercenary," he muttered into his coffee cup. "A gorgeous, well-read one, but a mercenary." He shut up when he noticed the owner eyeing him strangely. He just hoped Taylor would not show up with a string of police cars in pursuit.

He was still sitting there staring off into space and totally unaware of the passage of time when a car horn startled him out of his reverie. Looking up, he saw Taylor at the curb, behind the wheel of a jet-black Porsche. Oh, my God, he thought.

"Where did you get that?"

"I borrowed it from Professor Fruhling," she said. "And I do mean borrowed." She smiled at him, a broad genuine smile from her mouth to her eyes. Jeffers smiled in return as he walked to the car. Once again, he felt pretty chipper.

Jeffers slid into the passenger seat gingerly, subconsciously fearing the Porsche would emulate Cinderella's coach at midnight. The seat was of smooth brown leather and firmly padded. It gripped his form like a cushioned socket. Recessed into the dashboard were the usual gauges for speed, rpm, and oil pressure. Air conditioning was absent, but a fancy Alpine stereo above the center console broke the otherwise utilitarian appearance of the interior. With the transmission in neutral, the engine emitted a barely audible growl.

"This is Fruhling's car?" Jeffers was shocked, and the question came out squeaky. He had heard that Fruhling had money, but not, he believed, in the realm the price tag on a car such as this required. "I can't believe he would let you take a car like this. Just like that." He snapped his fingers.

Taylor put the car in gear and moved quickly out into traffic. The engine ran smoothly.

"It was really no problem, George. Max and I had a long talk, in a rather short period of time. We understand each other, if you know what I mean."

Jeffers certainly did not, and said so.

"Let's just say that we have similar views of the world."

"Okay, let's leave it at that." It was not really okay, but Jeffers had learned to recognize when he was not going to get any further information out of Taylor. It would have to do for the present. He looked out the window for a few minutes, watching the city go by.

"You know, as I recall, when we last talked you had different ideas about getting a car. What happened?"

"I changed my mind."

"Why?"

She shrugged, slightly, without taking either hand off the steering wheel. There might also have been a quirky little grin on her face, but seeing her only from the side, he could not be sure of that.

"It mattered what you thought," she said. Her eyes never moved from the road ahead.

It mattered what *I* thought! The phrase echoed around inside his head, touching off little sparkles each time he heard it. From the time they met, Taylor had demonstrated an ability to profoundly shift his mood by word or deed, and this was no exception. The aches and pains were gone, and the world was bright and shiny. Or would have been had the sun been out. After all, it had mattered what he thought. Jeffers felt like letting out a whoop and bringing out champagne.

"I knew you would play it straight in the end," he said, all the while forgetting how depressed he had been at the prospect that she would not. Taylor remained silent and did not look over at him. "I meant that. I think I know what kind of person you are." At least, he hoped he did.

"Do you, George?" When she finally spoke there was an edge in her voice. "Be careful you don't make me out to be something I'm not. I'm just Taylor Redding, that's all. I like what I do, and I do whatever I need to."

Her vehemence surprised him. "Hey," he said, "I was just trying to give you a compliment."

As quickly as it came, the iron in her voice vanished. "I appreciate that, but I wasn't fishing for one. I just am what I am."

Jeffers tried to digest that, and had some difficulty. There was an element of rejection in it. Still, she had said that it mattered what he thought. The one sentence was enough to continue to provide him with an inner glow. It also emboldened him to ask questions that had nagged at him for days.

"Taylor, as long as we are on the subject of what you are, can I ask you a few personal questions?" Her assent was cautious.

"You never told me why you call yourself the world's greatest female adventurer."

"I figured if I just called myself the world's greatest adventurer, you might think I was stretching the truth and not buy it."

Jeffers chuckled. At this stage, he would buy it either way. He scarcely noticed the city giving way to wooded countryside outside.

"So, why do you do it?" he asked.

"Hand you that line, you mean? Because I have good instincts, and they told me I should get involved in your business."

Jeffers noted the oblique move away from a subject that Taylor liked to employ. This time, he decided to press.

"Actually, I was more interested in why you go adventuring in the first place. The mercenary argument I don't buy."

"Why not?"

"Well, would you have split if I did not have this company money to draw on?"

Taylor wanted to lie, but found herself unable. "No," she sighed, "I would not."

"Then why? You've taken chances with your own life the past few days. I wouldn't risk my neck for what I could get out of that box, there isn't *that* much there, and I certainly wouldn't do it for kicks. You can't have any personal stake in this enzyme, and even if you were some crazy super-patriotic agent, I've told you I don't believe it's as important as everybody else seems to think. And Lord only knows it isn't because I am James Bond's twin, 'cause I'm not. So why?" Good speech, George, he thought, with a touch of sarcasm. Once you get your mouth rolling it does not stop. Nice of you to lay out all the reasons for her to dump you out the door. Count yourself lucky if she does not.

She did nothing, immediately. It was as though the road required all of her attention. When she did speak, it was quietly, softly, as though from a distance. Jeffers, who had grown accustomed to hearing her voice cut through any noise, had to strain to hear her.

"I wish you would just leave it, that I am what I am. Because you are not going to understand."

"Try me."

*Cattle die, and kinsmen die,*
*And so one dies one's self;*
*One thing I know that never dies,*
*The fame of a dead man's deeds.*

Taylor's recitation, ending with an emphasis on the last line, seemed to drop into a stillness in the car. For a while, the silence grew.

"That sounds like the Havamal," Jeffers said at last, and saw her nod. The old verse had sent a shiver down his spine. First ancient Chinese generals, and now this. She was right, he did not understand.

"Taylor?"

"Yeah."

"You're strange."

A giggle answered him. "I know," she replied when her mirth died down, "I like it that way."

Taylor's voice was pleasant enough when she said that, her face held only its customary tautness, but she let the sentence end and said nothing afterward. Jeffers, as he often did when he was unsure of the right words, played variation after variation in his head, saying none of them. The silence grew. Taylor seemed completely absorbed by the road, apparently unaware that there was anyone in the passenger seat. Jeffers watched her for a while, then turned, fearing that she might think he was staring for other reasons, and looked out the window. The German border passed, marked only by signs. The language on the billboards changed also, but that was all. Hours passed and Jeffers began to find even his cushioned seat uncomfortable, but Taylor gave no sign that she was interested in stopping. Daylight lasts a long time in the summer in northern Europe, but as dark was falling Taylor was still driving east. Jeffers finally decided that if she was going to ignore him he might as well try to sleep. He cranked the seat back as far as it would go and closed his eyes.

## NEU MECKLENBERG, GERMANY

IT SEEMED ONLY A moment later that he opened his eyes again, but when he did, they were looking at cloudy sunlight. The engine was still running, although the car was not moving. He pulled himself upright in the seat and saw that they were parked on the shoulder of a two-lane road. Taylor was outside staring at a map she had spread out on the hood. Jeffers got out also, feeling quite stiff as he did so. Taylor was leaning on the map as much to keep it from blowing away in the wind as to study it closely. The same wind blew numerous strands of hair that had escaped her braid across her face. She brushed them away with one hand only to have to slap the hand down again quickly when a gust blew the map into the air.

"Good morning," she said without looking up.

"I'm not sure yet," he answered. "My God, did you drive all night?"

"Not all night, George. I pulled over and dozed for a little while. I usually don't sleep a whole lot anyway."

Jeffers shrugged. "Okay by me. Do you know where we are?"

Taylor's smile was a bit rueful. "We should be close to Neu Mecklenberg," she said. "I think I may have taken a wrong turn back there, though."

She pointed down the road behind them. "It's not very well marked around here."

Jeffers gaze followed where she pointed and, as it did, he noticed the countryside for the first time. When it registered, his mouth fell open. "Jesus." The word came out slowly. "Taylor, are we still in Germany?"

"George, I didn't make that much of a wrong turn. We can't be more than ten miles from Neu Mecklenberg. Where did you think we were?"

"I don't know," Jeffers said. He turned slowly from side to side. "I think Tolkien wrote about this place. He called it Mordor."

The road ran through a wooded area or, at least, it had once been wooded. The trees were still there but, despite it being midsummer, they were completely bare, rank upon rank of dead, naked sticks rooted in the ground. A fire could have accounted for their death, but there was not a scorch mark to be seen. There was nothing but lifeless bark. The ground on which they stood was nothing more than brown dirt. There was no grass, no wildflowers. Not far from the side of the road was a lake. Its shores were as dead as the rest of the area. Faint iridescent bands of red and green covered the surface of the water.

"What the hell happened here?"

Taylor shrugged. "I have no idea. The old East Bloc countries weren't real careful about what they dumped or where they dumped it. Actually, that's understating it. They didn't care at all. You dump enough shit on a place, you'll kill everything there. I doubt you could ever find out what's around here. I don't think anyone kept records."

"But you said Neu Mecklenberg is near here. I mean, people live there, don't they?"

"It probably kills them, too." Her voice had gone completely flat. "Look, we're not going to hang around here any longer than it takes to get the information we need. For damn sure I wouldn't live near here. Not if I had any choice at all."

Taylor took one more look at the map. Then she folded it and tossed it behind her seat.

"Well, George, I'm going to go back and take that other road. Even if it doesn't get us to Neu Mecklenberg, we ought to be able to find someone we can ask."

Jeffers was glad to get back into the car. With the door closed and the windows up, he felt there was a barrier between him and whatever had tainted the land outside. Of course, the air in the car was the same as outside, but he tried not to think about that. A mile or two down the road they came out of the dead woods. A little farther on, grass and bushes returned. At the crossroads, Taylor turned north.

The town they reached shortly afterward was little more prepossessing than the countryside. The shells of three Trabis by the side of the road seemed to mark the boundary of Neu Mecklenberg. Drab buildings of concrete or brick lined the western side of the road. On the east ran a chain-link fence topped with coils of razor wire. In the distance, beyond the fence, was the hulk of an industrial plant whose half-dozen brick smokestacks formed the highest point in the vicinity. A gate in the fence barred an access road leading to the plant. The sign at the gate read, SACHSEN FABRIK.

"Well, well," Taylor said, "if it isn't the company from Herr Hochmann's files."

"But wait a minute, Taylor. I thought you said Helvetica-Chemie was going to buy that company because they were working on the designer enzyme technology. This place looks like it was built in the nineteenth century to make steel."

"I don't argue with that," Taylor said.

The plant like the rest of the town was built of dark red brick and concrete, the concrete so weathered and stained it was almost as dark as the brick. The windows they could see were so dirty as to be opaque.

"You know," Taylor said, "unless I've completely lost track of time, this is a workday and that place looks awfully quiet. Still, the name was in the file and Karl presumably met both Schwerin and this Dr. Schroeder in Neu Mecklenberg."

"In Neu Mecklenberg, but not necessarily at this plant," Jeffers pointed out.

"True. Maybe we should look around the town a little bit. We can always come back here."

Two blocks farther on, the fence turned and ran off along the northern border of the plant. Past it, along the road, was a row of identical apartment buildings. Each one was a rectangular prism, six stories high with the long axis along the road. They were built of concrete, now grimy with age and exhaust from the plant. The one nearest the fence showed more than the effects of age and weather and Taylor stopped the car to take a closer look. Part of the building was blackened as though it had recently been set on fire. Almost all the windows had been broken. Most were boarded up but some opened into empty apartments. Broken glass and trash littered the ground around the building even more than around the others.

"Feels like we've been transported to L.A.," Jeffers said. His laughter was forced.

Taylor did not reply. Instead she walked toward the front door. Someone had spray painted two large swastikas along either side of the door. The initials SRG had been sprayed across the top of the door and the wall above it. At the lower edge of one swastika was sprayed, *Nazis raus*. Another hand had partially blotted out the word "Nazis" and written *Fremde* in its place.

"Looks like they had a bit of a riot here," Taylor observed.

"Over what?"

She shrugged. "*Fremde* means foreigners. They may have had foreign workers at the plant. Past tense, I suspect."

"SRG. That's Fruhling's party," Jeffers said.

"Yup."

"Well, that's just great. I've got the old East German secret police on one side and a bunch of Nazis on the other. That's just fuckin' wonderful."

"Just chill a minute, George," Taylor said. She kicked absently at some of the broken glass. "Right now, there's nobody too close on any side, which is the way I'd like to keep it until we know what's going on. Whatever happened here is old news. When we bring the car back we can ask Fruhling for an explanation, but it will have to wait until then."

She led the way back to the car in silence. They both noticed a woman watching them from an upper story window in the building across the street. The slogan, DEUTSCHLAND DEN DEUTSCHEN, had been sprayed across the concrete wall of her building. Taylor gave her a smile, which was not returned, before she got into the car.

The downtown area was not large, nor was it very busy. It did appear older, the streets narrow and given to wandering curves, the buildings more carefully built from the dark brick, with second-floor bay windows and small sculptures at the cornices. The buildings were shabby, though, windows missing and roofs in need of repair. The little sculptures had been reduced to blackened lumps by soot and acid exhaust. There was no telling what they had been. Here and there graffiti had been sprayed, most of it the saying, DEUTSCHLAND DEN DEUTSCHEN.

"I don't think we're going to find a tourist office in this town."

That brought a chuckle from Jeffers. "You know, I've heard people say that about Cleveland, too."

"Yeah, well, they're right about that, aren't they?"

Jeffers chuckled again. "Okay, chief. I think I've got it back under control. Who do we tackle first? The Commies or the Nazis?"

"We tackle coffee first." Taylor pointed at a shop across the street.

There was no one inside except the proprietor and a girl at the cash register who was reading a newspaper. Taylor sat down and ordered two coffees. When he brought them, she stopped him before he could leave.

"Excuse me," she said, "I'm looking for a Dr. H. Schroeder. Do you know of him or where I might find someone who does?"

"Dr. Schroeder? You should find him at the clinic. Do you know where that is?"

"No."

"Just follow this road through town. The clinic is on the right just as you leave town."

"And should I just ask for him?"

"I would think so. He runs it."

"Ah, of course. *Danke schön.*"

*"Bitte."*

When she translated the conversation, Jeffers asked, "How the hell did you know he would know?"

"I didn't, but it's no surprise. I just had to assume the name was real. A town like this isn't going to have a lot of doctors. I think we should see what Dr. Schroeder's specialty is."

The clinic was where the shopkeeper had indicated it would be. It was a two-story structure set hard by the road. A fairly steady flow of people was entering and leaving, the most activity they had seen at any place in town. A roster of names inside the main entrance listed, "DR. MED. HEINRICH SCHROEDER, CHEF ARTZT."

"That's our boy," Taylor said. "Although I confess I'm puzzled how a doc running a small town clinic comes to be mixed up in something like this. You're sure this enzyme of yours doesn't cure low back pain or chronic halitosis or some such?"

"Taylor, at this point, for all I know it may cure PMS. I mean, what the hell do I know? I'm only the guy who designed it."

"Tsk, tsk. Come on, George, we better get it in gear here." Their conversation in English was drawing odd looks from people unaccustomed to hearing a foreign language.

"I'm coming," he said as he walked after her. "What are we going to do?"

"I'm not sure yet. Probably just play it by ear as we go. Just follow my lead, okay?"

"Sure," said Jeffers, who was trying to sound a lot more certain than he felt.

Dr. Schroeder's office was marked only by a plastic nameplate next to an otherwise plain wooden door. Beyond the door was an outer office occupied by a secretary who told them that Dr. Schroeder was not in the office. Did they, she wanted to know, have an appointment?

"No," Taylor answered, "but this is rather important. We don't mind waiting."

The secretary did not offer them seats. Instead she wanted to know if she could call Dr. Schroeder in the outpatient clinic and tell him what this was about.

Taylor put her hands on the edge of the desk and leaned forward so that she loomed right over the secretary's head. "I think that is an excellent idea. Please tell Dr. Schroeder that I am Charlotte Becker from Kiel. I'm a freelance writer, mostly for American magazines, but I've sold to *Der Spiegel* recently. My friend," she indicated Jeffers with a turn of her head, "is George Anderson of *Time* magazine from America. Please ask *Herr Doktor* Schroeder if he can spend a little time with us."

The secretary decided that a visit from two journalists was worth interrupting the doctor. Then, becoming friendlier as the implications sank in, she asked if they would like tea, which Taylor declined. The secretary also wanted to know if there would be a photographer. Not this visit, Taylor told her.

The first notice of Dr. Schroeder's arrival was his voice booming from the vicinity of the outer door. "Katrina, why am I interrupted for these reporters? I don't have time for this."

Dr. Heinrich Schroeder proved to be a middle-aged man who did not appear to have aged well. Thin white hair did not keep much of his scalp hidden. It flopped this way and that as though combing it would be futile. He had a broad, florid face with a sharp nose and bright blue eyes. A bad limp made it seem like he rolled from side to side as he walked. He stopped what he was saying when he saw Taylor and Jeffers but the glare he gave them said more of the same.

"We don't plan on taking too much of your time, *Herr Doktor*," Taylor said. "I'm sorry if today is exceptionally busy."

"Today is not exceptionally busy," Schroeder snapped. "It's normal. But when they opened the border in 1989, three-quarters of my staff left for the West. The only ones who came back had discovered they didn't like having to work hard to keep their jobs and they are not the ones I need. All I get from the West are stupid reporters who want to write about *Rechtsradikalismus* and the riots, but that doesn't help take care of the people who've been hurt. That's what you want, isn't it? I don't have time for it."

"No," said Taylor.

"Eh?" Schroeder stopped with a surprised look on his face. The answer appeared to have short circuited his diatribe. "What do you want, then?" he asked after a pause.

"May we talk inside?" Taylor indicated the inner office door.

"Of course."

Once they were seated with the door closed, Taylor asked, "Can we continue this in English? My colleague does not speak German."

"I speak English, although it is, I'm afraid, ah, what is the word?"

"Rusty?" Taylor suggested.

"*Genau.*" Schroeder let out a sigh and clasped his hands across his stomach. Then he shifted back to English. "Very well. You have interrupted my clinic but it's not to write about the riots. What is it then, that brings such famous journalists to Neu Mecklenberg?"

"We were told that you were involved in the development of this new technology called designer enzymes and we wanted to ask you about it. We were not aware there was such interest in any riots here, although we saw signs of it when we drove in."

Schroeder's face frowned. "I have not the slightest idea what you are talking about."

"Maybe the term is different here," Jeffers broke in. "Designer enzymes are artificial enzymes, designed to catalyze specific chemical reactions. Scientists expect them to be useful in making some kinds of drugs and so forth." He had difficulty getting the next sentence out as he tried to avoid saying Taylor's real name. "We were astonished to hear that a major breakthrough had been made in Neu Mecklenberg."

"Whatever you are talking about, you are in the wrong place. I run a clinic. I make no experiments and no discoveries."

"We were told," Taylor said, "that the work was done at Sachsen Fabrik and that we should speak to Dr. H. Schroeder in Neu Mecklenberg. Are you saying this is wrong?"

At her question, Schroeder smiled, but it was the rueful smile of a man who has indeed wasted his time. "Not entirely wrong," he said. "My younger brother, Helmut Schroeder, is the general manager of Sachsen Fabrik. He is also Dr. H. Schroeder, although his doctorate is in chemistry. He has become quite particular about his title of late, has my brother. Still, if you simply ask for Herr Dr. H. Schroeder in Neu Mecklenberg, you will most likely be directed to me."

"There's another Dr. H. Schroeder over at Sachsen Fabrik?"

"Yes."

Taylor looked across the room at Jeffers. "I'll be damned." She looked back at Schroeder. "Can you tell us anything about what your brother's company is doing?"

"Not really. I'm twelve years older than he is and we were never really close. I know that an investor group from the West bought the company from the *Treuhandanstalt* a year or so ago. I'm not even really sure of the date. I didn't know they were doing any work with any new technology. I doubt the *Treuhand* knew either. I'm told it went cheap. Certainly any work they are doing has not kept them very busy. If it had, we might not have had riots here."

"I see," Taylor said. "We would still like to talk to your brother about it. Do you think we can get in to see him?"

"I should think so," Schroeder said dryly. "As I said, they are not too busy over there these days." He picked up the telephone and dialed. A short conversation in rapid-fire German ensued. After he hung up, he looked back at them. "I spoke with Gunther Goetz, my brother's assistant. I'm afraid my brother is out of town until tomorrow evening. I told Goetz, however, who you were and what you wanted. If you stop by the plant around seven-thirty or eight o'clock tomorrow evening, he'll be there. You should go to the office entrance; it will be open."

"Good enough. We'll see him tomorrow then," Jeffers said. "Maybe you could show us around your clinic today, though. I would like to see how you are getting your work done here."

Taylor shot him a look that said she had not been interested in spending time in the clinic. Schroeder, however, beamed at the suggestion. None of the previous journalists had cared to see more of the clinic than was nec-essary to set up the photographer. Schroeder took them to his outpatient clinic, then up to the inpatient wards, along the way telling them how many of the town's children had asthma, how many had skin problems, how many miscarriages there were, how many people had cancer. Sachsen Fabrik was the cause of most of it, Schroeder said more than once. Jeffers found the recitation fascinating, if horrifying. Along the way they stopped by the room of one of the men injured in the riots.

"Turkish," Schroeder said, as if that explained the man's injuries. Then he rattled off an account of the man's status with fine clinical de-tachment. He was in a private room, Schroeder explained, to avoid any trouble on the wards. Jeffers was so intent on Schroeder's commentary that he did not notice Taylor, who marched along tight-lipped and grim-faced.

After lunch, eaten with Schroeder in his office, Taylor led the way back to the Porsche. She dropped into the driver's seat with a grunt and tilted her head back against the headrest.

"Taylor, are you okay?" Jeffers hung in the open door on the other side, his arms draped over the roof.

"I'm fine. Why should anything be wrong?"

"I don't know. You hardly ate anything at lunch. The food wasn't that bad."

"George, I'm allowed to be not-hungry every now and then. Now stop pretending to be a Jewish mother and get in the car."

Jeffers shrugged and did as he was told. "Okay. Where to?"

"Back to the Sachsen Fabrik plant, I think."

"Why? The other Schroeder won't be back until tomorrow."

"I know. I'd like to look around a bit."

"You think they'll let us?"

"For all the activity we saw the first time past, I wonder if anybody will notice."

The gate in the fence surrounding the plant stood open when they returned. It was, as far as they could tell, unattended. Taylor drove the car to a small lot and parked it. Only two other cars and a scattering of bicycles shared the area with them. Looking past the lot, there was a door set into the brick wall to their right with a sign reading OFFICES hung over it. Taylor assumed that was the entrance Schroeder had suggested they use tomorrow.

"Come on George, let's take a stroll." Taylor started away from the entrance, headed for the side of the building. Jeffers scrambled to catch up.

"Hey, Taylor," he said. "I've got a feeling we're not supposed to be walking around here."

"You're probably right, George, but nobody has said anything different. If we run into anybody, well, hey, honest mistake."

"Yeah. I hope they see it that way," Jeffers muttered, but he stayed with her.

The side and back of the plant was, if anything, more of a mess than the front. Overturned and rusted metal drums were strewn about the grounds. They were empty, but there was no way of knowing if they had been that way when they were dumped. Against one wall, a pyramid of drums had been stacked. Presumably, some of them were leaking because a fan of wet earth reached out from the pyramid. It collected in a little gully which joined a bigger gully and then vanished into a drainpipe. There was an odor in the air that Jeffers identified as benzene, along with others he could not place.

"Christ," he said. "One match and I bet you'd have a hell of a fireworks display."

"Not to mention a big hole in the ground." Taylor shook her head. "Somehow, this doesn't look like a hot biotech company to me."

"Me neither. I still haven't seen anyone here. What are you thinking, Taylor?"

"I'm wondering about Fruhling again. If the enzyme is valuable and the SRG needs money to operate, well, maybe there's a motive."

Jeffers shifted uncomfortably. "Dammit, I thought you had decided he was okay. Anyway, if he's our enemy, why did he lend you his car?"

"I don't know. Maybe to speed us off on a wild-goose chase. I can't square in my mind someone like Fruhling working with an ex-Stasi agent like Schwerin either, but it's only Fruhling's word that Schwerin was Stasi."

The wind picked up, strengthening the chemical stench around them. Taylor wrinkled her nose in disgust.

"George, I'm sorry I suggested coming out here. Let's go back."

"And do what?"

"Wait for tomorrow. I still want to hear what Dr. Schroeder has to say."

Back at the main entrance there was a man standing by the Porsche. He was a slim man of perhaps forty years, wearing a dark suit. He was busy jotting something in a notebook but looked up as they approached.

"This is your car, I assume. Would you mind telling me who you are and why you are here?" His voice was soft but insistent.

"I am Becker," Taylor said. "My colleague is George Anderson. We are both journalists. Do you speak English? Herr Anderson is American."

"English is not a problem," he said. "You would be the two journalists Schroeder called about. I thought you were told to come tomorrow evening."

"We were told that Dr. Schroeder of Sachsen Fabrik would see us tomorrow," Taylor said. "We thought we would come to look at the plant in advance. I don't believe I know your name."

"I am Goetz," he said. Both of them recalled that name from the conversation with Schroeder at the clinic. "You should not be walking around here by yourselves," he continued. "It's not safe."

"I can believe that," Jeffers muttered, which brought a sharp look from Goetz.

Goetz turned back to the car and kicked one of the front tires. "I guess one of you is a very successful journalist," he said.

"I can generally sell my work," Taylor said smoothly, "which is more than can be said for some."

Goetz stiffened at the remark and his face was not pleasant when he turned back to face them. "I suggest you come back tomorrow to see Dr.

Schroeder. This plant is off-limits to unescorted visitors. Alternatively, of course, I can call the police."

"Not necessary," Taylor said. "We were just leaving."

"Well," she said as they drove out through the gate, "this Schroeder got himself a real pleasant fellow for an assistant. I wonder what you do to get help like that? Call Rent-A-Jerk maybe?"

"Oh, come on, Taylor. Give the man a break. We were trespassing, you know."

"A minor point," she replied. "You noted, though, how he reacted when I talked about selling my work? I was just trying to say something reasonable—after all, this is a fancy car for a young journalist—but he looked like he'd been sucker-punched. I'll bet this place doesn't sell much of anything anymore. I'm surprised the *Treuhand* found anybody to buy it, cheap or not."

"Taylor, that's the second time I've heard that word and I have no idea what it means. What is the *Treuhand?*"

"Oh, sorry. The *Treuhandanstalt* is sort of like a German version of the Resolution Trust Company. In the States the RTC sells off assets of dead banks, right?" Jeffers nodded. "Well, the *Treuhandanstalt* is responsible for selling off the old East German industries. It's really quite a problem. Most of them have lots of people on the payroll but, like here, don't make anything anyone wants to buy. Poor quality or obsolete usually. And it's politically difficult to shut them down and have people lose their jobs."

"You mean because of the riots."

"That's part of it. As I recall, the first director of the *Treuhand* was assassinated. It makes it a tough sell to unload these places."

"I'll bet." Jeffers was silent for a moment. "Taylor, what if somebody knew that a place like this was about to get something valuable, like a patent on the designer enzyme technology?"

She grinned at him as though she were a teacher whose prize pupil had just won a contest. "A most interesting thought, Dr. Jeffers, and one that's been going through my mind too. If a hypothetical someone knew that, why he'd buy the place for a song. The *Treuhandanstalt* would probably be so happy to have a sucker they wouldn't look too closely. When the patent is filed, this plant becomes worth real money."

"Jesus, maybe it really is Fruhling."

"Maybe," she said, "but are you forgetting your friend Dr. Bieber? He says he has a designer enzyme in his freezer and he's got a direct connection to this company."

Jeffers's face twisted into a grimace. "Bieber doesn't have the balls. He just doesn't have the balls for something like this. I know what he says he's got in his freezer, but, like I said before, I'm not sure I buy that either. Not without proof."

"Okay." Taylor left the discussion there. A few minutes later she pulled the car over to the side of the road and stopped.

"Taylor," Jeffers began a few minutes later, "what are you doing?"

"Aren't you curious?" she asked.

"Curious about what?" Jeffers's reply was wary. "When you get more cryptic than usual, I get nervous."

The grin on Taylor's face seemed justification enough for his wariness. Then she said, "Curious about how this relic of a plant has cracked a major problem in biotechnology. Curious about why Goetz was so insistent about booting us out. Sure, we were trespassing, but you wouldn't act that way about a mountain of scrap metal and used chemicals. Aren't you curious about what it is that he doesn't want us to see?"

"Of course I'm curious," Jeffers said. "I thought that's why we were going to come back to see Schroeder tomorrow."

"Right. I said that, too. Do you think he'll tell us what's going on?"

Jeffers searched her face before he answered and saw nothing except, maybe, amusement. "Probably not," he said. "At least, we won't know if he's telling the truth."

"Precisely. I think we owe it to ourselves to get a good look at the inside of this place before we see him."

"What! Taylor, we just got thrown out of there. You're the one who said we should wait until tomorrow."

"I know. But something about this bothers me. Don't laugh, George, I do have, well, sort of a sixth sense for trouble."

"Believe me, Taylor, I'm not laughing."

Under other circumstances, he might have enjoyed the puzzled look on her face.

# Chapter 16

## NEU MECKLENBERG, GERMANY

It was after midnight when they returned to the plant. This time Taylor parked Fruhling's car by the burned-out apartment building in a spot that was invisible from the street. Taylor hefted a black flashlight that had been packed with the Porsche's road-emergency kit. Jeffers did not need her to say anything to know that she was eager to go. They walked from the building to the main gate of the Sachsen Fabrik plant. It was still open.

"Great security," Jeffers muttered.

"From what I saw when we were here earlier," Taylor said, "it didn't look like this gate had been moved in years. Just keep your eyes open, though. I'm sure our friend Goetz has gone to bed by now and I'd hate it if anybody here felt they had to wake him."

They hiked up the road to the parking lot, the dark bulk of the old plant looming large in front of them. It brought to Jeffers's mind fantasies of a haunted castle, with turrets and towers peopled only by ghosts or vampires. He was not sure, though, whether he would prefer those to the security detail that was more likely waiting for them. Of course, he told himself, there was not much evidence of any kind of security around the plant, not during the day and not now either. The road was completely unlit, as was the parking lot when they reached it. There seemed to be no lights in the plant ahead. With the moon hidden by clouds, anything that was not right in front of them was invisible.

When they reached the building Taylor turned left, away from the direction of the door to the offices. A few minutes' walk brought them to an area that looked like a loading dock. Four huge metal doors were set into the side of the building, all closed. On the far side of the dock, Taylor stopped by a small door, one that looked as though it was intended for people. She flicked the light on for just long enough to see a sign for the shipping department by the door.

"Well?" she asked.

"Do you think it's alarmed?"

Taylor shrugged. "It's possible. Look at the size of this place, though. I can't believe they retrofitted every door and window in this place with an alarm. The offices probably are alarmed but I'm betting this area isn't. Anyway, there's one sure way to find out."

Taylor fished a small tool from a belt pouch. She fitted one end of it into the lock, then jiggled it a few times. The door swung inward with a creak that was loud enough for an alarm all by itself. They drew back into the shadows at that, both holding their breaths. No sound of running feet followed. There was no siren.

"So far so good," Jeffers said. Taylor held a finger up in front of her lips, then waved him on with her other hand.

The shipping office on the other side of the door was empty. The flashlight picked out a few papers on the desk but nothing to even show that the area was in regular use anymore. A corridor beyond led them into the main area of the old plant. The interior was cavernous, partially filled with huge machinery that neither Taylor nor Jeffers recognized. Almost all of it looked old, with patches of rust and caked grease visible in the flashlight beam. None of it was in operation, although they could not guess if it was shut down for the night or forever. No one else seemed to be around.

They wandered among the old machinery for a while until they turned into a corridor that ended ahead of them in a door that showed light underneath it.

"Somebody here?" Jeffers whispered.

"Maybe." The flashlight was already out.

They crept closer to the door, Taylor, it seemed, effortlessly silent while Jeffers was convinced that his footsteps were audible out in the parking lot. Jeffers wished he had never agreed to come back to the plant. It was too risky. Someone would see them. There would be a camera up in the dim rafters. Whatever they were looking for would surely be alarmed and heavily guarded. He was going to spend the next ten years in a German jail, assuming that Goetz didn't simply shoot him and bury him in the ooze out back. The pounding of his heart rang in his chest and his head. It made it even more difficult to concentrate on walking without giving off echoes in every direction.

The door ahead was set in the far wall of a crossing hall. They had almost reached it when a loud snort came from that hall on the righthand side. The sound shocked both of them into immobility. The guard dog leading a submachine gun–armed guard that Jeffers imagined did not, however, materialize. He looked back at Taylor and saw a knife in her hand. Jeffers swallowed hard. Where was the gun he had taken from Schwerin? Back in the car, of course. Mentally, he cursed himself for a fool. A second snort followed the first.

Taylor moved ahead, keeping as close to the machinery at the side of the corridor as possible. Jeffers followed, the gun he did not have still in his mind. As they approached the intersection, they could see that a security office had been built in the cross corridor. It backed up into an alcove just past the door showing the light, and then projected forward into the corridor. The three sides of the office that stuck out into the corridor had glass walls that went up to a height of ten feet. Behind the glass, they could see a desk that stood in front of a bank of television screens attached to the back wall. No one was visible in the office but, as another snort made clear, that was where the noise was coming from. On the far side of the office, they could see an open door. There was no cover between them and that door, but there was no one in the office to see them, or so it seemed.

Without a word Taylor rushed for the door to the office, leaving Jeffers to wonder if he should follow. When she reached it, she stopped and Jeffers could see her relax. Then she gave a small hand signal for him to join her. Inside the office there was a still form lying on the floor. It was a man in some sort of uniform.

As Taylor bent over him he let out a loud snore, which was the noise they had heard out in the corridor. Along with the noise came a smell that forced Taylor back upright. She had been to breweries that were less pungent. The man was dead drunk. An empty vodka bottle on the floor next to him and another standing in an open desk drawer corroborated that impression. Jeffers looked at Taylor's knife and wondered if the man's binge had been luckier for him than for them.

Taylor, meanwhile, wrinkled her nose and tried to ignore the smell to concentrate on the television screens at the back of the room. They showed a series of lighted hallways, all empty. Presumably the area under surveillance was behind the door to the left as those hallways resembled nothing they had passed. Taylor studied the controls under the screens for a moment. Then she hit two buttons. When she hit the first one, all the screens went dark. The second was followed by an audible click from the door outside the office. Taylor walked over to it and tugged gently. It opened smoothly, without a sound.

The area on the other side of the door looked modern. A false ceiling of acoustic tile had been dropped from the high rafters of the factory making the halls indistinguishable from a standard office building. Fluorescent lights made the halls, with their white walls, impossibly bright compared to the gloom on the other side of the wall. Dark rooms, at intervals, opened onto the halls.

"Well, I wonder what we've got here?" Taylor asked, keeping her voice to a whisper.

"I have no idea," Jeffers said. "Do you think it's safe coming in here and leaving him out there?"

Taylor shrugged. "I doubt he's going to wake up unless we do something stupid. Even if he does, I doubt he'll be good for much. If I do something about him, though, there goes any chance of getting out without them knowing tomorrow that someone was in here. It's worth the chance, I think, to take a quick look around."

The first four rooms proved to be laboratories. They also looked modern. Jeffers catalogued the equipment as they went. There were laminar airflow hoods with stacks of tissue culture flasks, incubators with more flasks inside them, liquid chromatographs on benches and, in one room, a machine that made short lengths of DNA. Each of the laboratories also had shelves full of more mundane glassware and reagents. Several computers sat on desks in each of the rooms. When Jeffers looked at them, he saw they were the type of PC that could be ordered through the mail from a variety of clone makers.

"This doesn't make sense," Jeffers muttered.

"What do you mean?"

"These labs, they've been stocked with the kind of equipment you would need for genetic engineering. I mean, the stuff is here, mostly, to make designer enzymes. But look," his arm swept around the hall. "All the doors are open. Normally you want an air pressure difference between the lab and the corridor, either to prevent outside organisms from contaminating your stocks or, if what you've got is dangerous, to keep it in the lab. Those flow hoods, you can tell from the HVAC gauges they're not hooked up." The contempt in his voice grew with each sentence. "They've got flasks in the hoods, but you can't do tissue culture with the hoods just sitting there. Same thing here," he tapped a tall gray gas cylinder next to an incubator. "The $CO_2$ isn't turned on. And all these computers. There isn't anything I've seen with the muscle to do protein design work."

"Maybe we should check the rest of the rooms," Taylor suggested.

"Okay. I just don't want to take too long. The sooner we're out of here, the better I'll like it."

"Just a quick look," Taylor said.

It turned out to be a very quick look as the rest of the rooms were empty.

They returned to the entrance while Jeffers wondered if the door would open from their side without someone to push the button in the guard's office. He did not voice the fear to Taylor, though, because he was becoming concerned that he had sounded anxious too many times already. The door would either open or it would not. His obsessing about it was not going to affect the result one bit. In fact, it opened without any difficulty. Taylor looked as though she had never given the question a thought. Jeffers just hoped that the thoughts that had been in his head had not also been evident on his face.

Outside, the drunken guard continued to snore loudly. Taylor walked back to the office and leaned over the guard to turn the camera back on. The switch that turned them off, however, did not turn them back on. She hesitated a moment, then decided to leave. It was possible, even likely, she hoped, that the turned-off cameras would be attributed to the drunk. Certainly, if he awoke before his relief arrived, he would say nothing. It was better, she told herself, to bet on that than to keep punching buttons. She had probably already had her evening's share of good luck. Don't push it too far, Redding, she told herself.

They were silent all the way back through the plant and down the road to where they had left the car. There was no sign it had been disturbed when they reached it. Only when they were inside did Taylor turn to Jeffers and ask, "You're saying the place is a fake, aren't you?"

"Absolutely." He tried to stifle a yawn with his fist. "The place looks like a designer enzyme production lab ought to look, at least if you don't look too closely, but there's no way anything has been produced, or even designed, in there. There's just no way. What I don't see, though, is how this all fits together. I mean, what's the point of setting up all that equipment if you're not going to use it?"

"Potemkin village," Taylor said.

"What?"

"Years ago, in imperial Russia, the czar would go out occasionally to visit peasant villages to see how the people were doing. One of his ministers would go ahead and make sure the houses on the route were fixed up and that the people there had good clothes and food so that when the czar got there, it looked like life was dandy. Same principle here. Could this rig fool Hochmann into buying the place?"

Jeffers started to say, "Of course not," then took it back quickly. He was silent for a few minutes while Taylor started driving. "Well," he said slowly, "you could always say the heavy computer work was done elsewhere. And all the hookups are there. You could turn everything on for a visitor. It probably wouldn't fool somebody like Teuschlein, but I got the impression he doesn't get that much input into the business deals. The business types, no, they wouldn't know." Herb came to mind. "And, if you actually *had* an artificial enzyme, well nobody might look too closely. Teuschlein would never see the place. It wouldn't be necessary." He almost spit that last word. Blalock had once said that to a stock analyst who had been curious about what Jeffers's lab looked like.

"Hmm." Taylor went a few more miles before she said anything else. "That explains the lack of security," she said. "There's really nothing to guard and you're probably better off without a whole bunch of drunken sods who're going to babble about how they're all guarding this lab where nothing goes on. Tell me though, to pull this off, you would have to have the enzyme. Right?"

"Absolutely. You need the enzyme and the patent to keep people from really inspecting the labs. Damn!"

"My sentiments exactly. I think we ought to keep our evening appointment with Dr. Schroeder tomorrow," she said. "I'd say we'll have some rather pointed questions for him. It ought to make for an interesting conversation."

"Where are you going now?" Jeffers yawned again and was too late to hide it.

"Leipzig," she answered. "This car is too conspicuous for a town like Neu Mecklenberg. We're stuck killing time until tomorrow and, right now, I'd feel a lot better if I could be sure where Schwerin is or who else he might talk to."

Twilight was just beginning the next day when they drove back to the plant. As much as he wanted to confront Schroeder about the enzyme, Jeffers was not happy with going to Sachsen Fabrik again. It seemed all too likely to him that the previous night's intrusion had been discovered and that Schroeder would have used the intervening hours to either flee or gather a group of thugs to serve as a reception committee. Jeffers had a mental image he could not shake of walking into the plant to find a squad of stormtroopers with machine guns waiting for him. At least, this time he was not going to leave the gun in the car. He made a show before they left for the plant of pulling out the pistol he had taken from Schwerin and sticking it in his waistband.

"If there really is a squad waiting for us, George, I don't think that's going to do a lot of good."

"Well, it's better than nothing," he muttered. "What do you suggest?"

"Let's wait and see what happens. I doubt that *Herr Doktor* Schroeder wants to call any more attention to himself than is absolutely necessary."

"Well, fine," Jeffers said, "but I'm still taking the gun."

The lights were on in the office area of the plant, and the entrance, as Schroeder had promised, was open. Sachsen Fabrik was as still as the night before. Only a few lights showed in the manufacturing areas. When they passed a doorway leading from the office section to the manufacturing floor, it was like looking into a dark cave. No one came to meet them, so they walked along, checking the nameplates on the doors as they went. Although the corridor lights were on, the offices were dark.

"Dollars to doughnuts he's split," Jeffers said. Taylor shushed him with a wave of her hand.

Just then there was a thump and a shuffling noise around a corner ahead of them in the general direction of Schroeder's office. "Well," Taylor said softly, "I think I'll take you up on the doughnuts."

Schroeder's door was not quite shut in its frame. Light showed through the narrow opening. A light rap on the door was followed by what might have been a reply from inside, but the words could not be discerned. Taylor looked at Jeffers and shrugged. He put his hand on the grip of his pistol as she pushed the door completely open.

Schroeder was in his chair, the upper part of his body slumped across the desk. He did not move as they came in. There was no question of who it was. The facial resemblance to his brother at the clinic was obvious.

"Oh, shit!" tore out of Jeffers.

Both of them were at the desk in an instant. They tilted his body back into the chair to see what had happened to him. His muscles were slack, offering no resistance; blood rolled out of his mouth to drip off his chin. Taylor pushed two fingers against his neck, then cursed quietly.

"No pulse," she said.

There was a sensation building in Jeffers that made him wonder whether he was going to vomit or have diarrhea first. "He's dead?" Jeffer's voice seemed to squeak as the words came out.

"That's usually what no pulse means," Taylor said dryly.

Jeffers gulped. "Suicide?" he asked.

"Not a chance." She pulled open Schroeder's shirt to reveal a wound in his chest. "That's a knife wound. There's no way he did that to himself. Anyway, there's no weapon here."

"What's this?" Jeffers had turned to poke around the desk as a way of avoiding looking at the body. What he found was a bloodstained sheet of paper with handwriting that stopped halfway down the page.

Taylor plucked it from his hand being careful not to put her fingers on the bloodstains. "It's a letter to some customer of his. Former customer, I guess, because it refers to problems over a shipment that Sachsen Fabrik never delivered. I guess he was writing it when whoever killed him showed up, but it has nothing to do with us that I can see."

She tossed it aside and joined him at the desk. "Maybe there's something else here that's worth a look."

Jeffers looked at the papers spread out across the desk with despair. Everything was in German. Taylor might be able to go through all of it to find something useful, but he was helpless. That was when his eyes fell on a key lying on top of a stack of papers. A small white tag was attached to it by a string.

"What about this?"

Taylor took the key from him and looked at the tag. "That's curious," she said. "It's a key to his brother's office."

"Why do you think it's curious? Why wouldn't he have a key to his brother's office?"

"Because." Taylor tried to put her thoughts in order. "His brother said they weren't close. And there's a tag on it, for Chrissakes. Why would he need to put a tag on the key to his brother's office unless he almost never used it? And if he almost never used it, why would it be on top of these papers? There has to be something in his brother's office that has to do with what's going on at this plant. I'd bet on that."

Behind them, the dead body of Helmut Schroeder was slipping forward in the chair. At about the same time Taylor reached her conclusion, the body reached the point where the chair could no longer hold it. It fell off, landing on the floor with a thud while tipping the chair over as well. At the clatter behind him, Jeffers jumped nearly a foot in the air. When he saw the cause of the noise, he let out a shaky laugh.

"Oh, hell, that's all it was." He said it much too loudly.

"Shh."

"What?"

"Right after the body fell, there was a noise out there." She indicated the main office. "Sounded like a door being opened and some footsteps."

"There was nobody out there when we came in," Jeffers protested. He did not want anybody to be out there.

"Somebody killed him fairly recently." Taylor was at the door to Schroeder's private office, peering outside. "I think we'd better have a look. Come on, follow me."

She slipped through the door without making a sound. Jeffers, however, was rooted where he stood. If there was a killer out there, going out to find him did not seem like a good idea. Then, he realized that Taylor had already gone. Dammit, dammit, dammit was all he could hear in his head. He did not want to go out there, but she was expecting him to watch her back. He could hardly stay where he was. Once again, she had maneuvered him into doing something crazy.

"Well, I can't leave her," he muttered.

With his heart pounding so hard he could feel it in the top of his head, he edged out of the office. It was quiet out there, absolutely still. Into the silence came the sound of footsteps in the manufacturing area. Unbidden, a vision popped into his head of Taylor walking along with someone coming up behind to stab her in the back. It would be his fault.

"I'm coming Taylor," he shouted and ran out of the office area.

There was not much light out where the machinery was, enough to see not to trip but not much else. The machines cast even deeper pools of shadow around them, easily wide enough to hide a dozen men in places. Jeffers paid no heed. He was running full speed, trying to see where Taylor was. The pistol, supported only by his belt, was not properly settled there. The possibilities of it falling out as he ran or, worse, of shooting himself in the groin seemed very real, enough so that he tried to reposition the gun without breaking stride. In doing so he failed to watch his footing. Jeffers skidded on some oil left on the floor and went down, sliding on his knees. When he looked up, he was facing back the way he had come. A figure detached itself from the shadow back there. Taylor? No. He realized it was a man's form starting toward him. Toward him! With a curse, he jumped to his feet. The other stopped, uncertain, as though he had not expected to see Jeffers pop up so quickly after the fall. There was just enough light for Jeffers to recognize him as Klaus, or rather, Schwerin. It was also enough light for Schwerin to recognize Jeffers. The gun! the gun! The command ran through Jeffers's mind, but hand and brain were tuned to separate channels. While Jeffers struggled with himself, Schwerin's hand moved to reach under his coat. My God, Jeffers thought, I'll stand here like an idiot while he shoots me. With a convulsive grab, he yanked the pistol out from his waistband. Schwerin saw the gun come up and never completed his own movement. Instead he darted down a side corridor amongst the machinery. Jeffers was left to curse himself for his inaction. He should have had Schwerin right then, and he knew it.

On the other side of that row of machinery, Taylor heard Jeffers fall and then the sound of running feet. Closed switchblade in hand, she hurried toward the noise, arriving just in time to see Schwerin dart across the corridor and disappear into a forest of large vats. Taylor flipped the blade open when she reached the place Schwerin had been last visible. The area ahead was almost completely dark; the vats and the machinery above them blocked most of what little light there was. As she moved into the darkness, she dropped her bandana on the floor outside. With luck, she thought, Jeffers was all right and would notice it when he came past.

Maybe it was a sixth sense that warned her first, but the corner of her eye caught a movement in the dimness. Her free hand whipped up in a block against a threat that was more felt that seen. The edge of her hand connected with a bony wrist. The impact was followed immediately by a flash of light and a blast that almost drowned out Schwerin's curse. His gun flew from a hand whose fingers had gone temporarily numb. It skittered across the floor under the base of a vat and was lost in the darkness. Schwerin had planned an ambush there to take her prisoner, hoping to use the poor lighting as a cloak. Taylor counted herself lucky that he had moved in to put the gun right on her, almost in her ear, in fact. Had he kept it beyond arm's reach, she would have been helpless. She spent no time dwelling on how close a call it had been. Instead, she whirled to meet him, knife out ahead of her. At the sight of her knife, Schwerin backpedaled quickly. He gave a quick shake to his arm, and suddenly there was a knife in his hand too.

They circled slowly, moving away from the entrance, each knife point held on line with its target. Taylor could see that Schwerin held his blade stiffly, and when a band of light from above struck his face a sheen of sweat was visible. He had horribly underestimated this woman before, and his determination not to do so again interfered with his concentration. By contrast, Taylor moved in a relaxed half crouch. Her blade was constantly in motion, although the point never left its target, the handle held in a soft grip, thumb on top. Eventually, she thought, there will be an opening.

It came suddenly. Either imagining an opening, or losing his patience, Schwerin made a quick lunge. Taylor dodged easily to his open side, and slashed. The knife cut across his forearm. At first she thought she had cut only the material of his suit jacket, but then she heard him gasp. Trying to ignore his wounded arm while keeping his guard up, Schwerin backed away. Feinting on a low line and coming in high, Taylor pressed the attack. Schwerin barely avoided being speared by the first thrust, but in doing so his guard came down, and he was wide open. Taylor saw her advantage and moved in. She would have had him then, but her left foot skidded on a bit of slick pavement.

Keeping her balance was impossible, the leg flew completely out from under her. Damn that leg! went through her mind, as she felt herself fall. She slapped hard with her left hand to break the fall as she hit but could not keep the right elbow from smacking into the ground. Pain shot through her arm, and the knife flew away. It landed just out of easy reach.

As she looked up at Schwerin she could feel her stomach knot, and a scream begin to build inside. Her iron rules saved her then. The scream died, stillborn. The stomach she ignored. She might die, but she was not going to yield, not even to her own fear. That there was no one to see how she behaved other than Schwerin was irrelevant. It mattered to her. Instead of the scream, she coughed up a laugh.

"Come on, then, if you can! You've still got six feet to go!"

That gave him pause. A disarmed opponent, flat on her back, should not be hurling challenges. Unless there was a trick somewhere.

The brief hesitation gave Taylor time to think, and her discipline let her do it. The situation was far from good. Her knife was too far away. If she made a grab for it he would be all over her. Similarly, there was no way she could gain her feet without being spitted in the process. It was not hopeless, however. Schwerin still had to reach her with the blade. From the way he held the knife, she could tell that he would not throw it. If she could make him lunge, and miss . . .

Taylor had seen Schwerin follow her eyes when she gauged the distance to her knife. Abruptly decision came. She would feint toward the knife, hoping that Schwerin would stab straight at her. Once he started to move, she planned to roll the other way. With luck, she would be able to land a kick with her right foot. That would buy her enough time to draw the other knife from her sock and get up. The plan was full of ifs, but it might work. She was going to bet her life on it.

It had taken scant time to make up her mind, but as she did she could see Schwerin's eyes narrowing. He had come to some decision of his own. It was time. Taylor started for the knife, looking for his answering move. It never came.

Instead, a small thunderclap filled the corridor. Schwerin spun away like a top and fell past her. Behind the place he had stood, outlined by the slightly brighter light between the vats, was George Jeffers. He stood, still as a statue, feet planted apart, both hands clamped on the gun. Taylor stayed down, awaiting a follow-up shot. It did not come. Instead, the statue slowly loosened, arms coming down like an oversized plastic doll. The gun came to rest, aiming at a nondescript patch of concrete between the two men. He walked over to Taylor, his free hand held out.

"Nice shot," she said, taking the hand and pulling herself to her feet. "Not bad timing either."

Jeffers had in fact run past the vats, only to turn back when he remembered seeing the bandana. Neither Taylor nor Schwerin had been aware of his entrance, so absorbing of one's attention is a naked blade. Jeffers had seen the tableau with Taylor on the ground as he entered, and he had known that he would freeze again. The next thing he knew, the gun was out and fired. For the life of him he could not remember either aiming or pulling the trigger. The fact that he was shooting a man in the back did not occur to him until he saw Schwerin fall.

He had not killed him, as a groan from the floor indicated. Schwerin was lying on his left side, softly moaning. The bullet had struck over the scapula. The bone had stopped the bullet, which was why Schwerin was alive, but in doing so it had shattered. Schwerin was lying very still, breathing shallowly. Anything to avoid moving that right arm. Jeffers stood over the man. He was not gloating, but neither was he feeling any remorse. There was a job to finish.

"Klaus, or Schwerin, whoever you are, I need information. Not an exchange of information, you are just going to answer my questions. I know you *verstehen* English, so don't try pretending you don't."

"Get fucked."

"That's rather impolite," Taylor put in. "It's also stupid. Now there is certainly the matter of Dr. Schroeder, who seems to have had a problem with a sharp object of yours, and I'm sure the *Bundesnachrichtendienst* is going to have some questions for you, but the shape you're in when they find you is entirely up to you. If you're not feeling talkative, or we don't like your answers, I'll just pack your wound with some of this nice slime at the base of the wall. By the time you are found, I'll bet you will have a beaut of an infection. I wonder how much they'll have to chop out to clean it?"

Schwerin's face contorted into a snarl. Taylor merely shrugged and gestured at the filth littering the floor. The fight went out of Schwerin all at once.

"All right, all right. What do you want me to tell you?"

"Did you steal the designer enzyme from Hank Davenport in Amsterdam?"

"Yes."

"Yes what? What did you do with it? What happened to Davenport?"

"Dammit," Schwerin protested, "I'm shot."

"You'll be worse than shot if you don't talk," Taylor warned.

"Okay, okay."

"Not okay!" Jeffers yelled. "What happened to Hank? Goddamn it, talk!"

Schwerin grunted and pain spasmed across his face. When he looked up after it passed, he found no sympathy in either Taylor or Jeffers. "I don't know what happened to Davenport. We met him at Schiphol Airport, told him we were from the conference organizing committee. It was easy. He never suspected anything was wrong. After that, I don't know. Karl took him; he had instructions to get rid of him. If you want details, you better ask Karl."

"It's a bit late for that." Taylor's voice was as calm as if she was giving a cookie recipe.

Jeffers shuddered at the exchange. Hank was certainly dead and Jeffers decided that he did not want to know the details.

"What did you do with the enzyme?" Jeffers asked. He had to move the questions away from what had happened to Hank.

"I gave it to a man," Schwerin said.

"Not good enough," Taylor said.

"I don't know who he is," Schwerin said. "I was to call him Herr Professor. That's all."

"What?" The question came from both of them simultaneously.

Schwerin had met this Herr Professor, but the description he gave was not helpful. Herr Professor was of average height, with straight dark hair and a round face. Taylor tried several ways of tricking him into giving an inconsistent description, but none of them worked.

"This Herr Professor was the one who told you and Karl to meet Dr. Jeffers in Amsterdam?"

"Yes."

"And what were you supposed to do?"

"Find out who he really was, then get rid of him, too." Jeffers swallowed hard.

"And how did you know we were here?"

"I got a call."

"Just like that," Taylor said sarcastically. "We always have the phone company announce our whereabouts to all interested parties. I think I know who called. Goetz was Stasi too, correct? He called you, didn't he?" Schwerin nodded. "Is he Herr Professor?"

"No, he's not."

"Did he have you kill Schroeder?"

"Goetz said the orders were to kill Schroeder if he was . . . more of a risk than a help."

"And, of course, Goetz knew that he was about to become that," Taylor finished. She turned to face Jeffers. "I think we ought to go see the other Dr. Schroeder tonight," she said. Then, turning back to Schwerin, she said, "Don't you go and get lost now. We'll send somebody back for you."

"Are you thinking the other Schroeder is Herr Professor?" Jeffers asked as they walked back to the main entrance.

Taylor shook her head, but there was some uncertainty in her voice. "I don't think so. I don't think Schwerin could have consistently maintained a false description like that, not wounded like he is. Also, whoever Herr Professor is, he's ordering around a bunch of ex-Stasi types. The good medicine man just doesn't seem cut out for that role."

"Then we're back to Fruhling again. He was the one Schwerin contacted."

"Which is a pretty good reason for it not to be him, but that's hardly conclusive either." Taylor shrugged. "Of course, you wouldn't expect someone with Fruhling's right-wing credentials to be working with the Stasi, but, when you come right down to it, except for labels, there isn't that much difference between the two. If it is Fruhling," she declared, "I'm going to keep his car."

The other Schroeder was still at the little hospital. He appeared rapidly after Taylor told the nurse at the front desk that the matter was urgent. The expression on his face alternated between puzzlement and anger when he saw who was there.

"What is this about?" he asked. "When I get an urgent call at night, I do not expect to find journalists."

"It is urgent, I'm afraid," Taylor said. "I'm sorry to have to tell you, but your brother was killed tonight."

For an instant, there was a flash of pain across the old man's face, then he clamped a mask over it. When he spoke, his voice was tightly controlled. "How do you know this?"

"We had an appointment to see him tonight," Taylor explained. "When we got there he was dead. A man named Schwerin, who used to work for the Stasi, did it. My partner," she indicated Jeffers, "shot him. He's still alive, up at the plant."

"Stasi," Schroeder murmured. "Still today, Stasi. I was always afraid Helmut was too closely tied to them." For a moment he seemed lost, his eyes focusing somewhere beyond the far wall. Then he came back to himself. "You have not told the police yet." It was a statement, not a question. They both nodded. "Why is that? It is not a rush to extend your sympathies, I'm sure of that."

"It is because of why your brother died," Taylor said. "That, and because we think you are involved, too. We were going to meet with him to discuss what we know about the Sachsen Fabrik designer enzyme. He may have been killed to prevent that discussion. We came to you because there was a key to your office on his desk."

Schroeder's eyes narrowed as she spoke. "I *told* him this would come to no good. I *warned* him that it did not feel right. I thought it was a mistake and I was right. Well, you want to know the story of Sachsen Fabrik."

"Yes," said both Taylor and Jeffers.

"Come on, then."

He led them back to his office, entering cautiously as though he was uncertain of finding it empty. There was, however, no one there. He poured some liquor from a flask in his desk into three small tumblers. Taylor and Jeffers refused the offer, so he shrugged and drank two of them, one after the other.

"Sachsen Fabrik was a chemical company for a long time; commodity chemical for the most part," Schroeder said. "When it became clear that the DDR would not survive, and Helmut saw it sooner than most, he came to the conclusion that Sachsen Fabrik could not survive in the world market. Biotech research made much more sense, so he said. I know he managed to build a company within the company to pursue it.

"After the Wall fell in 1989, he was going to change Sachsen Fabrik completely to a biotech company. It didn't work. He couldn't make it work! That probably doesn't surprise you, but remember, Helmut had no real understanding of the problems. He had run a chemical company that shipped most of its products to the Soviet Union. He thought he could do this and, of course, he couldn't. He was desperate for a way out, I know that. Then, he found a group who had access to this enzyme technology. I don't know how that was done. He never told me. I do know they wanted to set it up for sale and be certain that the origin of the technology was believed to be, shall we say, other than the real origin. Helmut arranged for them to buy Sachsen Fabrik, not a hard thing to do, and then made the project records look like they go back over three years."

Taylor and Jeffers looked at each other. If Sachsen Fabrik had been falsifying records on the project for that long, it was hard to see how it fit with Davenport's disappearance.

"I think we need more information on the people who own this company."

"I can do that," Schroeder said. He walked to a row of cabinets marked PATIENT FILES.

"Helmut would not listen to me when I told him of my concerns," Schroeder explained. "I told him that once the company had been sold, these people would no longer need him. Of course, he just told me that I should tend to my clinic and leave the politics to him. He said this would be child's play compared to living with the Party. He did at least agree to safeguard some of the documents." Schroeder pulled a thick file out of one of the drawers. "This is a patient of mine who died after a long and complicated history of asthma. The chart is officially here for my review. No one else would ever look here. You'll find what you want clipped in behind his hospitalization in 1978."

Taylor hefted the chart with a grim smile. The papers had been perfectly hidden, right in plain sight in an unlocked file cabinet. No one would ever have found them. She leafed through to the place Schroeder had indicated and, indeed, clipped into the medical chart was a sheaf of papers having nothing to do with medicine. Quickly, she began skimming through them. It was not long before she let out, "I'll be damned," and looked over at Jeffers.

"What is it?"

"I think I have the name of the man who coordinated this deal with the *Treuhandanstalt.* Come here and tell me what you think."

Jeffers walked around to where he could peer past her shoulder. He took one look and let out a gasp. The name at the end of Taylor's fingertip was that of Martin Bieber.

Moments later they were outside again. Schroeder had assured them he would take care of contacting the police, although both Taylor and Jeffers suspected he planned to make a trip to Sachsen Fabrik first. That was likely to prove unpleasant for Schwerin, but neither of them was very concerned about that. Schwerin in all probability deserved whatever happened to him.

"Well, George, what do you think of Bieber now?" Taylor had her eyes on the starless night sky.

"I don't know. I mean, I suppose he has the connections to pull off buying a company, but all the rest of this? Christ, I'm losing track of the number of people who've been killed. I just can't believe this. Anyway, he doesn't fit Schwerin's description of Herr Professor either."

"George, don't take this the wrong way, but is it possible that the way you feel about Bieber is, shall we say, professional jealousy? I mean, could the man know what he's doing?"

"Dammit, Taylor, you asked me that once before. No way! Well, maybe. I mean, oh, shit, I just don't know anymore! Maybe Bieber does have what it takes to set this up."

"Or maybe he has what it takes to make a designer enzyme," Taylor said. The look she got from Jeffers was an ominous one but she pressed ahead. "Hear me out, George. We know that Bieber got money from H-C to work on designer enzymes, right?" Jeffers nodded. "Now, would I be right in assuming that if Bieber then makes a designer enzyme, H-C owns it?"

"Probably," Jeffers said. "There are all kinds of contracts about discoveries, but if they were funding his work on designer enzymes then, yes, they would own it."

"Okay. Now, let's suppose friend Bieber has figured out how to make one, but he doesn't want to give it to H-C. Instead, he comes up with Sachsen

Fabrik and makes it look like they found it. Now Sachsen Fabrik owns the enzyme, but Bieber really controls Sachsen Fabrik. H-C has to buy Sachsen Fabrik to get it and Bieber walks off with the lion's share of the loot. Of course, once H-C gets the patent they'll just close that old plant and throw everyone out of work, so much for Schroeder's scheming, but maybe that explains what's going on. Your enzyme could have been stolen just to slow you down until their deal goes through."

"Either that," Jeffers said, "or Bieber has my enzyme and is using it to make the deal work just the way you said. Dammit."

"Maybe. We're just guessing right now, George."

Thinking was not Jeffers's strength at that moment. "I said before, when we were in Frankfurt, that I smelled a rat. I *cannot* believe that Bieber has made an enzyme on his own. That *has* to be my enzyme he has got."

"Yeah. All of which ignores the short, round-faced Herr Professor, although maybe he's just a stooge for Bieber. If we could trace him to Bieber, we'd have it, or if we could show that Bieber's enzyme really is yours, that would do it too. That's assuming that Bieber has any enzyme at all. We don't really know that there was an enzyme in that bottle. Could have been nothing but salt."

Jeffers rubbed the side of his head, as though to soothe an ache. There was an important point buried in the discussion, and he was missing it. It was the same feeling he remembered from exams in the past, of questions whose answers he knew, but lost in the transition from mind to pen. "That's not true Taylor. It can't have been a fake in the bottle. Bieber needs that enzyme to make this deal work. You can be sure Hochmann won't pay for something unless he can check the analysis himself. If the product is the real thing, maybe people wouldn't look too closely at the Potemkin village they set up at Sachsen Fabrik, but the product has to be real. So it has to be there. The problem is, how to prove it's mine."

Taylor thought about that, and stayed silent until they were within sight of the car. Then she asked, "George, an enzyme is a large, very complex molecule, right?"

"Yes, of course. Go to the head of the class."

She ignored the sarcasm. "Well, if Bieber or anyone else made one independently, would it have to be exactly like yours, even if it had the same function?"

"No, no. Not at all. Most of an enzyme is like girders and beams, to hold the essential parts in the right orientation. There is no single way the sequence has to run, except in certain critical areas. Even from species to species, enzymes that have the same function can have different structures."

The answer suddenly exploded in his head, and he burst out laughing. It was so obvious.

It was not that obvious to Taylor. She looked at him as though she was measuring him for a straightjacket.

"Sorry, I should explain," he said, wiping tears away from his eyes. "You were absolutely right with your questions. The odds of two people independently generating the same structure are infinitesimally small. The one I made has several characteristic features in its NMR spectrum that we can use to identify it. Even if Bieber went ahead and made an enzyme with the same function as the one I was working on, just to spite me the way he was implying, it's still going to have a different spectrum than mine. All I had to do was remember to think like a scientist, instead of a bloody spy." Taylor made a face that he ignored.

"NMR?"

"Yeah, nuclear magnetic resonance. Something I used to do a lot of before I met you. There will be an NMR machine at the institute in Frankfurt. All we have to do is grab Bieber's enzyme, and give me about three hours on the instrument. Either it's my stuff, or it isn't."

Taylor considered the idea. What Jeffers was talking about was way beyond her experience, not only to do but even to evaluate the possibility of success. She hated to move outside her own sphere of competence, but perhaps it was time to bank on Jeffers. If it worked they would have the next, maybe final, link. She came to a halt by the front bumper of the Porsche.

"I like the idea." Habitually, she chewed on her lower lip before continuing. "We had also better move fast, because God knows when Schwerin was supposed to report or who he really was supposed to report to. If nothing else, that snake Goetz will know by morning at the latest that somebody took out Schwerin. If we're going to have Stasi chasing us, I'd just as soon have as big a lead as possible. Of course," she chuckled, "we're going to run straight to Fruhling, who may or may not be a crazy Nazi." She pulled out a one-mark coin and made a show of examining both sides. Then she held it out to Jeffers. "Your choice, George, frying pan or fire." She chuckled again.

Jeffers waved the coin away with a grimace. "How do you propose to get to Frankfurt tonight?"

The sweep of Taylor's arm took in Fruhling's car and much of the street. "Now I'll show you some real driving," she said.

"That's what I was afraid of," said Jeffers.

# CHAPTER 17

## NEU MECKLENBERG, GERMANY

ALTHOUGH JEFFERS WAS NOT anxious to find out how Taylor was going to reach Frankfurt that night, he had to agree that they needed to be there. He also had no alternative to Taylor driving because he was not about to suggest himself as the driver—aside from the fact that it would be a night ride along unfamiliar roads, Jeffers had never driven a stick shift. He settled into the passenger seat with a fatalistic sigh. Taylor's driving could prove every bit as nerve-racking for him as the earlier part of the evening. Sitting there, trying not to think about how fast they were going, gave him his first opportunity to think about what had happened.

"Tell me," he said. "What would you have done if I hadn't shown up back there?"

"You mean at Sachsen Fabrik?"

"Yes."

She told him the plan she had concocted. Her voice stayed even.

Jeffers gave a low whistle when she finished. He had no doubt she would have done just as she said.

"Were you scared then, Taylor?"

The silence in the car after he asked that question drew out well beyond any ordinary conversational pause. In the darkness, he was unable to see her expression, how it was set or whether it changed. As the gap lengthened, Jeffers became convinced that he had stepped over an invisible line, had pushed into a forbidden area. Just when he had begun to feel that she was treating him as an equal, he was certain he had torn the delicate fabric of the conversation. She told you once she did not want to talk about feelings, he told himself. You had to go push her. Presumptuous fool, he thought.

Her answer, when it came, took him by surprise, both in what she said and the simple fact that she said it at all. "Certainly I was scared," her voice was low and controlled. "Although that is not something I usually care to discuss. Only fools and liars will insist otherwise, and I'm neither. But what counts is how you act, not what you feel inside. Remember what I told you about ice and fire."

Back to the old fire and ice, Jeffers thought, as he listened.

"You know, how you felt when you had to jump out of the plane?" Jeffers nodded. In the future, he was going to have a hard time forgetting. "Same principle. I just cover it better than you do. Hell, the first time I jumped I was petrified. But only on the inside."

"If it bothered you that much, why did you go up in the first place? Or did you do it because you were scared?"

Taylor shook her head, "no," at the last. "No, not that. I jumped because I was told I couldn't do it. You don't really think my upwardly mobile, Volvo-and-carseat-parents were going to let their daughter jump out of an airplane, do you?"

That started Taylor thinking about that first jump. It had not been her parents who had started the uproar, although they had contributed to it. It had started out as a silly thing, a doc at the clinic nit-picking about what she could or could not do, so Taylor had told him she wanted to jump. It had come to her out of the blue, as it were, but when he made a big deal out of it Taylor became stubborn. Her parents' reaction had just made her more insistent. A truly stupid way to make decisions, she told herself, but it had seemed important at the time. She remembered getting up the next morning, knowing she was going to jump and scared stiff of doing it. She remembered being scared that she would ruin her leg for good, being even more scared that someone would see how scared she was. She remembered thinking that if something went wrong, she would blame it all on the doc. She shook her head at the recollection. Blaming someone else for her behavior was stupid too. She had done that once. Never again. Afterward, though, the feeling had been so sweet, floating free in the air, knowing that she could make her own choices and beat her own fears. Parachuting had always been special after that.

While Taylor was wandering through her memories, Jeffers tried to conjure up an image of a parent, or anyone for that matter, saying "no" to Taylor Redding. What a scene that must have been! It occurred to him that it might also explain what had happened to her leg. He was about to ask her, when his eyes fell on the instrument panel. Quick arithmetic told him that the Porsche was shooting along at nearly 140 miles per hour. He swallowed hard, and decided he would find another time to ask about the leg.

# FRANKFURT, GERMANY

ONCE THEY ARRIVED IN Frankfurt, the urban location of the institute proved a blessing. They were able to park the car away from the building, carefully locked of course, in a well-lit and -traveled area. Had the building been in the countryside they would have been forced to choose between a conspicuous parking lot or an insecure side road. It would have been a difficult choice. Taylor was not about to take chances with Fruhling's car.

Gaining entrance to the institute was not a taxing chore. The building had been erected during the initial reconstruction phase after the war. Security at an academic institution, in those days, had not been a major preoccupation of the designers. Consequently, the building had multiple entrances, low-level windows and ledges. Also favoring them was the general laxness in regard to security found in any academic community. Jeffers was well acquainted with this mind-set from his university years. Security guards, when they made rounds at all, were hardly aggressive. Even if the face was unfamiliar, a person who appeared to be going about his business was rarely challenged. This tendency was reinforced by the well-known proclivity of many scientists for bizarre hours. The principal theft risk in such a setting was personal belongings, and they were usually not lying around at night. Most of the really valuable equipment was too esoteric or bulky to steal, although the disappearance of personal computers was chronic. Such conditions had also prevailed at NaturGene until the takeover had brought in Jim Thompson and his no-nonsense ideas of industrial security. The Frankfurt Institute was a research institute with, as far as Jeffers knew, no major industrial or military links. He expected, therefore, the usual academic version of security. As long as they were not overly noisy and avoided the guard desk at the main entrance, they had good odds of success.

In the actual event, getting in was even easier than Jeffers expected. While making a quick walking circuit of the building they spotted a half-open ground-floor window, located on a side away from the main street. Scrambling through it, Jeffers first while Taylor watched the rear, took but a moment. Immediately beneath the window on the other side was a small study desk, probably belonging to a student. Jeffers used the desk as a support to help him through the window, and in so doing ground dirt from the shrubbery bed below into the papers and X-rays on the desk top. He felt a twinge of regret when he realized what he had done. Someone was sure to be very upset in the morning. There was no help for it, however. He turned to help boost Taylor through, a process that wreaked further havoc with the material on the desk. They found themselves in a darkened laboratory. The illumination through the windows revealed a coat tree, with several long white lab coats hanging from it. Jeffers helped himself to two of them.

"Here, try this on for size," he held one of them out to Taylor.

The fits were not bad, although the sleeves on Taylor's coat were too short by several inches. Jeffers did not see this as a major problem, lab coats were never tailored to fit. For their purposes, the camouflage would be adequate. The stains and abrasions on Jeffers's jacket and shirt were mostly hidden by the coat. Unless a guard happened to notice that his suit coat was on under the lab coat, he looked, with his tie on, more the picture of a scientist than he ever had at work. The marks on his face could not be remedied, of course, but usually clothing was more important than features in placing a person. Taylor was, frankly, less satisfactory. Her loudly patterned, high-necked shirt and loose pants were at once too expensive and too *avant-garde* to be work clothes for either a technician or a graduate student. Fortunately, most of it could be covered by buttoning the coat all the way. A bonus was finding the owners' plastic identification cards clipped to the coats. Apparently, the American custom of clipping them reversed, with the photograph hidden from view, was followed in some places in Germany as well. No one would know that the face on the card did not match that of the wearer.

Set to impersonate late-working researchers, they stepped out into the corridor. The halls proved to be empty. Lights showed in an occasional laboratory or office, but their occupants, during that period of time, seemed to require nothing that was not already at hand. Having been in the building recently, it did not take long to locate Bieber's laboratory. It was dark, the door locked.

Jeffers allowed himself a short sigh of relief. His impression of Bieber had not been of a man given to working long hours, so he had not really expected to find the room occupied. Until they reached it, however, the possibility had lurked in his mind. Had that been the case, well, they could always have held him at gunpoint while they checked out the enzyme. But it would have been awfully embarrassing to be wrong.

The locked door hardly slowed them at all. Taylor palmed a small tool from one of her pockets. She slipped it into the lock and, leaning against the door, wiggled her wrist a few times. The door opened silently. Jeffers stepped through the opening and flicked the light on.

"Dammit! What are . . ." The expression burst from Taylor in a low but forceful tone, as she reached for the switch beyond Jeffers.

Jeffers held up a hand to stop her, having the immediate impression that he was trying to flag down a charging bull. "Whoa. Hold on a moment." Miraculously, the bull stopped in midstride. "This is a lab we're burgling, not a bank. A light on here, with people in the lab even at this hour, should not draw too much attention. But noise in a dark lab, while we blunder around, that would get security interested."

"Fair enough." Taylor cooled down as fast as she had become intense. "This is more your turf than mine. I'll follow your lead."

My lead, how fabulous, thought Jeffers. So now observe while the great criminal mastermind, George Jeffers, violates an unlocked refrigerator. He hesitated, with his hand on the door handle. What do I do if it's not in there? Probably have to find Bieber and beat the story out of him. All of which will look terrific if he is actually telling the truth.

He yanked the door open with sufficient force to topple several small items on the shelves. The little vial, with its powdery white contents, sat in front of him, precisely where Bieber had placed it the previous day.

"Thank God," he breathed.

Jeffers took the bottle out, gingerly. He turned it in his hand, watched the white flakes tumble against the plastic wall. The white layer at the bottom looked awfully unimpressive. Hardly worth four deaths. Assuming, of course, it was what he thought it was.

"What do you need?" Taylor's question snapped him out of his reverie.

"$D_2O$," he replied. At the blank look on Taylor's face, he tried again. "$D_2O$, deuterium oxide. Heavy water. It's probably on one of those shelves with the other chemicals." He had to have at least a small volume of it. The machine he would have to use would not work without it. "We also need a special tube for this. It will be clear glass, about an eighth of an inch wide, and six inches long. Think of it as an anoretic test tube. We'll have to check all the bench drawers; they could be kept anywhere."

The laboratory had two soapstone-covered islands, projecting from the outside wall, that formed double-sided lab benches, plus a single-sided bench at the far wall. Running from beneath the bench top to the floor of each were rows of metal drawers and cabinets. Taylor went to the rear of the lab and began to systematically check each drawer. Periodically she would hold an object up for inspection, asking if it was the type of tube he wanted. In each case Jeffers looked briefly, then shook his head. Jeffers started in on the chemicals. They proved to be alphabetically arranged on shelves running down the middle of the two islands. The German labels were not a problem; chemical formulas are constant. What did bother him was the absence of the $D_2O$ from the shelves. It was not in the place it should have occupied, so he checked every bottle. It simply was not there.

He began to feel a sense of desperation building inside. It had to be in the lab, but where? In the end, Taylor stumbled on it. She had finally found a packet of the slender tubes in one of the drawers, sealed in a clear plastic baggie. When Jeffers came to check her find, he saw a small brown bottle, about three inches high, next to the tubes.

"Ah, both at once. Now we're in business." He surveyed the other paraphernalia in the drawer and picked up a small Leroy pen. "You know, this place is kept so damn tidy, I find it hard to believe anybody works in here. I mean, you can't work without creating at least a little mess."

"Maybe they just spend extra time cleaning up at the end of the day."

"Come on, Taylor. To keep it like this they would have to start cleaning the moment they walked in." Jeffers had had a compulsively neat roommate one year at college. It had not worked out well.

Jeffers pulled a small pipette from an open box on the top of the bench and inserted the large end into a rubber bulb that had been placed next to the box. With it he sucked some liquid out of the bottle labeled $D_2O$ and squirted it into the bottle containing the enzyme. The powder dissolved immediately. Again using the pipette, he transferred the solution to one of the tubes.

"God, talk about a quick and dirty experiment." He shook his head. "Well, now all we have to do is find the NMR."

"Where would they keep that?" Taylor asked.

"It'll have to be in a separate room, either by itself or with other instruments that everybody shares. Just look for a sign that says to keep out if you have a pacemaker." At Taylor's questioning look, he explained, "The magnetic field interferes with their operation. It's strong enough to grab hold of anything ferromagnetic that gets too close. You also better keep your distance with those credit cards. The field will erase that little magnetic strip on the back." Jeffers thought he saw consternation on Taylor's face as he spoke, but she said nothing.

They left the lab then, the precious sample sticking halfway out of the front pocket of the coat Jeffers wore. They made no attempt to tidy up the lab behind them, there would be time enough to worry about that if Bieber turned out to be telling the truth. They found the room with the spectrometer by the simple expedient of checking every room on a floor, and then moving to the next one up. Although they were cautious passing any lighted doorway, there were still no people in the halls. Their luck held, and they were not challenged before they reached their goal. It came after what felt like an endless series of doors, but in reality was only three floors of the building.

The door was adorned with the customary warning Jeffers had expected.

The interior light was on. Taylor passed the entrance silently and quickly, to stand at the other side of the door, while Jeffers pushed it open. As he did so, his right hand crept under the double layers of jackets to find the butt of his automatic. For an instant he felt like a child playing cops and robbers. Except that he was not a child, and the gun was real. Jeffers also could remember many loud arguments, when he worked at the university, over the allocation of machine time, but this would be the only time he knew of it being taken at gunpoint. As the door moved a hinge squeaked, unnaturally loud in the nighttime silence.

"Crap!" he shouted, and bolted through the door, gun out.

Taylor had followed Jeffers in, moving rapidly away from him once he had passed through the door. They confronted an empty chair at the console. The machine was running on automatic.

Jeffers stuck the gun back under his jackets and wiped the perspiration from his forehead. He had known it was most likely that the room would be empty, but he felt relieved regardless. Unlike Jeffers, Taylor had not been particularly tense when they had moved in. With the finding that the room was untenanted, she stopped and stared at the machine with undisguised fascination.

It was the only occupant of the room. The main console, of gray metal, was about the size of an upright piano. The area where the keyboard would be protruded farther forward, and was flat. It served as a holding area for the chart paper. Behind it, the main console rose. In the center of it a small oscilloscope screen showed a trace moving horizontally, back and forth. Clusters of knobs, switches and lights were present below and on both sides of the screen. On closer inspection, she could see that the console was not a single piece; rather it was composed of subsections that could be slid in or out for replacement, much like the components of an expensive stereo. Adjacent to the console, on its right, was an open metal framework that held a minicomputer with its tape and disk drives. Bolted to the side of this, and at right angles to the main console, was a large cathode ray tube, and, directly below, a teletype terminal. The empty chair reposed in front of the terminal.

Next to the palpable complexity of the console and its accessories, the magnet itself was anticlimactic. Set away from the console, to one side of the room, it resembled nothing so much as a silver oil drum on stilts. The drum was really a high-technology thermos, encasing the magnet in an outer wrap of liquid nitrogen and an inner wrap of liquid helium. At the unimaginably cold temperatures near absolute zero that the liquid helium provided, the magnet became a superconductor, capable of generating the powerful magnetic fields necessary to distinguish one atom from another in complex molecules.

As a whole, the machine could be seen to have originated as a commercial item that had been extensively customized. Although Jeffers had hoped for a machine straight from the assembly line, he was happy enough with what he saw. It was almost as much a relief as the absence of a live operator. Most of the components bore the imprint of a major German manufacturer, whose instruments were heavily used in the United States as well. Jeffers, in fact, was quite familiar with the line, and, therefore, would have no difficulty understanding the controls and, more importantly, the computer. He had dreaded the possibility, ever since they had reached the institute, of finding the machine to be a "home brew," built and programmed in some unique and incomprehensible manner. That nightmare would not come to pass.

He stepped to the console and twisted one of the tiny black plastic knobs. A liquid crystal display next to it rapidly dropped to zero. Taylor could read the German inscription "spinning rate" below the display, but could see nothing that had either been, or had stopped, spinning. Jeffers, on the contrary, did not need to be able to read the lettering. He punched a two-letter code into the teletype to stop the instrument's program, then twisted another knob just below the first. He found it unexpectedly hard to make that move—he was interrupting someone's experiment, an egregious breach of etiquette that he, in the past, would have considered on a par with seducing said person's wife. As he turned the second knob, a high-pitched rush of air emanated from the silvered magnet. It ended with a sound akin to a popping cork. At the top of the magnet housing, centrally located between two hose connections, a glass tube wearing a plastic collar appeared. It bobbed there, supported by the uprushing column of air. The tube was similar to, but much wider than, the one Jeffers had.

"It figures. Wrong probe in."

"Is that a problem?" Taylor asked.

"Not really. What's going on is that all we want to look at are the hydrogen atoms, protons really, in this thing. The probe for that will have a different size bore. It's probably in one of those cabinets, and I'll just have to change it."

"Anything I can do here?" she asked.

"No," he answered, "it's really a one-person job anyway."

Truth was, he did not mind the extra work very much. It gave him more of an opportunity to strut his stuff, and that he welcomed. In this arena, he knew he would perform well.

Taylor, he noticed, for all her obvious interest in the instrument was carefully keeping nearly the full width of the room between her and the magnet. It puzzled him, until he realized that she must have taken to heart his warning about coming too close to the magnet.

"Hey, Taylor, you don't need that much space. Six feet or so should do fine. Trust me, I wouldn't take chances with your credit cards."

"You better not. My limits are higher than yours."

"Ow. Hit me where it hurts, why don't you?" He clapped a hand on his wallet. "I'll bet the highest limit is on the Bloomie's card, too." He could see that her retort had no feeling in it, and wondered if her real concern was not for the cards. Maybe she was worried the magnet would grab the brace. He considered the possibility, but said nothing. It had been dumb to bring the topic up in the first place.

"Well, I better get started. Hold this, will you?" He flipped her his wallet. Taylor caught it, and stashed it in a pocket of the lab coat.

After removing the tube and its collar from the top of the magnet, Jeffers put them aside and turned off the airflow. Then he turned his attention to the metal locker at the other end of the room. The probe he wanted was, as he expected, packed in the cabinet. It nestled in what could have passed for a flower box, carefully cushioned by Styrofoam. Removed from its packing, it was a short length of brass pipe a few inches across, with a flange at one end to which three screws were attached. The delicate equipment that made it function was totally hidden behind the metal.

Jeffers held it carefully across his knees as he squatted underneath the magnet. The position he took looked horribly uncomfortable, folded nearly into a ball with his head twisted up to watch as he unhooked the probe that was already in the machine. He did not notice the contortion; it was routine. Slowly, he slid the probe down, out of the magnet. It was of necessity slow going, when the magnetic field generated by the superconductor resisted any movement of the metal within its core. Finally, it was out, and replaced by the one taken from the cabinet. Jeffers bounded from the magnet to the console. Time to get under way! There was renewed energy in his movements. Fatigue was banished for the present. With the probe in place, he fitted his tube into a plastic collar of its own, and, with the air jet turned back on, stuck it atop the magnet. Using the control for the airflow, he gingerly lowered it into the center of the magnet. It came to rest with a click as the airflow shut off.

He turned his attention, then, to a thin black notebook that had been left on the flat plate of the console. This log gave the approximate settings for each of a bank of knobs at the lower left of the console, depending upon which probe was installed. It was not entirely luck that placed it there for Jeffers. Such a logbook would have to be present somewhere, in any such instrument room. Again, language was no barrier. The book was almost entirely numbers and symbols. When he was finished with the book and the dials, the central section of the console produced two peaks on the small oscilloscope screen. They were nearly mirror images, one produced when the trace moved right, the other when it came back to the left. The gap between them was at the center of the screen. A ghost of a smile flitted around his lips. He reached up and depressed the center button in a row of three above the screen. The button stayed down, now illuminated from behind. There was a soft click somewhere in the innards of the machine, after which a small green light came on. The trace on the oscilloscope changed to a straight line near the top of the screen.

Jeffers turned around in the chair to face Taylor. "I have it locked now, but I'll still have to shim it properly. That may take a little time." Taylor looked blank. The words were English, but the sentence made no sense to her.

Jeffers wondered what she made of all the activity. He had, from the corner of his eye, watched her watch him while he worked at the console. He knew she did not understand what he was doing, but he would have been unsurprised had she echoed back every move he had made. He wondered, but there was no time to go into it.

Instead, he turned back to the bank of knobs he had used before. There were sixteen of them, in two rows, each labeled with a different permutation of $x$, $y$, and $z$, some with exponents. A thin metal plate that normally covered their recessed area had been thoughtfully taped open by a previous operator. Carefully, he began to adjust them in sequence. Each knob was moved slightly, his eyes watching the trace on the oscilloscope to see if it moved higher or lower. Always, he tried to manipulate each knob to bring the trace as high as possible. When no further increase could be gained from a knob, he moved to the next one. After working his way completely through the series, he began over again.

At first, Taylor watched this proceeding with the same concentration as before. After a while, she began to wonder how long it would take. After it took longer, she became concerned. All she could see was Jeffers, motionless, at the console. His left hand rested on one of the knobs, his eyes on the screen, and frequently he would make an almost imperceptible change in the setting of a knob.

"God's sakes, George! You don't have to send this to the Nobel Prize committee."

"I know, I know," he said, "but if we don't get a decent spectrum it is all going to be worthless. Remember, I have to make this comparison from memory."

"Sorry. You know what you're doing." Which he did, and she did not. She chided herself for her impatience, and recognized that the problem was simple. She was useless. Even standing guard on the door was an exercise in futility.

Finally, Jeffers was satisfied with the settings. Using the knob by the LCD he started the sample spinning, and proceeded to make further, similar adjustments with two knobs mounted on a panel above the others. Taylor thought she was going to scream if it went on much longer. Fortunately, it did not quite reach that point.

"That should do it." Jeffers pushed his chair away from the console and stretched. "What we're going to do is pretty simple. The magnetic field makes all the atoms, you can think of them as spinning tops, line up in one direction. Then we hit them with a radio frequency pulse that tips them over. We pick up the signal they give off as they flip back, and the computer turns it into a spectrum. Since the field around any one atom depends on its neighbors, each one, or most of them anyway, has a characteristic signal."

Sure thing, Taylor thought. She might as well explain an internal combustion engine to a savage.

Jeffers tapped a string of commands into the keyboard. The large screen above the terminal went dark, then came on again. A complex signal, with the overall shape of an exponential decay began to build up.

"Off and running," he announced. "There is really nothing to do now but wait, probably about an hour.

"There are ways to check on whether it's ready while it's still running, but I can't be sure all the commands for the more complicated functions are the same as what I know. I would rather wait than take a chance."

"No problem," she replied. Lacking a chair to sprawl across, Taylor was letting the wall hold her up. "There is one thing I am starting to worry about, though. The more you show me, the more I am starting to believe how complicated these spectra are going to be. How sure are you that you can tell the difference without having your own to check them against?" Jeffers had seemed pretty confident when he had proposed the idea, but Taylor was beginning to wish she had voiced this question a few hours ago. The machinery looked impossibly arcane, and she knew there would be no way that she could have any idea whether Jeffers was right.

Jeffers frowned at the question, partly because it was a good question, and partly because the same question had been bothering him. It was always easier to feel certain before you sat down to work. "I ought to be able to tell," he said slowly, "especially if it is different than mine. It might be harder to be certain if they look the same. But, if all the comparison points I'll use are the same, then the samples are almost certainly the same."

"Almost certainly."

"Yeah," Jeffers shrugged. "I mean, we could be empirical about it, and just go ahead and shoot Bieber anyway."

"Now, look who's the bloodthirsty one!" Taylor laughed. That had been just what she needed to release her tension. "George, when it's done, you look at it. You say 'yes' or 'no,' and we'll take it from there. I'm satisfied you know what you're doing."

And I ought to be, too, he thought. Lord knew, he had been doing this sort of work long enough. He wondered if doctors had this feeling, when they were brought a sample or a test result with a patient's life waiting on their decision. Could you ever be so confident of your knowledge not to doubt, just a little, when the stakes were high? And if you were that confident, did it mean you were also a fool?

The hour passed, but in the drawn-out manner that occurs when there is nothing to do but mark time's passage. Taylor had exchanged her side wall for the rear one by the metal locker. Slouched in the corner formed by the locker and the wall, she had a good view of the door without being immediately obvious. She waited quietly, almost as much a part of the furniture as the locker she leaned against. The room was air conditioned to the point of frost, but that, too, she was able to ignore. She simply waited, mind in neutral, but watchful. Jeffers had a harder time. He was used to cold instrument rooms, so the temperature was not a problem, but he was also used to working with the machine while he waited. Normally, the computer memory could be split, allowing the operator to work with one area of the memory, even while the computer continued to operate the machine. However, while he had been happy to find the principal operating commands the same in Frankfurt as they had been in Ohio, he was not going to tempt fate by trying any fancy maneuvers. There had been too much customizing done to the machine's hardware, there could easily have been some done to the software as well. A mistake could shut him down, and he was not looking forward to trying to decipher a German software manual. All of which left him nothing to do but watch the screen count off the number of scans the machine had made, and invent new ways of cracking his knuckles.

He did give it the full hour before typing in the command to stop scanning. He followed it with several more commands, and the screen blinked off as the computer began converting the data into a readable spectrum. When it flashed back on again, it showed him the cross section of a mountain range, etched in bright green dots across the cathode ray tube. He reached for a group of four knobs, labeled A through D, on the console. As he turned them, the mountains contracted, then expanded, and twisted around their axes. When he was done, they were again orderly and upright. Satisfied, he turned from the screen, and struck a single key. The machine began to print out the image it had constructed. He went back, three times, to enlarge particular regions of the plot, but that was more to meet the needs of his stomach than his head. All it had really taken was to look at the full picture once.

Taylor came up to stand behind him, and looked silently over his shoulder while he worked. She had her answer, from the set of his face and the way he held his body, without ever asking a question.

"This is your stuff." It was a statement of fact, rather than a question.

"Yes. No questions, no doubts. It's mine." Jeffers swiveled the chair around to face her. His lips were compressed to a thin line, anger beginning to show on his face. "That goddamn bastard Bieber. Liar and thief, dear God. And Hank's dead, I'm sure, because of it. I vote we find the *Polizei*, or whatever they have around here, and fix his ass properly." He began to rise from his chair, as if propelled by the force of his words.

"Whoa, George, please." Taylor halted his progress with her outstretched hands, although she did not quite touch him. "We don't want the police. Not here, not now."

"Why not?" he demanded. "We've got this schmuck cold. Look, Taylor," his tone changed suddenly, "if there is some reason you *can't* go to the police, let me know. I swear to God, I'll leave you out of it. Not that I don't owe you more than that, but I can promise that, at the least. But Bieber has got to pay for this."

"I have no argument about his paying for it. But think a minute." Taylor turned partially away, and stepped back, avoiding the appearance of a toe-to-toe confrontation. "First of all, I have no old business with the police, at least none that I know of. But there has been, you will remember, some sundry unpleasantness in Amsterdam recently and also in Neu Mecklenberg. I doubt either one of us would enjoy being officially tied to it. We *might* resolve it satisfactorily, but I hate to bet too heavily on the intelligence of the police."

She was going to continue, but Jeffers jumped into the momentary pause. "Are you suggesting that we just kill him, and call it a day? I don't think cold-blooded murder is my style."

"Mine neither. But you didn't let me finish. We don't have all the answers here. Bieber is a crooked scientist, and he has your enzyme. Right?"

"On both counts."

"That's fine as far as it goes, but it doesn't go far enough. Somebody else picked up the enzyme from Schwerin and gave it to Bieber, and somebody else arranged the events in Boston. Somebody else is Herr Professor. Don't be surprised if the somebody else is also Stasi, which means I think we want to find out about them as soon as possible. Bieber is going to be our best lead to 'somebody else.' That's why we don't want to hand him to the police right now." She watched Jeffers carefully, looking to read his reaction in his body.

"All right. At least, we finally know where to go, and I'm glad of that." Jeffers tone had returned to normal. "I guess we ought to pay Dr. Bieber another visit."

"Most definitely," Taylor had her impish grin in place, "and there's no better way to handle a busy appointment schedule than to get a good early start."

"You mean, like now?"

"Exactly."

"All right, partner!" Jeffers remembered where he was barely in time to deny himself a whoop, and settled for throwing a haymaker at the air. He quickly popped his sample out of the magnet. The machine itself could be left until someone came in later in the morning. "There is one problem," he said as he returned to Taylor, sample tube in hand, "I have no idea where Bieber lives."

"That's okay. There should be something in his office with his address on it."

Backtracking to Bieber's office was quicker, and easier, than finding their way from it to the instrument room. Despite that, it was a tenser trip. The time they had spent had brought them to the early hours of the morning. Even at a research center, not many people worked that late, and those who did with any regularity would be known to the security people. Indeed, they saw no lights on in any of the offices or laboratories they passed through. Fortunately, they encountered no security personnel on the trip, either.

Bieber's office door offered no greater resistance than the adjacent laboratory door had a few hours before. Once inside, Jeffers drew a deep breath, and decided to turn the lights on. He really had no other option. They had no flashlight, and groping around in the dark was unattractive. The office looked just as it had two days before. The desk was tidy, almost bare, books and journals were neatly arranged. Jeffers could believe that Bieber used it the way some families used their living room, primarily for show and occasionally to receive guests. In this instance, Bieber's neatness came to their aid. Bieber's file drawers seemed to contain, in neatly indexed folders, every scrap of paper he had ever received. There was even one marked HUMOR that contained clipped, or scribbled, jokes and cartoons. There were several files labeled OFFICIAL CORRESPONDENCE and another two that were labeled only CORRESPONDENCE. The latter files were packed with Bieber's personal letters. Some of them held his home address.

"That should do it," Taylor said as she copied down the address. "Now, there are just a couple of items we need."

The side door from the office to the laboratory had a deadbolt, but the latch was on the office side. She pushed the door open and went through. As she did, Jeffers had a last-minute thought of his own. He went into the lab, and headed for a small crushed ice machine he had seen earlier. He quickly scooped a full load into a Styrofoam bucket, and stuck the sample tube into the middle of the ice. While he did so, he could hear Taylor going through a drawer in one of the aisles. With his bucket set, he retreated to the office to wait. It was not long before she came back through the door holding a flashlight and a coil of flexible insulated wire.

"I remembered seeing this stuff before. Lord knows, we need the light. Christ! What are you doing with that?" She pointed at the bucket.

Jeffers immediately felt defensive. "It's more stable when it's kept cold. A couple of hours, no problem, but I don't know when I'll get a chance to refrigerate it. And I'm certainly not going to leave it here."

"Easy, easy. I wasn't suggesting you should. This is one of the things we came for anyway. Besides, it adds authenticity to the outfit. What thief walks around with a bucket of ice? Come on, let's go. We can leave that in the back seat." Almost as an afterthought, she ripped the woman's picture on Bieber's desk out of its frame and stuffed it into one of her pockets.

The walk back to their point of entry was uneventful. The lab coats they left where they found them. They headed out through the same window, causing further damage to the unfortunate graduate student's notes. The entire time they had been in the institute, they had neither seen nor heard a guard. At last, Jeffers could appreciate Thompson's point of view. It had been too easy.

# CHAPTER 18

## FRANKFURT, GERMANY

BY THE TIME THEY returned to the car, Jeffer's emotional roller coaster had again careened to a high point. Never mind that it was four in the morning. He had successfully rescued his enzyme. Spirited it away he had, in the dead of night, and now he was going to get the thief. Almost as important in his mind, maybe just as important, was that Taylor had seen that he could be cool under pressure. That he could get a job done. A sensation of unquenchable energy ran through him as he turned these thoughts over in his head. The fatigue of earlier in the evening was a thing of the past. For the moment, at least, he was beyond such mundane feelings. It struck him that a large part of his elation at his exploit derived from a desire to impress Taylor. He hoped he had done so.

Taylor gave him a quick smile, highlighted by the street lamps, as she put the Porsche into gear. "What d'ya say? Let's go get the bad guy!"

"For sure." At that moment Jeffers could hardly have said anything else. The look on Taylor's face had been pure joy. He wished that he could capture that somehow, put it in a picture, keep it on his desk. Far better than the one Bieber had on his desk. The one on Bieber's desk!

Jeffers sat forward so fast that the seat belt ratchet caught, causing the belt to gouge into the side of his neck. "Oh, Hell!"

"What's the matter? Did we forget something?"

"Yes! That picture on Bieber's desk."

"Picture of a woman?" Jeffers nodded in response. "No problem, I have it."

"Who is it?"

A puzzled look came over Taylor's face. "I have no idea. Wife, girlfriend maybe. Cousin for all I know. Does it matter?"

"Of course it does." A horrible thought was forming in Jeffers's mind. "How do we know he's alone?"

"Ah, I see your point. Well, we'll see when we get there, I guess. Just have to play it by ear."

"There's just one thing, Taylor. You wouldn't, I mean . . ." Jeffers trailed off, finding it impossible to ask the question for fear the answer would be "yes."

"You mean, would I kill her if she happened to be there?" Jeffers said nothing. "Geez, George, what do you take me for? I wouldn't waste her just for sleeping with the guy. All that proves is that her taste in men is as bad as her taste in clothes. Steal her car, yes. Kill her, no. If she's there, we'll deal with it."

Jeffers relaxed and sat back. He had learned that he could trust Taylor's word. In fact, he began to worry that he had irritated her by considering the possibility. There was no way he could read that from her face and he was not about to ask. He resigned himself to trying to suppress his new anxiety over it.

Finding Bieber's address was uncomplicated; Taylor drove as though she had prior knowledge of the city and they made few wrong turns. It proved to be a 1960's vintage apartment building, in a well-kept neighborhood. They parked a block away and walked to the front entrance. The streets were completely deserted, creating the eerie feeling that they were exposed in front of a multitude of hidden watchers. The front door was equipped with a deadbolt lock, which defied Taylor's attempt to quickly jimmy it open.

"Damn!" That from Jeffers. "I thought Germany was one of those efficient well-run places where people don't have to lock their doors."

"Don't we wish," she answered. "It does tend to be efficiently run, and that goes for security too. With the exception, I guess, of academics." She checked up and down the street. "Let's try around the side. Maybe it has an outside fire escape."

It did not, but there did turn out to be a flight of steps leading down to a basement-level door. That door was bolted as well. The depressed stairway, however, screened them from casual observers. Given time to concentrate on the lock without worrying about looking natural, Taylor had it open in a few minutes. The entrance gave onto a dim hallway illuminated by a single, naked, low-wattage bulb overhead. Doors from the corridor led into areas housing the building's heating facility and storage bins. Behind the last of the doors was a staircase leading up. Unlike many modern buildings, in which the stairway from the basement debouches at a different point on the ground floor than the stairs from above, these were continuous. They took advantage of this to avoid the lobby altogether, with its potential risk of a night watchman. On the second floor, they left the stairs and took the elevator up four more flights.

Bieber had a corner apartment on the sixth floor. The corridor was well lit and empty. From one apartment, a radio program in German could be heard. Otherwise, there was no indication of any activity. Bieber's door had a conventional lock, without an added deadbolt. It fell prey, in short order, to Taylor's manipulations. As it clicked open, she gave thanks under her breath that they were not trying this stunt in New York City. Her earlier response to Jeffers to the contrary, Germany was not nearly as locked up as many parts of the United States.

The apartment beyond was almost pitch black. Once inside, they let the door close and waited a few minutes to give their eyes a chance to adapt to the dark. Even then it was hard to make out the contents of the room, but enough was visible to find a clear path along the floor. Taylor handed the flashlight back to Jeffers and moved out first. They could see well enough that they would not risk a light yet. She moved slowly in linear fashion, both hands checking the space in front of her, ready to be withdrawn at the lightest contact. Jeffers followed, a soldier trailing the point through a mine field. A stumble there, against an unseen coffee table, or an elbow brushing a vase could be catastrophic. The room they were in turned out to be fairly large, likely the living room of the apartment. Two doors were at the far end, distinguished by areas of deeper darkness. A snore emanated from the left-hand one, settling the question of where the bedroom was. Inside it, the dark mass of a bed could be visualized beneath an open window. Enough city glow came in through the window that the area around the bed could be dimly perceived. There was only one body in the bed.

Taylor's smile was invisible in the dark, but present all the same. She had been concerned about the possibility of a bedmate from the time she had thought of this excursion. Despite her confident reply to Jeffers, it would have been inconvenient at the least, and possibly dangerous. This was a piece of good luck. She signaled Jeffers silently to stay where he was while she went forward. Bieber was sleeping on his side, his head toward the window. From one of her pockets, Taylor brought out the coil of wire she had pilfered from the lab. It was long enough for her to grab a loop in each hand and still have a length of slack wire in between. This she converted into a large loop. Abandoning silence, she rushed in to pull the loop down around Bieber's head. The sudden contact roused the sleeping man. Instinctively, he tried to roll away from his attacker. That only made it easier for Taylor to yank the wire down so that it was completely around his neck. Quickly, she pulled the wire tight. By the time Bieber thought to scream, the wire had closed his windpipe.

"You want to live, you keep it quiet," she hissed. "Try to yell and I'll rip your head off. Understand?"

Bieber, after a frantic attempt to pull the wire noose loose, sagged in surrender. Taylor relaxed the tension on the wire, just enough to let him breath and talk. Jeffers meanwhile, had moved up with the flashlight on, shining it directly into Bieber's face. His right hand held the pistol. In the glare of the flashlight, it was obvious that the other side of the bed had seen use that evening. *Just as well I took so long at the laboratory*, Jeffers thought.

"Good morning, Herr Professor. It is a pleasure to see you again. We took the liberty of letting ourselves in." His voice was rock steady, which surprised him.

Squinting into the light, Bieber could not make out the figure in front of him, but he could see the gun. *"Was zum Teufel?"*

"Oh, come on, Bieber. We met in your office two days ago. I'm here to find out exactly how you got that enzyme."

"You!" Bieber glared at Jeffers. "You should think more of what will happen when the police catch you, whoever you are."

"I'm Jeffers, remember?"

"No, you're not. Dr. Jeffers died a week ago. As for the enzyme, I made it, I told you. I and Gerhardt. Fruhling has the enzyme you were looking for, why don't you go aim your gun at him?"

"Hmm. Let me put it this way," Jeffers replied, "I was in your lab tonight. I reconstituted the enzyme in $D_2O$, and ran the NMR spectrum on your institute's five hundred megahertz instrument using a pulse width of nine microseconds and a sweep width of three thousand hertz." Jeffers rattled off a string of numbers giving the peak positions he had seen earlier. "You want more parameters, I'll give them to you. The spectra match the ones I ran in Cleveland. That should tell you who I am and what I already know. Now, I want to know who got it for you. And if you don't start talking quick, I'm going to get really angry and blow your balls off." For emphasis, he shifted the aim of the gun slightly. A white-hot rage was building inside of him. It sent shivers along his limbs and bunched the muscles along his jaw until they ached.

"Five seconds, Bieber. Should I give you a countdown?"

*"Lieber Gott!* No! Please!" All at once, Bieber broke. His composure, so carefully maintained to that point, vanished. He sat there, tears visible on his cheeks, bubbling and begging. "Don't, please please don't. I never, ever wanted, ever planned. God, this all wasn't supposed to happen!"

"But it did, didn't it? And now the accounts are due. Talk!" Jeffers barked at him. He was aware of another sensation underneath the anger, that of raw power.

"Jeffers, please, it wasn't my idea. Not my doing at all. Müller, Gerhardt

Müller, came to me a while ago. He came to me, understand? Schroeder sent him, Schroeder from Sachsen Fabrik. He knew I was working on the enzyme project. That was no secret, but he also knew I had the contract with H-C. He offered me a deal. Schroeder wanted the patent on the technology; he said he could sell it for a lot of money to a Western firm if we made it look like the enzyme had been developed by Sachsen Fabrik. I would be free of H-C and they would split the profits with me. I admit it, I was greedy, but that's all. I didn't do anything else."

"Bullshit!" Jeffers nearly spat at him. "I just got done telling you that I know that's my enzyme you've got. That wasn't your enzyme Sachsen Fabrik was going to peddle. Don't bullshit me!"

"I'm not. I won't. I know it's yours. My project failed; we didn't get the enzyme we were after, didn't get near it. We went down a blind alley! It would have taken years more work and Schroeder wouldn't wait. He sent Müller back. He told me that Schroeder had a connection that could get the designer enzyme for me and then the deal would go just as we planned. I was supposed to carry Müller as a fellow. Not to be a postdoctoral fellow, just to have the position and the mailing address. I fixed the records for him. That's all there was to it, believe me. I didn't know anyone would get hurt!"

"Which makes you greedy but innocent and I don't buy it," Taylor said. "We know about the group that bought Sachsen Fabrik."

"What? All right, yes. No! It's not what you think." Spittle flew out of Bieber's mouth along with the words. "Schroeder wasn't just going to sell the patent; he wanted to sell the whole company. They were going to pay me off when the deal went through, but Schroeder's group was going to control all the rest of the money. They came to me because they knew I could arrange the deal with the *Treuhand.*"

"I think they also knew that you wanted the enzyme bad enough you were ready to lie, cheat, and steal to get it. You were even ready to kill for it, weren't you?" Taylor's words hit Jeffers almost as hard as they hit Bieber. The gun hand started to shake and Bieber flinched away from it, toward Taylor, who forced him back into place.

"None of this was my idea!" Bieber yelled. "It was Schroeder's idea. Confront him! He'll tell you."

"Schroeder's dead, Bieber," Taylor said. "He's dead and Müller's Stasi. How long did you work for the Stasi, Bieber?"

"What? No! No, I never, ever. How would I know Müller worked for the Stasi? I mean, he came from the east, but I had no reason to think . . . The Stasi is gone, along with the rest of the DDR."

"It sounds like you made a great deal of effort not to think," Jeffers said. "Your friends at the ministry are going to enjoy hearing who you work with."

"No, damn you! I told you I didn't know. Schroeder was in charge."

"I don't think so," Taylor said. "Schroeder wasn't giving the orders and someone gave an order to have him killed. Who else did Müller talk to regularly?"

"I don't know. Wait!" he shrieked as the wire tightened. "You're right, Müller did not take orders from Schroeder. The other way around, maybe. There was a man named Walther Huebner. Müller spoke to him now and again and he never wanted anyone around then."

"Huebner?" The question was in Taylor's voice. That was a new name.

"I don't know who that is and I tell you again I don't know anything about the Stasi," Bieber said.

"Bieber, didn't you ever wonder about all of this?" Jeffers asked. "Müller is just a poor scientist working for a bankrupt company in the east that has a little scheme to steal my enzyme. Didn't you ever think that there had to be more to it than that? Who is Müller, really?"

"I don't know. It seemed better not to ask, not to know."

"I bet your parents were real good at that, too." Jeffers shifted his weight a little. It was time to wind it up. "So, Müller's the bad guy, or whoever he works for is, and you're just the greedy little dupe who got caught. Where do we find Müller?"

"I don't know."

"Godammit!" Jeffers practically spit the words at Bieber. "I would love an excuse to pull this trigger. Hank Davenport is dead, and you're the fuckin' thief that made it happen. You damn well better give me a reason *not* to shoot." The tension in Jeffers's voice was unmistakable. Bieber recognized it and terror showed on his face.

"God! I can't think! Wait! Müller had a letter from someone named Jon Petursson that I saw. It said he was expecting Müller soon. The address was in Reykjavik, Iceland."

"Iceland?" Taylor's voice showed surprise. "I don't suppose he showed it to you, so I'll assume you were reading his mail. What else did Müller get?"

"I don't know. No, I swear that was the only time I looked. It was only that he had gotten several from this person."

"All right. How long has he been gone?"

"I last spoke to him three days ago. He said he would be gone for a while."

"Meaning you tipped him off about us?" Jeffers asked, rhetorically. It figured. Müller must have set Schwerin and Karl on them just before leaving. To tidy up, one might say. It did provide the missing link between Bieber and what had happened in Amsterdam. Likely, Müller or his boss had given the order to kill Schroeder. Müller seemed to be a good candidate for Schwerin's Herr Professor.

"Bieber?" Taylor's voice was low, but far from soft. "I want you to think very carefully about what you have told us, and also about what you are going to say tomorrow. Because if it turns out that you have lied, or if you think that you can go to the police, we'll be back. But not, immediately, for you. That photo in your office, you know, is an excellent likeness."

"No! You . . ." The shout tore out of Bieber's throat but ended in a gurgle as Taylor pulled the wire tight. Eyes wide, struggling for breath, Bieber flopped back on the bed.

"Quiet now," she loosened the loop again. "Just a reminder I thought you would want." She looked up at Jeffers. "George, see what's in his medicine cabinet will you? Tape, pills, that sort of stuff."

Jeffers returned with a handful of pill bottles, but no tape. He read the names off to Taylor.

"Ah, a good sleeper," she said at one of the bottles. "Be a sport and get Dr. Bieber a glass of water and three of those." When Jeffers returned with the water, Bieber took the pills docilely. "Good, that should put him away for most of the day. We just need to hold him until they kick in." While she held Bieber secure with the wire, Jeffers tore a bedsheet into strips. He tied Bieber's hands and feet, then gagged him, after which Taylor released the wire.

"Sweet dreams, Martin," Jeffers said, touching the barrel of the gun to his forehead in mock salute. "Remember to be discreet."

They left the apartment the same way they had come in, again leaving the elevator at the second floor to walk down to the basement. On the staircase, Jeffers asked Taylor, "That threat you made. You don't really know who that woman is. And, anyway, I thought you wouldn't."

"It's not hard to find out a person's name," she answered, "but in fact no, I would not. However, *he* doesn't know that, and when he finds the picture gone, he'll draw the appropriate conclusions."

Jeffers did not press the issue any further and they continued down. The basement was just as they had left it, empty and silent save for periodic murmuring of machinery. A low-budget film about the last two survivors of mankind might have used a set like that building in the time just before dawn. Outside was quiet, too, permitting them a measure of relaxation. A thief would still have cause to worry, even after leaving his target, but they had taken nothing out with them that had not gone in. The only real risk once they were out the basement door was that Bieber might free himself before the sleeping pills took effect. Even then, Taylor doubted he would call for help. There was too much for him to lose.

"I can't help but think, though," Jeffers said as they walked along, "that I should have finished him right then, when I had the chance. A few hours ago I thought I was all set for it, but somehow with him blubbering around like that, I just lost it. Didn't want to do it, I mean."

"I have no problem with that, George. He is a thief and a schmuck, no doubt, but I quite believe he didn't realize what would happen to your friend. Anyway, think of how he has to live now. His only chance to keep any of what he has is to try and cover this up, sit on it so it never comes out. Great life, huh?"

"Well, I just hope I haven't fucked it up, that's all."

"George, if he really needed to be dead, I had him around the neck, remember? It would have been quick and quiet."

"Oh. Right. You know, it's as though all I can see of that scene is the tip of the gun and his face. Everything else is a blank right now. I guess I'm just not cut out for this kind of work."

"Like hell. George, you were great today." She gave him a quick pat on the back. The touch was light and quickly withdrawn, lest the intent be misunderstood, but it was there. Afterward, all he could remember of the walk was the tap behind his right shoulder.

# CHAPTER 19

## LANGLEY, VIRGINIA

CHARLES N. OLIVER WAS A most unhappy man. His physical distress derived from his stomach, where a miniature volcano rumbled. Periodically it erupted, sending a lava flow of acid upward to the back of his throat. Repeated episodes left him with a sore throat and a deep pain in the middle of his chest to go with the gnawing sensation in the middle of his stomach. Antacids were futile, even though he ate them like candy. Eventually the pills his doctor had prescribed would bring it back under control, but when it was this bad, he knew from experience, relief was days away.

The proximate cause of this grief was mental and focused on a report that had been filed by the case officer assigned to watch Fruhling. Mr. Marden had observed George Jeffers, in the company of a girl, meeting with Fruhling in Amsterdam. Marden's file sat on Oliver's desk next to the report. Oliver would bet after reviewing that file that if Marden reported Jeffers, it was Jeffers. Marden clearly had a reputation for reporting only items he was certain of. There was nothing else in the report regarding Jeffers. That was also to be expected. Marden had been ordered to report on Fruhling and that was what he was doing. In some respects, Oliver thought, Marden must be a bit like a wind-up toy. Once wound up, it went through its routine without deviation until it ran down. Oliver let out a small sigh, and some gas, at the thought of the missed opportunity. He could not really blame Marden for not leaving Fruhling to trail Jeffers and that, of course, was part of the problem. While it would be nice to see a little initiative in the field, what could you expect when initiative was too often the way to being canned, and too seldom the route to promotion? A man like Marden was simply reinforced in his own tendencies by such a system.

No use crying over that again, he thought. The crucial point was that Jeffers had been in Amsterdam. How had Jeffers gotten to Amsterdam? Not only how had he gotten there, but why was he so obviously uninterested in contacting the authorities? In Oliver's estimation, the man was a total zero when it came to being a man. In fact, he would have bet any amount of money that there was no possibility of Jeffers's escaping assassination and going to Europe on his own. Nor did he believe Jeffers could have been dissembling in the past, to hide parts of his background. Dr. George Jeffers might be the consummate wallflower socially, but he was prominent enough in science that his life was a public record. No place to hide other training or experience. None of which changed the fact that Jeffers had been in Amsterdam. None of which changed the fact that shortly after Jeffers had been spotted, there had been trouble in Amsterdam. One bully for hire was dead there. Not long afterward, a company executive was murdered in his plant in Saxony and another thug was found in said plant with a bullet in his back and a major case of amnesia. Oliver had a contact in German intelligence who had identified that thug as Reinhard Schwerin, late of the Stasi. It just happened that the police reports from the town mentioned an American named George Anderson who had been there that day. The description of Anderson just happened to match that of Jeffers. Fruhling (he knows he is being watched, damn him!) sat quietly doing nothing. Superficially, doing nothing. All unrelated coincidences, then, with Jeffers's appearance. Not bloody likely. And who was the girl, and what was her role? Oliver was sure this girl was the same one the police reports from Boston had mentioned. Fortunately, the meeting with Fruhling had been photographed. Oliver could recognize both Jeffers and Fruhling in the print, but not the girl. The quality of the photograph was only so-so but Oliver thought that the computer jockeys would be able to sharpen it up. For the time being, the girl's identity and her allegiance remained mysteries. They would not remain that way, but Oliver had a hunch he could not spend too much time finding out.

Oliver sighed again as the assault on his esophagus was renewed. The desk in front of him was piled with reports and files, most of them in urgent need of his attention. They languished, however, while he tried to fit the facts he had into a rational pattern. It was no good. No matter how many times he ran it through his head, there was not enough information. A solution was going to have to wait until he found Jeffers. That, and he had to know about the girl. Oliver popped another antacid tablet into his mouth and reached for the phone.

Later that day the photograph of the woman came back from the lab looking much sharper but still unfamiliar, so Oliver passed it to his contacts at the FBI. It had been years since he had worked in counterintelligence but he still knew enough people there who would work with local police forces and quietly pass the information back to him. The picture traveled to Boston where it was shown to the people who had been in the Kettle

Drum as well as a number of others who could be connected to the kind of activities that interested Oliver. In fairly short order there was information coming back, although, as always, it was fragmentary and often inconsistent. The woman in the picture was the same woman who had been in the Kettle Drum, although the bartender continued to deny having seen her. Several other people the police spoke to recognized the woman in the picture. Unfortunately, these individuals supplied a total of five different names for the woman, ranging from Becky Andrews to Taylor Redding. Four of these had driver's licenses giving different addresses. When checked, no such person lived at any of the addresses. One of the names, Taylor Redding, belonged to a person who had died six years before, according to the death certificate on file. Becky had been the name given by the girl in the plane. That memory caused Oliver's pen to fly across the office and bang off the wall.

Another bit of information was even more disturbing. The woman, whatever her name, was an associate of one William O'Brian. The name initially meant nothing to Oliver, but his friends at the FBI thoughtfully supplied a dossier. O'Brian was a successful Boston businessman and, apparently, an equally successful crook. Two items stood out. First, O'Brian served as a conduit for money and guns headed to the IRA. Second, O'Brian also funneled information on IRA activities and sympathizers in Boston back to the FBI. Oliver had to smile at the inclusion of that last datum in the file, information that really should not have been given to him. It was a message, really. The FBI considered O'Brian's information to be solid. That was why his other activities were tolerated. The FBI was not going to bother O'Brian as long as his information was good and they did not want Oliver to bother him either. That was okay for the present, Oliver thought. O'Brian was an American citizen on American soil and to act directly against him would be problematic, both for Oliver and the agency. Except . . . Oliver flipped idly through the pages as he thought. Could O'Brian have ordered the woman to kill Lorenzo to get at Jeffers and the enzyme? If it really had the sort of value that Thompson had claimed, well, O'Brian was the sort of man, with the right connections, to go after it. Oliver closed that folder and pushed it aside. If it turned out, in the end, that O'Brian had given the order there would be time to deal with him. The ban on agency action within the United States would not save him then. His role as an FBI asset would not save him either.

Oliver got up and paced back and forth in his office. He had to find the woman again, that and he had to find out more about her. His first step was logical and obvious. The chief of station in Germany was an old hand whom Oliver knew well. The man would do what was necessary without creating a fuss. Oliver sent him a message instructing him that if Jeffers and the woman contacted Fruhling again, Marden was to abandon his surveillance of Fruhling and follow them. He was sure the contact would occur; it was just a question of when. His second step, done almost as an afterthought, was to have the names provided by the Boston police run through the agency database.

He promptly forgot about the names because, just then, Thompson called again. Oliver was getting tired of Thompson's calls, with their insistence that he get Jeffers back, as though that were the only problem confronting the world since the end of the Cold War. Thompson should know better. He had been with the Company long enough, had known Oliver. He ought to know where Oliver's priorities were right now. Thompson seemed to sense Oliver's irritation, it was hardly disguised, because this time he said he had some new information to provide. Thompson had tracked Jeffers to Europe by tracing the man's phone and credit card activity. Thomson was certain Jeffers had not gone voluntarily; he knew him too well to believe that. He was also sure it was not just a thief on vacation with Jeffers's cards. Thompson's people had spoken with someone who had been able to identify Jeffers, apparently in the company of a woman, possibly the same as in Boston. What Thompson wanted now was help.

"I need some assistance in Berlin," he said. "That's where the trail goes, but we haven't been able to pick him up yet. I don't exactly have a lot of people to work with, not our kind of people anyway. I've got to get to him before he moves, or is moved, out of the city. We may not be able to pick him up again if that happens."

"Do you have a man there now?" Oliver asked.

"Yes."

"Okay. Understand, I can't call out the cavalry, but I will set it up so that your man should be able to get the help he needs. I'll get back to you today with the details." That seemed to satisfy Thompson.

Oliver leaned back in his chair after he hung up the phone, his mind half on the conversation and half on his stomach. He would bet that Thompson had known before today that Jeffers was in Europe. The bastard thought he could scoop up Jeffers on his own and look good to his brass while Oliver had to explain to the director what his group was doing to justify its existence. Except, guys who spend the day signing people in at a front door make lousy field agents. You ought to know that, Jim. Glad you finally admitted it. The ploy irritated Oliver. Had he been alerted to the possibility that Jeffers was in Europe, Marden might have been able to snare Jeffers and the girl in Amsterdam. Amsterdam—that was the other thing that bothered Oliver about the conversation. Thompson was placing Jeffers in Berlin at a time that Oliver knew, from Marden's report, that the man was in Amsterdam. Thompson's information, therefore, was unreliable. So much for high-tech spying, Oliver thought. In the end, there was no substitute for a good agent in place, although he decided he was not going to break that news to Thompson just yet.

Another message went out to the CoS in Germany. It informed him of the commitment that Oliver had made to Thompson. There was, however, one added instruction. Whatever "help" the CoS arranged for Thompson's man, he was to see to it that the man was steered away from Saxony, Amsterdam and Fruhling. He was to be kept away, in fact, from any place that Jeffers and the girl were likely to be. That ought to keep Thompson out of his way, Oliver thought, while he settled matters. Oliver might be short on both assets and information, but that did not mean he wanted any of Thompson's company spooks in the middle of his case. Not now.

He was still ruminating on Thompson's call when the records group called. One of the names on that list was in the database. Taylor Redding, apparently, had been mentioned in a report filed by a case officer in East Africa. Oliver looked at the printout, then looked back at his notepad. The period covered by the report was after the date that appeared on Taylor Redding's death certificate in Boston. Either someone was using the *persona* of a dead woman or this Taylor Redding had gone to some effort to appear dead. Either way, the information reinforced the feeling he had developed about this woman. Good thing, he told himself, he had gotten rid of the company people. There was going to be no time to deal with outside observers. What he needed to do next was to see the original report and speak with the case officer whose name, he saw, was Bill Waggeman. He just hoped the man was someplace accessible.

"The way this case has been going," Oliver muttered to himself, "he's probably been posted to Mogadishu."

## AUTOBAHN 9, GERMANY

A GUSTY, WORDLESS SNORE answered Taylor Redding's question. She took her eyes briefly from the road to glance across to the passenger seat and found Jeffers asleep. He lolled back against the headrest of the seat which, not being adjusted for his height, permitted his neck to hyperextend. Damn near have to be out cold to tolerate that position, she thought. Could hardly blame him though. Start your day off early with some sleuthing, finish nearly twenty-four hours later with a burglary, splice some murder, attempted and otherwise, in between and he had a right to be tired. For herself, Taylor did not feel too badly. Fatigue was one of those feelings that could be shunted aside, at least on a temporary basis. The two or possibly three hours of driving she had ahead of her would not represent a problem. She knew from experience that she could manage thirty-six, maybe forty hours without sleep. After that, legs grew lead weights, every muscle group ached, and the mind congealed like cold fat. That limit was still in the future. The prospect brought a momentary pang. It would be nice to be able to do without sleep entirely. She had never needed very much and had trained herself to manage on no more than three to four hours a night. Even that she begrudged because sleep always brought the possibility of dreams with it. Given a choice, she would rather be active all night, or if not that, at least spend the night reading, anything but sleeping. She shook away that train of thought. She needed to concentrate on what she was doing.

Lack of sleep aside, there were few problems as she ran through her mental checklist. Her left leg, the one that had betrayed her earlier in the evening, ached dully. She expected that. The surprise would have been had it not ached. The right elbow throbbed where its bony prominence had smacked into the factory floor. It was tender when it brushed anything more substantial than her sleeve, and doubtless was bruised and swollen as well, but she had free use of her arm. If those were to be the only consequences of falling flat on her ass in a knife fight, she would not complain.

Having reviewed her physical status, her mind drifted back to the status of her job. The answer to the original problem, of course, was clear. The trail of the enzyme had led to one Gerhardt Müller. The more interesting questions were, who did Müller really work for and what else was he involved in? The obvious thing to do was to chase down Herr Müller and throw a monkey wrench into whatever machinations he had created. She was uncertain, however, if Jeffers would see it that way. He had his enzyme back and might well think he had enough information to blow Müller's cover and operation just by talking to the right people. Maybe he would want to quit. If he did, did she want to take an unpaid vacation and keep going? Strangely enough, she was not looking forward to the thought of going off alone. Now, where did that come from? Simple gratitude, she told herself, for a timely shot that had saved her skin. No, that answer did not satisfy her.

The idea of partners, and of Taylor Redding, had never mixed well, although she could not attribute this to any conscious design. She had worked with others, certainly, but always either for them, or they for her. That had even been true of her time with Sister Angelica's missionaries in Africa, which was easily one of her fondest memories. Sister had organized her small group, and much of the surrounding countryside, with a thoroughness the elder von Moltke would have admired. They had preached the Word, taught the children and aided the sick, all while managing a marvelously efficient gunrunning and intelligence operation for the local insurgents. Taylor had worked for a pittance, "We came to serve God, not to get rich," as Sister liked to mangle Cortez, but it had been so grand an adventure she had not minded. (Actually, she had gotten lucky one night near a roadblock, after the region had gone all to chaos. Chance favors the prepared mind.) Still, for all the shared hardship and camaraderie, the hierarchy had been clear. "God's will be done," Sister Angelica was fond of saying, and it was too, just as soon as Sister decided what it was. No partnership there, except perhaps between Sister and God. One of Sister Angelica's contacts had been an American agent named Bill Waggeman. Taylor had served as the go-between and discovered that Waggeman often wanted information that had nothing to do with the mission's operation. They had worked together, too, but she would hardly call it a partnership. They were just using each other: Waggeman to have an independent asset there; Taylor to use the situation to learn whatever he could teach her. No other job had even come that close to a partnership, and when Taylor went off on a lark, she always went alone.

The fact was, she had come to like working as a partner with Jeffers. Now that was a strange thought. Back when she had talked her way into his business, it had been on the hunch, since proven correct, that an adventure of major dimensions could be found. Jeffers was an inescapable piece of extra baggage. Inept and naïve, he had seemed likely to be dangerous to himself and possibly to her also. Had there been any way of leaving him in New York, she would have done so. Yet, it had not worked out that way. Jeffers had been adaptable and helpful. He had also been rather sweet that previous, unmentionable, afternoon.

"The Lady of Ice and Fire," she repeated softly, then looked quickly to make certain he was still asleep. "I like the sound of it." Maybe she should have it printed on a business card. No, that would never do. A business card should be austere. The reputation should be gaudy, not the advertisement. How about "Redding and Jeffers, Adventurers"? Now, *that* was a *dangerous* thought.

A foolish one, too. Certainly, no good would ever come of it. Such thoughts led only in one direction, and that was impossible.

"Goddamn it, Taylor," said a voice, hers, in her head. "You know the rules. Who better?"

"Rules are made to be broken," she argued back.

*"Not mine."*

Maybe George would not want to go to Iceland.

## NEAR MUNICH, GERMANY

JEFFERS AWOKE TO SUNLIGHT streaming through the windshield into his face. He blinked a few times, squinted at the sun, and tried to sit up straight.

"Oh-h-h!"

The groan rose from below his diaphragm. His neck had frozen into position and gave every indication that it would break rather than bend. He dug fingers into the muscles along the sides of his neck, trying to knead them back to malleability. As he did so, he became aware of an equally sore region just above the base of his spine.

The aches and pains were enough initially to distract him from his surroundings. When he did look up, he was impressed. The Porsche sat, idling, before a sturdy metal gate set into a stone wall. Visible through the gate was a wide expanse of green lawn running up a gentle slope. At the top of the hill was a large manor, done in white and set stone. Next to him, Taylor was conducting an argument in German with a voice that issued from a metal grille in the wall next to the gate. As he looked around, the voice cut off and the gate swung inward, silently.

"Officious turkey," Taylor muttered. With the car in first gear, they rolled slowly up the drive to the house.

"Where in God's name are we?"

"Ah! The sleeper awakes. For a while, I thought resuscitation was going to be necessary." She looked over at him and grinned. "You slept right through some of the worst bumps I've ever seen on an allegedly paved road. As for where we are, this is the home of your friend and collaborator, Max Fruhling. We do need to return his car, in case you have forgotten, and I thought we could continue our tradition of early morning social calls to also answer some questions we both have."

"This is Fruhling's?" As they drew even with the front entrance, the scale of the structure became more apparent than it had been from the gate below. Two wings, invisible from the base of the hill, extended from the rear of the main building. The sprawling building looked as though it could easily have housed a regiment.

"If it isn't his, there will be more than two very surprised people in a moment. But it fits the description he gave me the other day. Besides, using his name got the gate opened."

"Oh. I suppose this also means that what happened last night was real, too?"

"Quite real," she said sunnily. Jeffers glanced quickly into the rear seat. The sample tube was there in its ice bucket, tilting a jut, as much of the supporting ice had melted.

Taylor stopped the car across from the front door and got out as a man in livery came to meet them. Jeffers, ice bucket in hand, copied her. The chauffeur acknowledged neither of them, climbed into the car and drove it around to the far side of the house. They were left standing alone in front of the open door.

"Well," said Taylor, "why don't we go in and see if we can cadge some breakfast?"

"Breakfast! Taylor, breakfast is a bowl of Wheaties with milk and a cup of coffee. What you do in the morning isn't breakfast. It belongs on the cover of American Gourmand."

Breakfast was, in fact, available in the kitchen. It came hot and in bulk. The rapidity with which it appeared, and the smug look on Taylor's face, suggested to Jeffers that the stop had been planned in advance, and in detail. Jeffers had expected to be ravenous, but after the food arrived he found himself full after only a few bites. Conversation tended to receive a low priority from Taylor while there was food on the table, so he amused himself by taking inventory of the room. Like the house itself, the kitchen was constructed on a grand scale. The wooden table at which they ate could have easily sat eight, the cooking area looked capable of satisfying a reception for a hundred and fifty. There were interesting contrasts, too; old iron skillets were hung on the wall above a Litton microwave. The morning sun, warming him through the window, interfered with his concentration. He counted the jars in a spice rack twice, then proceeded to lose track of the room entirely.

"George, are you still with me?"

The question snapped his head up. The resulting pain in his neck brought him back to full wakefulness. Whatever Taylor might have been saying, he had completely missed it. With his eyes, he examined her closely, looking for some reciprocal sign of exhaustion and found none. Yet he knew she had driven all night. So much for his own vaunted workaholic character.

"Sorry. I missed what you said."

"I said that we need to make a decision today."

"Sorry again. I must be dense this morning. What decision is that? Wait a minute!" He cut her off before she could answer. "You're thinking of chasing Müller to Iceland, aren't you?"

"Yes, of course. Why not? That's where Bieber says he went and, all things considered, I'm inclined to believe him."

"I can think of several reasons." The idea had been in Jeffers's mind since the moment they had pried the information out of Bieber. "We have really done what we set out to do, haven't we? We know who took the enzyme, and we have it back. We know what happened to Hank—" surprisingly, contemplating that no longer gave him shivers—"and we cleared Fruhling, which in a sense also clears me. Müller's cover is gone, as soon as we report what we know. Seems to me that's a pretty good job. I just can't see the two of us charging after Müller ourselves. The man's clearly professional; we'd be playing way over our heads. I think I've had enough of this Stasi, or whatever these people used to work for, to last a lifetime. So, I think it's time to call in the cavalry, so to speak. If it's earning your pay you're worried about," he continued, "God knows, you've done more than enough. Far as I'm concerned, the whole lockbox is yours, and if Herb and Sir James both have a stroke about it, tough shit."

In the ideal world, as it existed then in his mind, she would have agreed with his reasoning. Then she would give him an address and phone number in Boston, and they would catch a plane to the States. That world's existence proved to be confined to his brain.

"It's not just a question of money—or rather, it's not a question of money at all. The job is not done, and I know it and you should too. 'He either fears his fate too much, Or else his desserts are small, that puts it not unto the touch, To win or lose it all.' "

The quotation put a sharp rein on Jeffers's imagination. Did it really look as though he was running out on unfinished business? "I don't really think I'm being a coward about it. Not now." It sounded defensive, and he knew it as soon as he said it.

"George, I have never thought you were a coward, and I don't now. I was speaking in regard to me, because that is the way I have to be. I can see how you might have taken it though."

"Oh, hell, that's okay." He waved at the air between them. "Until very recently I probably would have agreed with you if you had called me a coward, and please don't try to act as though it would not have been true. I probably still am, underneath. What was that quote anyway?"

"It's from a poem by a Scottish nobleman at the time of the English Civil

War, guy named James Graham of Montrose, the Great Marquis. Probably my most favored historical figure." As always when the conversation turned to history and adventure, Taylor's voice lit up with animation.

"Ah, historic verse at breakfast! Taylor, you are a wonder." Montrose meant nothing to Jeffers, but he could postpone asking for more details because, just then, the most obvious reason to leave Müller alone popped into his head. "Taylor, I won't argue that the business isn't finished, but we don't have to chase Müller to do that. I know who set this up."

Taylor's response was not in verse. "Who?" The question was almost an order.

"Hochmann."

She stared at him. "How did you come to that conclusion just now? Or should I ask, how is it that you are suddenly sure of this?"

Jeffers shrugged, then decided that his neck didn't appreciate that motion either. "Because it all fits," he said. "Look, Hochmann didn't buy the enzyme technology when he had the chance. Now he needs it. Bieber wants the enzyme to upstage me and keep his reputation from taking a hit. Then you have Schroeder over at Sachsen Fabrik who would latch onto anything that would bail him out of the hole he was in. Hochmann sends Müller to Sachsen Fabrik to set up the biotech scam, then he has Bieber set up the deal with whatever that German organization is called. The only thing left was to steal the real enzyme, which I made very easy for them, although I suspect that if I hadn't sent it with Hank, something would have happened in Cleveland. Hell, something did happen in Cleveland: the fire in our labs. I guess grabbing the enzyme from Hank was probably easier than stealing it from the lab, no risk of getting the wrong bottle, plus Hank had with him all the info I was sending Fruhling. Meanwhile, H-C quietly buys control of Sachsen Fabrik, Bieber 'discovers' the enzyme, Sachsen Fabrik patents it, and H-C owns it." Jeffers finished with a flourish, slightly out of breath.

Taylor did not look completely convinced. "I don't see why they would bother with Bieber at all. Why not just have Sachsen Fabrik discover it?"

"Because Bieber is credible and has the right connections to make sure people don't look too closely."

"George, I'm not sure you've really got everything tied up that tightly."

"Tight enough," he said. "Once we report what we know, they'll go after Hochmann. Müller becomes irrelevant."

"Maybe Müller is Hochmann's hired hand." Taylor's tone lacked conviction. "Even so, George, we need to go after him. Why did Müller go to Iceland? I don't know and that worries me. I can't see letting someone like that run around loose while we hope the authorities get enough information

from Hochmann to shut down whatever machinations we *don't* know about.
That's why I'm going. You might also consider to whom you are going to
report what, if you go home. Müller must control a number of people, some
we've found and some we haven't, including agents in the U.S. There has
to be a leak at your company and possibly with the feds too. How secure
are you going to be if we don't get Müller first? The Stasi were very much
feared before the DDR fell and these are the same people, even if they're
working for somebody else now. Anyway, if it makes any difference at all,
I think I've told you what I think we should do." Having said that, she fell
silent, suddenly intent on deciding whether a scrap of egg on her plate
warranted an excursion with her fork.

Jeffers considered her words. Unfortunately for his desires, her comments
about security made sense. Sir James was going to have a fit when it was
pointed out, but there was no help for it. There had to have been a leak.
So, where did that leave him? Four men dead already, including one very
innocent scientist. Far more innocent than himself, for that matter. There
was one more point in what she had said, one that he had almost missed,
so casually had it been made. She had clearly stated that she was going,
but then in her last sentence there had been a definite stress on the 'we.' It
occurred to him that this was as close to a direct request as Taylor ever
came. She was asking him to come with her. The realization was a shock.
Part of his mind told him to be sensible. He should go home, talk to Thompson. No security problem could be worse than running after Müller. But if
he turned her down, she would leave. No address, no phone number, no
more Taylor.

"Answer a question, Taylor?"

"Ask."

"Is this really something we should do, or is this just another Taylor
Redding adventure?"

"George, I won't deny it'll be an adventure, a good one too. But look at
what Müller leaves behind him. Stopping him is important. Chances like
this don't come often."

"Well, then," he said lifting his coffee cup, thinking as he spoke that he
would regret it, "let's put it to the touch."

"Ah, now there is a truly heartwarming sight!"

At the unexpected interruption, Jeffers looked around. Fruhling was
there, standing in the doorway to the kitchen. Neither of them had heard
him arrive, nor did they know how much of the conversation he had heard.

"Forgive my appearance," he said. Indeed, he was garbed in bathrobe
and slippers, his hair wildly unkempt. "It is not my custom to receive guests

in quite this manner. However, as the delightful young lady explained when we talked, this is not a routine visit."

"No, Dr. Fruhling, it is not," Jeffers replied after seeing that Taylor was going to remain silent. "I'm not sure whether I should be apologizing or asking for explanations. Maybe a little of both." Fruhling grinned at that. "Maybe we owe you some explanations too. How much of this do you know?"

Fruhling took it as an invitation and walked over to the table, taking a chair opposite from Jeffers. "When 'Becky,' as she was calling herself, came to see me that night, she had decided that I was not the enemy you sought. In return for the car, she gave me a good summary of events. I think I am current up to your departure from Amsterdam. If you like, you can bring me up to date."

"Sure," Jeffers shrugged. "There's just one thing though. If you knew we still suspected you after our first meeting, why didn't you say something instead of betting that we would work it out ourselves?"

That brought a dry chuckle from Fruhling. "What else should I have said that I did not say that day? You cannot mean to tell me your suspicions would have been allayed had I merely told you not to worry about me."

There was no real reply to that; Jeffers knew Fruhling was correct. He dropped that line of talk in favor of Fruhling's request and launched into a narrative of the preceding days, omitting nothing that he could remember. When he mentioned the name Walther Huebner, the one Bieber had given as someone Müller spoke with, he could see Fruhling tense.

"You know that name?" he asked.

"I do," Fruhling said. "I know that he worked in *Abteilung XXII* of the Stasi, the section charged with working with international terrorist organizations. I do not know of this Müller, however."

"That name is certainly phony," Taylor said.

"Of course," Fruhling replied. "Why don't you continue, Dr. Jeffers."

That was nearly the end of what Jeffers had to tell. When he finished he pushed his chair back slightly and looked directly at Fruhling. He was not keen to be involved with international terrorists. The Stasi were bad enough. Thinking about terrorists, though, jogged another thought in his mind. Immediately he was upset with himself for not saying what he had intended to ask first. There were explanations he wanted from Fruhling. The image of burned-out apartments with SRG painted on the walls rose in his mind. Then, he thought, be tactful, George. Getting Fruhling to throw you out the door will not help matters.

"Dr. Fruhling, are you a neo-Nazi?"

*That* ruffled the older man's composure. In fact, for a moment, Fruhling just gaped at him. Well, Jeffers thought, I may not have been tactful, but Taylor keeps telling me to agitate people and see what they do. I guess we'll see what he does.

What Fruhling did first was to pull his features back under control. When he spoke, his voice was soft. "A neo-Nazi. An interesting question." He fixed Jeffers with a unblinking gaze. "You do know who I am, I assume. I was an officer in the German army during the Second World War. You can assume that, as such, I was a member of the National Socialist Party, in other words, a Nazi. I do not pretend that it never occurred. If you choose to believe, as some do, that once a Nazi always a Nazi, well, there you have it. But a neo-Nazi? A curious question, Dr. Jeffers."

Jeffers had the feeling that Fruhling had, somehow, turned the situation around and was now waiting to see what Jeffers would do. "We saw what was left after a riot in Neu Mecklenberg," Jeffers said. "They burned out the foreign workers, drove them out of town. The SRG Party did that. That's your party, isn't it?"

"Ah, the SRG." Fruhling made a steeple of his fingertips and looked at Jeffers over the top of them. "I founded the SRG Party and, yes, I have been closely associated with it. Be careful of saying that they are *my* party. They are not mine, not anymore than the Greens belonged to Petra Kelly. Not that I intend to end up the way she did, but that is off the point. Do you know what SRG stands for?"

Jeffers shook his head.

"*Schwarz, rot, gold,*" Fruhling said. "The colors of the flag of the Bundesrepublik. The SRG was founded as a nationalist party and, perhaps, with the reunification it has suffered from having its primary goal fulfilled. I still think it has a purpose, to lead the fight against Maastricht and to prevent the bureaucrats in Brussels from submerging us all in a European socialist state. That, however, is my belief, not everyone else's. Fools! What do they have but a bunch of young thugs parading down the street behind a *Reichkriegsfahnen* and shouting, '*Sieg Heil!*' at anyone who will listen. They have not the faintest idea of the horror that unleashed, nor would they listen if you told them. Idiots. One can be a German nationalist without glorifying either the Third Reich or Hitler. I was *there,* Jeffers. Sometimes I think we have learned nothing in the last fifty years—either that, or we have managed to forget what we learned. I make no apologies for who I am or what I believe, but I am not an idiot and I *do* remember. Does that answer your question?"

"I think so." Jeffers swallowed hard. "I think I'm sorry I brought it up. Maybe we should go back to where we were before I asked that."

"If you wish," Fruhling said. "What were you planning to say?"

"We'd brought you up to this morning's breakfast, and the decision we were talking about when you came in. What do you think? Is it the right move to chase Müller to Iceland?"

"Should you go?" Fruhling appeared taken aback by the question. "I do not see where it is for me to tell you what to do. I will make two observations, however. First, you have suggested that Müller works for Werner Hochmann at Helvetica-Chemie and that this elaborate operation was designed to allow H-C to obtain your material in a way that could not be traced to them. I know Werner Hochmann. He is, I think, capable of this. He would also have the resources and the contacts to hire these Stasi. There are also a great many people obligated to him, or Helvetica-Chemie, in one way or another. They are likely to include some whose cooperation will be essential for any official investigation that involves Helvetica-Chemie. I am not saying that he owns them, necessarily, only that it will take powerful evidence to make them move against Helvetica-Chemie. For that, you will need Müller. Dangerous as he is, Müller will be easier to tackle than Hochmann.

"The second observation is related to the first, and is something your friend had alluded to. I do not see why you should be convinced that Müller works for Helvetica-Chemie."

Jeffers's eyes opened wide in surprise. He had, in fact, just managed to convince himself of that. H-C had the motive to steal the enzyme and they were more likely than Bieber, far more likely, to have hired those men. "Who else could Müller work for? I told you everything we had, including what Bieber said last night. It all makes perfect sense this way."

"George," Taylor put in, "a great many otherwise rational people believe professional wrestling and the evening news make sense, too."

"Just so," Fruhling continued as Taylor lapsed back into silence. "You have a great deal of suggestion, without proof. I also would not put too much credence in what Bieber said regarding Müller's background. Under the circumstances he probably would have said that Müller worked for the pope, had you suggested it."

"All right, all right," Jeffers said with a sigh. "I was going anyway, and I will keep an open mind about Müller until we get hold of him. I don't suppose it matters too much what I think until that time anyhow. When we go, will we be able to count on your help?"

The older man shook his head. "I am afraid that will not be possible."

"Why not?" Jeffers replied, shocked. "I'm coming to believe you have a lot more experience at this sort of thing than either one of us, and we can use all the help we can get. For God's sake, we're both on the same side."

"Same side?" Fruhling echoed. He fixed Taylor with a stern look, to which she merely shrugged. Getting no further response, Fruhling turned back to Jeffers. "My dear Dr. Jeffers, I'm afraid that you have led a rather cloistered life. Please do not take offense; none is intended. I have only the highest regard for your ability as a scientist, and, speaking as a scientist, it is a privilege to be able to collaborate with you. However," his voice hardened to emphasize the word, "you are now moving from the world of science to that of *Realpolitik,* and the rules are very different. Yes, I am very pleased with the way it turned out with Bieber, and not only because I can now carry out the experiments we had planned. It has always grated on me that a man whose primary talent lies in knowing what to lick, and when, should rise to such a prominent position. That, I think, you have fixed, and I am glad to have been of some assistance. Nonetheless, do not assume that our interests will always run parallel, which is something you should have inferred from our discussion of my background. Gerhardt Müller is not my problem."

Fruhling paused for breath, then continued, "Understand, please, that I agree with you that the world would, almost certainly, be better off without Herr Müller. I also realize that if he continues on, at some future date he may become my problem. Right now, however, my immediate problem lies not with the Müller's of the world, but with the Charles Olivers."

At the unexpected mention of Oliver's name, Jeffers sat bolt upright in his chair, a startled expression on his face.

"Thank you for waking up," Fruhling said dryly. "Do you know who Mr. Oliver is?"

"CIA, I would assume." Jeffers tried to give his answer with an air of nonchalance. Of course, Oliver was CIA. So what? The look Fruhling gave him in return was pitying.

"All sorts of people work for the CIA," Fruhling said. "Some of them sit behind desks all day and shuffle paper. Others do not. You really have no idea who Charles Oliver is, do you?" Fruhling's tone made it less a question and more a statement of fact.

Jeffers acknowledged that with a shrug. "I guess not," he said. "I gather you do."

"Yes." Fruhling paused to straighten his robe. "Let us say that over the years I have developed excellent connections, both German and American. Quite possibly, I know more about Mr. Oliver than he does about me." Fruhling allowed himself a small chuckle. "Actually, the relative amounts of knowledge are not very important, are they? Your Mr. Oliver works in the directorate of operations and he has, in the past, been on the counter-intelligence staff and the covert action staff, which is why we know of each other. Recently, he was picked to head a new section on industrial espionage, which is why he is interested in you. Do not be fooled by his appearance and his cheap suits. He is a smart man who has spent many years in the field. I had expected him to become the next deputy director of operations and he may yet get that appointment. This is a dangerous man to have on your trail. I will tell you now that, following Dr. Davenport's disappearance, I spent an unpleasant few hours with agents of the BND. Take it as a given that they came at Oliver's instigation. I know that I am under surveillance for my political activities and, although that is no longer Oliver's area of responsbility, he now has another reason to take an interest in me. You should understand that I do not want him involved in my affairs but that is precisely what will happen if I am seen to be further involved with you two and Müller. Why do you think I sent you Wolfgang in Amsterdam? I realize he was not as much help as you could have used, but he was a *bona fide* student with no embarrassing ties, should someone investigate." Fruhling took a roll from a plate at the center of the table, then continued. "You know, when the two of you first showed up, I was sure you would turn out to be CIA."

Jeffers could feel his heart begin to pound in his chest. If Fruhling had reasons, as it now seemed, to be unfavorably disposed to the CIA, what might he do if he still thought Jeffers worked for them? "Dr. Fruhling, I am who I said I am. I don't work for the CIA and if Oliver has been having you watched, I'm sorry, but I've had nothing to do with it."

That brought a smile to Fruhling's face. In deliberate fashion, he tore off a piece of the roll and buttered it. "My dear Dr. Jeffers," he said, "I am absolutely certain that you are who you say you are and that you do not work for the CIA."

That was the response Jeffers thought he wanted, but, somehow, it did not feel like a compliment. Fruhling, however, was not finished. His gaze now turned to Taylor. "I am even secure that you do not work for them, *Fraulein*, although I have heard of your involvement, shall we say, with them in the past."

Taylor's grin suddenly vanished, to be replaced by an uncomfortable look, which was enough to make Jeffers feel even more uncomfortable. "I was, as you say, involved with an agency operation," she said. "That was a number of years ago."

"In Africa," Fruhling said.

"Correct. That does not mean that I work for them or, in fact, have any connection with them today."

"As I said, I do not contest that. Some of my BND contacts know of you as well. One of them told me you were pretty good, for an amateur."

Taylor bristled at that. "I'm better than pretty good and he knows it. And I'm not an amateur."

Fruhling was an old man in a bathrobe whose voice was barely above a whisper, but still he seemed to dominate the room. "Forgive the snobishness of a professional officer. I did not ask for details but I gather he was satisfied with the outcome. I am curious, though, as to why you do this sort of work, since it is not in the service of your government."

"I told you I'm not an amateur," Taylor said. "This is how I earn my living."

"A mercenary is what you are saying. But most mercenaries, to my knowledge, have learned their trade in an army, legitimate or otherwise, or an intelligence agency."

"I had good mentors," Taylor said. "They just weren't always the official kind. And, you just said you knew that I have worked with some of the official kind." She shrugged. "I learn fast, which is why I'm still around. Anyway, as long as my reasons don't cause trouble for you, they shouldn't matter."

Fruhling shrugged in return. "Each to his own taste, as the French would say. Or her taste, in this case."

"Thank you. You know," Taylor said, "you seem to have unusually good sources. I don't imagine you could get this kind of information without fairly high-level help."

Fruhling ate half the roll before he answered. "During the Cold War," he said, "my position was aligned with the BND and, usually, with the CIA, too. That state of affairs lasted for a long time and left me with . . . sources."

"Ah, and do they know you have such good sources?"

"If they did, I probably would not have them, don't you think?"

Jeffers had the sensation that the ground was shifting under his feet. There was an enormous amount of information in what Fruhling had implied, but not actually said. Taylor was grinning again as she watched him and it was dangerously close to a smirk. "You knew this all the time didn't you?" Jeffers said to her.

"No, not all the time. I made some fairly good guesses, but it was what Dr. Fruhling said this morning that made me sure. What is important is the old saying about the enemy of my enemy. I trust you know it. You don't have to agree on everything to work with someone where you have common ground. You just didn't want to believe what you saw. I'm sorry if I look like I'm laughing, I should not, but sometimes, George, you just look so damned shocked when the real world smacks you in the face."

I guess I owe Oliver an apology, Jeffers thought. Or do I? If we have "common ground" in science, why not work together there? "I am curious, Dr. Fruhling, just what your other interests are?"

"Dr. Jeffers, it is much as your friend said. I oppose Maastricht and I will do what I can to prevent its implementation. This, as you may expect, places me in opposition to official policy. Since I am confident that you have no particular interest in the treaty, nor do I think you are being used by anyone in connection with it, I will say that your interests and mine are not opposed at this time. I would prefer that our involvement, outside of science, stop there."

"I see. Tell me, would our area of shared interest extend to arranging tickets to Reykjavik?"

It turned out that it did.

# PART III

---

## ICE AND FIRE

# CHAPTER 20

## FRANKFURT, GERMANY

JAKE MARDEN DECIDED TO consider himself lucky. That was, he figured, the most positive way of looking at his present situation. Marden had worked in Europe for several years and had gotten to know a great many useful people. Consequently, when the chief of station had told him to keep Max Fruhling under surveillance, Marden had needed little time to assemble his network. He already had assets at Fruhling's university and it took little time to place someone at the conference Fruhling was to attend in Amsterdam. Fruhling had been kept under close but unobtrusive watch by one of Marden's operatives almost from the day of the CoS's order. It had gone well too, with no sign that the old man knew he was being spied on, just as it should be. Marden had a complete diary of what Fruhling had done, and with whom—complete, that is, with the exception of a few hours during the torrential thunderstorm a few days before, but Marden found that to be a negligible gap. Not the sort of problem he would pass along to Langley. All told, Marden had been satisfied. Sooner or later Fruhling would make a move, and when he did Marden was going to know about it.

Then, bang! A priority message arrived telling him to establish surveillance on Dr. George Jeffers, and to give that priority over Fruhling. The request had originated with the high and mighty Charles Oliver in Langley, so there was no question of what Marden was going to do. Still, it rankled. Oliver, of course, always wanted things done instantaneously, which was simply not the way fieldwork went. Marden privately doubted it had worked that way back in the days when Oliver was doing it himself either. It would beyond doubt ruin his chances of keeping close tabs on Fruhling, a point some bureaucrat would surely resurrect at a future review. If this Jeffers was so important, enough so that Marden had to drop what had been a priority assignment, someone should have given him some advance notice. Hell, he had seen Jeffers meet Fruhling at that conference only a few days before. At the time it had seemed like just another routine—that is, non-subversive—contact, and Marden had reported it that way. Had he known

239

there was anything special about this Jeffers he could have had the man tailed from there, rather than have to go out and find him. In fact, Marden thought, had it not been for his own efficiency in checking on whom Fruhling spoke with, he would not have even known it was Jeffers. Thank you, Langley, for your help in this matter! Having no idea what Jeffers had done to deserve this attention, Marden spent some time talking with the CoS over lunch. With the news he got, the entire situation began to make a nasty kind of sense. Jeffers was a scientist who had disappeared in Boston right around the time a CIA agent named Don Lorenzo had been shot. Those pieces suddenly fit together with news that Marden had been picking up from his sources in Germany. Jeffers is in Boston and Lorenzo gets offed. Jeffers disappears from Boston, shows up in Amsterdam, and one of Germany's lesser lights, Karl Schurmer, has his throat cut. Not too long after that, a known associate of the dead man, one Reinhard Schwerin, is knifed and shot in a small East German town, but has no idea who did it. Just coincidentally, an industrialist was killed there on the same day. An American "journalist," who met Jeffers's description, was in the same town at the same time. The coincidence was too great to dismiss. Put it all together, and you had to wonder what Jeffers had to do with Lorenzo's death. It explained Oliver's sudden interruption of Marden's assignment. Whatever else Marden might say about Oliver, the man had a reputation for getting satisfaction when an agent died. People who killed for a living gave Marden the creeps. Thanks for the warning on this one, Langley, he thought. It was a good thing he was used to working this stuff out for himself.

Shortly afterward, one of his assets reported that Jeffers was at Fruhling's home. Marden's orders said surveillance, so that is what he did. Jeffers was tailed to Luxembourg where he boarded a plane for Iceland. Iceland! What in God's name was this man, who had apparently left a string of bodies from America through Europe, going to do in Iceland? Had Fruhling hired him to take out someone there? Marden was not going to discount the possibility. Indeed, he included that assessment with the other information on Jeffers and sent it off in a priority message. Oliver would then turn the problem over to the CoS of Iceland Station, may the man have the joy of that assignment! Marden, meanwhile, could go back to watching Fruhling and hope that nothing important had happened while he was scrambling after Jeffers. The odds of that, he thought, were fairly good as the distraction had not taken up too many days. Looked at in that fashion, Marden could call himself lucky.

# REYKJAVIK, ICELAND

ICELAND. THE WORD CONJURED visions of a gigantic ice cube floating to and fro somewhere in the North Atlantic. Beyond the images afforded by free association, Jeffers knew little about the place. He searched back through the memories of his reading, looking for information, and came up almost blank. Leif Ericsson had left from there, he remembered, on his voyage to North America. No. He caught himself. It had been Greenland, hadn't it? Vikings had come from Iceland in the Middle Ages, he thought. Maybe not, although he was sure Iceland had been in that history somewhere. More recently, there had been disagreements with Britain over cod. He had read about it in the papers. Those three items, of which only one was certain, comprised his entire knowledge of the land. The realization was unpleasant, given the pride he took in the breadth of his reading. Taylor, though, had been there before. He had pieced that together from comments she had made. Why she would go there was another question. It hardly seemed the promised land for adventurers and troublemakers. But Gerhardt Müller had gone there, too. Müller, thief, murderer and by inference spy had gone to Iceland. Had arranged his trip carefully, if Bieber was to be believed. Why?

Keflavik, where the Icelandair flight landed, was primarily a large military base with a modern passenger terminal growing out of its side like a bud on a tree. Along with the other travelers they piled into a waiting bus for what proved to be a forty-five minute ride to Reykjavik. In between was nothing. The base might have been set on the moon, so little was around it. Once through the chain-link fence that arbitrarily marked the base's perimeter the emptiness stretched away on both sides, miles of low, rolling waves of weathered volcanic rock. Here and there among the rocks were patches of green moss, but nowhere did a tree break the horizon. Again, in Jeffers's mind, the question of why Müller had come arose. Accompanying it was the question of why anyone would come to such a desolate land.

Reykjavik, when they reached it, offered a sharp contrast to the bleak land that lay between it and Keflavik. A modern city had arisen, expanding inland from the shores of a large bay. It had both given rise to suburbs and grown right up to other towns to create a miniature version of the sprawling cities of the U.S. On a hill in the middle of the city rose the steep spire of Hallgrimskirkja like an Alpine peak. Jeffers figured that, even with his sense of direction, it would be hard to get lost. Judging by the construction activity along the perimeter, the city and its population were undergoing a furious expansion. Then just when the city, with its cars, lights and paved roads, was putting Iceland back into familiar realms, strangeness reasserted itself.

The new houses Jeffers saw under construction were not the wooden-frame style he was accustomed to, nor were they brick. A wooden frame was there, but to serve as a mold into which a concrete shell could be poured. It occurred to him then that the absence of trees he had noticed on the way in had to be a general phenomenon.

The airport hotel, the Loftleidir, might have been any large hotel in any large city. A rectilinear assemblage of steel and glass, it nestled up against the smaller domestic airfield. The interior lobby was both utilitarian and blandly cosmopolitan. Jeffers found an out-of-the-way place to sit while Taylor went to inquire about rooms. When he sat down, Jeffers felt certain that obtaining rooms would be a snap, nothing like the haggling required in Amsterdam. From the length of time Taylor was gone, however, and the look on her face when she returned, he could tell that was not the case.

"What happened?" he asked her.

"Nothing good. The best I could manage was one room here. None of the other major hotels has anything at all."

"That's bizarre." In fact, it made no sense to Jeffers. "Iceland hardly strikes me as a tourist mecca."

"It's not," Taylor had the attitude of someone stating the obvious, "but there aren't that many rooms either. All you need is more people than rooms and it doesn't matter whether you're at the Arctic Circle or on the Riviera. Anyway, there are some smaller places in town we can check for another room."

"Why? Taylor, you said we had one room. Why tromp all over the city looking for another one?"

"Because," she said levelly, "unless you want to camp in a tent, we need another room."

That was too much for Jeffers. "Like hell I'm going to camp in a tent. I don't mind sleeping on the couch, or even the floor if the room only has one bed, but a tent is ridiculous. If you're so damned set on the idea, why don't *you* take the tent? Me, I think we can manage with one room. You ought to know me well enough by now to realize I'm not going to do something stupid."

"That has nothing to do with it, George. I don't share rooms. Period."

"Why? Is that another rule? Sometimes I think you've got more rules than the Army."

"Don't make fun of me, George. I don't like it." An element of warning crept into her voice with the sentence.

The change was evident to Jeffers. "Look," he said, "I'm not trying to make fun of you." Respect aside, doing so was probably not a safe proposition. "I just don't understand what the big deal is."

"You wouldn't understand. Why don't we just leave it at that?"

"Okay." Jeffers threw his hands up. "We go look for another room." Arguing with Taylor was about as productive as arguing with his spectrometer.

For all its sprawl, Reykjavik was not a large city, at least not by the standards of countries whose citizens numbered in the millions, but going from one hotel to the next was like a connect-the-dots puzzle. Taylor insisted on trying in person, however, after several telephone calls produced only rapid "no vacancy" responses. The personal touch, unfortunately, was just as unproductive; the only difference being the amount of time it took to produce a final "no." Eventually, even Taylor had to give up.

"All right, enough!" She slapped her hands against her sides. "The damn city's full, I don't want a room in someone's house, and I agree a tent is ridiculous. Come on, I'll show you how to order a cheeseburger and fries in Icelandic."

Jeffers marveled at the almost complete change in mood that Taylor manifested. He suspected, though, that the lightness and gaiety were on the surface only. He doubted that, behind her wall, she was really reconciled to the arrangement.

While they ate, Jeffers returned to the real reason they were there, which was not to find a hotel room. "Taylor, this may sound dumb at this stage, but wouldn't we have a better chance of finding Müller if we went to the police?"

"Went to them with what?" she asked. "We don't know what he looks like, not really, we don't even know what name he's using. On top of that, the only way we could really prove he was up to no good would tie us to a chain of events on the Continent that would cause us problems. I thought you had been cured of the idea that there is any use for the police."

"Maybe so, Taylor, but if we don't know his name, or what he looks like, how are we going to find him? All we have is the name of that guy at the university. Do we just hang around and wait for him to show up?"

"To some extent, you're quite right. It's just like the situation we had a few days ago. If all Müller wanted to do was hide from us, I grant you, it would be damned hard to find him. But that's not why he came here. He has a job to do, and he has to do it. It's like ripples spreading from a splash in a quiet pond. Picking up those ripples, that's how we'll trace him. Also, don't forget that he won't have any idea we're here. Hopefully, by the time he does, we'll have him.

"Fine. But what kind of job is somebody like him going to do in a place like this and what could my enzyme possibly have to do with it?"

"I don't know yet, George. We're just going to have to play it by ear."

Their meal completed, and the tab put on Visa, Taylor announced that since Jeffers really needed to learn his way around, she would show him the city. With that she was off, again playing tour guide. Jeffers did not doubt that it was a useful, even interesting lesson, but after a while the afternoon seemed to drag on endlessly. A look at his watch gave him a shock. It had been endless! In Reykjavik, at midsummer, midnight is not much different than midafternoon in lighting, and in listening to Taylor, he had not noticed the closed shops and paucity of people. In spite of the hour, however, Taylor seemed reluctant to turn back. Jeffers, on this occasion was adamant. If she was not coming, she could go pitch a tent.

When they reached the room, after an oddly quiet final leg of the journey, Taylor immediately disappeared into the bathroom. Jeffers, meanwhile, dropped on the far bed, the room coming equipped with two of them, and pulled the shoes off his aching feet. While he waited for Taylor to reappear, he took stock of the room. It was fairly standard, a little small with a rather narrow door, but it could easily have been a hotel room in the United States. The only unusual item was the heavy blackout curtain that kept out the midnight sun.

After waiting what seemed more than a reasonable time, he yelled out, "Hey, what happened? Are you going to sleep in the tub, or did you die in there?"

When there was no answer, he waited a little longer. While he waited, he remembered the brace. Could Taylor be vain enough to make such a production of hiding the fact that she wore a brace? It was possible. He thought of all the times he had almost brought it up and regretted his inability to do so.

"Hey, Taylor, if it's the brace that bothers you, I already know about it."

"What?" The voice came back thinly through the door.

"Your knee brace is what. I bumped against it on the plane, and I've noticed it a couple of times since."

*"Knee brace?"*

"Yeah." Jeffers was looking at the floor as he spoke so he sensed, rather than clearly saw, the object that hurtled at him and raised his hands only by reflex to block his face. He had not noticed the bathroom door open.

It landed with a thud near his feet, and it took him a moment to recognize what it was. One end consisted of a padded circular band attached to two long braces made out of some dense plastic. The braces ended in a hinge where a knee would be. That was the part of the structure Jeffers had noticed before. Below the hinge, though, was a lower leg. An artificial lower leg. Taylor's sock and sneaker were still on its foot.

Jeffers looked up, his mouth soundlessly agape. Taylor was leaning with one hand on the wall for support. Her left pant leg dangled limply below the knee. Silently she worked her way closer to where he sat.

"Knee brace, huh? You can't draw conclusions when you don't know what you're talking about. Maybe you should learn." Her voice was low and tense. As she finished speaking, she pulled open the clasp at the waistband. Loose and floppy by design, the pants had no other point of support. Released, they fell in a heap at her foot.

Taylor's right leg, seen from the point it cleared her shirt at the upper thigh, was about what Jeffers would have expected, long and lithe. The left started out the same, but then narrowed rapidly at midthigh. It terminated right below the knee in a foot, the foot hanging there with the toes pointed backward and the sole forward. While he watched, she flexed the foot forward and back. The kneecap he noticed was a heel, the knee an ankle. Then he saw the scars. All at once, he realized this was not some bizarre deformity. The lower leg had been flipped around and surgically grafted with the ankle in place of the knee.

"Good God, Taylor! What happened?"

"What happened?" she mirrored back. "Cancer is what happened. An osteogenic sarcoma, if the name means anything to you."

It did not, but he still asked, "When?"

"I was fifteen," she answered. He made no response. "Well, come on," demanded Taylor Redding, "what do you think of my Van Nes? The tumor was right above my knee, so I had to lose my knee and most of my thigh. You can't do much, you know, without a knee. They told me they could use my lower leg, though, graft it like this so I'd have a knee. My foot holds my weight, no stump problems; all the nerves are there, my balance is fine. I can do almost anything you can do with a leg. It looks grotesque, I knew it would, but I wanted it. Come on. What do you think?"

For the moment, Jeffers was not thinking. He could not take his eyes from the horribly truncated limb she referred to as her "Van Nes." All at once, any feelings of irritation he had harbored over her behavior shrank to insignificance. Unexpectedly, he found himself blinking back tears.

"It doesn't make any difference to me, Taylor," he said carefully. "None at all."

"Oh, it matters, Jeffers," she answered in a dead-even voice, "It matters a great deal."

"Not to me." Just then, he could only think of the way he felt when she smiled at him. His words tumbled out in a sudden rush, unthinking. "It doesn't matter to me. Dammit, Taylor, I love you and I really don't care what it looks like." The astonishing thing was not that he said it, but that he still meant it after he said it.

"No!" Her composure broke with a scream. "No, you don't! You do *not* love me! I am *not* lovable!"

The vehemence rocked him back. Looking at her, he could see her hands clenching and trembling. Moisture glistened at the corners of her eyes.

"Why not?" he tried. "I meant what I said. What's past is past. I told you it doesn't matter to me. You're great, you really are terrific, and the way you go you'll have a great future."

"Damn you Jeffers! Don't you listen? I am not terrific, I'm Taylor Redding, and I don't have a great future. I don't have any future. None at all."

"What do you mean? You said you were fifteen, that means it's been ten years."

"Damn you again!" She cut him off before he could go further. "If you can't listen, maybe you should open your eyes and see!"

One hand went to the buttons of her shirt and began to open them. Deep in her mind, she screamed at herself that this was crazy, screamed at her hand to stop. Her hand, however, had acquired a mind of its own. Trembling, and fumbling with the buttons, she continued to pull the shirt open. When she finished, she shrugged her shoulders allowing the shirt to fall behind her, down to her wrists. Quietly, she stood in front of Jeffers.

Jeffers was quiet as well. He had previously fantasized about what she might look like unclothed, but now he was not seeing her body. Only the scars. The first one he saw was small, a rough circle nestled in the hollow of her throat. He wondered that he had never noticed it before, until he realized that the place was always covered, either by a buttoned collar or a scarf. On her chest were two half moon scars. Time, and a surgeon's skill, had left them little more than thin, irregular lines, but they riveted his eyes as effectively as if they had been broad stripes. They ran from behind her back around her side, the left one a little higher than the right, almost to her breast bone. It was as though someone had opened her sideways, like a clam, and then pushed her closed again. The right arm was marked too. From the inside of her elbow, down nearly to the wrist, the skin was curdled and darkened. What might have happened there, he could not imagine.

"I've had it back twice in my lungs, plus a few other problems," she said softly. "Once, you can get away with it, sometimes. That's what they told me then. Twice, forget it. It's just going to come back, again and again, and all they can do is keep cracking my chest and berry picking them. Sooner or later, they won't be able to clean it out. All I've had is a long, lucky run. It won't last and I know it. I'm dead, George. I just haven't gotten around to actually dying yet."

"Jesus Christ." The words came slowly. "Taylor, I didn't know. I'm sorry."

"Sorry?" The fire in her voice rose again. "Goddamn you. And goddamn your 'sorry.' I don't want it." Her entire body was shaking, as was her voice. The tears that had stood ready at the corners of her eyes now began to roll down her cheeks. "If I wanted you to pity me, don't you think I could have done it, long ago? That's not how I want to be seen." She stopped to wipe the tears away and her composure was back as fast as it had vanished. "Well, now you see how it is. How it really is."

Jeffers had to say something. He knew that. But what? A wrong word, a careless phrase, and the fragile hold she was maintaining on her emotions might break entirely. This was infinitely worse than the day in Amsterdam. He had an aching sense of her vulnerability and could guess at what it cost her to have him see her so.

"I am sorry, Taylor, and I don't say that to pity you. I'm sorry for what has happened. I'm sorry, I guess, for a lot of things, my own stupidity not the least of them. Taylor, I couldn't play the hand you were dealt. Certainly not the way you have. That's admiration you hear, not pity.

"Now, please," he asked, "put your shirt back on, that's better, and come over here. I'd like, if you don't mind, to see that knee they made for you."

# CHAPTER 21

## REYKJAVIK, ICELAND

LATER, THEY SLEPT IN separate beds or, at least, Taylor thought Jeffers slept, judging from his breathing pattern. Taylor, however, hung in the void, halfway between sleep and wakefulness, drifting from time to time closer to one extreme or the other. She had not wanted to get into the bed, had not wanted to go to sleep at all, but there was no choice. As little as she required, she still had to have some sleep. So, she lay there, helpless against the assault of her mind, which endlessly replayed the evening as well as the flood of other memories the evening had unleashed.

For Taylor, the morning felt like the proverbial morning after. She had slept a few hours, probably, but it would have been impossible to prove it from the way she felt. Fatigue, and a malaise that went beyond anything physical, were her principal sensations. She looked at the ceiling, without attempting to rise from the bed, and tried to remember the last time the night had been so bad. The worst of it was that the previous evening should never have happened, and would not have happened had she not allowed it. She should simply have pitched a tent, found a room in a house, come up with some alternative. She had known the possibilities and it would not have been hard to give a plausible reason for whatever she had chosen. Should have done that. Should have. The track does not pay off on "should have."

God, what a night! She had known, from the moment she got into bed that the flashbacks were coming, never mind that she could not afford them, not now, not so close to the heart of this adventure. They came of their own will, not hers, and sucked her into her past nightmare regardless of her needs. Not bad enough to lose a leg, no, that she had handled. It was the pain after they cut her chest, the pain in her arm, which would never be the same, after the medication leaked, the retching which seemed to go on and on without end. Those memories, those and the Demerol, that was what made her shrink back, want to hide from herself. First she had taken it just for the pain, later she had lived for it, watched the clock to see when each dose was due. The memory of being tied to it, helpless, was so shameful it was even worse than the pain. That memory brought others with it. All the faces that said, "Poor Taylor," even if the words were not said out loud, the knowledge that she had blamed everyone else for what she had become. She had broken away, invented her Ice and Fire and her Rules and given herself over entirely to those rules. That escape had been almost as bad as the pain before it. She remembered coming completely awake, at one point in the night, screaming, "I want out, I want out!" over and over. She always did, or so her parents had told her before she left home for good. It was yet another weakness she could not seem to subdue. Fortunately, Jeffers had proven to be a sound sleeper.

She glanced over at Jeffers in the other bed. He still seemed to be sound asleep. A minor piece of luck. She was not ready to pick up where they had left off. What was he going to think of her? It bothered her that the question was even on her mind. Why should his opinion be of any importance? Love, he had spoken of. Love and Taylor Redding were mutually exclusive concepts. She had decided that years ago. Yet, she was acting, or at least thinking, as though she were attached to the man. Ridiculous.

Taylor swung herself upright over the side of the bed and strapped on the prosthesis. Normally, it was an operation she did automatically, without thinking. Instead, the limb felt heavy and awkward, foreign, when she stood up. It was like that after flashbacks, the same way she remembered it feeling in the hospital and time after time in her dreams. God, she thought looking down, the whole apparatus looked ugly. Ah, well, it was not as though she had any choice in the matter and there was no point in wasting the morning staring at her leg. Flashbacks or no, there was work to do. Or was there? She wondered about that. Jeffers had come to Iceland on the word of a dashing and beautiful adventuress, not a crippled, cut apart and pasted together old cancer patient pretending to be a soldier of fortune. Pretending? The word stung her mind even though she had only thought it, not spoken it. The rest of the thought might be true, but, regardless of the scale of her accomplishments, she was not pretending about her occupation. Unfortunately, it could easily look as though she was, and appearances, for all that they were useless as a guide to the reality of a person, could be decisive in framing opinions. Jeffers might quit. For all her internal discussion about continuing alone, she had worked hard to bring him along. It was far easier to steal someone's car than their adventure. In the end, it was simpler to avoid the question and proceed as if nothing had happened.

The mirror in the bathroom covered the entire wall behind the sink. When she first looked into it, she saw a different face. It was pale, with hollow cheeks and sunken eyes. Only a few wisps of hair straggled across the bald pate. The body in the mirror was hunched over as though it could not stand up straight. Her face. Her body. She fought down an urge to retch and the image vanished. She touched the small scar in the hollow of her throat where the breathing tube had once been. Sometimes she felt as though it was still there. The mirror gave a wide enough view for her to see the top of the brace. She winced at the sight, then looked at herself in the mirror with disgust for having done so. This will never do, she thought.

Taylor kept her eyes fastened on the image in the glass and started her exercise. Slowly, in her mind, she molded her face, tightened it, until through slightly narrowed eyes she saw the picture of ice and stone she wanted. Hard and cold, that was the idea. The face satisfactory, she turned to the rest of her attire. When she was fully clad she cracked the door, hoping to find Jeffers still asleep. He was.

Poor Jeffers, with his talk of love and "doesn't matter." Sure, it doesn't matter. Next winter, maybe, they would take a trip to Bermuda. She would look just fine in a bikini. Taylor stopped that line of thought abruptly. It was probably not fair to Jeffers.

Back in the room, she regarded Jeffers's sleeping form silently. She had planned to simply go out alone, but realized how the appearance that would give could be misleading. Instead, she grabbed a piece of paper and scrawled a note.

"George," it read, "went out to start taking care of business. I'll check back this evening. If you're not here, I'll understand. Taylor."

It was far enough to the city center that a cab would have been convenient. Instead, Taylor chose to walk. The dash of cold water in the face she had in the room had hardly compensated for the lack of sleep, but it had served to wake her up. The wind off the ocean in the early morning was cool enough to chill, even in midsummer, and it picked up where the water had left off. As she walked along, she slowly pulled the rest of her armor back around her. The wind helped the picture that she framed in her mind. In it, she walked alone on a plain that grew nothing save boulders and ice. Ice on the outside, ice on a rock. By the time she reached Laekjargata, she was ready to face the world again. Not that she felt entirely well, she did not. But it did not matter how she felt, not as long as it was tucked away, safely out of sight.

Once there, she hesitated briefly as she searched for newspaper vendors. It took only a minute to find them, as they hawked their wares noisily on the street. Her papers bought, and it was papers plural, Reykjavik probably holding the world's record for per capita newspapers, she looked for a quiet place to read them. Before she went careening off across the island looking for Müller, she wanted to know what was going on locally. The outdoor chessboard, at that hour of the morning, was the ideal place for her. Physically, it was exactly that, a large chessboard set into the sidewalk with benches on one side and a comfortable hill on the other. Later in the day, if the weather held, it would have the look of a crowded miniamphitheater as passersby stopped to watch contestants play with nearly man-sized pieces mounted on rollers. In the early morning, it was deserted.

Taylor planted herself on the hillside, papers held down by a convenient rock. At first glance, the news did not seem terribly different from what she had read on her previous visit. The economy was in trouble and politics seemed as corrupt and vituperative as anywhere else in the world. Something had changed, though. Most members of the Althing, the Icelandic Parliament, usually came from one of four parties: the Independence Party, the Progressive Party, the People's Alliance, and the Social Democrats. They were squabbling among themselves worse than usual, which made the formation of a stable coalition government impossible. The Women's Alliance, the radical feminist party, still held half a dozen seats but, as usual, refused to join with any other party in a coalition. Two or three splinter groups also held a number of seats. One of them, the Progressive Conservatives, had enough support to make a coalition work with one of the major parties, but they were demanding an impossible share of power in return for their votes. Taylor frowned at the name. She did not recognize it. It appeared to be a recent splinter group formed by defectors from the Independence Party and the Progressive Party under the leadership of one Gizur Thorkelson. Gizur certainly wanted a whole lot in return for his support. Taylor shrugged and flipped the pages. Splinters might come and go, no matter how grandiose the ideas of their leaders. What next caught her eye was the front page of a rather thin paper. At the top, right under the banner, was a block of text set in a heavy black border suitable to a death announcement. Who had died? Nobody, it turned out. The text started out with, "Having regard to the fact that the people of Iceland cannot themselves adequately secure their own defenses, and whereas experience has shown that a country's lack of defenses greatly endangers its security and that of its peaceful neighbors, the North Atlantic Treaty Organization has requested . . ." Taylor recognized it as a portion of the defense agreement between Iceland and the United States. The articles on the front page seemed directed at that post-World War II treaty and they were far from favorable. The name of the paper was the *Progressive Conservative*. Same name as Gizur's party. Now that was unusual. It was unusual to find a splinter group with its own paper. If nothing else, it was economically difficult to start a newspaper, and there was not the kind of concentrated old wealth in Iceland that would enable an individual, such as Fruhling for instance, to bankroll the venture. Of course, she might not have paid attention before.

The question piqued Taylor's interest sufficiently that she paid more attention to it than its few pages would otherwise have warranted. After having read it, she decided that a more appropriate title would have been the "New Reactionary." The principal articles, which seemed to have been excerpted from other works by Gizur, had as a recurring theme the need to reestablish Iceland's neutrality. The Cold War was over, the theme ran, so who needed the Americans in Keflavik? Only the pressure of the Cold War had pushed Iceland into NATO, albeit only after some riots. Now that pressure was gone, and the Progressive Conservatives wanted to write off the base along with the Cold War. They also had some drastic ideas about how to deal with the EC on fishing rights. On domestic questions, she presumed Gizur leaned toward centralized planning given the invective he directed at the breakup of the state television monopoly. She wondered how much support Gizur really had, that he could put out the paper without expecting to go broke. It was an interesting question, even if it was not particularly relevant to anything. Then, an item on the editorial page caught her eye. The editor of the paper was a Jon Petursson, the same name that Bieber had mentioned as being on Müller's letters. Coincidence? It was hard to know; at times it seemed that every third Icelander was named Jon. However, according to the paper, this Jon Petursson taught economics at the university, and there was only one university. Taylor suddenly felt short of breath. She had a connection between the paper and Gerhardt Müller!

With that insight, the paper took on far greater importance than it had a few minutes before. She went back through the political articles more thoroughly, looking for any hint of outside ties. She found none. The isolationist flavor she had picked up the first time through held on rereading. There was an open letter, though, that she noticed. It was remarkable less for its content, essentially a repetition of points made elsewhere, than for its authorship. It was attributed to a student named Thorfinn Asgrimson, writing on behalf of a group of university students. A short article in the paper was by the same author. University professor, university student. It was not much, but it was enough linkage for Taylor to start.

She got up then, and stretched. She could see that this development had great promise. The involvement of someone like Müller with an oddball political figure had to portend a major event. The fates were going to be kind to Taylor Redding because there she was, right in the middle of it. All she had to do was figure out what it was. The prospect of action was not quite enough to drive out the memory of the previous night, nothing could really do that, but it helped her to ignore it. Her mind cleared for action, she began to lay her plans. She had originally considered going straight to Jon Petursson, as he was the only solid lead she had. The more she thought about it, however, the better it seemed to approach him indirectly by starting with the Thorfinn character. And where better to find a student than the university?

It was only a short walk back to reach the university. The main building was a large rectangular prism of gray stone seated on top of a low, terraced hill. In appearance, it reminded her more of a court house, or a government building, than a school. Other than an energetic soccer game in progress on the lower terrace, the building had an activity level appropriate to a school in the summertime. There was no barrier to entering the building and she wandered through the corridors for a while until she met one of the students.

"Excuse me, can I help you?" he asked.

"Yes, thank you. A mutual friend suggested that I could meet Thorfinn Asgrimson here. Could you tell me how to find him?"

For a moment, she watched the student watch her. She knew that he would take her for a foreign student. There were always a few of them at the university, and, although she was fluent enough in the language, her accent would never approach anything native. She hoped that her origin was the only question in his mind.

"I think he is in the soccer game outside. Look for the green shorts."

That had been easy enough. From the wording of the letter in the paper, Taylor had thought it reasonable that he would be around the university. A classroom or library would have been more likely for the budding political analyst, but Taylor was not going to sneer at what opportunity handed her.

She walked back out the front entrance and positioned herself to the side of the game. Played six men on a side with jerseys to mark the goals, it could have been a schoolyard game anywhere. Well, anywhere in Europe. The level of skill was far higher than one would see in an American soccer game. There was, indeed, a player wearing green shorts who Taylor assumed was Thorfinn. He was, perhaps, six feet tall with, for an Icelander, a dark complexion. The tan T-shirt he wore did not entirely conceal his pudgy build. The most distinctive part of his appearance, though, was a scowl that seemed to have been put on his face with a chisel. It varied only in deepening when he or a teammate missed a play.

"No wonder that kid looked at me funny when I asked for this guy," she said softly to herself. "He looks like a real joy."

As she watched the game, she noticed that Thorfinn spoke, that is in passages of more than one syllable, to only one of the other players. Nearly a head taller than the dour Thorfinn and with ash-blond hair, he was the schoolbook image of a Viking from days past. Shirt off, his lean and muscular torso glistened in the sunlight and cool air. The resemblance to the ancient Vikings ended there, however. His face was open and quick to smile or laugh. A greater contrast to Thorfinn would have been hard to imagine, yet from their interaction on the field they were obviously friends.

The problem remained. How to meet Thorfinn? The game was not going to last forever. When it ended, she had to be able to either talk to Thorfinn, or arrange to meet him at another time. Trying to catch his eye during the game was worthless. Thorfinn took as much notice of her as the building behind her. From what she saw on the field, being totally brazen and trying to pick him up after the game, from a cold start, did not seem like a good bet. Then the game itself offered her an opening. An errant pass flew past its intended recipient on a direct line to Taylor. She trapped it cleanly and looked up. Part of her would have dearly loved to dribble it back onto the playing field, as she had once been quite skilled with a soccer ball. There was no way, however, that the left leg would permit any fancy footwork. All possibilities were not ruled out, though. With a quick move of her right foot she rolled the ball onto the top of her instep and tossed it into the air in front of her. As it started to fall, she brought the leg up again bouncing it, this time, off her knee. At the top of its trajectory, she popped it a little higher with her forehead. Then, as it fell back she kicked up the left leg. The ball struck the reversed heel at the left knee, a far sharper blow than would normally be obtained from a knee. It boomed off in a high arc back to the middle of the field. Taylor smiled at the result. Thank God she had not muffed it! She looked around quickly to make contact with Thorfinn, but he had turned around, scuffing at the grass. Was there anything, short of a sledgehammer, that would make an impression on that man?

What she did get was, "Whoo! Nicely done!" from Thorfinn's friend, accompanied by a broad smile. She returned his gaze, giving him a thumbs-up sign as he returned to the play. He caught her eye, with a grin, several times after that.

Interesting. Every position had a flank. She had planned to use Thorfinn to turn Jon Petursson's, but maybe she could use this man to get to Thorfinn. The approach was becoming awfully indirect, but surely she felt old Captain Hart would have approved. That is, if he were alive he would.

When, at last, the game broke up, she strode across the field to where Thorfinn and his friend were talking. Thorfinn's response to her cheery

"Hello" was a grunt, followed by a quick departure. The other stood there, watching him go.

"You're friend's a real charm," Taylor said.

"Who? Thorfinn?" The question seemed to jolt the tall man out of his reverie. He turned to face Taylor. "He's always kept to himself, but lately . . . I don't know. I'm sorry. My name is Einar Jonsson." He brightened as the topic changed. "And you are?"

"Charlotte Becker, from Bonn."

"Ah, Deutschland! You speak Icelandic quite well, although the accent is, well, odd."

"Can't help it, I'm afraid. There is too much 'th' in the language. I'll never have it right."

"Sure you will. You took the trouble to learn it in the first place." He hesitated before his next sentence. "I thought that was a nice move you made. With the ball, I mean." A bit of redness appeared along the edges of Einar's ears as he saw the possible double meaning.

"Thanks," Taylor noticed his embarrassment but never showed her perception of it. "It just takes practice. I'm sure my accent will get better with some practice, too." She looked straight into his eyes as she said it, and kept her unblinking gaze locked in place.

Einar's reply was slow in coming. When it did, it was preceded by a nervous twitch of his lips. "Well, would you have some time to practice this evening? Perhaps over drinks?"

"Sounds fine to me. Do you have any place in mind?"

"Do you know Gaukurinn?" Taylor nodded. "Good, I'll pick you up at 2230."

She shook her head at that. "I would rather meet you there."

"It may be crowded. I would hate it if we had to spend half the evening looking for each other."

"I'll meet you at the bus stop then, out in front of the Laekjartorg. At 2230." She ended the discussion with a wave and headed back toward the town center.

The agreed-upon time gave her several hours to kill. What she ought to be doing, she knew, was going back to the hotel to bring Jeffers up to date. She was not doing it, however, for the same reason she had not wanted Einar to pick her up at the hotel. She did not want to go back there yet. Jeffers, she was certain, was going to decide to leave, but she could not remember the airline schedules. At that hour he might still be there. That was a meeting she would prefer to avoid. Instead of the hotel, she went downtown, going through the shelves of bookstores looking for anything written by Gizur or Jon Petursson. By the time the stores closed, she had noted several volumes for future purchase. Then she sat on the grass for a while, tossing pebbles at the ducks on the lake. Finally, it was time to catch her bus.

It let her off at the stop she had given Einar, a few blocks from Gaukurinn. There was no one at the small shelter when she got off. Could he have stood her up? She rather doubted it. Men were, dependably, like children at Christmas; they always went for the brightly wrapped package. What was under the wrap was another matter, but for the moment it was not an issue. Einar would show.

"Charlotte?" She turned at the question. The knack of answering to any name she decided on was an old and much practiced art.

"Oh, there you are. I was wondering if you would show up."

"If *I* would show up?" Einar laughed. "Surely, you are joking?"

"Well," Taylor said with a wry grin, "I thought you might find it boring to spend your evening giving language lessons."

"Under the circumstances, I will have to endure it. Shall we walk over? It's beginning to get chilly."

The few blocks between the bus stop and the pub were covered rapidly. Inside, it was beginning to fill, predominantly with young people in groups and couples. It was not so full yet, however, that they were unable to find a place to sit. It was a smallish place, with a spread of tables facing the bar and a set of speakers and instruments by one wall where a band had not yet appeared.

As Taylor settled into her seat, Einar asked, "What can I get you to drink?"

"Brennivin, please."

"Brennivin?"

"I first came here several years ago," she explained. "You don't think that I was going to drink the fruit juice you people called beer back then, do you? I got used to brennivin."

"We have real beer here now, you know. Maybe even German beer."

"Thanks, but I'll have the brennivin anyway."

Einar shook his head, and returned with two glasses of clear liquid. Taylor sipped hers slowly. It had a smoky, sweet taste. It also had a kick to equal vodka.

"I don't think I have ever met a German quite like you," he said.

"My mother is Irish. It accounts for a number of my habits."

Einar elected not to inquire about what habits were implied. "How long have you been here? In spite of what I said about your accent, you speak Icelandic very well, and brennivin is an acquired taste."

"Actually, I just got here yesterday. But I've been here quite a few times before. Mostly for vacation."

"Why here?"

"I like it. It's pretty. It's quiet, and I don't go for heat or beaches. I'm comfortable here." Nice to just be able to tell the truth, she thought as she finished.

Einar elected to toast that by tossing down the rest of his drink. Taylor followed suit and they went for refills.

"Tell me, Einar," she said when they returned, "what you do."

"I'm still a student, I'm afraid, for another year. Economics is what I like best."

"And are you also involved in politics, like your friend Thorfinn?"

"Like Thorfinn? No. Well, we used to . . ." He let the sentence trail off into nowhere. "How would you know that Thorfinn is in politics?"

"I read what he wrote in the *Progressive Conservative*. I assume we are talking about the same person."

"Yes, yes, the same. We both studied with Jon Petursson at the university. If you read through the paper, you must have noticed his name also. He is a close friend of Gizur Thorkelson, who is the Althing member who started that party. I don't know if you are familiar with his views on where Iceland belongs politically." Taylor nodded, having given herself a cram course earlier in the day. "We both, Thorfinn and I, found his ideas interesting. Thorfinn has stayed on to work with him."

"What kind of work?"

Einar said nothing, but stared into his glass. "I think," he said, "that I need another drink. How about you?" Taylor's glass was still half full, but she nodded in agreement. When he returned, she renewed the question.

"Mostly, he writes articles for Jon, runs errands for the paper or for Gizur's party."

"And your views don't agree anymore?"

"Not exactly. It's just that I've known Thorfinn since we were children." He broke off, staring past Taylor at the dance floor. "Do you really want to talk about politics tonight?"

You bet, was what Taylor thought. What she said was, "Not if you don't want to." From there, she let the conversation drift to inconsequential things: how she had first come to work on her friend Margret's farm in the north, how she had come to learn the language, what she was studying. She concentrated on the first two, where talking about real events gave her the advantage of going into considerable detail. As the alcohol flowed, Einar visibly relaxed and became more loquacious. When she saw this, Taylor steered the conversation back to the original topic.

"Politics," Einar snorted. "There I go again. You'd think I could find something more interesting to talk to you about."

Taylor smiled. He had not noticed who was guiding the conversation. "That's okay," she said. "I mean, it really seems as though something is bothering you. If you want to talk to me about it, I'm here to listen."

Einar was still staring at the dance floor. It was more a small open space between the tables and the bar but, since the band had started, it had filled with couples. The pulsating rock music in the background filled the void in the conversation. The man, Taylor was sure, had something to say. She just had to let him say it. She tried on her most wide-eyed looks and waited. Finally, Einar downed his drink with one gulp and turned back to her.

"All right. If you don't mind. Actually, I don't know if I should talk to you about it."

That sentence made Taylor all the more convinced that Einar should talk to her. "Einar, I can't imagine what it could be that you can't talk to me about it. I mean, what could be so secret?"

"Nothing really. Well, now I can see that I must look like a fool. All right. You know, or maybe you don't, what Gizur and Jon have been saying. That Iceland should be truly neutral, the way the constitution was originally written. Not the way we have it now. I have wondered how the economics of it would work out, particularly the more I learn, but I don't argue with the politics. Especially now, there should be no need to be tied to any power bloc."

"There's nothing wrong with having those political views. In fact, you probably have a lot of company."

"You're right, there is nothing wrong with those views, or with arguing those views. It is not arguments that bother me. Lately, Thorfinn has been coming up with catch words I do not like. On the order of "struggle" and "organizing" and "revolution." That is what bothers me. Since I laughed at him when he first mentioned it, he has said less and less. But I know he was organizing some group, mostly down by the docks. Precisely for what, I don't know, he never said. But he was very involved in this, expecting an "expert" friend of Jon's to come from Germany."

At that, Taylor had to struggle to keep her face neutral. Jackpot! "Do you know his name?"

"No, but I did tell Thorfinn that any expert in what he had been talking about was not a person to be involved with. So, what did he do? He laughed at *me*. Then, this 'expert' shows up and, I gather, it did not go well."

"How do you mean, 'did not go well'?"

"He did not like how Thorfinn was doing his job. Anyway, that is what Thorfinn told me. That it was so bad, they were going to bring someone else here from Germany to show him how to do it right. Now, Thorfinn won't tell me what it is that has to be done right, but I'll tell you what these Germans have to be." He leaned forward at Taylor, face flushed. "Terrorists," he hissed. Then he sat back, looking as though he would have liked to have his last sentence back.

Taylor sipped at her drink to buy enough time to formulate a reply. It was a reasonable deduction that if Müller knew Jon Petursson, then Müller was the German expert Thorfinn had been waiting for. In which case, Thorfinn was not organizing a political discussion group.

"Einar, I think we both need another drink. Would you?" He was a trifle unsteady getting up. Then, when he returned with full glasses she said, "So, big time international politics and nasty German radicals. Your friend Gizur sounds like a real modern Sturlung."

Einar gave her a sharp look. "I don't know that Gizur has anything to do with it. I think Jon just got a little carried away with the idea of the party and Thorfinn went along with him."

"My friend Einar, this goes beyond being 'a little carried away.' Someone is going to get hurt."

"Yes, I can see that. That is what bothers me, mostly. Understand, Thorfinn is my friend. I can't just stand by and do nothing, but I can't see anything that I could do. It's frustrating."

"I'll tell you what," Taylor said, as though the idea had crossed her mind for the first time in that instant, "I think I know how we can get help. If you are interested." Einar nodded quietly. He seemed far more sober than he had been just a moment before. "Good. I need you to get me some information. Can you tell me where the people are that Thorfinn has been with, and where is that German? Can you do that tomorrow without making anyone suspicious?"

Einar nodded again, but when he spoke, it was not to answer the question. "I can't believe what I have been talking about, or even how I got started on it."

"Oh, it's not so surprising. It's obviously been on your mind, and I'm easy to talk to." And the booze did not hurt, she added silently.

"Anyway, if you can do what I asked, do it and meet me at the lake at fourteen o'clock. Don't tell anyone and don't bring anyone."

"Okay, I can manage that. I've made a perfect fool of myself tonight, though, haven't I?"

"Why would you say that?"

"Just look. You asked me out, and what do I do?" He managed a rueful grin, "I spend the evening telling you about politics and my friends' problems. It doesn't matter whether you are a good listener or not, I should have been able to find something more interesting for you to listen to." He shrugged. "I don't suppose you will be going home with me tonight."

Taylor had to smile at that. "Einar, don't misunderstand me. I do like you and I do not think you are a fool. But, no, I am not planning on sleeping with you." She watched him closely for his reaction. There were obvious limits on how far she could carry the Mata Hari act in any case. Einar had given her a good opportunity to terminate the illusion. Even if his response was to leave, thereby ruining the next day's contact, she still had valuable information.

He did not leave. In fact, he started to laugh, a deep belly laugh that took several minutes to control. "You know," he said when he was again calm enough to talk, "I was thinking earlier that my luck was running too good to be true. I believe I can live with what I have. I would like to hear a little more about you though, and forget what we were talking about before. At least for tonight, if you don't mind."

That was not a problem. Taylor had a large fund of stories she enjoyed telling. Many of them were even true.

# CHAPTER 22

## REYKJAVIK, ICELAND

IT WAS LONG AFTER midnight when Taylor started back. The sun was dipping close to the horizon and looked as though it might actually arrive there. The wind had picked up, sending a line of purple clouds skidding across the bay. They brought with them a deeper chill than her blouse was meant for and they might bring rain as well.

She was going as she had come, alone. Einar had taken that rather well, considering that she had all but propositioned him in the afternoon. A nice kid basically, she thought. He had offered to take her back, but she had preferred the walk and the being alone. It gave her a chance to think and also to work off some of the alcohol. Her thoughts revolved around the evening. The conversation had confirmed what she had guessed, had hoped, from the first. Actually, it had gone well beyond, in its implications, anything she had considered. She had stumbled, that was the best word for it, into something big. Certainly it was big; oh, God, was it big! It was just the kind of job she had always dreamed about. A job that she would have given almost anything to have obtained. She chuckled out loud at the thought. She was giving up a great deal for the job. Jeffers would be gone by this time, of that she was certain. By staying behind, letting Jeffers go, Taylor was forfeiting the lockbox in Liechtenstein. Jeffers, if he was smart, would clean it out on his way home. If he did not, it was unlikely that he would deliberately conceal it from his security people. It would be gone, one way or another, long before Taylor could get there. There had been an awful lot of money in that box. Still, it was only money. Her situation was such that she would not starve without it. This job was a once in a lifetime shot, particularly for a short lifetime.

Eventually, the distance and the wind eroded the overlying exultation of her mood and she began to examine what would actually need to be done. It would not be simple. In fact, it was considerably more involved than any job she had undertaken before. Not that the complexity was a deterrent. Sister Angelica had always said that believing you cannot do a job was the first step toward not doing it. Taylor was not about to fall into such a trap. So, how was she going to handle it? Einar had to be met in the afternoon and his lead, hopefully, followed to Thorfinn's group. Since Einar might easily be followed, he would need to be observed before the meeting. Depending on the results, Thorfinn or Jon Petursson or both would need to be watched. All of this while keeping an eye out for Müller. There would be an obvious advantage to having a partner, but that was a problem. Taylor knew a number of Icelanders well, but she had always come to Iceland in the past to relax, not to work. The people she knew were not business acquaintances; involving them in a cloak-and-dagger affair would not be right. There was Einar, of course, but she was dubious about the idea. Einar had too many ties to the characters Taylor was interested in. Besides, he was just a kid! What would he do if it got tight? Memories of Wolfgang in Amsterdam surfaced. It was too bad Jeffers had left. Her fault for giving him the easy out that morning. She had liked working with him. The train of thought from her drive out of Frankfurt came to mind, and she shied away from the emotions. He had been dependable, though, she reminded herself. Hell, when it had counted, he had pulled the trigger. It was hard to ask for more. Unfortunately, it was also asking for the impossible. She began turning over in her mind ways of managing by herself, at least initially. Once she got started other opportunities were likely to present themselves and she could play it by ear.

By the time she returned to the hotel she had worked out an approach that, she felt, offered her reasonable chances of success. She also had a pleasant sense of fatigue, a byproduct of the hour and the long walk. A good night's sleep and an early start were all she wanted then. She opened the door to the room and found Jeffers there, seated in the armchair, waiting for her.

"Where the hell have you been?" he asked. The tone of his voice might have been appropriate to greeting an overlate teenager. The expression on his face would have been more suitable for greeting Dracula.

"Working," she answered. "And what the hell are you doing here?"

"Doing here?" Jeffers exploded up out of the seat and began to pace back and forth in the limited corridor between the beds and the wall. " 'What am I doing here?' she asks. As I seem to recall, it was you who argued me into being here in the first place. So, I'm here, all right? Or is it suddenly not all right?"

Taylor managed to get the door closed behind her, shutting the conversation out of the hallway. "I figured you would have left after last night. It only makes sense. I know you really didn't want to come in the first place. That's why I left you the note, to tell you it was okay."

"You were so sure I would split on you? Why? Because I found out that Taylor Redding isn't quite the Amazon she makes herself out to be?" Taylor nodded mutely. "Well, Jesus Christ! You complain that I don't listen. Look at you! Didn't you hear a goddamn word I said last night?"

Then it was Taylor's turn to flare. "Come off it, George," she said, "this is business, not a Frank Capra picture."

"Yeah. Well, maybe it was stupid of me to use the word 'love.' Lord knows, I don't think I've ever really been in love before, so maybe I haven't the right. But I'll tell you this, you're like nobody I've ever met before and you're as impressive as hell. I've seen what you can do, so why should I stop believing it because you've been cut up? You stand there and shake you head because you don't believe me. But that's because you don't love anyone, not even yourself. So, you figure I'll run out on you."

"George, it has nothing to do with love, nothing at all. You know it; you just won't admit it. You know what I am; you can't not know. Deep inside you'll wonder how strong I really am. In a bind, you won't believe I'll hold up my end. You start making allowances for me, or think that I am making allowances for myself, and we'll screw up good. It's always true, so you are better off realizing it and leaving. And don't think you need to stay to take care of me. Taylor Redding always takes care of herself, thank you."

They faced each other across eight feet of carpet, temporarily quiet. As they stood, Jeffers's expression changed from one of anger to one of sadness.

"Is that the bottom of it, then?" he asked. "That Taylor always has to take care of herself?" Jeffers recalled having read of people with cancer sometimes being treated as though they had leprosy. "Is it that you don't believe me because your old friends and family let you down when you got sick?"

"No!" she shouted, then more softly, "no. I can't tell you the story of ten years in ten minutes, even if I wanted to, but don't think that I'm a loner because everyone runs out on me, even my folks. It's not like that. Don't ever assume that my parents don't love me, or tossed me. They do love me, probably too much." A sense of pressure came into her voice, "If I asked, they would give me anything, clothes, car, school, name it. Thing is, if I took from them, I'd have to be the way they want me to be. I can't do that, and I won't take from them and then laugh in their faces. They can't deal with what I am and what it means. I guess it's hard to have your prized little daughter turn into, well, into me.

"To my folks, I'm a valuable old car. Warranty's expired, can't get spare parts. How do you keep it running as long as possible? You pamper it, never stress it, use it as little as possible. Hell, Mummy would be perfectly happy if I did nothing but sit around the house eating potato chips and watching soap operas. Can you see *me* watching soap operas?" The question did not seem to need an answer and Taylor did not wait for one. "So what other socially acceptable thing might I do? Go to school? So I can spend all my time getting ready for a career when I'll die before I've more than just begun? I have to face the facts. I don't want my obit to read 'Taylor Redding, 25, of Wellesley, a graduate student at Harvard, after a long illness.'

"I'm not looking for love, I'm not looking for understanding. I'm looking for adventure. That's where my immortality is. 'So great attempts, heroic ventures shall, Advance my fortune, or renown my fall.' Montrose wrote that once, but it fits me. I like this life. I can stand on my own two feet, even if one of them was made in Japan. Taylor Redding, the adventurer, is what I will write in the books. And I will write it large so people will remember that I was, that I lived, that I did deeds, that I did not go quietly into the night. And right now, I am onto something big."

"All right Taylor. Now I've heard the speech. I'm still not leaving."

Jeffers had trouble believing it, but there was a grin on Taylor's face after he spoke. Then he realized that it was relief. Everything was out on the table, there was nothing more left to worry about being exposed.

"I have to admit," she said, "I was regretting your having left. I can use a good partner. But," and the grin vanished with frightening speed, "if you start acting like you're my big brother, you are going to wish, for the rest of your life, that you had gotten on that plane."

"Understood," said Jeffers. "Now tell me, *what* is going on?"

"Have a seat, George," she indicated the chair he had started from, "this may take a little while." Briefly, she recapitulated the story of her meeting with Einar and their conversation at Gaukurinn.

"You have to understand that this all makes sense if you look at a little recent history. Iceland was occupied by the Allies during the Second World War, British first then Americans. Nobody asked them in, but Iceland had been a Danish territory and Denmark was occupied, as you remember, by Germany. After the war, Iceland got its independence and a new constitution which provided, among other things, that Iceland would be a neutral nation. Of course, after the war, the Americans only left temporarily. The Keflavik base turned into a big NATO base and Iceland, somewhat reluctantly, became a member of NATO. The chain of events didn't always sit so well here and, I guess, it still doesn't, even with the American presence being reduced now. Iceland used to trade quite a bit with the Soviet Union and I assume they're still trading with the Russians. Some of the biggest foreign policy problems have been with Britain, over fish.

"Now, Gizur has put this party of his together by grabbing people from the other parties for whom these particular hot buttons work. He's pushing these issues for all they're worth, trying to leverage them, through his control of Althing votes, into getting a chunk of the government. I can't tell whether he's getting frustrated because the other parties won't give him what he wants, or whether he has decided that he won't be satisfied even with a big chunk. Gizur is aiming at power here in Iceland. I'm sure of it." Her voice sharpened with that phrase. "Yes, he has a party and a paper, but he is nowhere near the top. Whether he is just impatient, or doesn't think time will improve his position, doesn't matter. He's looking for a short cut. That's what this bully boy underground is all about; there's nothing new about the tactic. He has had Jon and Thorfinn trying to put it together, but they don't really know how to do it. So, now he's gone for some professional help: Müller."

Taylor paused to see what effect she was having. Jeffers was quiet, an intense look on his face. "I almost pity Gizur, in a way," she went on. "I think, if he wins, he'll put his ideas into action. That will mean booting NATO out of Keflavik. But I wonder if Gizur, or any of them, really understand what Müller is. I get the impression that they think he is a kind of professional terrorist, somebody from the German radical underground. That is, I think, a rather naïve view given what we know about him. Apparently, Müller is supposed to be bringing in someone from Germany to take over running the organization on a day-to-day basis. Remember that Müller has been talking to Walther Huebner, whom Fruhling identified as someone the Stasi used to work with and train terrorist organizations. I'll bet that he's working for Müller and that he's the one who's going to take over the organization. Ultimately, it will be Müller, not Gizur, who controls the power structure. I'm sure that, quite early on, Gizur will discover that he is no more than a figurehead."

"Okay, Taylor, just wait a moment." Jeffers had both hands up in the air. "There's something here I just don't get. I'll grant that Müller played in the secret agent major leagues. Okay. But now you're describing a scheme to take over a government here. For what? The Cold War is over, the Soviet Union is gone; what's the point? Answer me that?"

"I'm not sure of the answer, George. Maybe Müller's just out for himself, to use his connections and his skills to grab his own kingdom. That sort of thing has happened often enough in history. Some war ends and all of a sudden you have all these men with combat skills no one wants, so they find ways to keep fighting on their own. I can't imagine a former Stasi officer has a whole lot of attractive career options right now. What better idea than to grab your own country? Like I said, if Gizur wins, he's going to discover that Müller is the one who really controls the power structure. With NATO gone there won't be any force here to act as a counterbalance. Cushy retirement for Müller and his cronies, don't you think?"

Jeffers was silent as he tried to digest the information. One item stuck out. "Let's grant," he said at last, "that this scheme is a reality. I don't see what my enzyme has to do Müller's revolution."

"I think I can explain that," Taylor answered. "I imagine this operation is going to need a lot of money, and these guys don't have a government to fund them any more. I'll bet the money Schroeder thought he was going to get out of H-C for your enzyme would have wound up in Müller's hands. I can't be sure it would have been enough to finance a revolution, but it's possible. Meanwhile, working for Bieber is a great cover, no fixed schedule, no real need to do anything. Your enzyme was also the means to buy Bieber, to make the cover possible. Bieber's a perfect one to suborn, lot's of good connections and influence, and he wanted that enzyme. Regardless of what he thought, once he had taken the bait, Müller had him forever."

"Terrific. Hank Davenport gets killed to set up a cover and fund a revolution. But it doesn't quite fit, Taylor. At least, what happened in Boston doesn't fit."

"I agree with you there. A messy public hit is a poor way to set up a cover. But the rest makes sense. Certainly, what Müller is up to now makes a great deal of sense."

"So what you are telling me," Jeffers said, "is that my enzyme was supposed to jump-start this revolution. I've heard of the impact of science on society before, but this is ridiculous. The thing is, though, we've got the enzyme back. You sure don't look like you think this is over."

"That's right, George. There are lots of ways to get money."

"And you think now it's up to us to put an end to Müller's schemes and, maybe, save a country in the process."

"That's about the size of it."

"Hmm. Do you think we'll get medals?"

"I doubt it, George."

# CHAPTER 23

## REYKJAVIK, ICELAND

THE FOLLOWING AFTERNOON FOUND Taylor standing at the shore of the city lake, apparently gazing at the jet fountain near its center. The day was overcast, with a wet, raw wind that had recently carried rain and promised to do so again. The weather was both friend and foe to her. Friend because it cut the number of people outside to a minimum stripping away cover from observers. Foe because it was aggravating to have to stand out in it. Taylor could ignore such aggravations. She was pleased with the weather.

She stood at the water's edge tearing a couple of slices of bread into small bits for the ducks that clustered near her. In this weather, she was the only one feeding them. Her eyes did not really focus on the fountain or the ducks, however. Instead they swept the area around the small park searching for Einar. Would he come and would he have the information he had promised? More importantly, how careless had he been in getting it? She had no way of answering those questions so they just circled around her head until finally she saw him, beanpole frame hidden under a poncho, approaching from the opposite side of the lake. She made no move toward him, rather she waited watching the areas behind and to the side of him. There was no one in sight.

"Charlotte!" he called, "I am here."

"I can see that," she said. "There is no need to shout." She waited until he had reached her position. "Did you find out what I asked about?"

"Yes."

"Good. I have made my contacts as well." She held up her hand to stop him as he started to speak. "Not here. We should go somewhere dry to sit down. Does anyone know you are here?"

"No."

"Also good. Walk with me and don't look around. One of our friends will be following."

They walked a few blocks to a cafeteria-style restaurant. Taylor bought coffees and a fish platter for both and they settled into a booth. Through the window she saw Jeffers walk past. He looked in briefly and flashed a thumbs-up sign.

"Einar, I'm going to have you meet one of the people I spoke with. He is an American. Call him George." The youth nodded in reply.

She and Jeffers had agonized over this part the previous night. The issue had been whether to allow Einar to meet Jeffers. There were many advantages to preserving Jeffers's anonymity, not the least being the ability to avoid detection if Einar had trouble keeping his mouth shut. These were outweighed in the end by the desire to show Einar an additional participant. It would make it all the easier to pretend that there was even more help available. As Jeffers again walked past the window, Taylor returned the sign. Jeffers saw it, nodded and headed for the entrance.

Jeffers had found it equally unpleasant standing outdoors watching Taylor wait. By design, he would be the hidden reserve in the event the Icelander was followed or did not come alone. There was an air of unreality about the scene, walking slowly back and forth through the grove of small trees near the lake, always keeping in sight the girl at the fountain. The hard butt of the pistol prodded him in the side as he turned and made the scene real. Taylor, with Fruhling's help he imagined, had managed to get the weapon across in the checked luggage. When they had prepared to leave the hotel, she had insisted that he carry it.

"How many shots left, George?" she had asked.

"I don't know. I only fired that once, but I don't know if it was full when I picked it up."

"Well, pull the clip and check it." He had looked uncertainly at the weapon in response. "Oh, sweet Jesus," Taylor had exclaimed, "here, I'll show you." She had slipped the clip out to reveal three bullets. "Oh, well, let's hope we really don't need any firepower. If you have to use them, make 'em count."

Jeffers thought about making them count every time the pistol reminded him of its presence. Aside from plugging Schwerin in the back, he had never fired a gun in anger. In spite of that, he was in completely premeditated fashion standing guard with a semiautomatic pistol and three bullets waiting for what? If he had to shoot, would he?

From his position he saw the tall man in the poncho walk over to Taylor. It was an effort he found, to avoid concentrating on the pair, and instead look around for other interested parties. He saw none during the time they stood by the fountain. When they left, he trailed behind, the images of violence and gore that floated through his mind in complete contrast to the quiet street. After Taylor was seated in the cafeteria, he walked past to give the agreed-upon all-clear sign. When she returned it, he went in to join them.

"Einar, please meet my friend, George," Taylor said in English as Jeffers sat down.

They exchanged greetings, but Jeffers noticed that the young man continued to watch him afterwards. It was a bit unsettling, Jeffers not being used to causing concern in others by his presence. Then, he realized that his appearance was probably the issue. The bruises on his face were beginning to heal, but they were enough in evidence to imply that the man wearing them was no stranger to violence.

Taylor ignored the brief byplay. "I have filled George in on what you told me last night, so there is no need to repeat it. What we need to know is where Thorfinn's group meets."

"Yes, of course," he answered still looking at Jeffers. "There is a warehouse in the old harbor, not far from the ferry dock, that they use, at least the ones that Thorfinn has used to help him organize things. I think many of them use it as a meeting place regardless of whether Thorfinn is there."

"You mean they all just hang out there?" Taylor was incredulous. "No wonder Müller sent for help. It sounds like a damned social club."

"More of a gang than a club," Einar responded. "This is something I learned this morning. The man who has been doing most of the recruiting for Thorfinn is one Sigurd Arason. He's about twenty-two, twenty-three, used to work as a fisherman, but the captains he's worked for don't want him back. I'm not sure why, but he supposedly has a bad mean streak. That could do it, I suppose. Anyway, he's collected a bunch of others, I don't know how many. I think they listen to him more than to Thorfinn. You can expect some of them to be there late this afternoon."

"Einar, that was nicely done," Jeffers said. In fact, he though, it was a little too nicely done. "I'm curious, though, how you got the information. I mean, you didn't know all that last night, so, uh, Charlotte tells me. Did it make anyone suspicious when you asked?"

"Oh, no," he smiled, "I just asked Gudrun."

"Who is Gudrun?" The question came in stereo.

"Gudrun Jonsdottir."

"You mean, Gudrun Petursson?" Jeffers asked. Einar stared at him in stupefaction while Taylor fell prey to giggles she could not contain.

"Never mind," Taylor got out around the laughter. "George is very good at what he does, but social customs are not part of it." That was true enough, even if the implication about what George did was not. "George, Gudrun is the daughter of Jon Petursson, and is called Gudrun Jonsdottir. Very few Icelanders use surnames, just the first name and patronymic."

"Must be a real trip to use the phone directory," Jeffers muttered.

Taylor ignored the comment. "More to the point," she said, turning back to Einar, "how does she fit into this organization?"

"She doesn't really," he answered. "I mean, she's only sixteen."

"Then how does she know?" Taylor demanded.

"Oh, that's simple. Jon talks to her about almost everything."

"Now hold on! Jon Petursson is trying to put together an underground and he discusses all the details with his sixteen-year-old daughter?"

"Please, it's not what it sounds like." Einar drained his coffee and took a bite of fish before continuing. "First of all, Gudrun is not going to talk about this with anyone, except Thorfinn or me. Second, you have to understand a little more about Jon." The silence that followed encouraged him to continue. "Thorfinn and I might as well have been part of Jon's family when we were younger. We spent a lot of time at his house; he is the main reason we went to the university, and Gudrun always used to tag along from the time she was six or seven. It was like that until about three years ago. That was when Jon's son, he was ten, died." Jeffers looked across at Taylor as Einar spoke. Her expression was closed, unreadable. "It was bad after that. Jon's wife never got over it; she killed herself about six months later. That's when Jon really began to get involved with Gizur and his party, and otherwise just pulled into a shell. Now, aside from Gudrun and Thorfinn, I don't think he talks to anyone unless it's about work or the party. As I told you, I've sort of drifted away recently also."

"Well, it doesn't sound good," Taylor commented after Einar had finished. "Neither Jon nor your friend Thorfinn know how to make this work. Left to themselves, they will go nowhere. Müller, that's who your German is, does know what to do, though, and he'll get that collection of toughs working for him. Your friends will wind up frozen out, although I'm sure they will be kept around to take the fall if things go sour. Do you know where Müller is?"

"No, only that he is out of town for a few weeks. Listen, I'm not stupid. I can see that the way it's going my friends are going to get hurt and I don't want that. It's all very well for Thorfinn to talk about struggles and policies until he starts doing things that will get people hurt. I just don't want that, and I don't want them hurt either."

"I can't promise," Taylor answered, "but we'll do our best. The worst route would be to just let it go on. Now, George and I need to make some plans, and I think it would be best if you left. Meet me here at this time, in two days. I don't want to see or hear from you, until then."

As he left, Taylor turned around in her hands the slip of paper bearing the address Einar had given her. "So, George, what do you think?"

Jeffers had been quiet through most of the conversation, especially after his gaffe. He took his time before replying. "I think it's crazy, that's what. A couple of college kids and a nutty professor playing at revolution with a politician who may, or may not, be playing with a full deck. What's a crack spy like Müller doing with them?"

"I rather doubt that it matters a great deal to Müller," Taylor said, still looking at the address from varying angles. "Remember, Müller isn't going to care about these guys; they are just the tools he needs to use. He will take the toughs that are there and build his own organization within the shell of Gizur's party, hide his own underground as it were underneath another one for an extra layer of security. That may not have been what he was expecting to do, I have no idea what Jon led him to believe, but, short of quitting, it's the only way to go from here. I think we just happened to show up right at the beginning."

"So, what do we do now?"

"George, those people are expecting someone from Germany to take over Thorfinn's role and get the Reykjavik organization going the way Müller wants. I think," she paused to draw the sentence out, "that person is going to be me."

Jeffers's mouth opened but no sound came out at first. When words did emerge, he found himself saying, "I don't know, Taylor." Actually, he felt that he did know. The idea was preposterous—crazy—and he did not like it at all. No, not one bit. "You can't just stroll in there and pass yourself off as a terrorist serviceman. There's probably a password, and you don't know it. What happens if they catch on? Or if Müller gets in touch early? Or if the right guy shows up? Or any one of a hundred other possible problems? And don't hand me that line about having to take risks in this business. This is too risky."

She answered his concern first with a laugh. "I remember you once saying to me that if it were me having to take a chance, I'd jump at it. Well, it's that time, and I'm going to go for it."

Jeffers felt an uneasy feeling building inside. True enough, he had said it, but that was before he knew very much about the woman across from him. The free and easy laugh, no tension at all, was not a manufactured veneer. She was really looking forward to this.

"I get the impression," Jeffers said slowly, "that you like taking wild chances, that you like them to be necessary. You really don't care if you get killed, do you?" There was a sadness in his voice. "In fact, maybe that's what you're looking for. Is it?"

"What? To get myself killed? No." She stopped while she debated silently how far to carry the conversation. "You have to understand that I don't find the possibility a tremendous deterrent. It's going to happen, sooner rather than later, and the end for Taylor Redding isn't going to be very pleasant. That is, unless I buy it real quick on a job like this."

Abruptly, she leaned forward at him, eyes intense. "George, have you ever been to Gettysburg?"

"Only in books." Jeffers looked puzzled. What in God's name had Gettysburg to do with either Iceland or Taylor Redding?

"I've been there. Walked all over that battlefield, as a matter of fact. Let me tell you something about it. After two days there of very bloody but inconclusive fighting, the Union and Confederate armies were still facing each other, neither having gained an advantage. That next morning, Lee ordered a frontal assault by Pickett's and Pettigrew's divisions on the center of the Union line at Cemetery Ridge.

"Now, Robert E. Lee is probably my second most favorite historical person, but that was a horrible mistake. The top of Cemetery Ridge doesn't look that high, or that far, from where the Confederate lines were, but let me tell you, it is a longer and steeper climb than it looks. They had to form up in the open, no way of hiding what they were doing. And they went in, with no cover, twelve thousand men and their officers. They were all veterans, a crack unit. They must have known, could not have avoided knowing, that there was no way in Hell they were going to make it over that ridge. But they tried. Came close, too. Old man Armistead, old enough to have been sitting on his porch instead of leading an infantry charge, led his men right to the stone wall of the Union lines. Richard Garnett rode his horse alongside his men, a fat target if there ever was one. He got to within a hundred yards of the wall."

"I'm not sure I see the point," Jeffers replied. "If you remember, they lost there, Taylor, and they lost the war too."

"I remember. Don't you forget, in the end I'm going to lose, too. The point is, when the outcome is inevitable, it's the effort and the style that is important."

"I see. And you live with style."

"Damn straight."

Jeffers said nothing immediately. There was an image in his head of those gray lines on a long ago summer day, trying to do the impossible. What, he asked himself silently, do you say to a woman who sees her life as a long charge into the guns at Gettysburg? Did she envy Armistead and Garnett their immortal reputations, purchased at the price of their lives?

"Okay," he said finally. "When are you going to meet these people, and what do you want me to do?"

Taylor slowed as she stepped through the unlocked side door into the warehouse. Even though the sky had remained overcast, the contrast between the outside illumination and the interior was enough to make the latter appear wholly unlit. Gradually, her eyes adjusted, allowing her a better view of her surroundings. Seeing did not help much. The rows of crates and boxes could have been present in any warehouse. There was nothing about them, that she could see, to make them distinctive. Neither eyes nor ears detected any sign of activity. That was probably because, in spite of the daylight, it was well past normal working hours. Certainly, the layer of dust that might have been expected on the floor or boxes had the place not been in use was absent. Now what? She could feel her stomach react to the anticipation of action. Risks are the spice of life, she remembered, and thank you, Sister Angelica. Of course, the good Sister had been assured of her place in heaven, when all was said and done. Taylor headed down what appeared to be a main aisle leading farther into the building.

"Ahoy, Sigurd," she called out, "where are you?" There seemed to be no advantage in trying to sneak up on her quarry. Were she, indeed, the person she was going to claim to be, she would approach openly. She passed more rows of crates, no different than the ones before, still with no sign of life.

As she moved past yet another side passage, she sensed movement behind her, but before she could turn, there was an arm thrown around her neck to choke her. That is, it started to. Taylor reacted immediately, before the choke was really in place. Her right arm swung back, connecting with a set of ribs left unguarded by the arm at her neck. There was a grunt behind her, and no pressure was applied to her throat. She did not wait for any, but drove her other elbow straight backward where it met yielding flesh. A gasp followed the impact and the choke vanished entirely. She pivoted on her good leg to face her assailant for the first time. A youngish face, with a scraggly blond beard, seemed to hang in midair directly in front of her, at shoulder level. Without any hesitation, she stepped in swinging her elbow to drive the outside of her forearm into the man's face. There was an audible snap as the cheek was smashed in followed by a spray of blood. The erstwhile attacker collapsed like an empty sack. The lack of attempt, on his part, to break his fall convinced her that she could safely turn her back on him. When she turned back around, perhaps three seconds after the attack began, she found herself facing four more men. For a brief time, nothing happened.

"All right," she said firmly, "which one of you is Sigurd?" There was no answer.

"Okay, your hospitality is as lousy as your security. I am here to do a job and I do not have time to play stupid games with stupid children." She stood with her feet planted apart, hands on hips, nothing in her voice or stance to suggest that she faced odds of four to one. With her right hand she fingered the still-closed switchblade she had slipped out of her sleeve as she had turned around. "I will ask once more," she said, "who is Sigurd?"

"Are you the one Gerhardt sent?" countered the one standing at the far left.

"Am I the one Gerhardt sent?" she parroted back in a mocking tone. "Who did you think I was? Madonna?"

She could sense their indecision. It showed in the sideways looks they exchanged among themselves, in the absence of any attempt to dominate her. That was all to the good; she almost had them. A low groan came from the floor behind her. Hopefully, the man she had downed was going to stay down, even if he regained his senses. He would have to, she decided.

Finally, the one on the left spoke again. "Very well. I am Sigurd. But I still do not know who you are. You have not given me the proper phrase, and if you are who you claim to be, you are three weeks early."

"The proper phrase." No surprise that there would be a password. Even Jeffers had pointed that out.

"As for who I am, call me Anna. That will do as well as any other name. As for when I was supposed to arrive, I work by my timetable. Not Gerhardt's, not anybody else's. And as for the 'proper phrase,' " as she spoke the words she covered the distance between her and the nearest of the men with rapid strides. Before the man realized what was happening, her arm swung up and the switchblade flashed open. She halted it with the point pressing up under his chin. To avoid having it sink into the soft tissue, he was forced to come up on tiptoe.

"Fools!" she snarled. "You answer to me, not I to you. That is why I have no phrase for you. But you," she indicated Sigurd, "will now identify yourself properly to me. If not, I will move the knife up, about ten centimeters."

Now for the moment of truth! She could all but feel the tension around her. The man she had hoist on her blade looked over at Sigurd with wide fearful eyes. A drop of blood drew a thin, red line down the blade. She wished that she could know how Sigurd would react. She had, obviously, no idea of the code Gerhardt had given Sigurd. In fact, she assumed it existed only because recognition codes were usually given by both parties. Whatever Sigurd said, she would have to take it as genuine. Would he be bright enough, and suspicious enough, to give her a false code so that she would betray herself? Would he be cold-blooded enough to risk a man's life by trying it?

"It usually rains in Bremen on Thursday," Sigurd said slowly.

"Good," she replied. At least, she hoped so. With a single motion, she pulled the knife back and shoved the man into one of his fellows. "I am satisfied with your identity. Do you have any further questions about mine?"

If Sigurd had truly known his business, he would have attacked then. Taylor had worked long enough with both Sister Angelica's shadowy network and Bill Waggeman to know that you never accepted a person's *bona fides* without the correct code. They, however, had been real professionals, working in a very unforgiving environment. Taylor had also known hirelings of Sean, and even of Billy O'Brian, who could be persuaded to accept other forms of proof. She had decided to bet that Sigurd fell into the latter class.

"I have no questions, Anna," Sigurd answered. "Gerhardt said that you would have instructions for us. If you will tell me what they are, I will do my best to carry them out."

"That is better." Taylor refolded the knife and slipped it back into its hiding place under her sleeve. "Have two of your men get that," she indicated the fallen man with a wave of her hand, "to a hospital. Make sure that it is reported as an accident, and make sure that when his mouth starts to work again he keeps it closed. Within three days, you will have three apartments available in Reykjavik, and another in Kopavogur. Use the names of friends or relatives, not your own. I will supply cash if it is needed, you are not to use credit or checks." To emphasize the point, she pulled a sheaf of bills she had taken from the pack and tossed it onto the floor at Sigurd's feet. She watched while he picked it up and counted it. From the look on his face, she guessed that the money had allayed any remaining doubts about her identity. "When you have made these arrangements, put up a note in the bus station saying 'Anna, have found a place to stay.' I will meet you at Ingolfur's statue at noon, the day you put up the note. Be there alone. If I do not see that note by the fourth day, I will find you and the results will be unfortunate. One more thing for now. One of your security problems is that Thorfinn talks too much. He is still useful as a writer, so he is not to be touched, but there is to be no contact between any of your men and him. Understood?"

"Yes, Anna." There was nothing but respect in Sigurd's tone.

"Then vanish. I will see you when you put the note up."

They left quickly, two of them half-carrying their dazed comrade. Taylor was left alone in the warehouse, with none to see the big grin on her face. It had worked perfectly! She could hardly have asked for a better result. Given just a little time, she would own Gizur's organization in Reykjavik. Gerhardt and his German friend would have trouble finding the group, not to mention controlling it, by the time she was done. The only part of the evening's results that she wanted to complain about was the damage to her shirt. She looked a bit ruefully at the damp red blotch on the right sleeve. Oh, well, maybe some hydrogen peroxide would salvage it. The grin had resumed its customary place as she left the building.

# CHAPTER 24

## LANGLEY, VIRGINIA

THE PILE OF PAPER that overflowed Oliver's 'In' box had not improved and neither had his dyspepsia. It seemed that every time he tried to act on Lorenzo's murder, or even thought about the case, he was handed another snafu. It was in the midst of dealing with another one of those when Marden's message landed on his desk. Iceland! What in God's name were Jeffers and the woman going to do there? Oliver actually did not care so much about what they were going to do as what he was going to do about it. The proper thing to do, at least by the book, would be to contact the chief of station in Reykjavik, let him know what the situation was, and have him find out what the two of them were up to. There was just one problem and that was the Reykjavik CoS. The man was relatively new in his position but Oliver knew enough about him to know that he would follow the book, far too strictly for Oliver's comfort. In a case that might well end up with action against an American citizen, the last thing Oliver wanted was a CoS who thought that the Intelligence Oversight Law made good sense. This was a man who would probably decide that such activity was a sufficiently important covert action to be referred back to the covert action staff for authorization. Once that happened, the only sure thing was that quick action would be out of the question. Hell, Jeffers and the woman might both die of old age before an action was agreed on.

Well, if that was the case, then there were ways to bypass the CoS. Oliver had done it in the past, especially when he was working for counterintelligence. Oliver picked up Marden's file and went through it again. This man was probably the right tool for this job. The file suggested that Marden was very sure of himself and tended to resent anything he saw as interference in his operations. Not a bad choice, Oliver thought, for a somewhat irregular job. A message went out, both to Marden and to his CoS in Germany, instructing Marden to follow the pair to Iceland and to avoid all contact with the CoS in Reykjavik. Quite distinct from the CIA, Oliver knew that the DIA had both agents and assets in Reykjavik. Oliver was willing to bet that he knew the DIA people better than the current CoS did. Oliver made a few more calls, followed by a brief lunch with an old acquaintance. The result was another message to Marden, one that gave him a contact in Reykjavik. Simultaneously, it gave Oliver a discreet channel through which he could contact Marden, one that completely bypassed the CoS and his apparatus. Marden had never operated in Iceland, but Oliver figured that, since he was chasing Americans rather than natives, it would not be a major problem.

Shortly after Oliver had completed Marden's arrangements, one of his earlier inquiries bore fruit in the form of Bill Waggeman's arrival. Waggeman proved to be a tall black man with thinning hair and a salt and pepper moustache. His age could have been anywhere from thirty-five to fifty-five.

"So, what's up at the Pickle Factory, Charley?" Waggeman said after he settled in to one of Oliver's side chairs. "I thought you were on the nerd patrol these days."

Oliver winced. Waggeman just sat there with the casual arrogance Oliver was sure came from too long an association with Special Operations' knuckledraggers."Don't remind me," he said. "I called you because of a report of yours from a few years ago." Oliver passed the folder across his desk to Waggeman.

"Sure, I remember this. What does Africa have to do with technology surveillance?"

"It's a name I'm interested in," Oliver said. "Taylor Redding."

At the name, Waggeman smiled. "Taylor Redding. What's she into this time?"

"I take it you're not surprised to hear the name." Oliver was surprised. The report was years old. "Recognize her?" Oliver passed over the Amsterdam photograph. Waggeman nodded. "What can you tell me about here?"

"I assume you've read the report?" Oliver nodded. "Okay. I'll skip the operational details. Special Operations was supporting the insurgent group there at the time. Our best conduit to get weapons in and to get humint was through this missionary group, a bunch of nuns, if you can believe it. A Sister Angelica ran it, and that's a misnomer if there ever was one. I don't know how long she'd been in the bush, a couple of decades I guess, but she was as tough an old bird as you'll ever find. Anyway, they had this young kid from the States working at the mission; that was Taylor. Initially, we thought she was there on some school or church thing."

"I take it she wasn't."

"Good guess. I mean, it seemed a little odd anyway, a kid from Wellesley, Massachusetts, in an area as unsettled as that. All you'd get from her was that she'd gotten the idea to come from an uncle of hers, Cyrus Redding. Anyway, it was pretty easy to see what she was doing for the mission and, shit, I really needed an asset there who wasn't bound, hand and foot, to Sister Angelica."

The expression on Oliver's face was skeptical. "Do you honestly expect me to believe that you and some nun took this kid from the suburbs and trained her to be an intelligence operative?"

Waggeman spread his hands out, palms up. "What do you want me to tell you? She was there; I needed someone; she fit; I used her. She started out pretty raw, didn't know a lot of practical stuff, you know, the sort of bright eager kid who usually gets killed. I'll tell you, though, she learned fast, wasn't afraid of anything. Show her something once and she'd soak it up like a sponge. We got a lot of good information through her."

"I'll tell you what it sounds like," Oliver said. "It sounds like goddamn Nancy Drew goes to spy school."

Waggeman laughed out loud. "Yeah, but so what? In a situation like that, Christ, you'd try to recruit Nancy Drew."

"Did you try to recruit Redding?"

"Yeah. She wouldn't bite. Don't know why, anymore than I don't really know why she was there in the first place. What's she done?"

Oliver did not quite answer the question. "Did you know there's a death certificate that says she died before you met her?"

"No, I didn't. I can believe it though. Taylor was a pretty spooky kid."

"Interesting choice of term," Oliver said and they both grinned.

"You still haven't told me what this is about," Waggeman said.

In response, Oliver gave him a barebones sketch of the problem: the missing enzyme, the missing scientists, the trail through Europe. "I need to know what's going on and I'm willing to bet that she has that information. Do you know anything that I could use as a hook that would work with her?"

Waggeman shook his head. "If you mean blackmail, I think the answer is no. At least, there's nothing I know that would give you a hold on her. Money might work."

Oliver seemed to ignore that. "What about this uncle of hers she told you about? Did she tell you anything about him? Maybe we can get to her through him."

Waggeman shook his head again. "Won't work, Charley. I was curious, so I found Uncle Cyrus years ago."

"And?"

"Cyrus Redding was one of the old OSS operatives. Unfortunately, he's been dead longer than that certificate says his niece has been."

"Damn! Do you want to try contacting her?"

That brought a sharp look from Waggeman. "Charley, you said they were in Iceland. I'm going to stick out there worse than she did at that African mission and if she sees me pop up like that," he snapped his fingers, "she's going to know something is funny. You'll be better off using the people up there to approach her."

This time it was Oliver's turn to shake his head. "That, I am not going to do. I've got someone in there myself and I'll work through him. I'll pass him your information and see if he can buy the information I need."

"Be careful, Charley. She'll blend in well up there. She speaks Icelandic, you know."

Oliver's eyebrows went up. "You're kidding."

"No, not at all. Things like that stick in your mind. She told me she speaks that and German as well. I believe her, too. During the time we were in Africa, she got quite fluent in the local dialect."

"I'll pass that along, too, but I'm not going through our station people."

Waggeman was watching Oliver carefully, his face expressionless. "Mind if I ask why you want to avoid our people?"

Again, Oliver did not quite answer the question. "We had a man killed in Boston recently," he said.

"You think she did it?" This time, it was Waggeman's turn to look surprised. "Well, I would think she could kill if she had to, but I wouldn't figure her for an assassin."

"It has been several years since you knew her," Oliver pointed out. "Regardless, I want to know what she knows about this case. If it turns out that she was involved in the killing," Oliver's voice turned ominous, "let's just say it's useful, sometimes, to be outside regular channels. You ought to know what I mean."


# REYKJAVIK, ICELAND

JEFFERS WAS NOT SURE which sensation he liked least, that of looking like the archetype of the dumb American tourist, or that of being a peeping Tom. The camera equipment with which Taylor had outfitted him equipped him for either role. It hung around his neck like a millstone, the thin, synthetic strap digging into his skin no matter how he slung it, unless, that is, he supported it with one hand. He wondered if elephants felt the same way about their trunks. It was not the camera itself that was the source of all this emotional and physical discomfort; that marvel of plastic and circuitry weighed next to nothing. Rather, it was the lens attached to it, a thick black snout that elongated and retracted Pinocchio style. The scientist in Jeffers was capable of recognizing it for the optical triumph it was. The lens zoomed with superb definition from wide angle well into the telephoto range. The number of lens elements required to achieve this feat at reasonable shutter speeds accounted for both the weight and size, the characteristics that left Jeffers feeling like a tourist. It was the telephoto ability in particular that made him intermittently feel like a peeping Tom.

Taylor had wanted pictures of Gudrun. In fact, she had nearly turned the city upside down looking for just that lens almost immediately after leaving the cafeteria. Taylor wanted to know the girl's routine, and she wanted a photographic record of it. Not just a photograph to identify the girl—no, she wanted pictures of where she went and who she saw and notes as to when she did both. She wanted the photos at wide angle so that she could identify the surroundings, and she wanted telephotos to identify people, without having Jeffers come too close. There was nothing specific that Taylor wanted, as she had put it she did not know enough yet to know what to want although a bedroom scene, if one came up, was always welcome; it was just information that might prove useful. The concept made sense to Jeffers, but he still felt like a damn peeping Tom, hanging around the street corner waiting for the girl to come out of her house.

After half an eternity of waiting, the door opened. He swung the camera up for a close-up shot, then rotated the lens to frame the girl against the building. Shots taken, he lowered the camera and followed her at a safe distance. He spent the rest of the day in that manner, photographing shops she went to, friends she met, places she walked past. To judge from the number of casual conversations Jeffers monitored, on the sidewalk or in a store, Gudrun knew half the population of the city. There was nothing Jeffers could see that distinguished any one conversation from the others. How Taylor proposed to glean any significant insight from the photos he had no idea. It also occurred to him to wonder, as she flowed from one greeting to another, whether she was as discreet as Einar said or whether Thorfinn's underground was common knowledge. While such talk might do their work for them in scuttling certain political schemes, it was also likely to raise Gerhardt Müller's ire. Would Müller hurt a sixteen-year-old girl? Probably. It did not seem fair, to Jeffers, for a child to be endangered by the dirty politics of others, but, of course, it had not been fair for Hank either. Nothing he saw answered any of his questions. When Gudrun returned home, Jeffers set out to find a one-hour film developer.

* * *

Arrival in Iceland was no great thrill for Jake Marden. At best, he was a full day behind Jeffers with no idea of where Jeffers would go, no contacts, and damn little money. He could not think of a worse conceivable way to begin a mission and it was all because rear-echelon Oliver had forgotten how to work with the field people. He had been told in no uncertain terms not to contact the CoS in Reykjavik, an instruction that bothered him more than anything else about the assignment. It suggested infighting at the agency, something Marden wanted nothing to do with. His aggravation was further compounded by having to spend most of his first day finding a room. Somewhere in that city, he thought, there had to be a usable safe house, but where? He could hardly put a note up in the embassy cafeteria. This was yet another item Langley should have arranged. He had, after all, transmitted the message about Jeffers's destination the day before, but all he had been given was a contact name for emergency communications only. The result? Sharing a youth hostel room with two German punkers and a Danish snob.

Marden was out early the next morning in search of a lead to Jeffers; the company hardly made him want to linger in the room. He planned to check hotel registers first. He doubted that Jeffers would have any reason to suspect that his cover was blown and, consequently, should still be out in the open. If that try failed, Marden knew he would need to find locals who would be willing to keep an eye open, preferably on the basis of no more than a promise of money.

He had checked at two hotels, without success, when a glance down the street made his jaw fall open. He forced a cough and looked down, to avoid drawing attention to his surprise. The bastard was right there in front of him, just a little farther down the street. Jeffers was standing there, partially turned away, speaking to the girl Marden had seen him with in Amsterdam. There was no sign that Jeffers had seen Marden. Oh, fabulous day! Jake Marden's innate knack of being in the right place at the right time was going to save a mission that Langley had almost screwed up beyond repair. As Marden watched, the pair split up but neither one headed toward him. Marden's next decision was made without hesitation, almost without conscious thought. Oliver would have a fit that both were not monitored, but Marden had a real situation, not a book of standard operating procedures, to deal with. For Marden, it was a simple choice, one that did not even need the years of experience he had. "Go where the money is" was Willie Sutton's justly famous law. Marden would stick with the dangerous one, with Jeffers.

The girl hardly required immediate attention although, he laughed mentally, she might deserve very close attention under other circumstances.

Jeffers set an easy pace, obviously having no idea he was being followed. Marden had always prided himself on his abilities in the field, and this was another case in which they were so helpful. He would tail Jeffers and Jeffers was never going to know it. The trail did not lead far, only a few blocks to a street of low stone and brick homes set amid carefully tended shrubs. Here, Jeffers did not stop, but began to mark time. Marden allowed the distance between the two to lengthen. It was obvious to him that Jeffers was waiting for something, or someone, but what? The camera Jeffers carried argued that there would be no violence, at least not immediately, but Marden patted the butt of his semiautomatic for reassurance anyway. It proved to be a long wait, long enough to make Marden antsy that Jeffers would spot him or, worse, that some innocent would approach Jeffers and spark a confrontation.

At length, a door opened in a building across the street and Marden saw Jeffers snap a couple of pictures. From where Jeffers aimed the camera, his target was clear.

Jeffers was after a girl, ash blonde and beautiful, who looked no older than her midteens. Was this Jeffers a pervert, having some fun on the side? Marden discarded the idea quickly. Doubtless, it was the girl's father who was the real target. Still, he felt a twisting sensation in his guts. His older daughter would be near the age of the one in Jeffers's lens. From what he remembered of her as an eight-year-old, she might even look a bit like that girl. He was not certain though. It had been years since he had known, for sure, where his ex-wife had moved. He shook himself as his thoughts began to wander from the job in front of him. It would never do to be woolgathering and lose track of Jeffers at this point. For the rest of the day, Marden followed as Jeffers stalked the girl across the city. Although Marden was tense and alert for trouble the entire time, it was uneventful. Jeffers did nothing but take pictures. On several occasions Marden tried to work closer to the girl, to better identify the people she spoke to and to try to form an idea of what she was doing. In the end, however, it was futile. He dared not come too close, because Jeffers was watching. The few scraps of conversation he did hear were, of course, in Icelandic and incomprehensible. Once he realized that he had no other option, he watched passively as Jeffers followed her back home. From there, Jeffers led him to the Loftleidir. That brought a silent yell of triumph to Marden's mind. The desk of the Loftleidir was where his emergency contact worked.

*    *    *

"All right, Taylor, there you have it," Jeffers spread the pictures in front of her on the table, "a day in the life of Gudrun Jonsdottir. Please tell me that you can make something out of them."

"The one thing I can say for sure is that you need some practice in focusing and composition." Having said that, she hastened to say that she did not really mean it. Then, "There's nothing that jumps right out, but you would have known that when you were there. It's more to have a baseline, to work out who she sees and talks to habitually. Some of them may turn out to be useful. Give me a moment to look at them, please."

Where Jeffers had merely glanced at the pictures, Taylor spent time, more than a moment, looking at each one, making notes of companions and background details. When she finished she tossed three of them in front of Jeffers.

"Not what I was expecting, but what do you make of these?"

"What do you mean?" Jeffers asked in return. "One at a fruit stand, one with a friend in front of a museum, the other in that downtown shopping area. Why?"

"You took all three of them with a wide angle setting, right?" Jeffers nodded. "All right, look toward the edge of the field, here and here and here," she pointed. "The same man is in all the shots."

Jeffers followed the finger. In each photo there was a stocky man with a blazer and an open collar white shirt. His features were difficult to be certain of in the wide angle image and small print, but the thinning blond hair was the same from picture to picture.

"That's odd," Jeffers said slowly, "those three places are nowhere near each other."

"Exactly. So, either someone else is following Gudrun, or they are following you."

"Great," Jeffers flopped on the bed, "here we go again. What do you have in mind?"

"For the moment, I am going to prop that chair under the door knob, and get some sleep. There's really nothing else worth doing tonight."

The next morning, Taylor was intentionally slow about getting out of the hotel. It was not from fatigue—she was properly thankful for a night free of flashbacks—but in the hope of spotting the man who had so unexpectedly appeared in Jeffers's photos. Taylor had to admit, to herself and to Jeffers, that she had no idea about the man's identity. For an unknown pursuer to appear, just as she was getting to the meat of the case, was unwelcome. Still, it could have been worse. The man might not have been obliging enough to come within Jeffers's field of view on several occasions. In that case, they would have remained unaware of him. At least, this way she could reasonably expect him to look for Jeffers at the hotel, and, in so doing, give Taylor a chance to retake the offensive.

She was not disappointed. The man was there, apparently absorbed in travel brochures in the lobby. He could easily have been a tourist, killing time waiting for a bus, but he matched the photograph exactly. Taylor walked to the door with Jeffers, turning her head as if in conversation, but in reality just keeping the man in view. He watched them leave, and once satisfied that they were going out, went to speak with one of the clerks. Taylor's last glimpse was of him, and the clerk, headed for the elevators.

"Well, that answers that," Taylor announced.

"What does?"

"He's not going to follow us now. For sure, he's headed upstairs to check out our room."

Jeffers hesitated. "If you don't mind my playing devil's advocate, can you really be sure he's not just a tourist headed up to his own room? I mean, it *could* have been coincidence, him showing up in the pictures."

Taylor shook her head. "It's possible he's heading to his own room, but no way is he an innocent tourist. Not carrying a heavy sidearm, he's not."

Jeffers had thought he had become accustomed to Taylor's thinking, but that comment left him gaping. "Taylor, I got as much of a look as you did. How the hell do you know that?"

"Elementary, my dear Jeffers," she replied. "You can tell from his coat, his collar, and the way he carries his arm. With practice."

Taylor had originally planned to avoid any contact with her friends in the area, but the appearance of the stranger had forced a fast reevaluation. They now urgently needed a new place to stay. She was not going to chance waiting for Sigurd to come up with a safe house. An elderly couple she knew in one of the Reykjavik suburbs proved quite suitable. They had no living children, so there was extra space in the small house, and Taylor was a frequent enough visitor that there was no surprise at her appearance. Of course, they would put up Taylor's friend, too. Not *boy*friend, the point was clearly made, just friend. In a way, Jeffers found a cover that mandated separate sleeping arrangements a relief. He had enough problems on his mind without that one.

With Jeffers safely stashed, for the moment, Taylor went back to the hotel. Their room looked just as she had left it, on the surface. What was not the same, however, were the minute telltales she had set before leaving. A slip of paper here, some hair there, a whole series of tiny clues that screamed out that the room had been searched. Whoever had been there had taken pains to hide the search. That was also useful. The searcher believed his identity secret, and wanted to keep it that way.

Taylor's next move was back downstairs, where she broached the subject to the desk clerk, and met with an emphatic denial.

"Look," Taylor said, "there is no point in arguing, because I know you let the man into our room. It doesn't matter to me that you did; you have no problem with me. I'm just interested in some information, that's all." She continued her argument by giving the clerk a brief glimpse of dollar bills.

The money, eventually, proved persuasive and the clerk admitted that a man named Jake had inquired about Taylor and her friend. Lubricated by a few more bills, the clerk said yes, she had let him into the room. After the bills changed hands, the girl said nothing more, but from the narrowing of her eyes, Taylor could see that the conversation was not over. Taylor waited, and was rewarded.

"They sometimes ask me to pass along messages. They pay for that."

"Who does?"

"I'd rather not say."

Taylor flashed more money, but got a negative shake of the head in response. "Then why mention it?" she asked.

The girl looked everywhere but at Taylor before she spoke again. "They left a letter for Jake, it came just after he was here. I'm supposed to hold it until he comes back."

"I could see that it gets delivered," Taylor answered. "If you agree." She leaned on the counter laying out a row of bills in such a way that they were visible only to the clerk. The clerk nodded and the money moved across the counter and vanished. In its place a sealed white envelope appeared. Taylor thanked her and left, the precious envelope tucked into one of her pockets.

It was a major effort to restrain herself from opening it before she returned to Jeffers, but she managed. It sat, then, on the table between them, as they both looked at it.

"What's in it?" he asked.

"If I had opened it, I'd know. I thought you would be interested."

"I am, I am. Do it already."

She tore it open, to find inside a folded piece of paper with a note typed on it.

"Urgent, urgent," it read. "Meet at kiosk by Laekjargata 0900 hours for message from uncle. Wear red handkerchief in pocket, carry *Morgunbladdid*. I will ask you when the Yankees will win again. Tell me the Mets are better. Will check for you each day."

"Sounds like something's up, but what?" Jeffers asked.

"Wish I knew." Taylor worked on her lower lip before continuing. "Clearly, the home office wants to talk with the guy who tailed you. What we want to know, is what they have in mind. I think you better be the one at this meeting."

"Shit! How am I going to pull this off?"

"Easy. Wear the red handkerchief, carry the *Morgunbladdid* and root for the Mets. If these two were supposed to know each other there wouldn't be all this code crap. All you have to do is pick up the message and vanish."

The concept had had little appeal for Jeffers when Taylor first mentioned it. It still did not appeal to him as he stood at the kiosk the next morning. He had learned, however, to shove unwanted feelings below the surface while he went about his business. The street was crowded, which he took as a good sign. It reassured him, however superficially, that nothing too violent could occur. He wondered if the man named Jake was in that crowd somewhere, unwittingly watching Jeffers pick up a message intended for him. It was the sort of joke he knew Taylor would love, if she could have been sure it would happen. While he was thinking about it, a light tap on his shoulder startled him and he turned around. He found a short man wearing a gray sport jacket and equally gray face in front of him.

"Excuse me," the man said, "do you think it will be next year before the Yankees win again?"

Jeffers managed to keep his composure and reply with a shrug, "I don't much care. The Mets are a better team."

At the mention of the Mets, the face in front of him winked. The man shook his hand and whispered, "I hope it's fun," and was gone. Jeffers looked down to find a small envelope in his hand. The entire transaction had taken only seconds.

When he and Taylor opened it together, they found two pages of closely typed notes, all of it gibberish. Jeffers looked helplessly at Taylor. "What is this?"

"Code," was the laconic reply. "It's a damn code. This guy, Jake, obviously has the key, but we don't."

"Can we crack it, maybe?"

"By which millennium? Damn, this could be anything and I've got no idea what."

"Wonderful," Jeffers said. "For all we know it could be an order to kill us."

"I would think that's unlikely, George, since he probably is an American agent. Also, if that's what it is, then it's a little verbose. Still, I agree that we can't be sure and there's no time to play games."

"Although," Jeffers added, far more coolly than he thought he could, "it also implies that there is no immediate danger because whatever he is being told to do, he hasn't been told to do it yet. Otherwise why send an order?"

"Good point," Taylor acknowledged. "Especially since this kind of thing is not broadcast, it's a fair bet that only he and whoever issued it are supposed to know. I would think if we can act first, and get him out of the way, we should have plenty of time to take care of our business. Once we've done that, we can worry about this, whatever it is. We just need to come up with a way of getting rid of him without killing him."

"Why the sudden scruples?"

"There's an old saying," Taylor said, " 'Paybacks are a bitch.' Believe me, we don't want to kill this one. Besides, I've got a cute and nasty idea."

Leaving Jeffers with a late breakfast, which he did not really want, and small talk from their host, which he really did not want, Taylor went to the bus station as quickly as she could. The note from Sigurd she had hoped for was there. She took the note down and carefully folded it and put it in one of her pockets. One hurdle down!

From the station, it was back to the hotel. The desk clerk did not seem surprised to see her. Once again, the sight of money proved an excellent opener for the conversation. Taylor wanted to know if Jake had returned to the desk yet. The clerk noted that he had, but that she had told him that Taylor had gone out early with a mention that she would be back around noon. Jake had paid for the information and said he would return then as well. The clear expectation was that the information would be equally valuable to Taylor, which it was.

Taylor was not quite through. She peeled off a few more notes, and said, "You might let him know, when he comes back, that we returned early and left again. We did ask, however, about a restaurant for us and a friend for dinner tonight and you recommended the Rjupa. We said we would try it. If we see him there tonight, I'll double what I just gave you. Since you should also be able to charge him for information that he can verify, you should do rather nicely." From the clerk's smile, Taylor was certain she had reached the same conclusion.

It was, Taylor thought as she walked out, a perfect setup. If the clerk played it straight, Jake would show up unsuspecting. If she decided to double-cross Taylor and try for an even larger payoff from Jake, well, the man would probably still show up. He would just be on the lookout for a trap, figuring that the knowledge gave him an advantage. The way Taylor had it planned, it would make no difference. It remained only to find Sigurd and launch the underground's first operation.

Sigurd met her according to their previous plan, quite proud of himself for having finished his job well ahead of the time limit. Taylor seized on his mood, and presented her plan as a reward for Sigurd's performance. Sigurd loved it. Of course, he could arrange what she needed. Yes, the afternoon provided plenty of time.

Jeffers, when she returned, was less sanguine about the idea. "This scheme of yours has me sitting there solo when he shows up. What's the plan if he doesn't want to wait to see who I meet, but comes straight over?"

"Figuring out what to do shouldn't be too difficult. Usually, all you really need to know is your opponent's intentions and what his capabilities are. Actually, even one of them should be sufficient."

"Hah. Is that something your pet Chinese general wrote?"

"Not quite in those words," she answered. "Actually, I heard it that way from an old teacher of mine. Name of Sister Angelica."

"Sister, huh?" Jeffers had a look that fell somewhere between puzzled and disbelief. "Well, since I can't be sure what instructions he had before the message we intercepted, we don't really know either his intentions or his capabilities. Did learned Sister have a quick answer for this situation."

"Sure," Taylor did not hesitate. "Shoot first."

"Jesus Christ! What kind of parochial school did you go to?"

"Our Lady of the Hard Knocks," she replied.

So it was that Jeffers found himself alone at the Rjupa that evening. He was conducted to a table for three and coffee appeared without his asking for it. Shortly afterward, Jake appeared. The sight of Jeffers, at a table with three place settings, brought a thrill to his mind. The clerk's information was good, the confirmation was sitting right in front of him. No doubt about it, dump old Jake Marden into even this Godforsaken, volcanic wasteland and he would come up with good sources. It was with immense satisfaction that he took a table giving him a good natural view of Jeffers. He ordered coffee and some soup and prepared to give the impression of taking a lengthy dinner. For Jeffers, the paramount urge was to stare at the man he knew was watching him. Since that would be a dead giveaway, he stared, alternatively, at the other diners. Taylor had not gone into the details of her plan, but, as he shifted his gaze from a couple who had noticed him, he caught a glimpse of Taylor standing in the doorway. She winked. He was so intent on the wink, that he almost missed the action.

Jake had downed his coffee, and half finished his soup, when he became aware of something very wrong with his stomach. Something wrong with the soup? He started to get out of his chair, but the wrongness coalesced into outright nausea that was beyond his control. It caught him as he had gotten halfway up. A mix of soup, coffee and stomach juice vomited out across the table, spilling onto the floor and splashing on the back of the diner at the table in front of him.

With cries of "Are you all right?" and, "What happened?" Taylor and two men rushed to Marden's side. Everyone else in the room studiously tried to ignore the mess, grateful that they did not have to help. Quickly, the trio helped Marden to the door, while a third man appeared to help the staff in cleaning up. Once outside and shielded from prying eyes, Taylor stabbed swiftly with the syringe one of Sigurd's men had pirated from the hospital that afternoon. So racked with misery and retching was Marden that he never noticed the needle. He noticed nothing, in fact, until the world turned fuzzy, after which he noticed nothing at all.

Later that night, two seamen half-carried, half-dragged a comrade aboard a trawler. "Too much liquor," was the only comment they made as they carefully tucked him into a bunk. None of the crew disputed their assessment. The man was apparently so drunk he did not even notice when the engines started.

Marden awoke, much later the next day, to find himself on a pitching vessel, out of sight of land. Neither English nor German made any impression on the crew. Sign language for "radio" or "turning around" drew only laughter. It was going to be, he decided, very unpleasant explaining all of this to Charles Oliver.

# CHAPTER 25

## REYKJAVIK, ICELAND

AFTER THE EVENING OF Marden's disposal, the days became progressively busier with Jeffers occasionally waking in the morning to find Taylor either asleep in bed or just arriving with that intention. All her time and effort poured into Thorfinn's former organization. To Jeffers, it sometimes seemed that the effort went a little too far.

"You know," he commented one evening, "at the rate you're going, you will create exactly the organization I thought we were going to prevent."

"In a sense, you're right," she replied, "or you would be if I had time to do more than just start. There is, however, one critically important point. That is, the presence of a mole, i.e., me. Whenever we need to, we can pull the plug on the whole apparatus."

What Taylor had left unsaid, primarily because it seemed self-evident, was that her view of the apparatus was dramatically changing. Even initially, she had been able to see that it was not the hopeless collection of amateurs that Einar had described just as it was not the professional organization that Müller wanted. The earlier members, those Thorfinn had originally recruited, tended to be students, or friends of students, Thorfinn had met through the university. By and large, they fit the description Einar had provided. They shared a strong conviction about Gizur's positions and programs, and spoke forcefully about putting them into effect. Forceful speech, however, was their forte. There was little, if any, organization with groups meeting in members' houses and all of them having some contact with Thorfinn. At some point Gizur, or perhaps Müller, had recognized that Thorfinn had constructed a debating society. Such groups make poor storm troopers. That realization had led to pressure on Thorfinn to do better, or be put aside, and led directly to the recruiting of the group Taylor had met in the warehouse. These recruits were more to Müller's taste, but they were also totally beyond Thorfinn's ability to control, hence Müller's displeasure on his previous trip.

The speed with which Sigurd had completed Taylor's first assignment, and then the performance of his men in getting rid of Marden had shown Taylor that there was considerable potential in that crew. The same events had cemented Sigurd and his men to her. After all, within a few days of arriving, she had led them against the CIA! Sigurd was eager for more. Where "Anna" had first obtained his obedience by force and bluff, she now held his genuine loyalty. It convinced Taylor that although her initial objective had been only to deny Müller access to the group she might, in fact, be able to create an organization of her own.

Taylor knew what needed to be done. Meetings were rotated among the safe houses and no meetings were permitted anywhere else. New members, a limited number of the same type as Sigurd's toughs, were brought in through a series of small cells. A few of Thorfinn's old comrades were included, but most of them were completely cut off, just as Thorfinn was. Members were encouraged to report on anything they saw or heard, with the news all being channeled indirectly up to Taylor. It was, to all appearances, a textbook example of an underground, with one major exception. Taylor kept, for herself, a complete roster of names and contacts. For an underground, the mere existence of such a compilation could threaten the very being of the organization and was a major mistake. In Taylor's case, it was not a mistake.

Taylor pressed ahead with the construction of her group, frequently ignoring her needs for sleep and food, and often insisting that others do the same. The need for speed was prompted by the uncertainty about not only Müller's return but the arrival of his compatriot whom she believed would be Walther Huebner. They had learned from Einar, via Gudrun, that Müller was in Ireland. This was no miracle of intelligence, Gudrun had heard her father call Müller, found the number and passed the information along. It caused Jeffers to wonder if she was really the innocent that Einar portrayed. In the normal course of events, who checks the phone numbers their parents dial? While it gave Müller's location, it did not provide the date of return, as Gudrun had reported only seeing the number, not hearing the conversation. Since Gudrun checked the number, did she also eavesdrop on her father's conversations? Einar refused to consider the possibility and Taylor did not want either herself or Jeffers to speak with Gudrun. The fewer direct contacts they had, the safer they were. By the time the information arrived, Taylor had no interest in chasing Müller to Ireland. She knew he was coming back and she was sure the organization would provide a way of dealing with him when he did.

The first order of business was knowing, as soon as possible, when Müller arrived. For this purpose, money flowed to airport customs officials, and several German tourists found themselves victimized by inexplicable delays on arrival. More money went to other airport personnel for "future" considerations. Still more money went to acquire several cars. As Taylor saw it, these were things Gizur's organization ought to be doing anyway, and by keeping her people busy it helped avoid pressure for actions like robbing banks that Taylor wanted to avoid. Funding these activities required calls to Liechtenstein for more money. The needs were beyond what she had stuffed into her pack. The amount of money dispensed stunned Jeffers, initially. It even bothered Taylor.

Taylor hoped that all of the preparation would pay off with Müller being detected at the airport. Even if they missed his arrival, however, it would not be a complete loss. Müller had left a plan by which he would reestablish contact with the organization the day he returned and Taylor, of course, had it. Thorfinn was to be the primary contact, but that would be Müller's first surprise. Thorfinn would have nothing to tell Müller. He would not even know how to reach anyone. There was probably some risk to Thorfinn's safety in this, which was troubling in view of their commitment to Einar, but as Taylor was fond of saying, some risks had to be taken. Müller also had a series of backup contacts, but Taylor had been careful to change all of the routines. Müller was unlikely to have any independent success in making contact unless he happened to accidently spot someone he knew. That possibility could not be entirely ruled out, but the odds were relatively low since Müller had probably followed the same pattern as Taylor and met very few people directly. If the airport gave her advance notice, Taylor planned to reduce that chance to zero by having anyone Müller had met out of sight. In all, there was a good chance of finding Müller and isolating him.

Once that had been accomplished, a messenger was to contact Müller. A messenger sent by Taylor. That would be Müller's second surprise. The messenger would inform him that the organization was under new and tighter management. A meeting to discuss the situation would be offered. What would Müller do? Taylor figured that he would accept. The idea was not unreasonable that someone eager for favor would push aside the old, incompetent leadership. Even if it did not smell entirely right, Müller was unlikely to abandon his project. He would go to the meeting.

That was to be the sting. Müller would be met by one of Taylor's people. He would have a great deal of information for Müller, some of it in writing. The last was a heinous breach of protocol, but there was no one in the baby underground who would realize it. The individual involved had been selected by Taylor based on Sigurd's reports, a man whose character was not the strongest and who had never met Taylor. Their meeting, of course, would be betrayed. The information carried by Taylor's unsuspecting plant would be enough to bring down Gizur and his party. It would also snare Müller. There would be enough time, Taylor hoped, for her and Jeffers to leave the country before any roundup netted people who could identify her. Compared to that maneuver, it would be a simple matter to straighten out the misunderstanding behind Marden's assignment. She hoped.

While Taylor molded the revolutionary underground, Jeffers had more than enough to keep himself busy. He became Einar's primary contact, the conduit through which the bits of information gleaned from Gudrun flowed. When Gizur and Jon met at the university, Jeffers knew about it the day before and was there to photograph it when it happened. When Jon had a quiet lunch with a Russian official, again Jeffers was there, camera in hand. Einar also kept him informed of Thorfinn's activities but they were mercifully few. Thorfinn had taken his isolation as a personal rebuke and kept largely to himself. Even so, trying to keep tabs on the activities of Gudrun, Jon, and Gizur was an almost impossible job. It had Jeffers wondering how one went about recruiting a helper.

Then, just as they were settling into a routine they were jolted out of it by Müller's return. Jeffers found out when he returned to the hotel one evening to find Taylor anxiously awaiting him.

"What's up?" he asked, "You look like you're ready to burst."

"I am. Müller's back."

"Terrific. Where is he?"

"I don't know."

"What do you mean? I thought you said he was here."

"I did. Let me explain. One of the people we bought checked him through at Keflavik. No doubt about it, a Gerhardt Müller, German passport, Irish stamp, and a previous Iceland entry. Unfortunately, it took the turkey over a day to let us know. The problem is, I don't know where he's gone."

Taylor did not look pleased, nor, as her explanation made clear, was she. None of the methods Müller had arranged for making contact on his return had been used. Instead, he had just melted into the background, leaving them without any means of putting their own plan into operation. As usual, the first casualty of the battle was the battle plan.

"Betrayal?" wondered Jeffers. Was someone, Einar perhaps, playing a double role? It was possible. There was no way to check what Einar said to either Jon or Gudrun. Einar did not, however, know very much of what Taylor was doing, so any treason of his would be limited in effect. Limited probably to Jeffers's skin.

Taylor took the comment in stride. "It's always possible," she said. "I can't be entirely sure that one of the men who has met me does not also have an independent way of contacting Müller." The calm statement jolted Jeffers. He had only visualized himself on the bull's-eye. "It's something to keep in mind, though I would guess that the real reason for his change in plans has nothing to do with us."

"Okay, Taylor. Let's skip the reason. He hasn't tried to make contact, and we don't know where he is, so our plan is out the window. What now?"

"Simple. We go to our usual backup plan. We improvise. Where do you think he is headed?"

"Well, the logical person for him to contact is still Jon. Of course, the other possibility is that he will see Thorfinn, which could be unfortunate if there has been a leak."

"I thought of that." There was no humor in Taylor's smile. "I arranged for him to spend a few days with friends. I do agree with you that he will probably see Jon, no matter what he plans to do afterward. Gudrun should know about that. In fact, she may well know where he is going. That little turkey has been very useful."

Jeffers frowned at the last sentence. He had never spoken to Gudrun, never really met except through a lens or Einar's words, but "turkey" did not seem right. There was no point in arguing about it though. They had more pressing problems.

"I assume you want to find Müller fairly fast," Jeffers said. "I have a meeting arranged with Einar for the morning, but I could try to reach him tonight,"

Taylor considered it, then shook her head. "Let it wait. There is always the possibility that Müller had a delay of his own and will try to make contact tonight."

That hope turned out to be groundless. When morning came there had still been no word of Müller so Jeffers went out to the chessboard, his prearranged spot, to meet Einar. The boy had a mischievous grin on his face when he arrived.

"Guess what?" he asked.

"Müller's here," Jeffers replied flatly.

Einar's jaw dropped. "How did you know that?"

"Come on," Jeffers laughed, "you didn't think that you were my only source did you?" He saw the amazement on Einar's face and decided there were aspects to this lifestyle that he enjoyed. "I do need to know what else you know though."

"Only that he met with Jon for an hour and a half yesterday, then left."

"That's good, but where did he go?"

"I don't know, George. Gudrun only knows he was there. She said she couldn't hear the conversation."

The implication was that Gudrun had tried to listen. What did she really think she was doing? "She must have heard something. No clue at all?"

"None, George, honestly." Einar was starting to sweat and it occurred to Jeffers that the boy was afraid of him. Either that, or the risks inherent in this enterprise were finally dawning on him. Jeffers favored the latter. No one was afraid of George Jeffers.

"All right, all right, I believe you. Now tell me, is Jon at the university today?" Einar nodded. "Good. Look for me back here at noon. If I'm not here then, I will be this time tomorrow." Amazing, Jeffers thought, I'm starting to sound like Taylor.

Sounding like Taylor was not going to be enough. He was going to have to start acting like Taylor too. He began to feel sweat on his own skin in spite of the cool breeze. Even if Gudrun did not know where Müller had gone, there was one person who did. Jon Petursson. Jeffers remembered the series of photographs of Gudrun he had taken to learn her routine. None of the people in the pictures had ever proved to be worth the trouble of learning their names, but the pictures were going to prove useful after all. They were the lever by which he would move Jon Petursson.

He left Einar with a brusque goodbye. He was going to have to move rapidly as the pictures were back at the hotel and he would have to go there before going to the university. When he picked up the pouch he could see his hand shake, whether with tension or excitement he was not certain. Damn it, Jeffers, he told himself, now is not the time to have the shakes. Think of Hank Davenport.

From his previous surveillance, he knew the location of Jon's office, and gaining access to the university was no more difficult than on previous occasions. The office door was open, the professor writing at his desk when Jeffers arrived. He walked straight through the door and closed it behind him, a little shocked at his own temerity. Jon, absorbed in his work, looked up at the sound of the door closing to find Jeffers standing directly in front of his desk.

"Good day," Jeffers said in English.

"Who are you?" Jon asked. Irritation was apparent in his voice.

"That is not really important. You are Jon Petursson, correct?" Jeffers did not wait for the acknowledgment. "You have information about a person I need to find."

"I do not know you or what you want." Jon had half risen from his chair so that Jeffers could see that although he had once been tall and thin, middle age had bloated his waist as well as grayed his hair. The expression on Jon's face was a mixture of indignation and fear.

"I am looking for one Gerhardt Müller," the words spat out with a vehemence that surprised Jeffers and made Jon flinch. "I believe you can tell me where to find him."

"Müller? Gerhardt Müller?" Jon sat back in his chair. "I know no such person and, therefore, can hardly tell you where to find him. Now, have the goodness to leave."

"I'm afraid I can't leave yet. Let me refresh your memory about Gerhardt Müller. He is a spy and a thief and a murderer, and he works with your precious party." As he spoke the words became increasingly clipped and harsh. Jeffers knew, intellectually, that Jon was unlikely to answer any such question freely but he could feel himself coming to an emotional boil. Far from not voicing the words, it was all he could do not to shout them. "Where is he!"

Jon Petursson's face had gone as gray as his hair. "Get out!" It was more of a whisper than a command. "Get out or I will call the police."

"I will not get out and you will not call the police," Jeffers said flatly and with force. "You have one more opportunity to answer me and I suggest you do it or you are going to regret it for as long as you live."

"Don't be a fool."

"Wrong. You're the fool." From his jacket Jeffers pulled the packet and tossed it on the desk.

Jon looked at it, without moving. The outside was blank, no clue to the contents, yet he made no attempt to open it.

"What is this?"

"Go ahead, open it," Jeffers urged. "It's quite safe, but it will tell you why my questions must be answered."

Slowly, and with trembling fingers, Jon tore open the flap. Out spilled the photographs of Gudrun. Jon looked at them, turned one or two around in front of him, and said nothing. Jeffers waited, equally silent. At last, Jon spoke.

"What is this supposed to mean?"

"It means," said Jeffers, "that I know where she goes, and whom she sees. I know when she goes out and when she comes back in. It means that you will tell me where Gerhardt Müller is."

There was another silence. Jon rocked back and forth in his seat, covered his eyes with his hands for a while, then looked back at the pictures.

"You would not," he said pleading.

"Try me."

Jon shuddered. His face sagged and when he spoke next his voice was broken. "Gerhardt Müller is in Akureyri," he said. "I cannot tell you precisely where because I do not know, but it is not such a big place. Are you satisfied now? Will you leave me alone?"

"Not quite yet." Jeffers had to assume that the name Akureyri would have meaning to Taylor. For all he knew, it was in Argentina. "I want to know what he is doing there. Please remember, I will know very soon if you are lying."

Jon picked up one of the pictures. "Gudrun," he said to it, "the young man wants to know what Müller is doing in Akureyri. What should I tell him, Gudrun? What shall I tell him?" Tears began to roll down his face. "Müller is in Akureyri to oversee the arrival of our weapons. They are coming by boat. I do not know more details." He turned back to the picture. "I think I was right to say it. I think I was."

Jeffers left him there, the color print clutched tightly in one hand, and closed the door quietly. He felt none of the anger that had coursed through him so violently only moments before. There was also none of the triumph he had expected to feel after confronting his enemy and breaking him. It was puzzling. He had watched Taylor pull almost the exact maneuver on Bieber to shut him up, in fact it had been that memory that had triggered his thought of the pictures in the first place, and aside from a brief concern that Taylor might not have been bluffing it had not bothered him a bit. But he did not feel good at all when he left Jon's office. Truth was, he was slightly sick to his stomach and felt far more a heel than a hero. Some victory! Bludgeon the answer out of an old man by threatening the daughter he cherishes. The daughter who will now know what her talking did to her father. But that father was working with the man who had Hank killed. Do the ends justify the means? Sometimes, according to Taylor Redding. Was this one of those times, and, if so, what should he be feeling? It seemed he ought to feel sorry, but sorry for whom? For the girl? For the father, perhaps, who would sacrifice all his plans for the daughter who had already betrayed him? Or for George Jeffers, who was finding at that very moment, that he had more in common with Gerhardt Müller than he cared to admit.

Taylor was not in the room when Jeffers returned and, having no idea of where to look for her, he was forced to wait. During his enforced idleness he had to relive his confrontation with Jon Petursson many times, each time with increasing distress. When she did arrive, he blurted out the information on Müller before she had even finished stepping through the door, and proceeded directly from that to pouring out his own mixed emotions. He finished with an immense sense of vulnerability, not at all sure how she would react.

Taylor turned to finish closing the door before she spoke. When she did, she said, "Believe me, I understand. It's not easy to watch someone break. The people I worry about are the ones who enjoy that, not the ones who agonize about it. But it's no different than it was in Amsterdam with Karl. You do what you have to do, and you get over it."

"That was different, Taylor. Those two guys would have killed me, just like they did Hank."

"Would you feel better if Jon had come at you with a club and you had to knock him down and beat the information out of him?"

"Probably," Jeffers said. "This way I feel like I'm no better than Müller. It feels so dirty."

Taylor reflected that Sister Angelica had once told her that a hand could get just as dirty working in a garden as in handling shit. The difference was that in only one case did it stink.

"George, he put himself into this position of his own free will. Nobody forced him into this party; nobody forced him to set up an underground. It was as much his idea as it was Gizur's, as best I can tell. I think he has to accept the consequences of his own actions.

"That information you got is critically important, and I don't think what you did to get it is all that horrible. The only person who came to grief earned what he got. All operations should be so selective."

"And what about Gudrun? Use her to betray her father and then use her again to break him? Her only fault was an accident of birth. Is it fair to her?"

"Life is not fair," Taylor snapped back, then quickly reined herself in. "Sorry, but I'm the wrong person to talk to about unfairness." Jeffers felt his face go red as she spoke. "All I can say is, take a moment. Think about all that's happened, all of it, and what is involved."

Jeffers turned away toward the window and looked out, silently, at the city. Red, blue and green rooftops made a crazy quilt above the busy streets. He stared at the pattern for a while and tried to think. What had to go into the balance? The work of a decade stolen, almost lost. His friend of many years murdered as part of a diversion. A man he never knew, killed in Boston. The people on the streets below him, there were consequences for them too. Did that justify what he had done?

"I guess," he said, "that's another way of telling me the ends justify the means."

"Sometimes," said Taylor Redding. "Not always, that's the road that leads to things like the Inquisition. But not never, either. Sooner or later, that leaves you defenseless."

So, now for the moment of decision, George. What do you do? Say, "Sorry, I'm in over my head," and wash your hands of it? He knew what Taylor was going to do, that was easy. She would be off on her private path to glory, all questions answered by her own rules. If a worthwhile job required a stolen car, or airplane, or whatever, she could do it because sometimes the ends justified the means. Taylor might accept a joust with a windmill, if the price was right, but if she could, she would figure out a way to steal the wind beforehand. Rigging the game was legitimate. But not everything was okay. She would not run drugs, bad for the "reputation" she had said. How was it so easy for her to know where to draw the line? That was not the real problem; she obviously managed. But how was he George Jeffers to do it? Until the past few days in Iceland he had been merely reacting to pressures, which made it easy to justify his actions to himself. For the first time, though, he had consciously reached out to manipulate people to produce a result he wanted. It was not the textbook myth he had learned of open confrontation between good and bad, of the Earps standing up to the Clantons at the O.K. Corral. It was not even the stuff of his beloved spy thrillers, where it was clear who was good and who was not. Could he accept the reality of an imperfect world, that the concept of "fair fight" was a contradiction in terms? He doubted that he was ever going to be completely comfortable with that philosophy, but there was no practical alternative. Not unless he was going to throw a tantrum every time impossible ideals ran into reality, or unless he planned to spend the rest of his life hiding in an ivory tower.

"It's all right. I'm okay." The look on her face had been one of concern and he appreciated it as much as he wanted to dispel it. "So, Müller is on his way to get his guns and other goodies. What do we do about it?"

"I'm going to Akureyri and stop him," Taylor replied. "Are you with me?"

Behind her words, Jeffers thought he could hear the rumble of the guns on Cemetery Ridge. "Of course, I'm coming," he answered.

The next few hours were packed with activity to prepare for their trip. Taylor had copies, painstakingly prepared, of the papers that gave the details of her organization. Names were there and meeting places. They also contained other interesting tidbits of intelligence that the organization had picked up. Who was sleeping with whom politically, sometimes literally as well; who had proved corruptible. Obviously, not all such information was reliable. Taylor had no illusions about that. Throughout her lists, she had attempted to grade the material from definite (the man is on the take because

I, personally, know he was paid off) to mere rumor (Petur heard from his grocer that so and so in the Fisheries Ministry is screwing a secretary in the Russian embassy). For the short time she had a functional organization, there was an impressive amount of information in the lists. Each copy was placed separately, one in a bank box, another with an old friend, and so on. Ultimately, those papers were their insurance against the very real possibility that Müller would win the showdown. In that case, the lists might ruin Müller anyway, and then it would be unlikely that both Taylor and Jeffers would have to worry about official reaction when they came to light.

Once the chore was done, Taylor asked Jeffers to find Einar. "Bring him with you, and meet me at the front of the Hallgrimskirkja."

"Why do you want Einar?" Jeffers wanted to know. He had long since blown his meeting.

"I'm betting that he will be steady," Taylor answered. "Just a hunch, but we can sure use some help. The dreck I've been working with all think I work for Müller. It was dicey enough to fiddle with the contact plans, we don't dare trust them on this." She paused to brush loose hair out of her eyes. "Please try and get him quickly, we've already taken more time than I like. Don't worry about being too discreet, we are way past the stage where that makes any difference. Now scat. I have to arrange for a vehicle and some supplies."

And I have to do it fast, too, she thought as Jeffers left. She had arranged, early on, a system with Sigurd for making contact in emergencies. A message and a large payment to a newspaper boy started it moving. Soon, Sigurd would be tracked down. All Taylor had to do in the meantime was go to the prearranged safe house and wait. It did not take long.

"Anna, what is the problem?" Sigurd asked as he entered the apartment.

"There is no problem," she told him imperiously. Sigurd, she had found, responded best to a stiff, authoritarian tone. "An operation needs to be carried out immediately. I will need a four-wheel-drive vehicle, left here, and three guns with ammunition."

Sigurd's eyes widened at the mention of weapons. The group had little in that line, and neither Sigurd, nor anyone else, knew of any way to obtain them other than theft from the NATO base. Taylor had found it a double-edged problem. On one hand, where weaponry was absent, it could not be used. That avoided operations she could not permit, but could prevent only by risking her position. However, it would have been out of character for the organization she was assembling not to have weapons. Taylor had played for time, under the guise of having Sigurd work out a secure way of obtaining a small number of sidearms. It seemed that this part of her timing had worked out well.

"Yes, Anna," he said, "I can have it all for you this afternoon. Who else will be going with us?" Sigurd had automatically included himself in the party.

"I have two comrades waiting for me," she told him in the same tone. "All that is required of you is that you bring the car and the guns. No, one more thing. You, and you alone, will bring the weapons. Clear?"

"Yes, Anna," Sigurd dipped his head in a short nod and disappeared through the door.

In a way, Taylor found, it was too bad this role had to end so soon. It had been a good one, a big, very big risk at the start, hard interesting work along the way, and evidence of success. Everything was set up just as it should be to convert the organization into a real power. Another month or two, the way she was going, and Iceland would never know what had hit it. At least, it was reasonable to assume she would have succeeded had that been her goal. Taylor had long admired the organization Sister Angelica had built, which had operated out of an unpretentious missionary church and shaken a pompous ruler and his government. It would have been interesting to see if Taylor Redding could have done as well. She had been taught how to do it, taught by a number of people who knew how to do it, and it was more that just interesting, it was tempting to see how well she had learned. Tempting, yes, it was tempting, but it was not going to happen.

Sigurd was back in less than an hour. Through the apartment window she saw him park an old Rover at the curb and walk to the door. He was alone.

She took the bag he handed her with a curt nod. There was more weight to it than visual inspection would have suggested, and a metallic clank issued from the bottom as it swung between them. A quick look inside revealed three semiautomatic pistols with spare clips. "Good. Please see if that will cover the cost." She indicated a wad of notes she had placed on a table in the corner of the room.

While Sigurd counted the money, Taylor inspected the guns. They were all of American manufacture, not surprising given the route they must have taken to reach her. Each had a full clip, with two spares apiece in the bag. They were clean and ought to perform satisfactorily.

"Is the money sufficient?" she asked.

"Yes. Certainly. Is there anything else you need?"

"Yes, there is. I want you to wait for fifteen minutes after I leave before you leave." She did not look for agreement, but quickly slid the guns back into the bag and left. She went directly to the Rover, gunned it to life, and pulled away. At the end of the block, she turned the corner and stopped to look back down the street. Sigurd had not come out. It was time to go.

# CHAPTER 26

## AKUREYRI, ICELAND

AKUREYRI IS APPROXIMATELY 270 MILES northeast of Reykjavik. The distance is most conveniently covered by airplane; about one hour is required for the trip. They could have done it that way, guns and all, there being no metal detectors for internal flights, but it would have left them without assured transportation after they arrived. Taylor would not chance it. That left driving, there being no railroad anywhere on the island. Two hundred and seventy miles is not all that much to a person raised on American interstate highways, or European autobahns. It is different in Iceland, where the road can seem as rocky as the barren landscape stretching away on either side.

The drive to Akureyri would have made quite a sightseeing tour; glaciers shimmered on the sides of mountain peaks, rivers turned white by the silt they carried roared past, and ever-changing patterns of bare tumbled rock touched the sky on a horizon devoid of even a single tree. They were not, however, tourists. Their minds were on their guns and on what might await them upon arrival. Such thoughts left little room for appreciation of the scenery. Any remaining urge to gaze at the view succumbed quickly to the harshness of the road which, in many places, was still unpaved. Taylor pushed the Rover as fast as the road permitted, a pace that shook not only the vehicle's suspension but that of the passengers as well.

Jeffers had an additional reason for not watching the scenery. Einar was there, and Jeffers had no idea of how he would react to what Jeffers had done at the university. Jeffers had gone to Einar's home to get him, and had found that Einar had not seen either Gudrun or Jon since his earlier meeting with Jeffers. The sudden trip, and the equally sudden metamorphosis of "Charlotte" into Taylor with pistols, had kept Einar's mind occupied. However, on their return to Reykjavik, assuming they returned, Jeffers was going to have to deal with the problem. Jeffers spent a good part of the trip thinking of unpleasant possibilities.

# LANGLEY, VIRGINIA

NO WORD. NONE AT all for more than two weeks. Some gap in reports was to be expected, especially under the conditions Marden was operating. It could easily take, for instance, a week to develop a contact to the point where there was information worth reporting. But not more than that. Two weeks without any report was too long.

The silence told its own tale to Oliver, and it was not a pleasant one. He had lost one man already; now the count might very well be two. All by itself, the thought was bothersome. It did not help that the deputy director was on Oliver's back almost daily, wanting to know if the Lorenzo matter had been closed. No discussion, of course, of how the case was to be closed. It was explicitly recognized that the deputy director was not interested in the details, which was to say that he did not want to hear anything a congressional committee might eventually hold against him. The lack of detail, however, reduced the case, and others like it, to a single sentence and made it easy for the deputy director to ignore the problems, of which he was unaware, and to be incensed over every day that the case remained open. It was not good for Oliver's stomach.

His secretary broke into his thoughts, via the intercom, to remind him that he was due in the deputy director's office for a meeting in five minutes. At which time, no doubt, Oliver would be reminded again that it was bad for morale to have a man gunned down in broad daylight in the middle of Boston and be unable to take any action in response. Oliver did not think he could stand the routine, "Why can't we get this finished? No, spare me the details, just do it," one more time.

Oliver lifted the receiver from the cradle. "June?" he asked.

"Yes," the secretary answered.

"Get me a flight reservation to Iceland, will you? As soon as possible."

"Iceland? You goin' into exile, boss? The meeting ain't even happened yet."

Oliver chuckled. "It never hurts to be prepared. But, seriously, I do want that ticket. Okay?"

Oliver felt considerably less gaiety than his chuckle conveyed. He never took his opponents lightly under any circumstances. In this case, two dead agents could easily become three, it had that kind of feel to it. *I am getting too old,* he thought, *to keep running into the field every time there is a screw-up.* Which meant, for Marden's sake, Marden had better be dead.

## AKUREYRI, ICELAND

SUMMER NIGHT OUTSIDE AKUREYRI was not much different from summer day. The only perceptible change in the light level was due, not to the hour, but to the solid gray wall of clouds that was rapidly covering the sky. The temperature drop that accompanied the grayness made them thankful for the woolen sweaters that had been stocked in the Rover.

Taylor did not take them into the city. Actually, city was probably too strong a term in an era when major cities counted their populations in the millions. For all that Akureyri was the major urban center in the north of Iceland, it was more properly a small town of 13,000 people. There was no mass of skyscrapers in front of them, just a concentration of low buildings overseen by an ultramodern church along the banks of Eyjafjordur. They drove south of the town and pushed on across the bridge spanning the narrows of Eyjafjordur, up the east coast past Svalbard. A few kilometers farther, a paved section of the Hringbraut curved away east, through a gap in the heights along the east bank. Taylor took them along it, then turned down a dirt side road to one of the nearby farms.

It had never occurred to Taylor before that the network of friends she had built up over the years could serve an operational purpose. She had always considered Iceland a retreat, a place to isolate herself from the world when she needed time to think. It was a good location for that, especially in the winter when the nearly perpetual dark woke ghosts in the minds of people, if not in fact on the barren lands. She had always stayed with one family or another, chance met in the beginning, and over the years had become close friends with several. The farm toward which she headed the Rover was run by one Eirik Helgason, his son and two daughters. Taylor had stayed with them on her first trip, having met Eirik along the road to Akureyri airport by means of getting his stalled car to start. Eirik was a solid man, although by his fiftieth year a little frayed about the edges. His wife had died a decade before Taylor first arrived, and the strain of the farm and family had taken a toll. Taylor's presence provided a welcome contact with a world where he had never traveled, all the more welcome for her predisposition to help with chores rather than merely pay for room and board. Bjarni, the son, was much like the father, primarily involved in running the farm and the family business. Initially, he had been cool and correct toward Taylor, although with the passage of years had come to treat her as another sister, albeit one who lived abroad. Both men were the sort of people one could turn to for help, no matter what the problem. As comfortable as Taylor had come to feel with Eirik and Bjarni, it was the two sisters she felt closest to. Margret, two years her junior, and Gudny, now sixteen, had been her buddies and confidantes. They had listened raptly to the stories Taylor brought, and had been just as attentive on the bad days of the early years, when Taylor's mood had been as black as the Iceland winter sky. As a family, they all knew as much of Taylor as she allowed anyone to know, certainly more than her own family did. The farm of Eirik Helgason, then, was a logical place for Taylor to stop. It was also a logical place to look for help. In the small world of Akureyri, Eirik and his children were as knowledgeable of events as anyone.

The house at which the dirt road ended was a one-story structure of concrete painted white, with a flat roof. On one side of the house, a field of tall grass swayed under the evening breeze. On the other, two horses and several sheep could be seen on a pasture whose verdant grass contrasted sharply with the bare brown hillside behind it. For a midsummer evening, it looked unusually quiet.

The quiet gave Taylor some unease as she knocked on the door, with Einar and Jeffers waiting behind her. Much can happen in a half year, which was the interval since she had last visited. A few years before, between her visits, Bjarni's wife had tired of the farm and left, taking their children back to her native Reykjavik. Before any words had been said on that occasion, Taylor had sensed the quiet resulting from the absence of the young children. Why the quiet this night?

It was a relief to see the door open, and find Margret, the older daughter behind it.

"Taylor!" she exclaimed, her face changing from anxious to open warmth. "I could use a pleasant surprise. Come in, please."

As Margret stepped back from the door, Taylor introduced her companions before entering. The invitation extended to all three, they followed Margret inside. As she led the way, she attracted more than a casual glance from both Jeffers and Einar. Slightly shorter than the average Icelander, she was well proportioned with bright red hair and green eyes, heritage of some long-ago Celtic slave. When they reached the living room, she dropped into an overstuffed armchair with a graceful swoop. Following behind, Taylor caught a glimpse of Kristinn, Margret's four-year-old daughter, peeking out from behind the couch. Taylor gave her a wink, which elicited a giggle and a grin before the child ducked behind the furniture on noticing the strangers.

"Well, it is good to see you," Margret said when they were all seated. She spoke in lightly accented English, having heard Jeffers's name. "How long can we keep you, and will your friends be staying? And, when everyone's back, we'll want a full account of your doings since we saw you last." She finished on a friendly, teasing note.

"Margret, please," Taylor protested, "I'd like nothing more than a long visit, but I can't. I'm here on business this time, and I would like to see if Bjarni or your father can help me with some information. Then, we had best be off."

At that Margret's eyes widened and she sat up straight in the chair. "A Taylor Redding adventure, here in quiet old Akureyri? I can't believe it, not unless I should stop believing all those other stories you've told."

Taylor could not avoid a blush. She was acutely aware of her companions' two sets of eyes being focused on her. "You can keep believing them, they're real," she answered, "and this business is real too. If Bjarni and Eirik are around, I'll tell you what's going on and see if they can help." She stopped when she saw Margret shake her head.

"Pabbi and Bjarni went to Reykjavik today. They won't be back for two days."

On one level, Taylor was glad to find a completely innocent explanation for the stillness at the farm, but she could also begin to feel that old knot form in her gut. She had counted on them, a priori, to help put her on Müller's track. Now she saw her chances of catching him red-handed and unawares substantially diminished. The disappointment was evident to Margret.

"Could I help?"

"No, I honestly don't think so. I need to find out what's going on down at the docks."

"Then, at least will you stay the night?"

"That we will," Taylor said, feeling the relief from Einar and Jeffers as she did so. They might as well. Eirik or Bjarni could probably have told them enough for her to pinpoint Müller's boat, even though they would have no idea what it carried. With them out of town, Taylor was going to have to proceed more methodically and that would have to wait for morning. Certainly, snooping around the waterfront at night, without the cover of darkness, was not a good idea. They would have to bet, that even with the delay, it would take Müller longer to finish his business than it would take them to find him.

"Since we're here for a bit," she continued, "I will tell you what I've been up to the last six months. But get Gudny first. This is about Australia and it's the real wild type she likes."

Then it was Margret's turn to look chagrined, and Taylor, instead of telling a story, wound up listening to one. Although, at present, it was about Gudny, Taylor knew from the past that it had really begun with Margret. Margret was, much like Taylor, bright, outgoing and energetic. When Taylor had first come to the farm, Margret had been full of plans to study engineering and have a career far beyond the confines of the farm, or of Iceland itself for that matter. It had all changed when, at eighteen, she had become pregnant with Kristinn. There was nothing unusual in Iceland about such an occurrence, nor was it unusual for the marriage to be planned for after the date of Kristinn's baptism. However, between the birth and the marriage the plans, as happens in Iceland and elsewhere, had gone awry. It did not mean that Margret would have trouble marrying another later—illegitimate children were not considered a problem—but it did effectively end her career plans. This, too, was not an uncommon occurrence. Overall, Taylor had thought that Margret had adapted well to the change (what choice was there?), and had thrown herself into the role of "lady of the house," for which Bjarni's wife had never cared. Still, Taylor was certain it rankled a bit beneath the surface. Gudny, however, had not handled it well at all, and had kept nothing beneath the surface. Whether out of feeling for her sister, or fear that she was seeing her own future, she had grown angrier and wilder as she grew older. The past few months, according to Margret, had been especially difficult. Gudny had been out late frequently, come home obviously drunk a few times and had to be fetched twice, although only Margret knew that. The family had been looking forward to Taylor's next visit on the thesis that Taylor, being wilder and crazier than anyone they knew, had the best rapport with Gudny, and would be the best person to try and talk some sense into her.

"The problem is, I don't know where she is tonight, and even if I did with no one else home, I can't go for her even if she needs it," Margret finished.

Taylor stood up. Suddenly, she was glad nothing could be done about Müller until morning. "Let me take care of it. She shouldn't be too hard to find."

"I'll go along with you," the offer came simultaneously from Jeffers and from Einar, both of them also coming to their feet.

"You two should really get some rest. I think I can manage to bring back a sixteen-year-old girl by myself," Taylor said dryly.

"Yeah, but that means you have to get past me to get to the door," Jeffers said, much to his own surprise.

"Crap. What is this, the Three Musketeers do a mitzvah?" She looked at them briefly, then yielded with a shrug. "All right, let's do it."

The weather had changed again while they had sat inside. The ground and the Rover were wet, evidence of a brief recent rain. Far from clearing, though, the sky looked even thicker and ground mist was starting to collect.

\*     \*     \*

The problem of finding a person in Akureyri was a completely different order of magnitude than finding the same person in, say, New York. Taylor, in fact, was counting on the size factor in her plans for tracking Müller. When it came to finding a girl who, after all, was not trying to avoid the searchers, it was even easier. Taylor knew the location of the few clubs in town and Margret had supplied the names of friends in whose company she might be. Armed with that information, it was not long before their search ended at the statue of the Outlaw, not far from the church. A small group of teenagers was clustered there.

When they asked for Gudny Eiriksdottir a boy giggled and jerked his thumb wordlessly toward the other side of the statue. Rounding the structure, they found the girl crouched on hands and knees. Even for Einar and Jeffers, neither of whom had ever met her, there was no question of identity. She was a younger edition of Margret with the same red hair and green eyes. A second look revealed some differences. Gudny was taller, with the lankiness of a fast-growing teenager, and her face sported a bumper crop of freckles where Margret's was almost clear. These items merely served to tell them who she was; beyond that her overall appearance tended to pull the eye away from physical details. Her clothes were wet, suggesting that the rain shower had fallen equally on her and the surrounding pavement. When she looked up, a blotchy stain was evident on the front of her shirt. Its origin was easily deduced from the distinct odor of alcohol and vomit. A pair of dry heaves racked her as they watched. She was a thoroughly sorry sight.

Seeing the retching, Taylor felt her own unease, sympathetic memories of days past. "I think it's time you went home, Gudny," she said.

The girl looked at her, as though not believing the evidence of her compromised senses. "Can't be Taylor. Go away elf, quit bothering me!"

The Icelandic words cut Jeffers out of the conversation, but not Einar. "There's no elf, and you're not seeing things. You're just a bit drunk, and more than a bit silly." It was his angry tone, as much as his actual words, that seemed to have an impact on her.

Her first attempt at getting up was unsuccessful. She toppled backwards from her crouch as she tried to rise, ending up braced with her hands behind her. From there she pushed off, swayed once, and finally managed to stand. For a moment, she just stood there, looking from one to another of the trio in front of her. A quiver could be seen on her lower lip.

"Oh, God! I'm sorry!" she cried. Rushing to Taylor, she burst into tears. Without a word, Taylor hugged her tightly until the sobbing stopped.

The return trip to the farm was considerably longer than the trip out as the mist had thickened, especially in the hollows. Taylor said nothing while she drove, but whether that was by choice or enforced by the worsening driving conditions was not clear. Gudny, in the back, fell asleep against Einar's shoulder and seemed undisturbed by the occasional jolts meted out by the road. The quiet gave Jeffers time to reflect that there was more to Taylor Redding than just ice and fire, regardless of how she liked to present herself.

At the farm, they half carried Gudny from the Rover to her bed. Taylor disappeared to the kitchen and returned carrying a basin of cool water and a wash cloth. After setting them on a nightstand by the bed, she shooed the others out and quietly closed the door.

# CHAPTER 27

## AKUREYRI, ICELAND

IT WAS WELL OVER an hour, maybe closer to two, before Taylor reappeared. By the time she did, the three left in the living room had become well acquainted with their various backgrounds, although both Jeffers and Einar were careful to sanitize recent history. Jeffers found it interesting to see that Einar was more amused at the role Jeffers had played for him than he was angry at being deceived. All at once, it made Jeffers's action at the university too much for him to keep secret any longer. With a deep breath, and being careful not to mention the reason behind it, he told Einar what he had done. When he was finished, there was silence. Quiet relief for Jeffers, at having it out in the open, quiet puzzlement for Margret, at not understanding what had happened, but Einar gave no immediate sign as to what he was feeling.

"I am waiting," Jeffers said after he had tired of waiting, "for you to tell me off, or attack me, or do something. What is it going to be?"

"Probably nothing," Einar said slowly. "I am not entirely a fool. Even if, at first, I did not understand what Charl . . . excuse me, what *Taylor* was doing, it did not take too long to figure out, even with only the little you told me. I have been a willing participant since then for two reasons. First, I have come to feel strongly about what Jon is doing. Not because I believe Gizur is wrong in much of what he says. I especially agree with him about the way Keflavik is now. The fact is, we would not have needed a defense force were it not for your feud with the Russians. Certainly, the base has been of no use in the fishing disputes. It is nothing more than a big aircraft carrier for you and if you and the Russians decide to shoot at each other some time, they are going to try and sink it, if you see what I mean. However, I can see that Gizur is just out to get power for himself. The politics are only an excuse.

"Second, I think I am one of a few people today who actually read the old sagas instead of using the volumes for decoration." Margret bridled at that. The videocassette recorder in the living room had clearly seen more use than any of the books. "It's hard to find an opportunity to match them today, but this looks like it might. I wish you could have avoided hurting him, but I can accept that you had no choice."

"And what about Gudrun?"

"She and I had a talk a few days ago about this when I began to think something might happen. She's just a girl, so I didn't go into the politics, but I think she will be all right."

"And why does being a girl mean you shouldn't discuss politics?" Margret asked with an edge in her voice.

"It means," Einar replied coolly, "that there are some things a child, in this case a female child, does not need to hear."

Margret seemed satisfied from the look on her face, but whatever she might have said was lost when Taylor came back into the room.

"How is she?" Margret asked.

"She'll live. We had what the diplomats are fond of calling 'a frank exchange of views.' She'll survive that too. I think she may have even heard it. We'll see."

"Well, thanks for trying. If she'll listen to anyone, it will be you." Margret paused and changed topics. "Now that Gudny's settled, why don't you sit down and let me in on what the big mystery is. There have been enough hints here in the last hour to make me burst."

Taylor answered her at first with her little half-grin. "I think it would be better if we just get some sleep, and then get going."

"Taylor Redding! If you think you are going to blow in and out of here like an Arctic wind and have an adventure practically right on my farm and not even tell me about it . . ." The sentence trailed off as she ran out of air.

Jeffers had not throughout the entire journey seen Taylor at a loss, until Margret delivered her blast. For a moment, both Taylor's expression and body seemed fixed in place, then they both dropped into a nearby chair. Saying, "I probably shouldn't do this," she went ahead and did it anyway.

The degree of detail Taylor gave surprised Jeffers, although he did note certain topics, such as the lockbox, were totally left out. Neither Einar nor Margret appeared to notice that the tale had a few gaps in it. Taylor ended with them on Margret's farm, temporarily balked.

"There are a few things I have left out, some important, some not. Talking about them now would not be smart—you'll have to take my word on it for now. As for the rest, it's always smarter to say nothing, but I think we'll resolve the whole business soon, one way or the other, so it won't matter. Bottom line, as I said, was I was hoping to talk to either Eirik or Bjarni. They're both in town a lot, and know a lot of people, so I thought we could get a quick line on Müller that way. As it is, we are better off getting some sleep."

"Bullshit!" Four startled heads snapped up at once. "If it's that fuckin' Irish boat you're interested in, I can tell you about that." The source of the flawless "American" was Gudny, who had come to stand in the entryway to the living room at some point during Taylor's story. As she became the center of attention, she realized that the wash cloth was still on her head, and she quickly pulled it off. Her expression belied her steady voice. Had she gotten any paler, she would have been translucent.

"Well, are you going to come in and tell us about it, or do you need to lean there and hold the wall up?" her sister asked, making room on the couch.

Gudny made her way slowly to the couch and sat down with a groan. "Ohh! My head feels like it's been kicked in. And I don't need to be told how it got that way! Not by you either, Taylor."

Taylor waited a moment, but when nothing further followed, she said, "Look, Gudny, I don't know how much you heard, but probably enough to know that this is serious. Some day, maybe, it'll be a good story, but right now it's real. If you can help, we will appreciate it, but we can't play games."

"Okay, okay, I'm all right. Well, no I'm not, but I'm not drunk now, my head just hurts and I need a moment." She took a deep breath and leaned back to rest her head on the back cushion. "That's better. You know, I know at least as many people in town as Bjarni and Pabbi do. I probably hear more of what's going on; they talk business too much. Anyway, Helgi was talking about the boat earlier tonight. He's got two jobs to start with, but he'll take any extra work he can get because Anna's pregnant and she wants them to have their own house when they get married. Of course, we know how *that* turns out." Margret looked as though she was going to say something, but Gudny did not give her a chance. "Damn it, Margret, I'm sorry but there was so much you wanted to do and now it's all spoilt!" The sentence seemed to hang in the acutely silent room.

"The boat, Gudny, the boat," Taylor urged. "We can talk about the rest another time."

"Right, the boat." Gudny stared up at the ceiling and continued as though there had been no interruption. "Helgi said that he and a friend got an offer to help unload this Irish boat. Worked with three men from the boat, two Icelanders not from here by their accent, and the other Irish, maybe. Moved a bunch of crates off the boat, trucked them up to the old haunted farm, and put them in the barn. That what you want?"

"Haunted farm?" Jeffers asked.

"Just an old farm north of here that has been abandoned for years," Taylor answered. "The three of us used to hang out up there quite a bit, so I know the layout. It's not really haunted, although plenty of people around here believe that it is. Did your friend see anyone up there but those three?"

"No."

"Three then. I would figure Müller to be there and Gizur too, more than likely. Under normal circumstances, that should be more than enough to stand guard out here." Taylor slapped her thigh and stood up. "Margret, I'll need two or three good-sized empty bottles." When she returned from the kitchen with three, Taylor said, "Ah, brennivin, how appropriate. It's time to make my favorite after-dinner drink, cocktails à la Molotov. And then, we had better get going."

"Now?" Jeffers asked, "What happened to a 'few hours' sleep'?"

"That was before I heard this. Right now, it's the middle of the night, and light or not people sleep; the weather is horrid; we know where they are; I know the ground and they don't know we are here. It's perfect."

"All right, you win. It makes sense. I'm sure your favorite Chinese general covered just this situation. Come on, Einar, let's get the Rover while our bartender mixes the drinks."

"I'm coming, too." Margret stood up suddenly and gave no one a chance to protest. "I know exactly what I'm doing. I know the road, and Taylor may have other things to do than drive. Also, if you need a bluff, Einar and I make a likely enough couple. We can make a good decoy at the house if you want to get at the barn across the back field. You can't do it, Taylor. Once you open your mouth, only the Irishman will believe you're an Icelander."

"If you're going, then I'm going, too," Gudny put in.

"No, you are not." There was no softness in Taylor's voice when she spoke. "Margret is right that she can be helpful and we can use her. You are so sick from tonight you have trouble standing up. You have no business out there like that. We would have to be looking out for you and we can't afford that. Remember what I told you about discipline. You have to have it before you get involved in things like this. I know that sounds harsh, but it's true. Even if it was not, we need you to look after Kristinn until we get back."

"That's not fair! Not after I told you about the boat!" Gudny fled to her room and slammed the door.

"Christ," Taylor said. "It's a wonder anybody has kids."

*    *    *

More rain had fallen while they had talked. The precipitation had attempted a return to the sky, but had succeeded only partially. The result
was a dense gray fog that hid all but the immediate vicinity from sight. The
Rover slipped slowly through it, a thixotropic fog that threatened to congeal
around them as they moved. The conditions turned the drive into a blind-
man's crawl, with the prospect of meeting a vehicle going the other way a
constant worry. Such an event did not occur, most likely because the hour
and the weather kept sane people were at home. If the fog was a hazard,
however, it was also a blessing. It provided a cover that night, at that time
of year, did not.

Margret killed the engine as the Rover made a climbing turn onto what
seemed to be a crest in the road. "From here," she said, "the road runs
down a hill and then past the farm." Taylor nodded, while the others listened
as Margret's hand traced a map on the cloud. "There's a little spur to the
left that heads to the main house, past that the road runs east around a low
hill and comes back to the main road. If I let you off here, you can walk
down the slope and cross the back field to the barn."

Taylor nodded again. She handed Einar one of the guns. His eyes widened
but he took it without saying anything. "Give us fifteen minutes, then get
started," she said. Normally, the walk would take far less time than that,
but these were not normal conditions. Walking down that loose, crumbly
slope could be every bit as treacherous as driving down the road. That point
in the road, however, was the closest drop off to the house Taylor was willing
to risk. The fog muffled sound, as well as sight, but only to a degree.

Carrying her Molotov cocktails stuffed into a bag, she and Jeffers planned
to move across the field to the barn, which was set about thirty yards from
the house. Once they had reached the barn, Margret and Einar would drive
around to the front and distract the watch that was certain to be around.
They would not have to hold his attention very long, just long enough for
Taylor and Jeffers to take care of the barn.

There were unknowns, of course. How many would be on watch? One
probably. Helgi had spotted three men at the farm. Add Gizur and Müller,
and it was still unlikely more than one at a time would stand watch. More
people at the farm? Always possible, but not likely. More men simply increased the chance of raising suspicions locally, and would not logically
increase security when the police did not normally go armed. So, it was
reasonable to play their luck as they were doing. "Pray to be stupid and
lucky, not clever and unlucky," Taylor remembered Sister Angelica telling

her once. Thus far, that night, they had been lucky. Lucky in Gudny's chance conversation with Helgi. Lucky in this miserable weather. Lucky in Müller's choosing ground that Taylor knew.

The thought of Gudny brought a frown to Taylor's face that was independent of the bad footing. That girl was in dire need of a swift kick in the ass, and when they returned (if?) that kick was going to be applied. Much as having Margret along was a help, Taylor recognized that Margret was taking these risks not for the sake of duty or adventure, but for Gudny's taunts. She pushed those thoughts away. There was no time to be worrying about Gudny or Margret now. A lack of concentration could easily get her killed, or worse, cause her to botch the job. The first prospect she could live with, the second she could not.

A short slide on the scree, and the accompanying stab of pain in her left leg, brought Taylor's mind back to the immediate task at hand. Tumbling down the slope on her rear would provide an embarrassment far worse than any she had been contemplating. The slope was not very steep, but its surface was also not as smooth as it appeared from a distance. There were little bumps and runnels everywhere and the crumbly surface easily dislodged underfoot. Artificial limbs were not designed with such terrain in mind. Taylor knew the hill well, and knew she could negotiate it, but had never tried it half-blind in fog carrying a sack full of Molotov cocktails. Another fifteen feet past her first slip told her that she would never make it. Only by handing the sack off to Jeffers, leaving her hands free for balancing, were they able to reach the base of the slope without mishap. At the bottom, a field of tall grass met them and stretched away into blank grayness.

"The barn will be that way," Taylor pointed at an undistinguished patch of grayness, and headed off into the wet grass.

"Looks like a great field for snakes," Jeffers muttered.

"Not to worry. There are none on the island."

The barn loomed up in front of them, just to the left of the line Taylor had taken and just at the set time. It was an old structure that seemed to be composed primarily of driftwood and turf. There was no light coming from the inside, and no way on their side of peeking in. From the direction of the road, they could hear a muffled rumble as Einar and Margret drove down to the house. There was no ground-level access to the barn from the side or back, so they waited on edge until the car noise stopped and they could hear voices.

Flattened against the wall, gun tucked into waistband and knife in hand, Taylor crept toward the front. When she reached the leading corner, she peeked around rapidly and then pulled back. No one there! Only one man had been on sentry duty, then, and he was now engaged with Einar and Margret at the house, as the voices revealed. There was a new lock on the door. Its main significance was to reassure Taylor that the prize really was inside. As a barrier, it did not hold out against her for more than a minute. With the door swinging freely, its minor squeak stifled by the turgid air, she ducked back to get the flashlight from Jeffers. Its beam picked out multiple crates in the interior stacked along both sidewalls, just as Gudny had said.

Stencilling on one crate read FARM MACHINERY, TRACTOR PARTS. A top slat looked loose, so Taylor heaved at it with all her strength. It gave way all at once, nails tearing out of the side, and fell to the floor. The Uzi submachine gun that she could see underneath had never been destined as a tractor part. For a moment, Taylor felt giddy. There was more firepower in this one barn than existed anywhere on the island, outside of the Keflavik base. Not for long, she told herself, and went back outside to get Jeffers. All they had to do was firebomb the barn, then rush the house while Einar covered the lone guard at the front. If their luck held, they would bag the entire group as Müller's men tried to wake up and understand what was happening.

As soon as she had stepped out through the door, however, she knew it had gone wrong. Jeffers was not waiting at the door with a bottle ready. He was crouched by the corner of the building, instead, gun aimed in the direction of the house.

"What's wrong?" she hissed, sliding back to his position.

"Listen!" he said, in a low, but urgent voice.

She strained her ears and eyes and then picked it up. Too many voices, too many shadows. Another man had joined the guard. Could they take both men out with a quick rush? The ground beneath the front of the house and the barn was mostly barren, splotches of grass interspersed with rocks of all sizes that were left over from some long-ago eruption, but it was level and hard. The distance could be covered quickly, even in fog and the early morning twilight. It might work. It had to.

"Why don't you give me those Molotovs," she said. One nice aspect of having no options was not having to spend time thinking about them.

Taylor lit two of the bottles and tossed them, one to each side of the barn. At the sound of breaking glass, she and Jeffers set off at top speed for the house. They had covered only a fraction of the distance, when one of the figures there turned toward the barn and shouted.

Einar and Margret waited, as they had agreed, before restarting the Rover. Even though Margret had driven the road many times before, she went very slowly down the slope. Einar did not complain about the lack of speed, he was thankful that her presence made it unnecessary for him to drive, but he did worry that Jeffers and Taylor (not Charlotte!) would arrive before them. To be in an epic and be remembered for failing was worse than not being in one at all. Soon enough, however, although it did not seem that way to Einar, the incline was behind them. A quick change of position then put Einar behind the wheel, so that he could drive the Rover to the front of the house. He brought it to a stop in the road, a good twenty yards distant. Dimly seen, near the house, was another Rover. Of more interest was the lone man standing in the drive ahead of them. Margret jumped out of the Rover and headed straight for him.

"Hey, there, have you got a bathroom?" she asked. There was an affected unsteadiness to her gait, so one might assume that she was not in full control of her faculties. At close range, the impression was heightened by the brennivin they had splashed on her face and shirt.

"Go home and use your own bathroom," the man said. "This is a private farm, not a service station."

"Go home?" she giggled, "I would, but the heroic Viking here," she indicated Einar, "hasn't any idea which direction to go. Probably just as well. Probably wouldn't be any good if I got him home anyway."

"Margret!" Einar's shocked exclamation was only partially faked.

"Listen here, *elskan,* I know what I'm talking about."

Einar waved his hands in the air and turned back to the guard. "I'm sorry to bother you so late at night, but we are lost and you can see she's not feeling too well." As he spoke, he climbed out of the Rover to stand beside her. It brought him to within a few feet of the guard. All he had to do was draw the gun and cover the man. It had sounded so easy when they had discussed it back at Margret's farm.

"Whatever she needs to do, she can do it behind a rock."

Einar had gotten his hand onto the pistol grip in the pocket of his parka, when the door opened and another man came out. "What is going on?" the man asked, as he walked over to join them.

Einar's initial relief that the newcomer was not Gizur, who would recognize him, turned to fear as the guard recounted their meeting. That question had been in German! The language was not a difficulty, Einar and Margret both understood it as did the man addressed, but it identified the speaker as Müller. He was not much to look at, short with a soft-looking face under dark curls, but it was not his appearance that made Einar's bowels clench. This was Müller the killer. Suddenly, the sagas and their heros were long ago and far away. Einar did not draw the gun.

"I do not see why," Müler said softly, "the young lady should not use our bathroom. Come along, I'll show you where it is."

That was wrong, Einar knew. Whether Müller was suspicious or not, Einar did not want Margret alone in that house. "I really ought to go with her," he said, "she's not very steady on her feet."

The only change on Müller's face was a slight narrowing of his eyes. "I'm sure she'll be quite all right. I think you should trust me on that."

Einar was not certain of what to do. They had not envisioned a shootout in front of the house, at least not before Taylor and Jeffers arrived, but he could not give in to Müller's offer. Einar was acutely aware that he had never even fired a gun, much less fired one at another person. Müller's right hand hung near the opening of his coat. Einar could imagine that if he tried to draw his gun, Müller would be able to kill him before he could shoot. There was certainly no chance of Einar being able to drop both men before they could react. Yet, he could not let Müller take Margret inside.

Avenge me, somebody, he thought, and started to draw the weapon. Abruptly, everything happened at once.

The flickering fire in the barn caught Müller's eye, just in the instant before he would have seen Einar's movement, and he turned with an oath. As he swung around, he saw two shadowy figures running away from the area of the barn. All at once, both the setup, and his peril, were clear to him. He shouted again, drawing a weapon from under his coat and firing as he did so.

Jeffers dove for the ground and saw Taylor do the same in front of him. The pistol was in his hand, rocking upward as three rounds fired off. The accomplishment pleased him, not that he had hit anything, except perhaps for the opposing hillside, but that he had acted properly. He had not frozen. Several feet ahead of him, though even at that close range she was partially obscured, he could see Taylor peering over a large rock looking for a target. Einar and Margret were completely invisible. They had darted for safety at Müller's first shout into the deeper mist on the hillside, with one of Müller's men in pursuit.

Suddenly, there was a rushing noise followed by a terrific boom with a red tongue of flame bursting through the barn roof as the fire ignited stored ammunition. A multitude of firecracker pops followed the big bang as individual cartridges sent metal and stone spraying randomly around the yard. The flame-triggered shooting forced everyone to the ground for a while. When it subsided, the confrontation quickly ground to a stalemate. Another

Icelander and a man who shouted instructions identified as Gizur had gotten outside to join Müller before the explosion. They took shelter among a cluster of large rocks between the dirt drive and the front of the house. The remaining man had posted himself in the doorway, using the wall to shield his body. In the fog, worsened by the smoke pouring from the barn, only the vaguest outlines of the opposing fighters were visible. The tactics were the same for all parties, crawl a bit to improve a position, fire at a half-seen shadow, all the while staying low enough to be hidden by the ground and the fog. Periodically a sharp crack and red-yellow flare cut through the murk as a gun was fired. There was hidden action as well on the hillside where Einar and Margret had gone, lurid muzzle flashes and the sound of gunshots were evident to those by the buildings. Who had fired, at what target, and with what effect were, however, impossible to say.

Under the cover of smoke and fog, Taylor tried to close the gap, both to Müller's group and to her Rover. She stayed low, snaking along the rock without regards to skin or clothing. The soupy air provided excellent cover, but it was not perfect and gusts of wind occasionally improved the view in an unpredictable manner. One such breeze showed her Müller, up in a half-crouch and trying to advance as well. She snapped off two quick shots and had the partial satisfaction of seeing him dive back behind his rock. Overall, Taylor knew their position left a great deal to be desired. Most of the cover on the rock field was provided by the atmosphere. If the fog lifted, it would simply be five on three; Margret, without a weapon, did not count. There was nothing about the personnel that would counterbalance those odds. In fact, it just made them worse. I am leading a goddamn children's crusade, Taylor thought morosely. She remembered well what had happened to the original one. Sometimes, unfortunately, knowing the ground well was not enough. Montrose, after all, had been in home territory at Carbisdale, for all the good it had done him. Taylor was going to have to make something happen, and she was going to have to do it fast.

She half rolled, in preparation for another try at moving forward, and as she did the remaining bottle in the sack clanked against a stone. She had forgotten all about it! She hefted it in her hand, an idea taking shape in her mind at the same time. Several wiggles and a roll bought a few more yards toward the farmhouse. It was hard to judge distances, and her arm was not what it once had been, but she would not have to be perfect. Taking a deep breath, she lit the oil-soaked rag that corked the bottle, keeping her body between the flame and the gunmen at the house. She waited, then waited some more, and just when she could wait no longer Jeffers chose that instant to fire twice from his position. Immediately, she leaped up and hurled the bottle at the house.

It struck, bursting into flame, just above the front doorway. The flaming liquid flowed down the wall and across the shoulders of the man who crouched there. His clothing ignited, almost simultaneously with his screams. The man flung himself to the ground, rolling and thrashing as he tried to extinguish the flames. Hearing his pain, his fellow turned to help him. As he did, he forgot what he was about, and stood up. The flames on the wall behind him sharply defined his silhouette. Taylor fired from a kneeling position, both hands on the gun, the left heel/knee giving her a stability that a normal knee would not. One of her bullets snapped a forearm, and, with a shriek, the man fell to his knees. That was enough for Gizur. He bolted for the Rover parked near the house without a backward glance for either his companions or attackers.

Müller hesitated for a moment, then pumped two shots in Taylor's general direction and ran to make sure that Gizur did not drive off without him.

Taylor saw the movement, and then, thanks to a small breath of wind, saw the other Rover. "Get to the Rover, pronto!" she yelled, and tried to follow her own advice with as much speed as she could muster.

On the hillside, Margret heard the screams, and then Taylor's call. She had lost track of Einar in the first frenzied minutes when they had run pell-mell from Müller. After that, she had worked at putting as much distance as possible between herself and the gunshots Einar was exchanging with the man who had chased them. This had led her, blindly, on a diagonal path upslope. When her brain had begun functioning again, she realized that the best place for her would be back at the Rover and, so, began working her way back down the slope. Winded by the unaccustomed strain of crawling on elbows and knees, she had paused to rest, partially concealed in a hollow within several feet of the Rover, when she heard Taylor's shout.

She nerved herself to get up and run for the vehicle when the sound of running feet froze her. The figure that burst through the fog, headed straight for her and the Rover, was not Einar. She clenched her teeth tightly, reached out and snagged an ankle as he went by. His eyes fixed on the Rover, the man never saw Margret until she tripped him. He sprawled headlong into the road ending up next to the Rover, but to her chagrin lost neither his weapon nor his senses. She was cold with fear, totally unable to move as he picked himself up and turned toward her. With deliberate slowness, he brought the gun up to aim at her face.

"Hai!" came a shout from the other side of the Rover. The Icelander turned back to find Taylor standing there. He swung the gun around, but it was way too late. Taylor's weapon was already aimed, and she blasted him point-blank in the chest. There was an immediate stain at midsternum and shredded tissue burst from his back as the bullet passed through him.

"Come on, come on! Get in quick!" Taylor waved Margret to the Rover, with only a brief glance at the crumpled figure on the road, to be sure there was no movement.

Jeffers also appeared out of the fog, climbing into the rear of the Rover as Taylor gunned the engine to life. There was no way to immediately head off Gizur and Müller. From the sound of the other engine, they had driven their Rover over the field and around the other side of the hill, planning to reach the road that way. The only option, then, was to chase them. Einar, however, was still unaccounted for. Was he hurt on the hill, or dead and beyond help? Taylor called his name as they started forward, but there was no human response, save for moaning by the house. Just then, a volley of shots rang out from farther down the road, near where the hill sloped down to meet it.

"Damn it, that's where he's gone," Taylor exclaimed, and drove forward as fast as she dared in the fog.

Einar had, indeed, planted himself there. He ran alongside and scrambled in as they drove around the bend.

"I thought I would be able to ambush them there," he explained as they rode, "but they weren't close enough to the hill for me to get a good shot."

The other occupants of the Rover left unsaid the thought that had the other Rover come close enough to give Einar the shot he wanted, Müller would have had an equally good shot at him, and probably a greater chance of being on target. Jeffers shook his head silently at the idea. As he watched Margret give Einar a quick peck on the cheek for his heroic try, Jeffers wondered if they had all gone as crazy as Taylor Redding.

The chase that ensued bore no resemblance to any Hollywood chase scene ever constructed. Its flavor, in fact, would have been best captured by a film of a turtle race. The thick fog and the bad road made all thoughts of speed impossible. The lights on the Rover did not help, either. They failed to make the road ahead any more visible, and they did help to pinpoint the Rover for anyone interested in trying for a lucky shot. Consequently, both groups traveled without lights, keeping track of each other by sound. The inability to see the fleeing Rover was a major concern for Taylor. It was not because she feared losing them—she could hear them well enough and they were as hampered by the fog as she. The possibility of ambush, similar to what

Einar had planned, nagged at her. A man could hide by the roadside and be well-nigh invisible until they were right on top of him. A few quick shots, in fact just one good shot at Taylor would probably be enough, and the game would be over. Of course, the risk to the man setting the trap would be extreme, particularly as Müller had no way of knowing how many experienced fighters were in the Rover and probably could not count on Gizur to come back for him, but the maneuver was what Taylor Redding would try were the positions reversed. She drove, therefore, gun in hand, straining to be sure of the road noises in front of her that assured her that no more than one man could have dropped back to counterattack.

In the end, the attack she feared never came. The greatly truncated event that passed for night in those parts also came to an end, and with it the cloud blanket began to peel itself off the ground. The scene that greeted them when the fog lifted was one of utter desolation. Bare rock, brown dirt and black lava stretched away in all directions. There were hills and valleys, the land was not flat, but the composition was the same everywhere. No grass, no trees, no sign of life. The road, never very good, was now nothing more than a bumpy track, barely different than the surrounding land. Up ahead, out of easy pistol shot, the fleeing Rover was visible.

"God in heaven, where are we?" Jeffers asked.

"Wasteland, George, real wasteland," was Taylor's answer. "Margret, any idea where this alleged road might lead?" Taylor's best guess was that they were heading roughly southeast, but that was of little help. Settlements in the Icelandic interior, where they existed at all, were tiny.

Margret shook her head almost before Taylor had finished the question. They were no place that she knew.

"Could they have an airfield out here?" Jeffers asked. "You know, like a bolt hole."

Taylor answered firmly, "I won't buy it, George. There's no natural place out here flat enough to land a plane, and clearing a field would need heavy equipment."

"Then, maybe," Margret suggested, "they just took a wrong turn in the fog."

Whichever answer was correct proved unimportant. Suddenly, there were brake lights ahead of them. The other Rover stopped briefly, and they could see Müller gauging the range over the sight of his gun. Taylor brought them to a halt outside what she judged his effective range to be and waited. Müller evidently agreed with her assessment, for he turned around again and drove on. When they reached the location Müller had been in, the reason for his stop was evident. Not too much farther ahead, the road simply ended in a wash of rock and dirt. Somewhere in the distance the road might have continued again, but even with a four-wheel-drive vehicle there was no way across the intervening stretch. The other Rover had stopped where the road ended. Müller and Gizur were visible scrambling onto the slopes on either side of the road.

"So, this is what it comes down to," there was excitement in Taylor's voice. "They're giving us a choice. We can try and wait them out; a poor choice for us. Whether they have supplies, I don't know. We don't. We can turn around and let them get away. That's another poor choice. Or, we can go down there and get them."

Deciding to go get them was easy. Actually doing it was a lot harder. The terrain was bare rock, not a tree, not a bush. The broken nature of the ground, together with large rocks and some odd-looking piles of old lava, provided some cover, but any approach on foot was going to be tortuous. Simply aiming to disable the other Rover would have been easier, but insufficient. A radio antenna sprouted from the rear fender, no surprise on a vehicle used in the uninhabited highlands. It would be harder to put that out of commission, than to put a bullet through the tires, and Müller, for certain, would be in position to cover his Rover. Which brought the problem back to tackling the men themselves. Müller and Gizur had split up, each climbing one of the slopes bordering the ravine through which the road ran. The reason for the split was unclear from the vantage point of the pursuers. Normally, one would expect two men together to offer far more effective resistance than two separately. Perhaps there was some quirk of terrain, not evident from where Taylor stood, that made the split advantageous, or perhaps Müller just did not trust Gizur in a fight. Whatever the reason, it did force Taylor to split her group as well. Jeffers would have to watch Müller. "Watch" was the operative word, and Taylor stressed it. There was no way Jeffers could be expected to take Müller out; it would be enough to find him and pin him down. Einar could be sent to flush Gizur out. It was doubtful that Einar could be persuaded to keep his head down, but Gizur's performance at the farm diminished the risk. Taylor would trail behind, initially to make sure that neither opponent tried to break out to the Rover. There was little choice about the role, on the broken ground her leg would be a hindrance. Given time, she would be able to join Einar. Then, with Gizur out of the way, the three of them would be able to take Müller. That would teach him to divide his force! All of which left Margret and the Rover. The two were not going to be totally defenseless for, as it turned out, Jeffers had brought with him the other semiautomatic pistol that they had carried from Amsterdam. It had sat, forgotten in a pack, until the moment they were leaving the Rover. It had only three rounds in it, and none of the spare clips Sigurd had provided fit, but it was better than nothing.

Taylor needed a deep breath when she reached the point of handing the gun over. Margret was more than just a friend, and Taylor knew that she had not a violent bone in her body. Asking her to guard the Rover, with only three bullets, was hardly fair. Unfortunately, there was no other choice, and wishing for what could not be was against Taylor's rules. It was also dumb.

The girl looked frightened, but she nodded and took the gun when Taylor held it out.

"I would suggest planting yourself in those rocks over there," Taylor indicated a site to the side of the Rover. "They will hide you pretty well, but you will be close to the Rover and have a clear view. It will give you a good shot if you need it. The question is, can you pull the trigger, if you have to?"

"I think so, Taylor," came the soft response.

"Most I can ask. Okay, folks, let's do it."

# CHAPTER 28

## REYKJAVIK, ICELAND

THE CHIEF OF STATION was having a rough time of it. He had been ever since Charles Oliver had materialized the previous day, demanding the impossible and being unreasonable when it was not delivered.

The tearing apart had gone on for a day and a half when Jon Christianson finally rebelled. "Look, Oliver, enough already. I have no idea where your man went, and there is no reason why I should. I didn't know he was coming. I didn't know he was here. You saw fit to bypass me with whatever directive you had for him, and I can guess what that must have been, so I am not entirely surprised that I can't find him now."

At the rebuke Oliver settled down, or at least, shut up. It was hard to blame Christianson for being unable to locate Marden. Oliver had known that from the beginning, but the combination of believing that the search was more effectively carried out when spurs were applied and the growing conviction that something horrible was brewing drove him on. When Christianson stood up to him, however, he came down like a holed blimp. Certainly, Christianson had tried hard enough to find Marden, but it had all been useless. There was no trace of the man, not a sighting, not a corpse. Marden's room had been bare when they checked it; no clues were there. They had questioned the desk clerk at the Loftleidir twice, to no avail. Yes, she had seen Marden, but the date she gave was weeks earlier. Yes, she had passed along the message. No, she had not seen him since. Her description of Marden had been accurate. There was no reason to doubt that she had seen him. There was also no reason to doubt that the message had been passed. The DIA man who had delivered the second half of Oliver's message had also confirmed that his drop had gone according to plan. His description of the man he gave the message to did not match Marden well at all, but, as Christianson pointed out, he had not been told that it was important to remember Marden's physiognomy. Christianson had not lost the opportunity to comment on Oliver's choice of channels, which raised Oliver's blood pressure, there being no good reply that he could make.

So, in the end, Oliver was left in the side chair of Christianson's office with an embarrassing problem. He was considering whether there was any way of resolving it that did not entail his spending the time in Iceland to do it himself, when they were interrupted by a man carrying a note.

Christianson scanned it quickly, then looked at Oliver. "I wish to Hell you guys would notify me when you are running a major operation in my territory."

Oliver stared at him in surprise. "I don't understand what you mean."

Christianson brandished the paper like a sword. "There's been an explosion reported outside of Akureyri," he said. "It sounds like a munitions cache went up."

At the words, the color drained out of Oliver's face. Somehow, he had misjudged the situation. Exploding munitions had to tie in with all the other events, and implied that he had greatly underestimated their scope.

Oliver's reaction was clear to Christianson. "You didn't know anything about this, did you?"

"No. Not at all. Where is Akureyri?"

"North coast. About an hour by plane."

"Get us there, just you and me for now. Some way, any way. And get me a gun."


## ODADAHRAUN, ICELAND


OUT OF SIGHT OF the others, and of the vehicle, Jeffers felt very alone. Lonely, not just alone. Nothing but dead black rock and gray sky. God, what an awful place to die! At the thought, he managed an inward grin. There was no good place to die, now was there? Certainly, none that he had ever heard of.

It was sheer madness, what he was doing, that was what it was. There he was, Dr. George Jeffers, Ph.D. product of Cal Tech and Stanford, author of many oft-referenced and highly regarded scientific papers, and winner of three prestigious research awards before his thirtieth birthday; there he was gun in hand stalking a professional spy and killer across a moonscape of ancient lava. It was crazy. The craziest of all was the sensation that flowed from his stomach to his head, and ran in tingling currents down his arms and legs. It was not fear, he realized, it was exhilaration, and neither the danger nor the aloneness could abolish it. Indeed, they fed it. As the thoughts flowed through his mind, the sensation of loneliness abated. He was still alone. It just no longer mattered.

He temporarily shifted the weapon to his left hand as he worked his way across a small ridge. The footing was constantly uneven. Almost any step could lead to a slip and a sprain. As he crested the ridge, a sharp crack sounded on his right. Split seconds later chips flew from a rock near his hand. He dropped to the ground, ignoring the scrapes occasioned by his brush with the rocks. He had been shot at! After a quiet moment had passed, he pushed himself up on his hands for a look. Nothing. Nothing to distinguish the loosely folded land in front of him from any other section he had passed. Cautiously, he got to his feet, but no sooner had he done so than another shot rang out. He dropped immediately at the sound and the bullet struck rock behind him. As he had gone down though, his eye had caught sight of motion in the direction of the sound. It was, perhaps, two football fields away, at least by line of sight. The ground, however, formed a shallow trough between the two positions. The gunfire had come from a spot two-thirds of the way up the opposite slope. Jeffers knew where Müller was, and knowing where to look was able to see him. That accomplishment did not seem to be worth much. From the first two shots, Jeffers had to assume that Müller could hit a man-sized target at that distance. Given Müller's history, it was not an unreasonable assumption. Jeffers had no illusions that he could do the same. Somehow, he had to get closer, without being shot in the process.

He hefted two small rocks in his hand, and tossed them a couple of yards to the right. When shots answered the clatter, he rolled frantically sideways in the other direction. After three rotations, he discovered a small, unsuspected ledge and dropped about eighteen inches. The shock of landing left him gasping for breath, but as soon as he had filled his lungs, he recognized it for a stroke of luck. The land had moved there, in recent geological time. A great slab, extending off to Jeffers's left had tilted downward to create a split-level effect. This portion of earth had pivoted, as it were, on a point near the ridge Jeffers had recently crossed. Its movement formed a wall that grew from a step, just behind Jeffers, to several feet by the time the other side of the trough was reached. If he stayed low, and kept to the wall, it would screen him from Müller.

Taylor Redding was becoming both displeased and extremely frustrated. She had known, just from looking, that it would be difficult ground to cross, but now that she was actually doing it she was finding it even worse. The left leg constantly slipped and shifted, causing a nagging ache in the rebuilt thigh. It also made her balance problematic, forcing her arms out from her sides and slowing her progress even more.

It was soon clear that she could not even maintain the slow trailing pace she had envisioned. Jeffers was out of sight to her left. No surprise there— she had planned on being able to watch the road so that he could move farther to the flank. Einar, however, was also out of sight ahead of her. That was not planned. He had been supposed to stay within her line of sight. The result, though, was that all three of them were isolated, the ultimate in divided forces. Inwardly, she cursed herself. It would be hard to think of any general so idiotic as to permit a force to become so divided. Nice work, Redding!

Up ahead of her, she heard two shots fired. Einar must have found Gizur. Then a cluster of shots, spaced apart, from far to the left. Damn! Jeffers was supposed to dog Müller, not try to tackle him. Out of sight and out of control. What a mess she was making of this! The self-reproach urged her to try for more speed, ignoring the pain in the leg. The land over which she was struggling had been sloping gently upward, but so intent was she on trying to divine the events ahead she did not notice a sudden pitch down. It was the left leg (of course) that failed to find ground beneath it. When it did make contact, she was already lurching forward and there was no hope of recovering her balance. She sprawled head first onto the ground with agony in her hip. For an instant, the world was black, then the uniform blackness resolved itself into the granular blackness of the old lava field.

"Oh, God," she groaned. With an effort, she pulled herself to a sitting position and checked herself over. No major damage was present, just a few scrapes and bruises, with the worst of those on her ego. Then she noticed the gun was gone. Down a crack between rocks as best she could tell, but definitely gone. Absolutely perfect. Everyone scattered to hell and gone, and Taylor Redding loses her gun.

"So, who told you life was going to be easy?" said a little voice in her head. Thank you, Sister Angelica, she returned silently. Now, please, shut up.

Gun or no gun, there was no alternative to going ahead. She still had her knives, and Gizur did not strike her as much of a fighter.

Another shot, followed by a shout, came from ahead of her and galvanized her back into motion. The sound had come from the other side of the slope in front of her. To go around it would mean having to go down to the road, walk past the spine of the ridge, and then double back. Einar must have gone over it, at some point and, unless she wanted to arrive after all was settled, so would she. It was not that steep, merely rocky and crumbly like the rest of the ground. Einar had probably scaled it with ease. For Taylor, it was both laborious and painful. By the time she reached the crest, she was half pulling herself along from handhold to handhold. When she did reach the top, though, she froze at the scene in front of her.

The land did not slope down on the other side. It dropped, precipitously to a flat and barren plain. The cliff was broken only by a terrace, really no more than a ledge, eight feet below her perch. On that ledge, locked in a hand-to-hand struggle, were Einar and Gizur. How two men, armed with guns, had come to a wrestling match she could only guess, but neither had any real experience with weapons. One pistol lay in the dirt near them, the other was nowhere to be seen. Taylor watched them each claw for an advantage for a few seconds that seemed far longer. Tall as Einar was, however, Gizur was just as tall, and more powerfully built. In the end, he broke free of Einar's grasp and drove a right uppercut into the younger man's stomach. There was pain on Einar's face as he fought to breathe, but even so he withstood the left jab that followed to his face. Withstood it for a moment, that is. The two punches had taken the fight out of him. A split second later, he could neither raise his arms nor duck the hard right hand that Gizur drove into the side of his head. Einar dropped like a sack of flour near the edge of the terrace, obviously unconscious from the moment the punch landed. Gizur straightened up with a grunt and turned around to locate the fallen pistol.

Up above, unseen and unsuspected by either combatant, Taylor reached for her throwing knife. It was not in its sheath! She looked down, with a sense of panic, her eyes confirming what her fingers told her. She did not remember losing it, but presumably it had fallen out at the same time as she had lost the gun. She had not specifically checked to make sure it had been there then. The switchblade was still there, but it was no good to her when everything rested on one throw. Below, Gizur had retrieved the pistol and was walking around to stand directly over Einar's head. There was no mistaking the look of satisfaction on his face. Then, there was no more time for thought. Taylor pulled her good leg under her, and leaped straight at him. Gizur looked up to see her in midair, but he had no time to act. The human projectile struck him across the upper chest and shoulders, knocking him over backwards. There was no more ground behind him. With a wail, arms and legs flailing, he went over the cliff and down twenty feet, where he landed on the plain. Except, the ground was not a normal plain; it was a geothermal basin. Instead of bouncing, he went right through the surface.

Taylor never saw the end of his flight. She landed in a stunning front fall that ripped her hands and forearms. Then her leg struck. Pain exploded in her mind, almost driving her to the edge of insensibility. She fought back from the brink, but with the thought in her mind that the leg had shattered. Broken past mending, she was sure; they would have to take it off. She would be a cripple for real, then, waiting out whatever time was left.

"Stop that!" It was a moment before she realized the shout was hers. Then she got her head up and looked around. No Gizur. Just Einar's still form. The pain began to ebb a bit, so she tried moving the leg. It hurt badly, but it moved. Not ruined, hallelujah! Standing was still out of the question, so she crawled over to the edge, dragging her leg. Down below, there was a jagged hole through what could be seen as a rather thin crust of earth. The characteristic smell of sulfur rose upward.

"Hellfire and brimstone. How appropriate."

Now that she looked closely, she could see the telltale patches of white to gray at the base of the cliff that warned of thin ground in geothermal areas. Beneath, judging from the smell, was molten sulfur. There was no point in spending further thought on Gizur. Staring through the hole in the ground sent a shudder through her body. She could just as easily have followed Gizur over the side. It was several minutes before she felt ready to move further.

The throbbing pain in the leg had decreased somewhat, but seemed to reach an irreducible level. It was obviously not going to go away promptly. The real test was going to be standing on it. If that construct of spliced bone and alloy was truly intact, it would bear her weight. If not, she might well wish she had gone with Gizur. Hastily, she swore at herself as her mind began to dwell on the idea. No matter what, the rules did not permit quitting.

Spurred on by those thoughts, she pushed herself erect, then put her weight on the bad leg. The pain was bad enough that she drew blood biting her lip to stifle a scream. The leg held, though, and slowly she was able to gain control of the pain. That accomplished, she turned to check Einar. There was no need to check pulse and respirations. He was beginning to stir. A quick quiz disclosed that he knew who he was, but where he was and how he had gotten there were mysteries. He then proved to be even less steady on his feet than Taylor was. It left her with a cruel decision. Einar, for certain, had a concussion and was going to need help just to return to the Rover. Taylor, herself, was hobbled by her leg. She did not want to bet on whether she could get back by herself, much less do so burdened by Einar. Meanwhile, Jeffers was alone somewhere across the road, facing Müller. Maybe he would be able to keep his head down, and stay between

Müller and the Rover, until Taylor could get to him. Maybe, she would be able to walk off the leg injury, and reach him soon. Maybe Einar's head would clear and he would be able to go back unaided.

"Maybe," she said to Einar. "If my grandmother had wheels, she'd be a car." Einar looked puzzled as she helped him up.

It took Jeffers scant time to scurry along the base of the dike. Once he had moved far enough laterally that he figured Müller would not be ready and waiting for his head to reappear, he moved to scale the wall. It was not a long climb—his head almost reached to the top of the dike when he stood up—but it was more difficult than it looked. The rock appeared bare and solid. However, let him grab a handhold, or plant his foot, and the rock turned to gravel. The worst came when a piece under his foot disintegrated just as he was ready to reach over the top. His hands were not properly planted and he went down on his backside. Nursing his sore buttock, and hoping he had not made enough noise to attract attention, he again attacked the wall. He made it over on the second attempt, spilling pebbles and dirt down behind him. From his new vantage point, Jeffers looked around and was struck with dismay. He could no longer spot Müller.

"Good move, George," he muttered under his breath. Taylor had been very specific. Do not engage Müller, just keep him in sight and away from the Rover. Jeffers was now zero for two, and he was uncertain of the third.

Once the initial cold sweat that accompanied his appraisal had passed, he was able to think about the situation. There was really no reason in the world for him to be surprised at Müller no longer being in sight. View it from Müller's perspective, he told himself. With shots exchanged, and Jeffers suddenly vanished from sight, it would be foolhardy to stay in the same position. Whatever else Jeffers had thought about Müller, he had never conceived of him as a fool. Ergo, the man had moved. The problem was, where? Jeffers scratched the side of his head and thought about it. He had spent most of his life solving mental problems of one type or another. He ought to be able to solve this one.

The bit of terrain which comprised Jeffers's field of view was a bit like half of a trowel, with one side slightly higher than the other. Jeffers had come over the crest to his right, the lower side of the scoop. Müller when he had fired had been positioned toward the closed end and on the higher side. By this analogy, Jeffers was now placed at the open end, and toward the high side. Muller would not have moved directly toward Jeffers's old position, nor would he have moved in an area that was exposed to that position. He also would not have come farther along the edge where Jeffers was now posted because he would not, Jeffers fervently hoped, be willing to give up his ability to cover his Rover. That left only the curved stern of Jeffers's rock scoop for Müller. If Jeffers were right, he ought to be able to work along to his left and take Müller in the rear. The risk, which he saw, was that if Müller divined his intentions, then Müller would have a clear field to Margret and the Rover. He hesitated, and then it struck him. Müller would *expect* Jeffers to interdict the route to the Rover, and that was where his attention would be focused. That had, in fact, been Taylor's plan. Only Jeffers's urgent need to take cover had placed him in a position that he would not rationally have taken. It was an opportunity he intended to exploit.

The footing was better than he had had before, enabling him to make rapid progress. Also, there were no shots to interrupt his movement. When he reached the closed end, he could see another problem present itself. The lava that had once flowed across this area had not been homogeneous. Over time, the softer, less resistant portions had eroded more markedly. The result was a section of deep channels and rock walls, as though a giant cat had clawed into the earth. He moved into the area with trepidation, shuddering with every corner he turned. After a short while of that, he stopped for a rest. Leaning against an eight-foot-high rock divider trying not to breathe too loudly, Jeffers began to wish he had done nothing more than what he had been told. Inevitably, he was going to round one of those corners and walk straight into Müller's sights. Suddenly, a noise from the other side of the rock intruded into his pessimism. Given the thickness of the rock, what he was hearing was only two feet away. There was no mistaking it. Someone was moving. Trying to be careful. Müller! Trying to make no noise at all, Jeffers edged to the vertical pillar which constituted the end of the rock section. For sure, he thought, the pounding of his heart was audible enough to give him away. Ear pressed to the rock, he could hear slow movement toward the other side of the same pillar behind which he was hidden.

Finally, a figure emerged from the cover of the rock, behind the slow sweep of a gun. Sheltered by a slight concavity of rock on his side, Jeffers pressed away from the sight and held his breath. Soon, most of Müller was in view. He was, indeed, concentrating on the other direction, oblivious to the possibility that Jeffers might be behind him. At that instant, Jeffers could have put a bullet in Muller's head virtually without risk. Once before, to save Taylor, he had shot a man in the back. This time, with his own life at stake, he could not do it. He might have rationalized it by saying that a corpse could not answer questions, but whatever the reason, he did not fire. Instead, he stepped out behind Müller and, with an ear-splitting scream, swung the pistol tomahawk style at the man's head.

Müller was fast, far faster than Jeffers would have believed. He did not freeze in surprise, but pivoted, gun held close to his body, ready for action. The movement took his head away from the arc of Jeffers's swing. Jeffers had a brief glimpse of hard brown eyes, all he would ever remember of that instant. Then, the butt end of Jeffers's gun smacked into flesh. As it did, there was a crack and, almost simultaneously, a deafening roar from Müller's gun. Jeffers felt a quick tug at his sweater and there was a scream. Seconds later, Jeffers realized that he had closed his eyes. To his surprise, he was still standing when he reopened them. The scream had not been his.

Muller lay on his back at Jeffers's feet, his face contorted with pain. The right arm was held tightly to his chest and it no longer held a gun. The left hand covered his clavicle, where the force of Jeffers's blow had broken it.

"I will be damned," Jeffers said. Looking down at his side, he found two neat holes in his bulky sweater. When he pulled the sweater up, he could see a short rip in his shirt and in the skin beneath it. As soon as he saw the wound, it began to hurt, but aside from some leaking blood it was an inconsequential scratch. Just one more half-inch . . . He did not finish the thought. To divert himself, first he retrieved Müller's gun and then turned to look at the man he had downed. In the interval, Müller had gotten control of his features. He had not moved, however.

"Herr Müller, I presume. I think you are my prisoner."

"Yes," Müller replied with lightly accented English, "since you have both guns and my collarbone is broken, I would not think anything else. What do you plan?"

Jeffers shrugged. "We will have to walk back to my Rover. I'm sure it's going to hurt, but I'll try not to enjoy it." He gestured with the gun. "Now, move."

It took approximately forever for Taylor to guide the dazed Einar back to the Rover. While she was doing it, a shout and a single shot were audible from the direction Jeffers had taken. After the shot there was only silence. Taylor could do nothing but shrug. Either Jeffers was all right, or he was not. If he was not, it became even more urgent for Taylor to reach Margret at the Rover. In either case, there was nothing she could do for Jeffers. When they finally arrived, they found Margret standing in front of the Rover looking anxious.

"Christ in heaven!" Taylor yelled to her, "can't anybody do what they are supposed to anymore? You're supposed to be behind that rock pile."

"I was, until I saw you and Einar coming up."

"Yes, and what would happen if Müller was coming from the other side at the same time? He would bag us all is what would happen. All right, now that you're here, give me a hand with him." As she watched Margret's face, Taylor felt the verbal slap, almost as though she, and not Margret, was the recipient. There was no help for it, though. Mistakes could all too easily become fatal.

Margret took it quietly and went to take Einar's free arm. "What happened to him?"

"Took a hard shot in the head. As best I can tell, he is okay, or will be with a little rest, but we will need to have a doc look at him. Sit him down back where you were and stay with him. I've got to go back and see what has happened with Jeffers and Müller."

"Can you make it?" Taylor's labored walk had not escaped Margret.

"No choice in the matter. Now . . . hoy! What's down there?" There had been movement out in the rock field. Urging Margret and Einar ahead of her, Taylor took cover by the Rover. Someone upstairs had decided to be kind, she thought. She knew she would never have been able to walk to the fight.

Soon it became clear that there would be no fight at all. Jeffers and Müller stepped into the clear and there was no doubt that Jeffers was the one in control. When she saw that, Taylor let out a whoop. Had she been able, she would have run down to meet them.

They put Müller in the back of the Rover after Taylor improvised a figure-eight bandage from an Ace wrap in the Rover's emergency kit. His face relaxed a little with the bandage providing support for his shoulder.

"We have no analgesics," Taylor said, "so that will be the best we can do until we get back to Akureyri. I'm sure the NATO base will be glad to send a chopper for you."

"No doubt," was Müller's sardonic reply.

Jeffers had been looking back and forth from Einar who was slumped in the back seat to Taylor's torn and dusty clothes. "You two look like you just got back from the Charge of the Light Brigade. What happened to Gizur?"

"I'm afraid Gizur has dropped from sight," Taylor said evenly.

Jeffers decided not to ask how literally she meant it. "I don't suppose it matters too much," he said.

"No, I don't think it does," Taylor said. She turned to their captive. "What did you think you were going to do here? Be the power behind the throne or actually make yourself king?"

Müller stared at her. "Don't be a fool," he said. "I don't do what I do for my personal gain."

That stopped Taylor, but only for a moment. "I'll be damned. I think I see. Müller isn't your real name, of course, but I'll bet that whatever it is, it sounds, shall we say, Slavic." Müller just glared at her. "Sure. That's the way it fits together, isn't it? That's why Fruhling had such good information on all the ex-Stasi, but he knew nothing about you. You're not German and you never worked for the Stasi. The KGB would be more correct, wouldn't it"

"Yes," Müller said. "You will find out anyway. I was a liaison with the Stasi, so, of course, I knew many of them."

"Russian," Jeffers said. "What in God's name did you think you were doing, if you weren't working for yourself? Hasn't anybody told you? The Cold War's over, man, it's all over. The Soviet Union is gone and it's all finished."

"It's all finished?" Müller asked. "You fool!" He started to laugh but the pain in his shoulder brought that to a quick end. "Jeffers, it's never over. Sure, the Soviet Union is gone, but so what? My people and your people are adversaries, we always have been and we always will be. Russia will recover her strength and when she does, it won't matter whether we are capitalists or something else. We and the West will still be adversaries."

"And against that, you wanted an advance position here, you or whoever your bosses are," Taylor said. "Yes, an unfriendly government here might not draw much notice today, not when everyone seems to have more immediate problems."

"So you're still going to pretend the Cold War's on, just in case we have another one in the future. Lovely. But what did you want my enzyme for? You want the naval base at Keflavik, but what did you want my enzyme for?"

Müller looked like he was going to laugh again, then thought better of it. "Your precious enzyme! *I* didn't want it; it's worthless to me. But Schroeder wanted it and Bieber wanted it and that made it valuable. It gave me Bieber and his contacts; it would have given me people inside H-C. It gave me advance money to use here. It would have brought more money that I needed here. For obvious reasons, this project was not, how would you say, well capitalized. It was just a means to an end, Jeffers, nothing more than that."

"And what about the U.S.?" Jeffers asked. "Tell me how you set it up there."

"No," said Gerhardt Müller.

"Don't give me 'no,' Müller. There's no one out here but us. I can either get answers or," Jeffers drew a finger across his throat.

What had worked before, however, proved valueless with Müller. "Go ahead, kill me," he challenged them. "What I have told you is nothing you will not know on your own. I won't give you anything else and threatening me won't change that. I am a patriot," he said proudly, "and if I have to die for my cause, I will."

"Patriot!" Jeffers spat the word out as though it were an obscenity. "The world wouldn't be in such a mess if we didn't have so many damn patriots. My country as well as yours. You kill innocent people and then call yourself patriots. What garbage!"

"Say what you like. It does not matter. I do what is necessary and I make no apologies. Now if you are going to shoot, do it." When Jeffers made no move, Müller taunted him again. "I thought not. You see, I do know a bit about you Dr. Jeffers. This is the real world, now, not a movie or a book. When you shoot a man in cold blood, you cannot simply turn the page. But if you cannot move out of your head and into the world, you should not meddle with it."

Müller's retort left Jeffers silent. He did not expect that kind of bravado from a prisoner with a broken clavicle. But it was not just Müller's manner that shut Jeffers up; there was something else about the comment that nagged at him. Then, all at once, it burst on him where he had heard the line before.

"Thompson! Jim Thompson! That's who your American agent is."

Jeffers's explosion caught Müller by surprise. It took him only an instant to compose his features, but that was long enough for Jeffers to have his insight confirmed.

Müller looked into Jeffers's face and saw that there was no chance of trying to brazen it out. "My congratulations, Dr. Jeffers. I suppose I deserve this for my overconfidence. I hope that it was the only item you still needed, for it is the last you will get from me." He was as good as his word the rest of the way back.

# CHAPTER 29

## AKUREYRI, ICELAND

COMPARED TO WHAT HAD gone before, the trip back to Akureyri was uneventful to the point of being boring. The road was visible this time; the place where first Müller, and then they, had turned wrong was obvious. Only in a dense fog could that sidetrack have been mistaken for a road in use. Müller, although a potential source of trouble for which they had to remain alert, stayed quiet. Even if he had been disposed to make a break, busted clavicle regardless, the jolting ride ensured that he thought of nothing but his shoulder. By the time they neared the city, he looked ready to pass out.

Einar they left at the local hospital. He was still a bit woozy and the rough ride had not done him any good either. He did not stay alone as Margret volunteered to watch over him. The arrangement pleased Taylor. She had grown fond of Einar, and Margret could use a good break. She was also glad that neither of them would be present when they brought Müller in. Consequently, it was just the two of them again, with a silent Müller in tow, when they reached Akureyri airport. The details of contacting the authorities, disposing of Müller, and clearing themselves of a myriad of questions and irregularities were in urgent need of attention. Taylor knew she had to handle them, but for once she felt devoid of inspiration. Everything was too anticlimactic and her brain refused to focus on the questions. Into this quandary, Müller inserted an urgent need of his own.

"Why don't you go ahead and take him to the john?" Taylor asked Jeffers. "Just stick next to him and he won't go anywhere. I need a quiet moment alone to think, anyway."

Oliver and Christianson arrived at the Akureyri airport with a sense of urgency at least equal to that of Taylor and Jeffers. The skimpy radio reports they had been able to pick up had told them only that an arms store had indeed been blown up at an isolated farmhouse, and that there had been a gunfight there as well. A team from Keflavik was being readied as they flew, and both men badly wanted to see the site before others began picking through it.

338

Oliver stomped across the field and into the small terminal building at high speed; Christianson, in spite of his longer legs, was hard pressed to keep up. It was as though Oliver had walked into a wall though, when he caught sight of Taylor. He stopped dead in his tracks. There was no doubt in his mind. She was the girl in the Amsterdam photograph, the one Jeffers had met at the Kettle Drum, the one he had unsuccessfully sent Marden after, the one who had made fools of them that night in White Plains. When he saw her, she seemed unaware of him, which was unsurprising as she had no reason to know him. Without a word, his hand dove beneath his jacket and emerged with a gun.

"Freeze! Oliver, if you shoot, I'll blow your motherfuckin' brains across the floor!"

Shock registered on three faces. On Taylor's, caught unawares and staring down the length of Oliver's gun with no place to hide. On Christianson's, also taken by surprise by Oliver's move and frozen with his hand still on his holstered gun. On Oliver's, as he and the others looked around to find the source of the voice in George Jeffers.

The bathroom where Jeffers had taken Müller was centrally placed on the first floor of the building. Emerging from it, he needed only a long stride to have a good view of either of the two large rooms that took up most of the ground floor. He now stood obliquely behind Oliver and Christianson. One hand gripped Müller by the back of his figure-eight bandage, the other held a steady pistol aimed at Oliver's head.

"Give it up, Jeffers," Oliver said as soon as he recognized his foe. "If you shoot me, my partner will drop you before you can do anything else. Besides, you'll probably miss anyway."

Jeffers ignored him. "I'm telling you, drop the gun. If you shoot, or I see your friend as much as twitch, I start shooting."

Oliver had trouble believing what he heard. "Since when," he asked, "have you become such a consummate assassin?"

"Well, I've already shot one in the back, so I don't suppose shooting you in the face will be such a big deal. And, this thing fires on automatic. I doubt I'll miss if I use the whole clip. Trust me."

Oliver went red with fury. "Goddamn it, you asshole! Don't you have any idea what she is? She's the one who killed your contact in Boston!"

"Wrong, Oliver." Jeffers had to fight not to laugh in his face. "The guy who had your man killed is your old buddy, Jim Thompson. And this is the scum that owns him." He brandished Müller by the wrap, bringing a gasp from the prisoner. The look on Oliver's face was one that Jeffers would cherish for the rest of his life.

"Excuse me, gentlemen," Taylor broke in, "but can we talk? We will be glad to sit down and give you the whole story. In return, we walk, free and clear. Can you deal?"

"I have the authority," Oliver answered, "but why should I?"

"Well, for one," Taylor said, "if blowing your cool and pulling a gun in the middle of an airport hasn't already created an international incident, starting a firefight certainly will. We are already attracting attention. Besides, once you hear what we have to say, I think you will be satisfied. We will also throw Müller into the bargain. A sweetener, if you will."

"Let's talk, then." Without looking at Jeffers, Oliver holstered his gun.

The three of them waited in a room with Christianson while Oliver spoke with the airport security, people at the Keflavik base, and a variety of people in Reykjavik. No words were exchanged until he came back to the room, having worked out an understanding with the Icelandic authorities. Then, they talked. It seemed endless to Jeffers. They went through the whole story with Oliver from the time Jeffers left the plane in Boston to the moment Jeffers saw Oliver draw his gun. Then they went through it a second time, and then Oliver started to ask questions about specifics. An occasional question from Christianson showed that he too was following the tale. When the conversation turned to Fruhling's involvement, Oliver pressed hard for details, and was clearly unhappy with the little he received. The extent and intensity of the questions at last made it clear to Jeffers why Fruhling had acted with such circumspection. A lifetime of seeing the unexpected happen had obviously made him loathe to leave any loose ends. In the end, Oliver came away with nothing about Fruhling other than the fact that the man had not been involved in this particular plot, which no doubt was just the way Fruhling had intended a question and answer session to come out. On the subject of Thompson, Oliver had little to say and that piqued Jeffers's curiosity. He had assumed the two men were old friends.

"Friends?" Oliver said in response to Jeffers's question, "Let's say we knew each other for many years. I guess nothing really surprises me anymore. People do strange things sometimes, especially if money or women are involved."

"And what do you do now?"

"That," Oliver said, "is for Washington to decide, not me."

That, Jeffers thought, was a deliberate dodge. Of course, if Oliver and company took too long coming to a decision, none was going to be necessary. Jeffers had definite ideas of his own.

Aside from Fruhling, Oliver remained dissatisfied with the account of the events around Lorenzo's death. Everything pointed to Thompson, but failed to give a good reason. Even after hours of discussion, Oliver returned to the question of why it had happened, scratching his head in frustration as each retelling duplicated the one that had gone before.

"All right, enough," Oliver said finally. "I have just one more question. You've done it, but I would like to know what in God's name made you think you could pull this off without getting killed?"

At that Jeffers threw back his head and laughed. "What can I tell you, Charles? In this business you have to take some risks."

Oliver left, shaking his head, and at long last it was over. They were free to go.

Jeffers asked Taylor about the Boston shooting later. "Oliver has a right to be confused about it, but you shouldn't be. Not any more," she said. When Jeffers gave her a puzzled look, she went on, "Oliver doesn't know about the lockbox, because that is the one major point we left out. Intentionally, of course, there is no need to trouble him with it. I think we can take care of it just fine by ourselves. Anyway, the lockbox is the key, if you will pardon the pun.

"You won't know for sure, unless you get it out of Thompson and in spite of what Oliver says, you will have to move very fast to get to Thompson before Oliver's people do. My guess, though, is that the plan was to take the key from you, or the agent, in Boston. It's possible that the killer thought the transfer had already been made, and that's why your contact was shot, although I think it's more likely he was suckered with the code name and killed to clear the way to you. In any case, Thompson could claim the key had been lost, and insist on moving the money in order to safeguard it. I can see how he could set up a dummy box, complete with appropriate papers, while all the time the money stayed right where it was. Then, after things cooled down, Thompson could go back and clean it out. That idea was probably what had occurred to Thompson when he convinced Oliver to give you a role and it explains why the hit in Boston was so out of line with the rest of Müller's operation. It had nothing to do with it! That was Thompson's own private game. I bet Müller never even knew about it. Of course, when you got away, Thompson was stuck. He couldn't block the money or even move it because then he wouldn't be able to secretly grab it for himself. After all, he'd just killed one of Oliver's men to get to it. He had gone too far to back out. He just had to hope that he could get his hands back on the key and the letter. That's the way I read it, George. Oliver will just have to be happy with only part of the story."

"Yeah, although I don't know how happy he was with the rest of it either. It seems unbelievable to me and I know it's true."

"It's not all that unbelievable, George," Taylor said. "Just because the Soviet Union is gone doesn't mean things are going to go smoothly with the Russians. You know, there are an awful lot of people now who chant 'democracy, democracy,' sort of like a mantra, but there's no guarrantee that just having some form of it will be a panacea. Remember, Hitler became chancellor democratically and I can't guess who the Russians will come up with in the end. Hell, a lot of Russian nationalists have been anti-Western since the nineteenth century. No reason to think that's changed. For all the trouble they're having today, eventually the Russians will get their act together. When they do, that base at Keflavik will be important again. If Müller had finished his job, well, no shots would have been fired and probably no one would have noticed until it was too late, but the balance of power in the Atlantic would have changed."

"Right," Jeffers said. "But we stopped his nefarious scheme and saved Western civilization from disaster."

"I might have put it more modestly, George, but you could be right. Anyway, you know the truth about your enzyme."

"I may know the truth," Jeffers said, "but that doesn't mean I'm happy with it. I put so much of myself into the project that it hurt to see that the only interest they had in it was as a way to manipulate people. I mean, for all they cared about its properties, it might have been salt. Same with Thompson spending all that time in my lab and going for beers after. There's something very cynical about that."

"It's a cynical world, George."

"Yeah. Looking back now, it's pretty obvious. I guess I just read too many spy stories. I always thought this stuff would be so . . . romantic."

That sentence brought him an odd look from Taylor. "What do you mean by . . . romantic?"

"Well," he started to say, then caught her looking at him. His face went red. "Crap, Taylor, I didn't mean it that way! Oh, never mind. It's over and done with. For now, I'm going to head back to Reykjavik. Are you coming?"

"Of course, why wouldn't I?"

"Well, Christ," Jeffers said, "the way Oliver was talking back there, I thought you were going to end up working for him." Taylor just smiled. "Oh, come on, I was kidding. You wouldn't. He was ready to kill you!"

"Hey, I wouldn't let a misunderstanding get in the way of a good job,"

Taylor said, "but no, I am not going to work for him. Governments tend to treat people like hospital supplies. You know, use once and dispose of properly. Not for me, thank you. I vote for Reykjavik."

# REYKJAVIK, ICELAND

SO IT WAS THAT two days after rolling into the Akureyri airport in a dirty Rover with a captured spy in the back, Jeffers found himself back in a Reykjavik hotel room. He was seated at the desk with his back to the door, a flagrant announcement that the adventure was over. He had spent a good deal of time trying, without success, to compose a letter to Hank's wife. How could he tell a friend, and the wife of his best friend, what had happened, and do it gently and with love? He could not, at least not on paper. In frustration, he tore to shreds the last of what he viewed as a series of inadequate attempts. The only right way was going to be to tell Paula in person, and he would do that as soon as he returned to the States.

His decision made, he leaned back and laced his fingers behind his head. He felt relaxed. There was absolutely nothing going on; the first time in a while that had been true. Even Taylor was not around. She had quietly disappeared several hours before. Wondering where she had gone led to thoughts of her in general. It was a pleasant train of thought. He was, in fact, so lost in his daydreams, that he almost fell over backwards when a foot stomped in the entry behind him.

"What the . . . ?" Recovering his balance, he spun around and the question died in midsentence. "Good Lord! Taylor, that's gorgeous!"

She was almost a different person, leaning against the wall just inside the door. A gray woolen skirt fell to midcalf partly covering a pair of high leather boots. Above it, she wore a silken blouse with a tiny black ribbon tie at the neck. Her hair fell straight about her shoulders, and the expression on her face was pure pixie.

"Do you like it? This was the first chance I've had to go shopping. It's been a long time, I think you know how long, since I've worn a skirt, but I thought this looked nice."

"Do I like it? Does it look nice? You have got to be kidding. I said it was gorgeous and I meant it. What is the occasion?"

Her answer was almost shy. "I thought that since tonight is our last night in Iceland, we might go out on the town. Just for fun. You did say, I believe, that you expected this adventure to be more romantic."

"I can't believe it," Jeffers sounded incredulous, "you are asking me out on a date? Of course, I'm going to say yes, and say 'yes' quickly, before you have a chance to retract it. I'm not going to let you off the hook."

It proved to be a most pleasant evening. There were shared experiences to talk of, and those helped to bring to life stories of other times as well. There were times to laugh at together, and times that called for shared sympathy. After a few drinks, Jeffers coaxed her out onto the dance floor. It was amazing, he thought, that he was coaxing any woman anywhere, but he felt comfortable with Taylor. Neither one was much of a dancer, but for a slow dance, it hardly mattered. Jeffers was surprised and pleased to feel her relax against him. If that moment could have been held forever, he would have done so.

At length, they came back to Jeffers's hotel room. Still his room, as always, but it did not bother him. This night was very different from all of those other nights. They went inside, closed the door, and he drew her close to kiss her. And felt her freeze. Solid.

There was no mistaking the change. The muscles that had been soft under his hands were now taut. The eyes were the hard, gray flint he remembered from their first meeting. They stayed where they were, lips just inches apart, for a moment. Then, Jeffers released her and stepped back. There was really nothing else to do.

"What's wrong, Taylor? What did I do?"

"Nothing, George. Nothing's wrong. No, everything's wrong." She turned away from him quickly. There had been, perhaps, a little buildup of fluid at the corners of her eyes. When she turned back a minute later, the eyes were dry.

"It's not you, George. It's me. I am what I am. I'm Taylor Redding. That's all, no more, no less. I've made myself what I am, and there's no way I can change it. Not now. I'm not even sure I would even if I could. There's too much I could lose for the little I would gain. That's all there is to it, George. We were partners, good partners, but that's all. There isn't anything more. I just *can't*." The sad finality in her voice could not be missed.

"I'm sorry, Taylor. I've said that before, I guess. Is there anything else I can say?"

"No," she shook her head, "there really is nothing to say."

Taylor said nothing else, taking her own advice. Jeffers was silent too, although his mind raced along looking for a good phrase. He failed to find one, and after the silence became awkward, Taylor left for her own room.

The next day, waiting for the afternoon flight to New York, was equally awkward. Jeffers still could think of nothing to say, and Taylor did not seem to want to talk. Their plans were set almost by default. Jeffers to return to Cleveland, Taylor to Boston. Neither one mentioned going back to Liechtenstein for the lockbox. Jeffers did not even want to bring up the subject. He did not feel he needed to; no matter when he went back, he was certain that half the money would still be there. Talking about it was going to bring up more painful topics and he avoided it. The five-hour flight to New York was silent, even though Taylor was awake for most of it. Jeffers spent the time trying to get his mind back where it belonged. Nothing was wrong, he told himself. The mystery was solved, the adventure over. They had been partners in that, strictly partners. Nothing more, nothing less. Well, maybe a bit less at the beginning, but that was irrelevant. Jeffers wondered where he had gotten the idea that a business arrangement should have a romantic coda? Certainly Taylor had never encouraged it so it must have been all in his mind.

Somewhere over the Atlantic, Jeffers decided that he ought to be thinking of what to do when he returned to his lab. That, after all, had been his true love for many years. The list of experiments he wanted to do was already lengthy when he had left, and he doubted it would be any shorter on his return. Probably, the laboratory had ground to a halt in his absence. Normally, it was all Jeffers could do to get his mind off his lab work. This time, he could not keep it there. His thoughts kept returning to Taylor despite all his mental admonitions.

He kept at it, though, and by the time they landed at Kennedy Airport he had managed to wrench his mind away from Taylor and back to his work. They picked up their bags and went through Customs without comment. Finally, in the busy concourse, it occurred to Jeffers that they were actually parting and he had not even said farewell.

"Taylor!" She stopped at her name and waited for him to continue. "I just wanted to say thank you, for everything, and goodbye. I don't think I'll ever forget it."

"Thanks, George. It was a good adventure, and you were a good partner. I'm sorry it couldn't go further than that."

"What are you going to do now?"

"Who knows?" she said. "Something will turn up. It always does. Now, you take care of yourself." With that, she gave him a friendly pat on the shoulder, turned and walked off into the crowd.

Jeffers stood where he was, watching the tall woman with the slight hitch in her gait move away from him. As he did, he realized that he was standing quietly, watching the best part of his life disappear. All at once, a life spent entirely within the walls of a laboratory seemed intolerable. There was a wild and fascinating world out beyond those walls, of which he had only had a glimpse. It was there for the taking, and anyone could have it if they were willing to take some chances.

"For once, George," he muttered under his breath, "don't wait until the next day to think of what to say.

"Hey, World's Greatest Adventurer!" he shouted.

A great many heads looked around at the shout, but he did not care. One of the heads was Taylor's. Eagerly, he galloped across the space between them, dodging other travelers who were not quick enough to get out of his way.

"Before you go, I have a question for you."

"Sure," she said. "What is it?"

"When something does come up, could you use a partner?"

The smile started in her eyes as he finished speaking and slowly spread across the rest of her face. "You bet, Mister secret agent," she replied. "You've got yourself a deal."

And they shook on it.